Magic at the Gate

"The action-packed fifth Allie Beckstrom novel amps up the magical mayhem.... Allie's adventures are gripping and engrossing, with an even, clever mix of humor, love, and brutality." — *Publishers Weekly*

"Devon Monk takes her story to places I couldn't have dreamed of. Each twist and turn was completely surprising for me. *Magic at the Gate* truly stands out." — Reading on the Dark Side

"A spellbinding story that will keep readers on the edge of their seats." — Romance Reviews Today

"Suspense is the name of the game.... I'm really enjoying this series.... Each book brings you a little bit further in to it and leaves you wanting more." — Night Owl Reviews

Magic on the Storm

"The latest Allie Beckstrom urban fantasy is a terrific entry.... This is a strong tale." — Genre Go Round Reviews

"First-rate urban fantasy entertainment." — Lurv a la Mode

Magic in the Shadows

"Snappy dialogue, a brisk pace, and plenty of magic keep the pages turning to the end.... This gritty, original urban fantasy packs a punch." — Monsters and Critics

"This is a wonderful read full of different types of magic, fascinating characters, an intriguing plot.... Devon Monk is an excellent storyteller." — Fresh Fiction

"Monk sweeps readers up in the drama and dangers of the heroine's life as it steadily changes and grows ... an intriguing read with fascinating characters and new magical elements introduced to the mix." — Darque Reviews

"The writing moves at a fast pace with plenty of exciting action.... This series just gets better and better with each new book." — Night Owl Reviews

Magic in the Blood

"Tight, fast, and vividly drawn, Monk's second Allison Beckstrom novel features fresh interpretations of the paranormal, strong characters dealing with their share of faults and flaws, and ghoulish plot twists. Fans of Patricia Briggs or Jim Butcher will want to check out this inventive new voice."
—Monsters and Critics

"[A] highly creative series. . . . If you love action, magic, intrigue, good-versus-evil battles, and pure entertainment, you will not want to miss this series." —Manic Readers

"One heck of a ride through a magical, dangerous Portland . . . imaginative, gritty, sometimes darkly humorous. . . . An un-put-downable book, *Magic in the Blood* is one fantastic read."
—Romance Reviews Today

"This series uses a system of rules for magic that is original and seems very realistic. . . . The structure of the story pulled me in right away and kept me reading. There's action, adventure, fantasy, and even some romance." —CA Reviews

Magic to the Bone

"Brilliantly and tightly written . . . will surprise, amuse, amaze, and absorb readers." —*Publishers Weekly* (starred review)

"Mystery, romance, and magic cobbled together in what amounts to a solid page-turner." —SFFWorld

"Loved it. Fiendishly original and a stay-up-all-night read. We're going to be hearing a lot more of Devon Monk."
—#1 *New York Times* bestselling author Patricia Briggs

"Highly original and compulsively readable. Don't pick this one up before going to bed unless you want to be up all night!" —Jenna Black, author of *Rogue Descendant*

"Gritty setting, compelling, fully realized characters, and a frightening system of magic-with-a-price that left me awed. Devon Monk's writing is addictive, and the only cure is more, more, more."
—*New York Times* bestselling author Rachel Vincent

STONE COLD

A BROKEN MAGIC NOVEL

Devon Monk

WITHDRAWN

A ROC BOOK

ROC
Published by the Penguin Group
Penguin Group (USA) LLC, 375 Hudson Street,
New York, New York 10014

USA | Canada | UK | Ireland | Australia | New Zealand | India | South Africa | China
penguin.com
A Penguin Random House Company

First published by Roc, an imprint of New American Library,
a division of Penguin Group (USA) LLC

First Printing, April 2014

REGISTERED TRADEMARK — MARCA REGISTRADA

ISBN 978-0-451-41793-0

Printed in the United States of America
10 9 8 7 6 5 4 3 2 1

For my family

ACKNOWLEDGMENTS

This book never would have seen the light of day if not for the wonderful people who have helped make it happen. Deepest thanks to my agent, Miriam Kriss, and my editor, Anne Sowards, who has an amazing knack for making each book better. A huge thank-you also to the wonderful artist, Mike Heath, and to the many people within Penguin who have gone above and beyond to make this baby shine.

To my first readers extraordinaire, Dean Woods and Dej-sha Knight: Your unflagging enthusiasm and support are appreciated more than you may know. Thank you. A big thanks to my family, one and all, for being there for me, offering encouragement, and sharing in the joy. To my husband, Russ, and sons, Kameron and Konner: Thank you for all your love and support. You are the best part of my life, and I love you.

And finally, dear readers, this book is for you. Thank you for letting me share these people, this world, and this journey with you.

Chapter 1

SHAME

The door behind Eleanor opened, letting in the March wind, a little rain, and the man I had come here to kill.

The man was a few years older than the photo I'd seen, black hair shot through with gray, white face gone pudgy behind square bifocals. His name was Stuart, and he carried himself like someone who was irritated with his own skin: stiff movements, coat clutched closed with one hand over his stomach, a scowl hammered into his face.

Not what I'd expect a murderer to look like, but then, killers came in all shapes and sizes.

After all, it took one to know one.

He gave the interior of the diner a quick glance. Didn't notice me because I looked right at home in a diner that hadn't passed a health inspection for a decade. And although it might be fun, I didn't go around introducing myself as "Shame Flynn, Death magic user, loyal friend, troublemaker, and the last guy you want to meet in a dark alley if you've done something naughty."

He didn't notice Eleanor either, but that was understandable.

Eleanor was a ghost.

She sat across from me, long blond hair flowing with an underwater grace as she moved. Soft features, sweet smile, she was beautiful when alive, and still beautiful when dead. She noticed me noticing him. Tipped her head a bit, narrowed her eyes. *What?* she mouthed.

I couldn't actually hear her because, hello, she was dead. But I'd learned how to read her lips over the last couple of years since she'd been tied to me.

"Nothing," I lied.

She, as usual, didn't believe me.

She scanned the diner, saw the guy take the booth just off to our right, looked back at me. Shook her head.

"Not listening." I stared at my breakfast so I didn't have to see her, poked at the waffles. My fork bounced off the hardened whipped cream.

She shifted through our table like someone forging a stream and floated in front of me, half her body stuck in the table.

"Jesus. Do you stay up at night thinking of ways to creep me out?"

No killing, she mouthed. Or maybe it was *no kidding.* I didn't say I was *good* at reading lips.

"Sorry. I made a promise. I never go back on my word."

She rolled her eyes.

"Fine. Lately," I amended. "I never go back on my word lately. That man." I lowered my voice because seriously, I did not need to draw attention to the crazy guy who was yelling at his waffles. "Has done unspeakable things to people. With magic. For years. He'll continue doing unspeakable things to people, with or without magic, because it's kind of his thing. He should have been dead a long, long time ago. I'm just taking care of business."

Terric. She pointed at my heart, which wasn't beating all that well today since it had been a while since I'd killed or consumed. A problem I intended to take care of as soon as the ghost got off her high horse so I could kill the guy.

I lifted my knife and started sawing at the waffles. "Terric doesn't need to know what I'm doing. If Victor had wanted him to know about the hit list, he would have given him a copy of it. Plus, Terric's not really a supporter of vigilante justice. Also, *he's* been avoiding *me*, not the other way around."

Not that I could ever get away from him. We were Soul Complements, Death magic, Life magic. Ever since the magical apocalypse a few years ago had made magic a gentle force, it was just us Soul Complements who could break magic into light and dark and make it do the old, horrifying things.

Well, and the old wonderful things too, but that wasn't really my department.

I was the guy who handled the darker side of magic.

I'd been a damn fine Death magic user back in the day. And now? Well, now I *was* death.

While it had its perks, it didn't come without a hell of a price. I carried death, but if I didn't let it loose, didn't let the Death magic in me consume and kill people, plants, or things, then it simply consumed and killed me.

Victor had been a teacher and a mentor in all things magic. The hit list he'd left for me when he'd died had been a blessing for my death hunger. Even so, I was never going to live to be an old man. If the Death magic in me didn't kill me, it was highly likely one of the murderers I was tracking would.

But I was damn sure going to live long enough to take out as many of the killers as I could before my time was up. It was just my way of giving back, and making the world a little more livable.

Today's cleanup was on aisle killer-in-the-booth-across-from-me. After him, I'd move on to the next on the list. Unless I found Eli Collins.

Eli was at the top of my own personal list of people who the world would be better without. A psychopath and magic user, he'd tried to kill me, Terric, and my friends. He was still suspect number one in the kidnapping six months ago of our friend Davy Silvers, who'd worked as a Hound to track down illegal magic use.

And he'd killed the first woman I'd thought I could take a chance on loving—Dessa Leeds.

I'd been wrong to take that chance, and she had paid the price for my poor judgment.

The only good thing about not finding Eli was that it gave me time to think about exactly how much agony I was going to put him through while I was killing him. His death was not going to be quick or painless.

There had been no hint of where he was holed up, no clue of what the government agency he was involved with had been doing since we'd thrown magic and bullets at each other.

But he couldn't hide forever. I'd catch his scent, and then he'd be dead.

A cold slap of pain hit my shoulder and forced my attention back on my surroundings. The grease and noise of the diner fell around me again, the heat of the air, the cool of the wind coming through the door.

Eleanor sat across from me, her hand up, ready to slap for attention again. She didn't need to.

Another man had stepped into the diner and was scanning it.

Terric Conley was a bit taller than me, dressed better than me, and had blue eyes and good looks angels would fistfight for. His hair had been white since the day when we were teens and I'd tried to kill him with magic, which was only the beginning of my life of bad choices.

Taken all together, he was the sort of man women fell

for. Unfortunately for women, he was the sort of man who fell for men.

He was also a hell of a Life magic user and, when we admitted such things, my friend and my Soul Complement.

He spotted me and started my way.

"Make room, Boy Scout's here," I muttered to Eleanor.

"Shame." He stopped at the table, glanced down at my plate of sawed-off waffles, strawberries, and whipped cream. "Breakfast? Why are you eating breakfast here? Now?"

"Mum kicked me out. What's wrong with here and now?"

"For one . . ." He glanced back across the diner, then at me. "This place is a dump. And secondly, you promised you'd go with me to a meeting today."

"*I* promised?"

"Okay, fine. I promised. Allie and Zayvion want you there. Us there," he corrected.

Allie and Zayvion were our friends, and also Soul Complements to each other. Zayvion had run with Terric and me when we were young bucks growing up in the Authority under Victor, and Allie was the daughter of one of the Authority's richest, and more conniving, members.

The Authority wasn't the same after the apocalypse. No need for a secret organization to keep the darker uses of magic secret since magic had been tamed and fully revealed to the public.

"Busy. Sorry." I hacked at the waffle with the wholly inadequate knife. Switched to the fork and shoveled waffle and whipped cream into my mouth. Chewed. And chewed. And kept on chewing.

Tough didn't describe this mouthful of particleboard. Kevlar had more give. And taste, come to think of it.

"Just . . . come, Shame," he said. "Allie wants you there."

Ever since Allie had gotten pregnant, she was all sorts of

unpredictable in the emotional department. I found it endlessly entertaining. Terric had taken to tiptoeing around her and doing everything she asked of him, and Zayvion had threatened to tie my spine in knots if I riled her up again.

I spit the waffle into the napkin. "If I don't?"

Terric raised an eyebrow. "You need me to threaten you?"

"Might be amusing."

"I can promise you the follow-through would not be."

Had some fire behind those words. Man could deal out the hurt when he wanted to. Apparently my not going to see Allie and Zay would make him want to.

"What the hell kind of meeting is it, anyway? You and I are no longer employed by the Authority."

"We aren't the head of the Authority," he corrected. "It doesn't mean we aren't a part of it."

The killer at the booth had finished his coffee and small bowl of oatmeal. He tossed cash on the table, pushed up on his feet, glanced over at me when he thought I wasn't looking, and walked out the door.

Damn it. He knew I was tailing him.

I could kill him from here. Without even standing up. Without even laying a finger on him. I could reach out, let the Death magic inside me pop his heart, blow his brain, drain his lungs.

Just the thought of it made my heart race.

Eleanor glared at me and shook her head, then pointed at Terric as if she was going to tell him what I was thinking.

I still hadn't quite figured out why she was so concerned about me. I was, after all, the bloke who had killed her and then hog-tied her spirit to my mortal coil. Another bad life choice.

I took a couple even breaths and shouldered into the death hunger, pushing it away. Terric was saying something, but I was a little busy, thank you, trying not to blow a kill zone a block wide.

Finally the hunger released and my heart came back down to human rhythms. It was painful and heady and I was still starving.

". . . drunk?" Terric asked.

"Yes." I had no idea what he was talking about. Hoped it was that we should get a pint or two.

While I'd been wrestling with my inner death, Killer Guy had strolled out of my reach.

Great. There went two weeks of hunting down the drain hole, thanks to Mr. We-had-a-date.

"Still drunk or already drunk?"

"What? Neither. Cover that for me, will you?" I said. "I left my cash in my other coat." I stood, wavered a little. I really needed to consume something, or someone, real soon now.

Eleanor pointed at Terric. *Life,* she mouthed.

I ignored her.

Why not? she mouthed.

"Reasons," I said to her.

"What?" Terric asked. He'd dug a bill out of his wallet and slipped it between the salt and pepper shakers.

"For the meeting," I said. "Why are we going? Is it about Davy Silvers?" I strolled toward the door and he followed. March meant rain, and today was no exception. I stepped out into the downpour.

Terric flipped his collar before taking the plunge to the sidewalk. "Weren't you listening?" he said. "Never mind. Don't answer that. No. Nothing new there. We still haven't found Davy, Eli, or where the government has them stashed."

"So, what is it about?"

We strode down a block or so to his car—double-parked. Every heartbeat from the people around us was a finger plucking rhythm against my spine. Forty-seven lives in the office building, twelve in the coffee shop, eight in the bank.

He didn't say anything more until we got into the car.

"How's Eleanor?" He couldn't see her unless he drew on magic to do so, but lately he made it a point to ask about her. Which she loved.

Women.

She smiled, then made pointy motions toward him again.

"Still dead," I said.

She slapped me in the back of the head. Ow. Brain freeze.

"Also, angry."

"What about?"

"Who can tell? Female things?"

She took another swing at me, but I leaned forward out of her reach, fake-checking my bootlaces.

Terric glanced over. "What is *wrong* with you today?"

Time to change the subject. "I could ask you the same thing, mate." I straightened, checking to make sure Eleanor was done with the smacking. She crossed her arms over her chest and stuck her tongue out at me.

I gave her a wink and a grin.

Terric started the engine. "What do you mean?"

"You're avoiding my question. You didn't get in until five this morning. You paced until six. It's what, nine o'clock?"

"Ten thirty."

"You've had three hours of sleep, which is the most I've seen you get all week. It's not like you to miss your beauty shut-eye."

He locked his jaw. Uncomfortable subject. I should probably just leave it alone.

So of course, I didn't.

"Come on, now, Ter. Gotta new guy working your night shift?"

He stopped for a light. Pedestrians without umbrellas took their time crossing the street.

"I've been . . . keeping busy," he hedged. "Looking into things."

"Do these things have names? Social Security numbers? Memory foam mattresses?"

He didn't say anything.

"Look at you," I said. "All mysterious and secretfying. Please tell me it is both a deep and shamefully dark secret you're hiding from me."

"I'm not hiding anything. Nothing you need to know, in any case."

"Those are not quite the same thing, are they?"

"Close enough."

I glanced out the side window. As I did so the blur of light surrounding him flared. Huh. Maybe it wasn't a new boyfriend on his mind.

Maybe it was magic. He had too much Life magic in him just as I had too much Death magic. And neither of us had much control over those magics.

There was a solution for this. We needed to use magic together, let the two magics cancel each other out. Of course, we both hated that because every time we used magic together, we lost a little more of our humanity.

Lately, I'd begun to think that hate it or not, maybe we should just use magic together anyway. And, yes, that was the exact opposite of what I'd tried to do over the last two years. But in small enough doses, it might be safe enough for us to use magic with each other, for each other. The same way carcinogens are safe in small doses.

And hey, humanity was overrated, right? So what if we lost a little more of our sanity, of our souls? We had people to kill, magic to feed, and meetings to attend. What was one more bad decision in my life anyway? I turned to Terric and decided to find out.

Chapter 2

SHAME

"You could have asked me to help with all that Life magic climbing the curtains in your noggin," I said quietly.

"So you could laugh in my face?"

"Harsh. Also, yes. Not like I haven't before."

"Maybe I just didn't want to deal with . . ." He shook his head.

"Me?" I supplied.

"Us," he answered.

"What about us?"

The traffic light turned and he was quiet for several blocks. Finally, "I don't know how to navigate this anymore, Shame."

"What's there to navigate?" I slouched down against the side door trying not to show him how much I needed to consume, to use magic too. "You need an outlet for all that Life magic crowding you up. I need to consume life. If we don't do it too often, if we don't do it too much, there's a slight chance we won't go insane and kill each other. Besides, it's not like we're going to die old men."

"It's an addiction. Us using magic together. When we

don't . . . the longer we go between using together, I can't . . . I can't think."

"Thinking's overrated."

"I feel like a goddamn junkie."

I waited until the truth of that cooled between us. He wasn't wrong. And I should know. "I haven't seen you in two weeks," I said. "Two weeks is a long time."

"I know."

"You could just get your own place and we could go back to permanently ignoring each other."

Since Mum kicked me out of the inn—the only place I'd ever called home—while she and her new love, Hayden, did a beam-to-basement remodeling on the place, I'd moved into the house I'd won—fairly, I might add—from my buddy Cody Miller back in the day.

And Terric? Well, he hadn't gotten over the last crappy boyfriend who had beat him and forced him to use Life magic for whatever the Blood magic and drug syndicate, Black Crane, had wanted him to do.

He had told me I owed him a couch for a few days. I'd probably been too drunk to say no. I didn't know when or how he'd moved in with me exactly. Hell, it was a big house. There was more than enough room. I had just expected him to leave by now.

"That wouldn't change anything. Wouldn't change us," he said.

"True. Pull over," I said.

"What?"

"Just." I pointed. "Pull over."

We were on the east side of the river now, a few miles out of St. Johns, where Allie and Zayvion lived, and where, I assumed, the meeting was being held.

He did as I said, which just showed what state of mind he was in. Terric never listened to me.

He put the car in park, then returned both his hands to the wheel. Stared straight ahead at the rain.

"Do it," I said. "Throw a little Life magic at me."

"I can't."

"Can't? Won't. Sorry, Ter. If I have to deal with the monster inside me, then a little turnabout's good for the gander."

That got a twitch of a smile out of him. "Your grasp of the English language is staggering."

"Shut up. Do it. Life it on up in here, and I'll Death it on down."

He took in a deep breath, half turned toward me. "You think it's that easy?"

"Drawing on Life magic? For you, yes."

"And what about all those people out there?"

I listened. I could count the heartbeats in the blocky apartment buildings on one side of us and in the beat-down row of nineteen forties cottages on the left. I knew Terric could do the same.

Death magic in me was obvious about its killing nature. The Life magic in Terric was a little more subtle in its cruelty.

Suffering a disease? Life magic might just side with the disease and accelerate it. Or it might decide that other latent things inside you should come alive.

To hear Terric talk about it, which he didn't often, it was an alien, calculating force that slipped through his fingers no matter how he tried to control it. To hear him talk about it, he never knew if it was going to heal or destroy.

Other people might be surprised that Life magic wasn't a blessing.

It wasn't news to me that life was synonymous with suffering.

"The people are going to be fine," I said. "We'll make sure we keep it contained in the car. It's why you came to pick me up, isn't it? To draw on magic, feed the need?"

"No," he said quietly. "I came to take you to the party."

"Party?"

He winced. "Meeting."

I did a quick check. It wasn't my birthday. I didn't keep track of other people's birthdays, but I was pretty sure it wasn't that either.

"Party?" I repeated.

"Baby shower. For Allie."

"Baby what? No."

"Shame."

"Hell no." I laughed. "Did Allie send you out to drag me in for a baby party?"

"No, Zay asked me for her. And I would have volunteered. You're supposed to be an uncle to that kid, a godfather."

"When the kid gets here and can blow out the candles, I'll be there to cheer," I said. "Baby showers are for girls."

"I'll be there. Zay will be there."

"Point stands."

"You are such an idiot. Fine," he said. "Don't. But I am. I am going to be around Allie, Shame. I am going to be around my friends, people I care for. Something I've avoided for almost a month now. This magic inside me . . . I need . . ." He clenched the steering wheel tighter. Then in a quieter voice, "I just want one damn normal day. You're the last person I want to ask, but . . ."

"You'll break your no-magic rule with me for a *baby* shower? Is it a gay thing?"

"It's an Allie and Zayvion thing." He turned toward me again. Blue eyes drenched in color, a depth that should reflect kindness, but instead gave the impression of fire. Madness wasn't far behind.

When Terric lost control of Life magic, he became a very alien thing. No emotions, no humanity. Just a calculating creature of power that twisted the world to his will.

We didn't need that. The world didn't need that because then I'd have to kill him.

"All right," I said to Terric, and to the madness within him. "I'll go to the party so you don't hurt anyone. But first we use magic so we can put on our sane masks while we're in public. We do a simple spell, here, in the car, nice and controlled, and take the overstock of Life down a notch."

He nodded once, stiffly. He hated this just as much as I did. Or, really, loved it as much as I did and hated that it was just one more step toward us losing our control of magic, or our humanity, for good.

I stuck one finger in the air and traced a very simple glyph for Burn.

It took Terric a second to notice which spell I'd chosen. "What? No," he said. "No fire inside the car."

"It's magic. It will flash so hot there won't even be ashes."

"Shame, this is my *car*. I just paid it off. No fire."

"I don't know, mate. I've already drawn most of the symbol. Too late to go back now."

"Just cancel it. There are a hundred better spells. Consume, Dampen, Flow . . ."

"Flow?" I asked. "Do you see a river that needs rerouting? No. Plus, I like Burn. Easy and quick."

"No fire. Use Dampen."

"Screw you, Life Boy. I'll cast what I want to cast. You best get busy calling up all the growing and thriving shit for me to knock down."

He licked his lips. "It's been a while."

"This isn't a confessional. Cast."

His left hand still gripped the steering wheel. The other clenched a fist next to him.

He wasn't moving. Wasn't casting. He was not doing much for a guy who wanted to use magic.

Fine. If talking wouldn't work, action should.

I didn't draw a spell. I didn't concentrate on pulling

magic from beneath the ground to fill the spell. I just relaxed a little, took a deep breath, and called on the Death magic snarling behind my mental chain link fences.

"Hey, Terric," I said, thinking maybe the element of surprise would knock him into gear. "Think fast."

Death magic hit him like a ton of . . . well, death.

Slammed him against the door. His head snapped so hard the glass cracked.

Crap.

Pain exploded through him, whipped back through our Soul Complement connection, riding the black fire of death coursing through me and into him.

Jesus. I'd expected him to block. He was fast. Faster than me. He should have seen that coming.

I grappled with the magic, trying to rein it in, but Death wanted its due. Heartbeat, blood, life. And Terric was right there for the picking.

Sweat slicked my face, scratched at my neck as I tried to drag Death back to me, back inside me. I hadn't meant to hurt him.

"Ter?" I said. "Are you breathing?"

Magic flared around him so bright it blinded.

I had one second to think that maybe we should have parked somewhere more private where people driving past wouldn't see the ridiculous amount of magic filling the vehicle.

I had another second to think that if I'd been smart, I would have cast a Block spell or an Illusion so no one would call the cops about the explosion about to go off in the car.

And the third second? Well, that's when I got busy fighting for my life.

Life magic roared out of Terric, pouring so hot it was hard to breathe. Liquid white shattered through the raging darkness of Death I was losing control of, canceling it, breaking it, burning it.

Light and darkness, life and death. Pretty even odds if you asked me.

But I'd caught Terric off guard, angry. And hungry. That was a dangerous misstep, like poking a raging lion, lighting a match near gasoline, or pissing off an uncontrolled Life magic user.

This was not going to end well for one of us. Probably me.

The pain between us shifted, nauseatingly so, to a sort of pleasure as the magic he called on and the magic I called on fought for the edge, fought for the advantage over each other.

I could feel Life creeping into me, filling dark hollows in me, firing across my nerves. Every muscle in my body clenched, just as I knew Death was biting off pieces of him.

Fight? Flight? Break glass in case of emergency?

Terric and I had done some stupid things with magic.

So far, we'd avoided reaching into the core of all magic that flows through the world and actually snapping that core in two—which is exactly how a magical apocalypse kicks off. Right now we were just accessing the magic we carried in us—Life and Death—and that was not strong enough to start the end of the world.

Still, I was pretty sure we'd just climbed to new heights of Mt. Dumb.

"Terric," I said. Or I think I said. I might have just thought it, since someone in the car was yelling, and I was pretty sure it wasn't me. "Take it down a notch."

The only problem? That wasn't Terric staring out of those brittle blues. That was Life magic, inhuman, calculating, brutal. Hungry.

Okay, so maybe I had underestimated how close to the edge of insanity he'd been.

If I let go of Death magic, I'd probably have a second or two of pure bliss as my body became completely and fully alive. After that?

Probably oblivion. Or obliteration.

Plus, that would mean Terric had won, Life magic had won.

Since I am a terrible loser, I wasn't going to let that happen. Time to tip the scales the best way I knew how: cheat.

I pulled a knife out of my pocket, cut my left palm. It instantly healed.

Thanks, Life magic.

I cut myself again, deeper. Got a few drops of blood before that healed too. Tried to think of my next move.

Jesus. I was getting a little drunk off all this Soul Complementy magic flying between us.

Spell. I needed a spell.

I carved the air with the blood-covered knife. It was not graceful. It was not precise.

Okay, so it took me two tries, because, damn. The amount of magic in this car. What a way to go.

Finally got it, got the glyph drawn. Laughed.

Terric, or rather, that inhuman vessel of magic over there, frowned.

I set the spell spinning with the tip of my blade.

Time.

It wasn't a spell I liked to use. You had to be connected to the other person in some way for Time to manipulate both you and your opponent's perception of it. Blood magic was the easiest way to accomplish that.

But as I said, Ter and I were joined by more than blood. I had his soul.

The other problem here was that Time was a damn hard spell to end. Instead of just canceling the spell, you had to make sure you were coming back into the reality of time exactly in sync with the natural flow of it.

That was as easy as landing a jumbo jet on the head of a pin.

Time washed out like a curling pinwheel of smoke, crashed over his head, crashed over mine, surrounded us.

Since I was the one who had cast the spell, I theoretically had control over whether it would speed things up or slow things down.

I opted for slow.

"Terric," I said as a year crawled by. "You need to listen to me, mate."

"You. Attacked. Me."

"I thought you'd block. You attacked me back. We're even. Except *you* have completely lost your mind. Control yourself, mate. Haul back on that Life magic."

"I . . . ," he started.

"Have gone crazy," I finished for him. Then a month or so later, "And if you can't get a grip, I will shut you down."

Something moved behind his eyes, something that looked a lot more like the man I knew. "You'd try," he said.

"You bet your weet sass I would," I said.

Even though Time was stretching each second so that it felt as if it were days and weeks, the overload of magic and hit of pleasure from using Life and Death was drunking me up a bit.

"We both put the magic down," I said. "On three."

I lifted my hand, so very, very slowly. He did the same, mirroring my movements.

"One," I said.

"Two." I waited, held my breath. Wasted a heartbeat or two savoring the high. Needed this to be right. Needed to get the alignment of our reality of time and time's real reality correct so I didn't kill us.

"Three."

He canceled Life magic, hauling back on it, controlling it. White fire snaked around his hand, a lightning storm come to rest in his fist.

While he was doing that, I was wrestling for control of my own magic. Not easy. Not fun. Blackness whipped around me, lashing hard enough to break skin.

It hurt. Everything hurt.

So: normal.

I flicked fingers and broke the Time spell. There was that thunder crack ringing and foot-off-the-cliff lurch of our perception of time readjusting.

I fell forever.

I'd missed the landing. I'd screwed it completely.

Nope. I nailed it.

We were sitting in the car, along the side of the road. Eventually I could hear the soft patter of rain over my pulse, which beat steady and strong.

Terric was breathing hard too.

But neither of us was exploded.

So: all good.

"What were you thinking?" he said.

I gave him a grin, licked the blood off my split lip, wondered how many more little cuts Death magic had left me with this time.

"You wanted to use magic with me but were afraid we couldn't control it. Which we did, I'd like to point out. I was tired of listening to you whine about it."

"I wasn't afraid of our control."

"Yes. You were. You'd be stupid if you weren't."

He swore softly, didn't meet my eyes. I wasn't the one who ususally told the truth in this relationship.

"So we're good now, right?" I wiped the side of my face on my arm. No blood. Maybe I'd gotten out of this one relatively unscathed. Or maybe there had been enough Life magic still in me it had healed up all the nicks. I licked my lip again. Blood was gone.

One point for Life magic, then.

"No," Terric said. "We are not good. Using like this . . . uncontrolled . . ."

"Speak for yourself, mate. I was plenty controlled."

He pressed his head back into the headrest and stared

out at the rain. "You hit me with Death magic, Shame," he said. "I could have killed you."

"Already dead. Also, good luck with that. Also, also, we're late for that baby shindig you wanted to go to."

He focused on something over my shoulder and out the door, as if he'd just noticed we were still in his car.

"One last thing," I said. "I think some of the people passing us called the cops. So getting the hell out of here might be in order. Unless you want to explain that magical explosion you just set off to Detective Stotts?"

"*I* set off?" He sat forward, turned the key. The engine purred. "You hit me in the face with Death." He glanced out his side window. "And you broke my window with my head."

"You were the one who wanted an outlet for Life magic so you could be stable around Allie and the baby Beckstrom."

"Beckstrom-Jones. They're hyphenating," he said. "And there is a difference between Death magic absorbing Life magic and being a dick, Shame."

"Don't I know it?" I said. "If I'd wanted to be a dick, I'd have broken more than one window."

"I don't think that's how it would go down."

"Oh?"

"Life always wins. Always."

I felt the best I had for the last couple weeks. I was pretty sure Life had won this time.

No need to tell Terric that, though.

"No, I just went easy on you, mate," I said. "If it was a fight, a *real* fight? I'd win."

"Why?"

"Because when it comes right down to it, you won't cheat to get your way. You're on the side of heroes, Terric."

"And you're not?"

I didn't say anything. I didn't have to. Hero hadn't been in my job description since the day I was born.

Chapter 3

SHAME

Allie and Zay's place out in St. Johns was a three-story farm-house that backed the Willamette River, and was within spitting distance from the formerly secret crystallized well of magic.

It was a pretty place with a rock wall fence and a garden they'd expanded again because the Hounds kept planting weird vegetables like bottle gourd, kohlrabi, and rhubarb in it when Allie wasn't looking. An old apple tree with a tire swing claimed the corner of the yard.

Hard to imagine two of the most powerful and danger-ous magic users in the world lived here. Hell, few other Soul Complements in the world could come close to challenging their magical mojo. If I had to put my last coin down on two people who would always, no matter the circumstance, come out on top, it was Allie and Zayvion.

Which is why I found the whole baby-on-the-way panic they had going kind of hilarious.

Terric parked the car next to several others in the alley behind the house. "Ready?"

"It's a baby bath—" I said.

"Shower."

"Whatever. I've got nothing on the line here. How ready do I have to be?"

I pushed out of the car, lit a cigarette, and filled my lungs with smoke. I wanted to roll up on the balls of my feet and stretch, I felt so good. That tussle with Life magic had taken the edge off the hunger inside me, steadied my heartbeat and all my other vital functions. I almost felt normal, human. Sure, it wouldn't last. But for the moment, it was plenty good enough.

I waited by the car, smoking, while he tried to pull his head together, tried to line up his thoughts. After he cast magic like that, he had to remind himself what a human did, and how a human acted.

Which was why we tried not to use magic in big doses, or at all, for that matter. It was just a delay of the inevitable. There was no way to get rid of the magic inside us. All magic came at a price, and we were paying out with our souls every time we used it. One day, Terric would no longer be Terric and I would no longer be whatever I was.

No rosy future for us. We both knew it.

We didn't talk about it.

He finally got out of the car and paused before shutting the door.

"Have your keys?" I asked.

Took him a minute before he answered. "Yes."

He was still just standing there. Looked a little lost.

"Did you bring a gift?"

He stared at me, and I stared right back. "For the baby? Or Allie, or however this thing works."

The last brittle edge of light in his eyes finally slipped away, leaving the deep blue of sanity. And with it, Terric.

Good. I relaxed a little. It was hell to see him losing ground. I knew one of these days, he wouldn't come back from our little meetings of magic.

"It's in the trunk." He walked back to get it.

"See you inside, then." I headed toward the house.

The wooden gate between the stone fence had little pink and blue balloons fluttering at the top of it. They'd tied more balloons to the railing of the covered porch and over the doorway.

I chuckled. It used to be all bullets and battles with these two. Now it was babies and balloons. My, how we'd changed. Well, at least how they'd changed.

I took the last of the heat out of the cigarette, flicked it into the wet flower bed, and jogged up the steps to the back door.

Eleanor was already ahead of me, grinning and excited. It didn't matter if they were dead or alive—women had this thing about babies. Also parties. So today was win-win for her.

I clomped across the porch, the voices from inside rolling out in that particular music of happiness and friends. I could feel their heartbeats, knew who they belonged to.

There were about a dozen Hounds in the house. I could hear the rhythm of Nola, Allie's best friend, Violet, her stepmother, and of course little Daniel, Allie's only sibling. Zay and Allie were there too, two hearts beating in rhythm.

Other than that, I quickly picked out Sunny's pulse and my mum's.

Great. My mother was here.

I paused at the screen door. Took a second to make sure the Death in me was deep-sixed. I hadn't seen Allie for three months. I hadn't seen my mum for at least two.

Allie and Zay never asked why I didn't come around. They knew. And frankly, this was going to be a short visit. No one wanted to watch what happened when a Death magic user lost control of his hunger in front of a pregnant woman.

But my mum didn't care that I was death walking. She insisted I show up at her dinner table occasionally.

". . . worry, you got this," Terric said as he slowly climbed the stairs behind me.

"What?" I said.

He paused. Then, "This attention problem of yours? There's a pill for that."

"Shut up."

I opened the door and braced myself for the wash of living—the heat, the tangle of emotions, laughter, and conversation.

I stepped into the kitchen. "Somebody pour me a drink. It's time to party!"

My mother, Maeve, turned from where she was pulling a platter of strawberries out of the refrigerator. "There's no booze at a baby shower. Wipe your feet, then give me a kiss and a hand."

"No booze? This isn't a prebaby kegger?"

"It's a party for Allie and the baby, son. Not for you." She set the strawberries on the counter and turned to give me a long look.

Mum was looking good, strong, just a sliver of silver catching in her long red hair, which was pulled back away from her face. She had on jeans, and a dark green sweater over a white T-shirt. Resigning as the head of Blood magic, and spending a few months with her boyfriend, Hayden, in Alaska had done good for her.

I hadn't seen her happier.

She put her hands on her hips and tilted her head. "You are looking better, Shamus. Whatever you've been doing lately, it sits well with you."

"Clean living and dirty work," I said. I reached over and popped one of the strawberries in my mouth and moaned a little in amazement. "What's in this?"

"Cheesecake. No more until after the presents."

I swiped two more from the platter before she slapped my hands away.

"Hello, Maeve," Terric said as he finally stepped into the room.

She pointed at me. "There's a bowl up in that cupboard. Fetch it down. Hello, Terric. How are you?"

"I thought my indentured servitude ended when you kicked me out of the house," I muttered.

"I kicked you out of the house when you were nineteen," she said.

"I'm well," Terric said, a little shakily. "Thank you."

Pitiful. The man could not lie to save his life.

"Nineteen? You did not." I handed Mum the glass bowl.

"Yes, I did. You just didn't listen to me."

"Pills," Terric said.

I flipped him off.

"So, is there fun out there?" I grabbed another strawberry while pointing toward the living room. " 'Cause the fun in here isn't."

Mum swiveled with the tray and dumped the berries into the bowl, her back to me, blocking my reach. I couldn't count the number of times she'd done that to try to keep me out of her cooking.

Unfortunately for her, I was taller than her now.

"Here," Terric said, "let me take that for you, Maeve." He lifted the bowl out of her hands, and out of my reach.

"Teacher's pet," I said.

"Thank you, Terric," she said. "There's a table set out in the dining room. Just put it down anywhere it fits."

"Got it," he said.

I started after him.

"Shamus," Mum said. "Stay for a cup."

I stared wistfully after the strawberries but knew better

than to push my luck. She had on that serious face that meant we could have this talk either here in the relative privacy of the kitchen or out there in front of everyone.

I poured myself a cup of coffee, added half a cup of cream, and a few tablespoons of sugar.

"You've been avoiding me," Mum said as she wiped her hands on a towel and turned to get more food out of the refrigerator. Deli platter. Looked delicious.

"I've been avoiding everyone, Mum." I took a drink of coffee, then walked over and gave her a quick kiss on the cheek. Not long enough for her to feel how cold my skin was, or how completely Death filled the shell of me. "Doesn't mean I don't love you."

That made her smile. I pushed the monster further away. Covered it with my best Shame face. Hoped she wouldn't see what I was now and how much ground I'd lost.

"Well, I'm given to understand people who love each other sit down to dinner every once in a while," she said. "Come by Friday. Bring Terric."

"Sure, okay. I'll do that." I was so not going to do that.

"Good," she said. "See that you do. Now, go on." She nodded toward the living room. "It's all friends here."

"I know." That's what made this harder. I walked through the door.

The living room was packed with people. Just about every Hound who had stood by Allie when the world had been about to end was lounging around the place.

Jamar, who still rocked the intellectual-tough-guy look, leaned against the bookcase talking to Sid, who was easy to mistake as a typical middle-aged accountant. Theresa and Beatrice were a study of opposites, Theresa being the kind of gal who looked as if she belonged in a military workout video, and Bea flying her boho, bright-colored scarves, frilly skirt, and easy laughter. I didn't see her whiskey-soaked boyfriend, Jack, around anywhere.

But Sunny was here, lingering in the shadows and giving off leave-me-alone vibes. She had stroked her dark hair back off her face into a single braid down her back. She wasn't wearing a stitch of makeup, had on black jeans, a gray long-sleeve shirt, and a black short jacket. The whole thing together should have made her look badass, which she was because—hello, Blood magic user and head of the Portland Hounds—but as the days and months had marched on without us finding where Eli and the government had taken her boyfriend, Davy, the sorrow was starting to crack her hard exterior, leaving her pale and pained.

All the Hounds except Sunny were holding plates predictably piled high with food. And also predictably, they all glanced up when I walked into the room.

I so hated that.

Dashiell Spade, the guy who used to work for Terric and me, had once said Death magic surrounded me like a dark shadow. He'd said anyone who had a brain in their head could see I was dangerous. Unpredictable.

Something to avoid.

The Hounds had some of the finest-honed survival instincts of any people I'd ever met. It was no surprise they were suddenly alert when I entered the room.

It bugged the hell out of me. I didn't like being noticed as what I really was unless I wanted someone to notice what I really was.

I didn't even try to hold up the Shame mask for the Hounds. They'd see right through it.

Instead I just sort of gave them all a nod and pointed at Sid's plate. "You'd better have left some scraps behind for the rest of us."

"With your mother in the kitchen?" Sid said with a smile. "The entire city won't go hungry for a week."

Sunny just stared at me as though we had unfinished business.

And that would be because we had unfinished business.

Jesus, why had I let Terric drag me here? Weren't pre-baby birthdays supposed to be a girls-only thing?

I looked around so I could complain to him about it. He was across the room talking with Zayvion, and he glanced my way as if I'd called his name.

I hated how much we could feel each other. Hated that we were getting closer and closer every time we used magic together, no matter how much we tried to stay away from each other.

He shook his head and looked away.

My mood, which hadn't been all that stellar to begin with, took a dive toward the nasty. Time to take my mood outside for a little nicotine therapy. I turned, digging in my pocket for a smoke.

And nearly ran into Allie Beckstrom herself.

"Hey, Shame. Long time."

The woman was gorgeous. She'd let her hair grow so that it fell in heavy dark waves down below her shoulders. It was tucked back on one side to show the ghostly shadow of the magical marks up by her temple, at the curve of her fuller cheek, and down the side of her face.

"Al," I said as I tapped a cigarette out of the pack, "you're looking beautiful, love."

She raised her eyebrow. "Beautiful for a two-ton freighter?"

I pulled out my lighter and gave her the full up-and-down. She had on slacks and a flowing blue and green shirt that didn't try to hide the swell of her belly. Seeing her, carrying life, cradling the life she and Zayvion had created, caught me flat-footed. I didn't have it in me to lie.

"Beautiful, as in absolutely lovely, darlin'. Zay's a lucky man, and I couldn't be happier for you both."

A deep shade of pink raced across her cheeks and she avoided eye contact for a second.

"You can be such a charmer when you want—you know that, Shamus?" she asked.

"Please." I pressed my fingers against my chest. "I am *always* a charmer. I meant every word. You're a stunner. If you ever get tired of Jones, you let me know." I gave her a wink, which just made her blush harder.

She didn't usually wear her emotions out in the open like this. Which made flustering the woman irresistible.

"You know you'd like it," I singsonged.

"You think?" She tipped her chin up a bit and gave me a sly look. "This"—she pointed to herself—"you couldn't handle if you tried. And there's no smoking in the house, remember? Ashtrays are on the porch."

"Right. I'll be back, then. *Do* start the party without me."

I took a step past her, but she reached out and pressed her fingers gently on my arm.

Suddenly it was hard to breathe.

"Don't leave, Shame. Please. I want to talk to you after the party."

And even though she looked soft and radiated life, the old toughness was right behind those pale green eyes.

I licked my lips and gently pulled my arm away. "Something wrong?"

She shook her head. "Later. Be here, okay?"

"It's been a while since you ordered me around. Even longer since I listened to you."

"You miss it," she said.

"As if." But yeah, I did. We'd had good times. We'd almost died; hell, I *had* died, but still, things were never boring when Allie Beckstrom was around.

Chapter 4

SHAME

I waited until my mum wasn't looking and then dodged out through the kitchen and onto the porch. No one else was out here, which suited me fine.

I lit a cigarette and paced, trying to slough off the high concentration of life, trying to make the edges of reality go away so I could deal with the "normals" a few minutes more.

Eleanor drifted over to the porch rail and floated up to sit on it, facing out toward the yard, one hand lifted to feel the rain, which fell right through her.

I leaned against the wall, one boot pressed against it, staring past Eleanor and smoking. Ignored the world, ignored the heartbeats, ignored the loudness, the warmth, the life. Pushed it all away until there were no bright edges, there was no sound. There was nothing I could care for. Nothing I could kill.

"Drink," Zayvion said.

And just like that, the world came crashing around me again.

Zay and Terric were both leaning on the porch rail facing toward me, beers in their hands. Eleanor had floated over to make swoony eyes at Zayvion, and what woman wouldn't? He was a six-foot-plus, dark-skinned, muscled, smoldering-hot-gaze, easy-smiling dude. He was also one of the most loyal, responsible guys I knew and head over heels in love with Allie.

Apparently the ladies liked those sorts of things.

". . . paying any attention to us?" Zay asked.

"Almost." Terric took a swig of beer, watching me.

"Heard every word," I said.

Zay leaned forward, offered me a beer. I took it.

"Aren't you supposed to be in there with the party people, papa Jones?"

"Allie's got it covered," he said. "I'm mostly here to kick out anyone who annoys her."

"That explains why you're out here with Terric, then," I said.

Terric shook his head and took another drink of beer.

Zay gave me a brief smile. "It's been, what, two months since I've seen you?"

"Three. I'm touched you've been keeping track, what with all the baby on your mind."

"Shame," he said. "You know you're welcome in our home. No matter what kind of crap you're mixed up in."

"Crap?"

"I was talking to Paul the other day," he said.

"So?"

Paul was Paul Stotts. Detective Paul Stotts. He used to chase down the illegal magic users in the city. Still did, come to think of it. But he was also the husband to Allie's best friend, Nola. Which made Paul our friend too.

Except when we were doing illegal things.

"He wanted to know if I'd noticed the upticks in strange deaths lately. About a dozen people who were involved with the Authority back in the day have gone missing."

Terric was giving me that graveyard stare.

"What am I supposed to know about this?"

"He said they've disappeared. Not even bones left behind. Not even ashes," Zay said.

"Disappeared could mean Cuba," I said. "It doesn't have to mean dead."

"Maybe. That's what he was thinking too. Until the most current disappeared."

"Oh?"

"They found a pile of ash in his backyard. With a single bone in it."

Shit.

"And how does that involve me? For that matter, how does it connect to the other missing people?"

"The ashes were in the glyph symbol for Death. Every last person suspiciously missing was a member of the Authority who had . . . a checkered past. All dead within the last couple months. There aren't many people in the world who can use Death magic strong enough to kill someone with it. Here in Portland, there's only one person I can think of who can do it."

"Come on, now, mate," I said. "If you're going to accuse a man, just come out and do it right."

"Are you killing people, Shame?"

"That's a question, not an accusation."

Zay just waited. He knew me. He usually knew when I was lying, which had often put a crimp in our relationship. So I looked over at Terric instead.

"*Et tu*, Terric?" I asked.

"Oh, I'm very interested in your answer," he said. "You've been gone a lot lately too, Shame."

"That's because you moved into my house"—I made air quotes—"'for just a few days' and haven't moved out. A man needs space. If you both think I've gone rogue, how come Stotts isn't here Miranda-ing my rights?"

"I told him I'd talk to you," Zay said.

I did not know Zay had that kind of pull with him. Interesting. "And?" I said.

"And make a decision on what happened next."

See, when Zay threatened, it was a subtle sort of thing. Unless he was breaking your fingers. He wasn't turning me in to Stotts yet if I could give him a good reason not to.

I swigged beer and let the cold and bitter wash through me. It would be easy to lie.

Except I wouldn't get away with it. Not with these two who were practically brothers to me.

"I don't know who Stotts is talking about," I hedged.

"Let's just settle on a yes/no," Zay said amiably. "You killing people?"

I hated it when he got specific. "Maybe a little."

Terric's eyebrows went up and Zayvion shifted his shoulders a bit. "Who?"

"Come on, Z. You can trust me."

"Who?"

"Might as well say," Terric muttered. "You know he won't let it go."

I sighed. "There is some business that is none of yours, Zay. This is that business."

Zay nodded, stared at his boot for a minute, his arms crossed over his chest. "You talk to me, or you talk to Stotts. That's the way it is."

"I don't remember you being my boss, Zayvion. This isn't the old days. You don't have any right to tell me what to do."

"Shame," Terric warned.

I didn't need a warning. I knew what Zayvion was—he was Allie's Soul Complement, which meant when Zay and Allie used magic together they were just as dangerous as Terric and me. They could, if they wanted to, reach into the core of magic and do the apocalyptic breakage too.

If anyone was ever going to end my life, if anyone *could*, it would be Zayvion.

"Who?" Zay asked. "Why? Two easy questions."

I held up one finger. "People," I said. Then held up another. "Personal."

Zayvion had this thing that happened when he was really ticked off. His eyes, which were brown, flashed with flecks of gold. It was worse back when magic was strong and he was guardian of the gates. Nowadays he had to be all kinds of pissed before there was even a glint of gold in his gaze.

His eyes washed with a metallic shine.

Oh-ho. My answers had not made him a happy boy.

"Last chance," Zay said.

"Or what?"

He blinked slowly. "Or I will have Terric hold you down while I shove a Truth spell down your throat."

I glanced at Terric. He lifted the beer bottle in a toast. "Your move, Caesar."

I tipped my head back and leaned against the house again. I could feel the heat of the heartbeats beyond those walls like a flickering bonfire across my back.

Ah, hell. Truth it was.

"Those people weren't just involved with the Authority," I said. "They were Closed."

Closed was the spell we used to use to take away people's memories, ability to use magic, and, sometimes, life. Usually it was cast on people who were dangerously against keeping magic secret and safe. Sometimes it wasn't.

When dark and light magic had been rejoined, healing it and also gentling it, everyone had gotten their memories back.

And once most people realized their lives had been manipulated by a secret group of magic users, they went a little bat-shit.

Couldn't blame them, really.

"Lots of people were Closed," Zay said. He should know.

He was Victor's star pupil. He had Closed a hell of a lot of people for the old man.

"You didn't Close them, Zay."

"How do you know?"

Here's the part I hadn't wanted to tell them yet. Certainly not at a baby party. "Victor left us something. Each of us."

At the mention of our old mentor's name, both of them suddenly went still. Terric had been his student too. Back in the day, before I'd hurt him so badly he couldn't use Faith magic anymore, he'd been training for the job Zayvion took. Guardian of the gates.

Now there weren't any more gates, and only Soul Complements could break magic into light and dark so that it had the destructive strength it used to have.

"What?" Zay asked with that calm that might make a person think he didn't care, in which case a person would be totally wrong. "What did Victor leave us?"

I reached into my pocket. "I don't know why I haven't shown you this yet." Behind me Allie's laughter drifted out through the door. "I guess I thought there were other, better things for you to be thinking about."

I handed them each a micro USB drive with their names on it.

"Where did you get this?" Terric asked. "Shame? When did Victor give this to you?"

"He didn't. After he . . ." I shrugged one shoulder. "After Eli killed him, I went over to his place. To look around. I . . . nicked a photo he had on his mantel. From that day we all hiked Mount Hood, remember?"

Zay nodded, studying the chip of plastic in his palm.

"Wasn't until I brought it home that I noticed the back of the frame didn't fit right. He'd glued three drives to the back of the picture. One with each of our names on it."

"What's on them?" Zay asked.

"Who says I looked?"

"Come on, Shame," Terric said. "We know you."

"Fine. I looked. He made a kind of picture album for each of us. Photos, some documents, things from when we were younger. I think there are pictures of your mom and dad, Zay. Your real mom and dad."

He'd gone very, very still. He didn't talk much about his parents. Oh, I'd heard the stock answer he gave to everyone who asked, but he was fostered out young. For all I knew, he didn't even remember what his biological parents looked like.

But Victor knew. Victor always knew everything.

"What else?" Terric asked quietly.

"On yours is information about Soul Complements. All of them. Us," I corrected, "throughout history. All the good, all the bad. On yours, Z, is Victor's diary. Every damn day of his life since he joined the Authority. A hell of a lot of secrets."

Finally Zay looked away from the drive. "What's on yours?"

"A classified list. People who were Closed. Dangerous people. People who now are unClosed, people who now have all the memories back of what they did, what they were capable of doing, and of what the Authority did to stop them, change their lives, ruin their lives."

"Why?" Terric asked. "Why would he give you that list, Shame? You're not a Closer."

"He didn't want their memories taken away again. Didn't want them Closed. He wanted them dead."

I drank and let them deal with that for a bit.

Terric scrubbed his fingers back through his hair, which just fell back over his eyes. "Jesus. He left you a hit list?"

"He knew what I was. What we each are. Who else was he going to leave a hit list with?"

"Us," they both said at the same time.

"Because you carry Death magic in your bones?" I said.

"No," Zay said. "Because we were Closers, Shame. Not

you. We dealt with these kinds of people. Not you. We're trained for it. We were *good* at it."

"Hey, now," I said with a grin. "Are you jealous your dead teacher didn't tap you for the job? 'Cause you're sounding kind of jealous."

Gold washed over his eyes again. And a thought occurred to me. Maybe with Allie pregnant and less than a month out from delivery, it was not the best time to rankle Papa Jones.

"How many?" Zay growled.

Terric glanced over at him, startled, then back at me. He shook his head just slightly, telling me not to push Zay any further.

So of course, I pushed. Just a little.

"Not your business, mate. Victor didn't want you to help, Zay. He left this for me. Me alone. So now you're going to leave it to me. Alone."

The muscles in his arms tightened. It might have been a few years since we were running hard, but the man had lost none of his edge. I was pretty sure if both of us had no magic at our disposal, he would kick my ass in under five minutes.

Okay, under one.

But that's not how things were anymore. He and I were pretty much on equal ground. Except as far as I knew, Zayvion wasn't controlled by magic. Zayvion wasn't ridden by it and fighting it every moment, losing his humanity to it. Because only Terric and I had been dumb enough to sacrifice our lives and souls for each other on the magic battlefield and literally shove both Life and Death magic into each other to survive.

We'd taken magic into our blood and bones and flesh in exchange for dying. No other Soul Complements had come together while drowning in magic as Terric and I had. No other Soul Complements carried magic in their bodies.

Zay certainly wasn't that stupid.

That was my job: making bad choices.

Well, mine and Terric's job.

"Zay, Shame," Terric said. "Let's think this through before anyone starts throwing punches."

Peacemaker. I rolled my eyes at him.

"We are going to make a deal, Shame," Zayvion said, a little calmer than a moment ago. "If you're taking someone down, you tell me. That way I can make sure Stotts is off your ass."

"What do you think Stotts can do to me?" I asked. "Death magic user trumps cop."

"He'll throw you in jail," he said. "Things aren't the way they used to be. Which means that if you decide to take someone out, the Authority doesn't have the reach or the power to protect you anymore."

I dug for a cigarette, lit it. "I don't need your help, Zay. Not with the list. Not with the police. This is my business. And you don't need to be a part of it. As a matter of fact . . ." I exhaled smoke and tapped ashes into my empty beer bottle. "There is only one thing you should be focused on." Laughter rolled out of the house again and I waved the cigarette in that direction. "That right there."

Zay pushed off the rail and took the distance between us in three strides. He stood there, towering above me, glowering.

"Angry black man hasn't worked since we were fifteen," I said.

"You want to kill these people, I won't stand in your way," he said. "But if you don't tell me who you're after *before* you go after them, I will shut you down, Shame." Gold rolled across his eyes again. Heat lightning signaling a storm. "I will take you down."

"I already have a mother, Z. Don't need you riding my back."

"Are you hunting anyone now?"

A car engine cut off and a door opened and thunked shut. Someone was coming this way. Not that I could see around Mt. Zayvion.

"Right this minute?" I grinned.

He cracked his knuckles and Terric strolled over—finally—and put his hand on Zay's arm.

"I'll watch him, Zay."

"Like you can," I started, then shut my mouth. Kind of a dumb thing to say because Terric of all people *could* watch me. We were bound at the soul. His magic, my magic. If I killed he'd know. He'd feel it. He'd probably felt it all along.

"Hell," I said.

"Before," Zay said again. "Tell me *before* you kill. So I can cover your ass, you idiot." He punched me in the shoulder, just hard enough it stung.

"Hey, now," I said. "Keep that up and it will get personal."

"Tell me you heard me," he said.

"I heard you."

"Terric. Zay," Dashiell called out from the yard. "You two killing Shame?"

"Not yet," Zay said.

"Good," he said. "I have news."

Zay tipped his head down just a bit, giving me one last look. I took another drag off the cigarette and exhaled smoke through my smile.

He pulled back and got out of my space.

Which was good. It wasn't easy controlling the Death magic when he was that close, burning that hard, pumping life with every beat of his heart.

"What's the news?" I asked.

I wiped the sweat off my mouth and paced over to the railings where Zay and Terric had been standing, needing some fresh air. My hand was shaking. Not out of fear. Out of need. That little magic trick Terric and I had pulled in the car had worn off already.

I needed to kill. Soon, to take the edge off Death magic's hunger.

Dash looked . . . different. I'd been so used to him in an office setting as our assistant when Terric and I had been, ridiculously, given the job of running the Authority in Portland after the apocalypse that I almost didn't recognize him in casual mode.

Dark thick hair, a little too long, looked like he'd combed it back with his fingers into a sort of messy, wavy thing. He had on black-framed glasses that actually looked good on him. But that's where assistant Dash stopped resembling day-off Dash.

Day-off Dash wore faded blue jeans and a heavy gray wool sweater that showed just a bit of the brown belt at his hips, and opened up at the neck in a collar held together by a single wooden button. He hadn't shaved, and the stubble showed cheekbones and a strong jaw. When he caught sight of Terric and smiled . . .

It was weird to know a guy you used to work with—a friend—was sort of into the man you were unwillingly tied to.

Weirder still to get that emotional echo of Terric's confused feelings about Dash.

Terric liked Dash. I thought he might like him a lot. But ever since the complete disaster that had been Terric's last boyfriend, Jeremy, Terric had been avoiding the whole relationship thing.

"The news," Dash said, "is that we have a lead on Davy."

"You know where he is?" I asked.

"We know where he's been."

"Where?" Terric asked.

"Spokane."

"You don't think he's there now?" I asked.

Dash shook his head. "We sent some people from the area to take a look around. The entire building is empty. No one's there."

"Do you have records? Eyewitnesses who saw him?" Terric had suddenly snapped into ex-head of the Authority mode. He was all about dotting i's and crossing t's during times like this.

At times like this, I was all about getting out of the work he'd want to saddle me with.

I pushed away from the rail. "Well, then. I'll leave you boys to it. Thanks for the beer." I took a step toward the house.

A shadow darkened the doorway, then moved just enough to let the light fall on her features. Sunny, Davy's girlfriend.

"If you take one step off this porch, Flynn, I will hunt you down. You owe me."

The others fell silent and each gave Sunny a measuring gaze, then looked at me to see what I'd do.

I didn't have to guess what she was talking about. I owed her a favor, and it looked like she'd come to collect on it.

Chapter 5

SHAME

Zayvion strolled over to Sunny, faced off in front of her, the width of his shoulders and body pretty much blocking her view of me. It effectively broke our staring contest.

"Let's have this conversation inside," he said calmly. "Over coffee. Have you eaten?"

"I'm not hungry."

"Plenty of food left." He placed his hand on her arm kindly.

So I must not be the only one who saw how badly Davy's kidnapping had worn her down. Zay shifted so she could see past him again.

She glanced at me. Waited to see what I'd do. She was too pale, lack of sleep shadowing her eyes. Being a Blood magic user, being a Hound, meant she'd seen plenty of shit in her days. But Davy disappearing wasn't just another shitty day on the job. She loved him.

And love made a person go through all sorts of hell.

No need for me to be one of her hells.

"You know what? I'm starving," I said. "Let's get some food."

"Fine." She turned, walked inside. Zay threw me a quick look of approval before walking in behind her.

Terric and Dash waited for me to follow, so that pretty much closed off my escape route.

While I was all for dealing with whatever Sunny wanted from me, the hunger that wouldn't be satisfied with food rolled knuckles against my gut and squeezed at my heart.

Death was hungry, and the Life magic Terric had fed it wasn't nearly enough to satisfy.

Plan: Give Sunny whatever she wanted, then go out and kill something. Also, drink more beer.

I strolled back inside.

Zayvion calmly announced that he and Allie had enjoyed everyone coming over, but that Allie was tired now, and could everyone please head home.

Apparently I'd been out on the porch long enough ignoring the living world that they'd gotten through gifts and food and all the rest of the baby doings.

Good-byes were said, hugs and handshakes exchanged, and the house cleared out pretty quickly.

"We need a beer run?" I asked when the last Hound, guest, and even Violet, my mum, and Nola were all on their way. "Be happy to score us some hooch."

"Plenty of beer in the fridge," Zay said, patting my shoulder as he walked past me toward the sink with empty coffee cups in his other hand.

Stuck with the living in a no-kill zone. Good times.

Dash had somehow talked Sunny into actually trying the food and was talking to her quietly in the corner of the kitchen while they both ate.

She leaned against the counter mostly watching me. I didn't know what she wanted, but I knew the favor she'd given me.

Back a few months ago I'd killed Terric's boyfriend. I hadn't told Terric about it. I hoped I wouldn't ever have to tell him, but if it came up, I wasn't going to lie or defend my actions. Jeremy had been a grade-A asshole. He'd hurt Terric.

I'd taken care of that problem.

But Sunny had helped me track him down and had kept her mouth shut about it.

So yeah, I owed her.

I grabbed a beer and strolled into the living room.

Terric was helping Allie move the gifts into the nursery, and I found myself standing around with my hands in my pockets.

Eleanor pointed at a couple of pastel bags left by the couch and pointed at the stairs.

"Fine." Anything to make this parade move a little faster.

I held up the bags as Allie walked back into the living room. "Want these somewhere?"

"I can take them." She reached out for the gifts and I took a step back. Her touching me was a bad idea right now. "I got it. Nursery's upstairs, right?"

She narrowed her eyes. "Are you okay, Shame?"

"Why?"

"You're helping."

"Funny. I'm aces, love."

"Upstairs, on the left."

I passed Terric coming down the stairs and ignored his raised eyebrow at the baby gifts in my hands.

Hall, wooden stairs, dark wooden railing. There were a couple of pictures of Allie and Zay on the wall, and an antique table on the landing. Left, second door down to the nursery.

It was a small room, painted a soft yellow with white trim. A couple of wooden birdhouses were attached to one wall, and the shadows of swallows in flight winged across the ceiling. A painted tree anchored the far corner, and sitting out on the branch of the tree was the silhouette of a gargoyle with his arm and wing around a child.

Eleanor floated in and pressed her hands over her smile. She loved this stuff.

It was . . . amazing, really. Like a little world where nothing bad could ever happen.

I hoped that was true. I hoped this kid would have a much better life than any of us. But as long as there was magic in the world, I didn't think that could ever be true.

Wooden floor, wooden dresser, wooden crib. A pile of stuffed puppies—no, hounds, at least three dozen of them probably given to Allie from the Hounds themselves—was artistically stacked on top of Stone, Allie's pet gargoyle, who held very still in the corner.

He burbled when I came in.

"Hey, Stoney, you big dork. You been keeping an eye on Allie and baby Beckstrom?"

He was roughly the size of a Saint Bernard, big round eyes, pointed ears, wings on his back. He sat on his haunches, peoplelike fingers wrapped around wolflike back feet. His gaze shifted from me to the floor just in front of his feet.

A pink puppy about the size of a plum lay on the floor.

"You want this?" I bent, picked up the puppy.

Stone hummed, a sort of harmonious vacuum cleaner sound. I grinned and walked up to him.

"Hold still."

His eyes followed my hand as I slowly raised the stuffed toy and balanced it on top of the other two puppies already on his head between his ears.

I could practically feel him shiver in pleasure.

"There you go, buddy. You look fierce."

He pulled his lips back away from a collection of teeth that would make a shark jealous.

I put the gifts down on the rocking chair as quietly as I could so as not to spoil the peace of the place somehow.

I turned.

"Hey," Allie said. "How about that talk?" She stepped

into the little room, and I stepped back so there was some distance between us.

"What can I help you with, Al?"

"I need to ask you a question."

I spread my hands. "All ears."

"Did you kill Brandy Scott?"

"Eli Collin's Soul Complement?" I asked. "I thought the doctors said she died of a heart attack."

"Her heart stopped beating." Allie leaned against the crib and crossed her arms. "But she was under careful observation in the mental institution, Shame. Constant care."

"And?"

"And you haven't answered me yet."

See, Allie knew how to get right to the point.

"She's dead," I said. "I don't see that it matters how she got that way."

"It matters to me."

"Why?"

"Because I think you did it. Zayvion doesn't think you'd be dumb enough to kill the only bargaining chip we had to get Eli and his boss, Krogher, to negotiate with us so we could get Davy and all those other people they've kidnapped back. But I think you did it because Eli killed Victor and Dessa. Am I wrong?"

"What do you want me to tell you, Al? I'm glad she's dead, even though we lost the bargaining chip."

"You killed her."

I didn't say anything, just stared at her.

She closed her eyes, then opened them again. "Hells, Shame. I can't believe this. You know he'll come for you. Eli Collins will walk right up to you and kill you in your sleep the first chance he gets."

"Let him come," I said. "I'd be happy to have a little heart-to-heart with him."

"And that's why you did it, isn't it? You didn't want to negotiate—you wanted to declare war."

"He killed Victor," I said quietly. "And Dessa. I'm not sorry Brandy's dead."

"Does Terric know?"

"I think this conversation has about run its course, don't you?"

"So he doesn't know."

I hated that she could read me so well, but then, she'd been a Hound for years, and a damn fine one. Plus, she knew me pretty well.

"You and Terric should leave. Out of the country, somewhere safe."

"Hold on," I said. "One, I can take care of myself and so can Terric. We're safe right where we are. Two, I didn't say I killed her, I just said I'm not sad about her death, and three, you need to let go of this. Put it down completely, Allie. Eli was threatening to kill me long before Brandy was dead. If he wants to kill me, he is welcome to step up to bat and give it a swing.

"But I do not want you getting in the middle of any of this. You do remember he took a stab—literally—at Zayvion a few months back? He has technology to pop himself into any room anytime he wants, and he knows where you live.

"So listen to me, love." I stepped toward her. "You are not to do anything to become a target."

She shook her head and looked away from me. "I can't just—"

"You can. *Just.*" I tipped my head to catch her gaze. "Do you understand how important it is to me that you stay out of this and keep that little godbaby of mine safe?"

"The baby will be fine," she said.

"We don't know that. You and Zay don't know that. The plan of you two not using magic or breaking magic until little Beckstrom-Jones shows up is still the right plan. A couple months and you can be in this fight up to your neck if you want," I said. "Until then, please, Allie." I reached over, touched her hand. "Stay far, far away from this."

Her eyes widened just a little at my touch. At the cold of it, the dead of it.

I pulled my fingers away and gave her half a grin. "Fine," I said before she could ask. "I'm fine. My magic's fine. It's under control."

She shook her head. "You think you're good at it, don't you?" she said as she walked toward the door.

"What?"

"Lying."

"Grading on a curve I'll pull an easy B-plus in bullshittery any day."

"You know I'll share what I know with Zayvion," she said as we walked down the stairs.

"Sure. Send him my way if he has any questions."

We walked out into the living room and Zayvion shifted in the love seat, making room for Allie to sit next to him, his arm around her.

He gave me a questioning look and I shrugged. She'd tell him what we were talking about or not. Lady's choice.

Dash and Terric sat as far apart from each other on the couch as possible, looking just as uncomfortable as it sounds. Sunny leaned against the bookshelf picking at a plate of fruit.

"Is this it?" I asked.

"This is it," Zay said.

"I expected as least Mum to stay," I said. "Not like her to miss out on a hunt."

"I asked her to give us some time," Zay said. "This isn't her mess to deal with."

And by that, he meant Mum wasn't a Soul Complement, and therefore wasn't a walking magical weapon.

Interesting.

I took the open chair. "Dashiell, mate, you're on. Tell us what you know about Davy."

Dash bent and pulled a file folder out of the messenger bag at his feet. "There's a company up in Spokane that handles testing for agricultural chemicals. Pesticides, fertilizers, that sort of thing. We've been getting the word out that we're looking for Davy, Eli Collins, and Krogher, the man who we think is keeping Eli under his employ and using him to kidnap the people who were infected with tainted magic back before the apocalypse. But we've been careful about our investigation, using only verified channels, verified people. So the search has been slow."

I glanced over at Sunny. She just stood there, a grape in her fingers, eyes trained on Dash. She was pretty much running the Hounds in Portland now that Davy was gone, but not every city was as organized as she was when it came to freelance magical P.I.'s.

Portland was one of the first to make strides in the Hounds being compensated fairly for their work, and for their work to be legitimized.

We might have a network of Hound eyes and ears here in town, but it wasn't the same everywhere. I was pretty sure the Hound situation in Spokane wasn't nearly as well run as what Allie had started and Sunny and Davy had perfected.

"We finally got eyes on the ground," he continued. "One of our people got into the plant and took a look around. "The entire place was cleaned out. Not a desk, test tube, or latex glove left behind. No record of a sale. Wasn't bankruptcy. One minute the company appeared to be in full operation. The next, it was gone."

"Odd," Terric said, "but not that unusual. They could have pulled up tent stakes for any number of reasons."

"Overnight?" I shook my head. "I'm going with Dash on this one. Company that size doesn't blow out of Dodge without some warning. So why do you think Davy was there?"

"Our person on the ground got this." He pulled out a photo, handed it to Terric instead of me.

Old habits die hard. Sure, both Terric and I had been Dash's bosses, but Terric had stuck with it twice as long.

"A Containment spell?" Terric said. "Anyone could have drawn that." He handed the picture to me. Concrete warehouse floor, yellow safety tape marking *x*'s and *t*'s where equipment or maybe pallets would have been.

But it was the spell on the floor—not drawn, burned into the concrete—that drew my attention. "This isn't Containment," I said, turning the picture upside down. "This is Crossing. See the faint double arc?"

Zay leaned forward and I handed it across the coffee table to him. Crossing was a spell that could be used for getting over a river or across a border safely. But Crossing could be used for other sorts of difficult passages if you had the will for it. Might even be used for getting out of shackles, getting out of a jail cell, or getting out of a warehouse.

And Davy had a hell of a will.

"It's both," Zay said. "Containment and Crossing. One on top of the other. Sunny, are they Davy's signature?"

She walked over, took the photo, her gaze tracing through the lines of the spell. "The Containment isn't him, but the Crossing? Yes." She handed Zay the photo. "Are we done talking about this? Every minute we waste here is a minute we lose finding him."

"Give us fifteen minutes to come up with a plan," Allie said, "and get some backups in place."

"You do that." Sunny walked toward the door. "Shame, you're with me."

"I don't think so."

"You owe me," she said.

Terric looked over at me and raised his eyebrows. "What do you owe her?"

"And I'll pay up," I said, ignoring him. "But I'm not driving three hundred and fifty miles to an empty warehouse without a little more info."

"What else do you need to know?" she asked. "That's his signature. He was there. Now he's not. You and I go find out where he went from there."

"Shame's not a Hound," Allie said.

"Meaning?" she asked.

"He won't be any good at tracking Davy."

"Hey," I said.

"You don't need Shame to help you find where Davy went anyway," she said. "You can do that. All you need Shame for is to kill the people holding him."

"I've got guns," she said.

"Guns won't be enough," Terric said. "And neither will Shame."

"Oh, come on, now," I said. "Right here. I'm sitting right here."

"We tried it that way." Terric threw me a look. "Shame and I together, we tried stopping Krogher and Eli Collins and the kidnapped people they'd carved up to hold magic. It didn't work."

What he was omitting was that we'd pulled on Life and Death magic against them and taken down half a hospital defending against the magic and tech Eli was using with his boss, Krogher. Terric had nearly died. Dessa Leeds had died. I'd come out of the entire event in a killing mood that wasn't anywhere near done yet.

"We'll find Davy," he was saying. "But no one is going to walk into a trap."

"How can this be a trap?" she said. "That warehouse is empty. You have eyewitness confirmation."

"Maybe," Terric said. "But if I were a government agency that wanted to get rid of Soul Complements who could stop it from using people—people like Davy, people like those they've kidnapped and turned into weapons—I'd start by luring a couple Soul Complements out into the middle of nowhere, then picking them off nice and easy in an empty warehouse."

"One Soul Complement," Sunny said. "You aren't invited, Terric."

"Where Shame goes, I go."

They had themselves a little staring match. Terric won.

Well, this was fun and all, but that hunger inside me wasn't backing off. Time to move this along.

"Dash, do you have someone on this?" I asked. "A Hound or two?"

"Try a dozen," he said.

Sunny exhaled loudly. "I'm going."

"They don't need you there," Zayvion said.

"Davy needs me."

"Alive," Allie said. "He needs you alive."

"So we sit here?" she demanded. "Do nothing?"

"We make a plan," Terric said. "And we gather information so we're not going into something blind. Dash, have the Spokane Hounds uncovered anything yet?"

Dash pushed his glasses closer to his nose and glanced at Sunny. "We have three leads saying they disappeared in three different directions. The moment they find out which one isn't a wild-goose chase, they'll call."

"And that's when we'll go get Davy," Terric said to Sunny.

"Good for you," she said. "Sit here and wait for all I care. I'm out." She started toward the door.

"Sunny," Terric said. "Don't go after him."

"See you around." She stormed across the room and slammed the door behind her.

"Tell me you have someone tailing her," I said to Dash.

"Several someones. Want me to put in a call so they keep her in the city?"

"She'll slip them," Allie said. "She's been a Hound for too long now not to expect someone to be shadowing her."

"Suggestions?" Dash said.

"Tell the Hounds to—" Allie stopped, took a deep breath, and held it.

Zay shifted and looked down at her, his arm up off her as if she suddenly couldn't bear the weight of it. He wasn't breathing either.

I scanned the room, expecting magic or some kind of attack. Nothing.

"Hello?" I said. "Are you two okay?"

They exhaled in unison. Allie nodded. "Fine. False alarm."

"False alarm for what?" I asked.

"Contractions," Zay said. He gave me a level look that did nothing to hide the fact that he'd gone a little wide-eyed for a minute there.

"The baby?" Dash asked. "Allie, do we need to get you to the hospital?"

"No." She brushed her fingers back through her hair and tucked it behind her ears. "It's false labor. Just giving us a preview for the big day."

I shifted my gaze back to Zay. He settled his arm around her again and was working the supercalm and supercollected. Nice cover-up, but I could see the panic in the twitch of his lips.

"Isn't it a little early for the baby?" I asked, just to watch Zay sweat.

"A little, but I'm not having the baby yet," Allie said. "This is fine. *Normal*," she stressed, taking Zay's hand and giving it a squeeze.

I delighted in the faint sheen of sweat that broke out on his forehead.

"You sure it's not the real deal?" I asked while Zay's heart rate kicked up a bit. "Baby could be here any second, mate. You sure you're ready for that?"

"I'm not in labor," Allie said, giving me a dirty look because she knew exactly what I was doing. "I'd know."

"Of course, darlin', 'cause you've done this so many times yourself."

"Shut up, Shame," Terric said.

"Just tell the Hounds to keep an eye on Sunny," Allie told Dash. "Contact and pay a few of them between here and Spokane to look out for her. If Sunny goes after Davy, we'll want to know where she is at all times."

"Sure," Dash said.

"And what are we going to do about finding Davy?" Terric asked. "If Krogher and Eli are on the move, they might be vulnerable. This could be our chance to pinpoint him."

We were all quiet. We'd tried looking for him all the standard ways, and plenty of nonstandard ways, for months. But wherever Eli Collins had him hidden, it was buttoned up so tight we had gotten nowhere.

That was the problem when your enemy buddied up with government insiders like Krogher. They suddenly had resources for a lot of things, including experimental magic tech.

We were at a dead loss for anything else we could do to find him. Well, anything nonmagical.

"If the baby's doing okay—" Allie started.

"No," Zay said.

"But you could find him, couldn't you, Zay?" she asked.

"We don't know that," he said.

Actually we did kind of know that. One of the tricks that Zayvion had picked up from being Guardian of the gates was he could go into a sort of Zen state and locate people in the city. He was especially good at locating people he knew, and he knew Davy very well.

Of course that was when magic was broken and strong.

"We could break magic," Allie said. "Maybe it wouldn't hurt the baby. I'm far enough along—"

"No," Zay said. He closed his eyes for a moment, and

Allie stared off into the middistance, then closed her eyes, listening to whatever he was saying to her in her mind.

The thing about Soul Complements is they became closer and closer until they could read each other's minds. Then they were in each other's minds more than they were in their own, and in a very short amount of time, they were no longer separate at all. They were joined so tightly they were something else, a combination of two people, two souls.

Allie and Zay had that kind of closeness. They didn't seem to mind it, so bully for them. But it was more than a little strange to see the two of them so easily slip into being just one of them.

I looked over at Terric. He had a kind of wistful expression on his face until he glanced over at me. Then all that emotion locked down tight.

Yeah. I didn't want that for us either. Shoving Life and Death in the same little cage would only end up with one or both of us bloody and broken.

"Well," Dash said. "I'll contact the Hounds, make sure they have eyes out for Sunny. I'll let Clyde know about it too, since I'm sure we'd like the current head of the Authority to know what we're doing, right?"

Terric nodded. "He should know."

"Good," Dash said. "If there's anything else I can do, please give me a call."

Allie and Zayvion opened their eyes at the same time. They had that sort of not-quite-them look on their faces.

Gave me the creeps.

Zayvion pushed up to his feet. "Thanks for coming by, Dash. Keep us in the loop. If one of the trails pans out in Spokane, I want to be a part of it."

Dash filed the photo and report away into his messenger bag. "I'll let you know if we get anything on Davy's location. But I understand you have other more pressing priorities."

"Thank you," Allie said softly.

This suddenly seemed like a good time to bail and go find me something to kill before Allie decided she was going to bring up the whole Brandy Scott thing with Zayvion.

"I'm off, then," I said. "Terric, you going to catch a ride with Dash?"

Terric frowned. "No. We came in my car."

"Then let's go, mate." I said my good-byes with a wave and a "later," then tromped out of the house, wanting distance between me and the living, pronto.

Terric lingered to talk to Zayvion, which left me out by the car smoking for a minute or two.

Dash strolled up to me. "You okay, Shame?"

"I've been worse. Including dead."

He leaned against the car, hands in his back pockets, and faced the house the way I was facing the house. "Do you have any idea what Terric's been doing?" he asked.

"Specifically?"

"Research of some kind," he said.

"He hasn't mentioned it. Why?"

"It's just . . . he asked me for access into some pretty old texts. He's been spending a lot of time looking for them. The word *obsessive* comes to mind."

"Magic, I assume? Old Authority stuff?"

"Not exactly. He wanted into some of Allie's father's records."

Allie was a sweet woman. Loved her dearly. But her father was a complete dick. He was a cold, hard bastard, who was also Eli's mentor. He had an obsession with mixing magic and technology. An obsession that had made him a very rich man and had given Eli the kinds of ideas that landed us where we were at—kidnapped Davy, and kidnapped people spelled up with enough magic and tech they were human bombs. Beckstrom had been a big player in the Authority, and yeah, he'd killed my father.

So in general, I hated the son of a bitch.

But his magic tech? The disks that could store magic, and the networked conduits underground that could channel magic? Damn. He changed the world with his technology.

I had no idea why Terric would be digging into that man's past.

"Which of his records?" I asked.

"A lot. Notes from decades ago. Tech records. I finally tracked them down."

"And gave them to Terric?"

He nodded again. "I might have scanned copies for myself."

I grinned and slid him a sideways look. "I forget how underhanded you can be. You make me proud. Going to give me a peek?"

"I'll send them over later today."

"Good. So, when are you going to ask Terric out?"

"What? Did he say something about me?"

"No," I said. "You like him. He likes you. Ask him out. Worst he can say is no."

"He did."

"What?"

"He said no."

I glanced back at the house. "Recently?"

"Couple months back. He says he's not interested in a relationship. That he likes me as a friend." He winced. "So that's that."

"Really?" I was tied to Terric's emotions. I knew he most certainly didn't only like Dash as a friend. I wondered why he was lying to him. "My bad, then. Sorry. I don't mean to meddle."

Dash chuckled. "You always mean to meddle."

"Not *always*."

He just raised an eyebrow. "Think we'll find Davy alive?"

"I don't think he's dead. Eli was having too much fun with him. Davy's *useful* to Eli or his bosses in some way."

"You'd think things would be different," he said. "Magic

gets healed so people can't use it to destroy. And instead of considering that a blessing, or a warning, people just find a new way to use magic to destroy."

"We are determined little bastards, aren't we?"

Terric stepped out of the house and Dash pushed away from the car. "That's my cue. You take care of yourself, Shame. Go kill something, okay? You're not looking so hot."

"Is it that obvious?"

"To me it is. You were practically salivating over Allie back there." He glanced over at me. "Lots of terminally ill who wouldn't mind an end to their contract."

"I'll keep that in mind. Also, you are a twisted, twisted man, Dashiell Spade."

He looked away to Terric, then back at me again. "I'm a pragmatist, Shame. You have a need for death. There's a merciful way to deal with that."

"Sure," I said. "I'll get right on it."

"One of these days, you'll listen to me. See you."

I watched him stride off to his car, watched him not turn to look at Terric, who was headed our way, watched him get in and drive off as if he couldn't feel Terric's eyes following him.

"You told him no?" I asked when Terric was close enough.

"About what?"

"Dating."

Terric paused with his hand on the door handle of the driver's side. "Of all the things to pay attention to, it's my love life? You seriously need a hobby, Shamus."

"I'm just saying, you like Dash."

"Crocheting, stamp collecting." He snapped his fingers. "Porn."

"What?"

"Hobby. Get one."

"Have one. It's bothering you. So, why shouldn't you date Dash?"

"Why do you think he deserves that?"

"Why doesn't he?"

Terric stared at me. The warmth and humanity drained away like a wave receding, revealing the stone cold inhumanity beneath. Apparently he had about as much control over the magic inside him as I did.

Death pushed so hard I could feel the cold of it behind my teeth. It wanted that. Wanted the magic roiling inside him. I took a deep, steadying breath, but the corners of my vision went shady and my heart thumped hard enough it was a bass drum in my ears.

We'd just used together too much. I wasn't going to do that to Terric again. Not so soon. Not ever, if I could help it.

This was getting ridiculous. My control was in the sewer today. Okay, lately.

"Because he doesn't deserve to be hurt," he said. Then he opened the door and ducked into the car.

I stood there until I could breathe right again. Maybe a few of the scrub oaks by the river died. Maybe a lot of the bushes died too. It wasn't just people I could pull life from, but people were always best.

The local vegetation was just enough to dampen the need. Barely.

If I was this close to the edge of losing control, Terric was even closer. Maybe he was right. No one deserved what he and I were. We were nothing but pain.

I opened the door and got in the car.

Chapter 6

SHAME

The house I'd won in a poker game was staked against the hills in Portland and surrounded by trees. The road snaked above it and the only way to get a good look at it was if you happened to glance up when you were navigating hairpin corners on the road below.

Terric had taken one of the spare rooms, and while he hadn't added a single item to my living room decor, which was no longer an armory of weapons, but was definitely still thrift shop chic, he had nonetheless made himself at home here.

Why had I let him stay?

For one thing, the man liked to cook.

I considered it one of his better qualities.

"Beer and ketchup." Terric shut the refrigerator door. "It was your turn to shop, Shame."

I pulled out my cell phone, dialed.

"What are you doing?" he said.

"Shopping. Hey," I said when the voice picked up on the other end. "Two large pizzas, vegetarian, pepperoni."

Terric rolled his eyes and grabbed us both a couple beers. "You're all kinds of class."

I hung up, took the beer, and popped the cap. "Back at-cha."

"Call me when it gets here," he said, walking off.

"Where you going to be?"

"Shower."

I paced and drank. Checked on the ferret I'd inherited from Dessa, the last person I'd loved and gotten killed.

The ferret, Jinkies, was asleep, curled up in the soft cotton blanket Terric had bought him.

Jinkies used to belong to Dessa's brother, Thomas, before he'd been killed by Eli Collins under Krogher's orders. I didn't know what secrets they'd gotten out of Thomas, but I was pretty sure his death had proved that having Eli Collins on board to help the government track all us Soul Complements down and kill us was worth the trouble.

Of course, Eli had a slightly different story. He said the government had kidnapped him and was forcing him to kill. But I knew the guy. He liked dealing out the blood and pain.

Somehow on the way to tracking down her brother's killer, Dessa and I had fallen, fast and hard, for each other.

Then Eli killed her.

I wandered over to my laptop set up on the table in the corner of the room. Checked messages.

Looked like I'd gotten a file from Dash.

Boy was quick.

I pulled out a chair, sat, and opened the file.

At first I wasn't sure what I was looking at. I had expected technical manuals, or research papers from Beckstrom Enterprises.

The scanned pages were handwritten and yellowed, and didn't look modern. Diagrams sketched glyphs I did not recognize connected together in ways I didn't understand, all working together in a manner I could not fathom.

Why the hell was Terric looking at this?

I clicked through a few more pages until something caught my eye.

Unbinding. It was the steps of an unbinding spell, mixed with a few other spells, carved into flesh with the blood of two people.

No, with the blood of Soul Complements.

This was a spell to unbind Soul Complements.

I wondered if it worked.

"It didn't," Terric said from behind me.

"Whose research is it?" I turned in the chair.

Terric was shirtless, drying his hair with a towel. The Void-stone-bullet scars from our last fight with Eli were still red knots of scar tissue sprayed across his gut, crisscrossed with marks from the surgery that had saved his life.

When I made my list of things to kill Eli for, Terric's near death at his hands was right up there.

"A woman named Doris Gables."

"Haven't heard of her," I said.

"She died in 1910." He tossed the towel over the arm of the couch and shrugged into the T-shirt he'd left there. "Allie's father was very interested in her theories and experiments with magic, particularly her research on the bond between Soul Complements."

"And you're interested in breaking that bond? Between us?"

He paused and gave me a long look. "Aren't you?"

"It would solve one problem."

"But?"

"Out on that battlefield in St. Johns," I said.

"Oh, so now you want to talk about it? Almost four years later?"

"Not if you're going to be a dick about it," I said.

He gestured with one hand, as if giving me the floor, then moved the towel out of the way and sat on the arm of the couch.

"You were dying," I said. "So I gave you the life I had left. I expected to die. I threw myself into Death magic aiming for one last chance to take that bastard Jingo Jingo out with me. I became Death magic. Not just a man who can use Death magic. I let it in me. And it's still there, in me."

"And?" he said quietly.

"You brought me back, you ass." I took a breath, let it out. "I didn't know how then, but I do now. You called on Life magic, and it answered you, *claimed* you, just like Death magic claimed me. Even if we weren't Soul Complements, we'd still be screwed by the magic we carry."

"True," he said. "That's why I've been looking into the old records. To see if anyone ever became carriers of magic, and how they may have handled it. Or didn't Dash give you those files yet?"

I grinned. "Maybe. I haven't gotten that far. Has anyone?"

"Carried a certain discipline of magic in their flesh and blood?" He wadded up the towel in his hand. "We're pretty much cutting edge on this gig."

"Delightful," I said. "Anything else you want to share with the class?"

"Nothing that comes to mind. Although I looked into the records on the transport device—the gate spell Eli has been using. It's a modification of Beckstrom tech. Powered by electricity and a configuration of crystals from the well in St. Johns. Probably has a five-hundred-mile range."

"So if Eli shows up, we can assume he's stationed somewhere in the Pacific Northwest. Not helpful."

"A little helpful," Terric said.

I made the so-so motion with my hand, stood, and started pacing. "And nothing on the radar about strange magics, or walking human magic bombs, or anything else that could turn us onto where the hell Krogher has Eli and Davy stashed?"

"If I knew, you'd know," he said. "Call when the pizza gets here." He pushed off the couch and walked back to his room.

I finally gave up on the pacing and flopped down on the couch. I could feel Terric's heart beating, just as I knew he could feel mine. It was annoying.

My fingers worked the heavy material of the couch, picking, pulling thread. Tearing. Destroying. There was a reason why all my furniture looked like it belonged in a junkyard.

I wasn't easy on anything around me. Or anyone, for that matter.

But the world was filled with life I could feed to this death. I closed my eyes and reached outward with my thoughts. Trees all around, roots holding the hillside together. It'd be easy to drain them, but doing so could trigger a rock slide. I did not feel like digging my way out of an avalanche if I screwed that up.

Farther off was the river. Lots of things living in there. Who would care if I killed off a couple dozen steelhead?

Death magic sprang to my will without even a word or glyph. Hunger coiled in my bones, in my mind, like an attack dog on a leash. I focused on the river, focused on the fish. Only a few. I would only kill a few. I held that image in my mind, of magic slipping, hungry and dark, into those slick silver bodies. Crushing cold brains, drinking rich blood.

"Yes," I whispered.

Death exploded, a thrown grenade dead on target. Fifteen fish. Fifteen small hearts stopped. Fifteen lives consumed. I inhaled, drank the lives down. Wanted more. So damn much more.

The doorbell rang. I stared at the ceiling and held my breath against the uneven, painful beats of my heart. Death wanted more. Death wanted the guy on the other side of the door.

Crap.

"Terric?" I whispered. The bell rang again. "Terric?" I said a little louder.

"Heard you the first time." He strode through the room and opened the door. We never locked it because, seriously? Who was going to break into this dump and try to kill two of the most powerful magic users in Portland?

"Thanks," I heard Terric say. There was a pause, and then the door shut again. "Kitchen."

He sauntered past. It took me a second, but I finally got my brain clear enough to walk into the kitchen. I needed more life than I'd taken from the fish. Pizza wasn't going to solve my problem, but it was going to be delicious.

Terric sat at the table, the pizza boxes stacked on top of the other, the top one open. Pepperoni. He hadn't bothered with plates. A six-pack of beer sat next to the boxes and the potted lucky bamboo Allie had given me as a housewarming gift was next to that.

"Sit," Terric said around a mouthful. "Eat."

The bamboo was woven at the base, seven trunks interlocked to form a sort of living basket. Vibrant green leaves reached out from the top of the bamboo, and as I watched, the entire plant grew half an inch or so.

Terric was slowly, carefully, feeding Life magic into it.

I sat down across from him, grabbed a piece of pizza, and tore into it.

The bamboo grew, new leaves curling outward.

If I drained too much life out of it, the plant would die for good. But if I pulled just as much life out of it as Terric was pouring into it, the plant would be fine.

I can't remember when we started doing this. We never spoke about it; just every once in a while the plant would end up at the kitchen table while we were eating and pretending not to use magic together, or out on the coffee table by the TV when we were arguing over a show and pretending not to use magic together.

So far we'd kept the plant alive.

I finished two slices of pizza before I felt up to the task. Then I carefully drained the life out of the plant. Which was good because the thing had grown another couple of inches.

Terric poured more into it. But not too much, because too much life was just as deadly as too much death.

"Dash is worried about you," I said, going for my third slice.

"He told you that?"

"He said you've been spending a lot of time digging into old records. Called you obsessive."

Terric chewed, chased pizza with beer. "Is this you asking me if I'm okay, Shame?"

"This is just casual dinner conversation."

"Our casual dinner conversation usually involves arguing over song lyrics, sports, and you asking me when I'm going to move out."

"When are you going to move out?"

"When you ask me nicely."

"Like that will ever happen."

He grinned and tipped his beer. "There you go."

"I'm willing if you're willing," I said.

"To do what?"

"Break our connection. Give it a try, anyway. If you want."

For a second, he stopped pouring life into the bamboo, and the leaves edged with brown because I hadn't adjusted for the pull.

But he picked it up again like the smooth son of a bitch he was and the plant greened up again.

"She tried it on herself," he said.

"Who?"

"Doris Gables. She tried breaking her Soul Complement connection with her husband and coscientist."

"And?"

"Turns out the only way you can break a soul connection is if one of the Soul Complements dies."

"Mmm." I dragged another piece of pie out of the box. "I take it Mr. Gables didn't make it?"

"No, he did. But it killed Doris."

He sat back and looked at the window over the kitchen sink where the nice normal world rustled and sunshined and otherwise went about its business regardless of Death and Life sharing a pizza.

"I was looking into ways we could deal with our connection," he said. "With our need to use magic together. Things other Soul Complements might have done."

"Besides go insane or get killed?" I asked.

He nodded. "I think we deserve a plan C, at least. Or if not us, Allie and Zay deserve some options."

"They seemed pretty happy to me."

"They are now," he said quietly. Yeah, I knew what he was worried about.

There were no happy endings for Soul Complements. And even though Allie and Zay were setting a record for Soul Complement ever-after bliss, there were dangers. Danger of losing who they were to the need of being joined as one.

And they were dragging a kid into the middle of that, of them slipping up one of these days and becoming something that wasn't quite human.

"How about the microdrive with Soul Complement information on it?" I said. "Might be something there."

"I'll look." He grabbed another piece. "Shame, today, in the car . . . I want to say—"

"Don't."

"—I *appreciate* what you did. For me. Death magic for the Life magic to consume. It helped."

Sure. That had been all about him. Only it hadn't. I'd wanted it as much as he did.

But I didn't tell him that.

"How's your head?" At his look, I added, "Where you cracked it on the window."

"It's good. Healed." He glanced away, guilty about it. Man had issues.

"I was the one who hit you, Ter. I was the one who got aggressive about the whole let's-do-magic thing."

"Speaking of. Burn, Shame? Were you really going to cast Burn in my car?"

"Got your attention, didn't it?"

"Yes. Which means you owe me. I own the speakers tonight."

I groaned. The house was wired so that there were speakers in every room. If you wanted to play music, just hook up the tunes and the whole house was rocking.

Terric had crap taste in music. Jeff Buckley and Counting Crows, for God's sake.

"No," I said. "Ask for something else. Anything."

"Anything?" He held my gaze as he finished off his beer. I had an idea of what was going through his head. Not because I could read his mind but because he'd threatened me with the same thing for the last three months.

A schedule.

Laundry days, shopping days, cooking days, and yes, bathroom-cleaning days. Please. I'd rather die.

"Forget it," I said. "You can have the speakers."

"You sure?" he said, already knowing what I'd say. "I'm feeling the urge to go full-on Portishead."

Gag.

"Better than getting domestic with you, mate. I refuse to check off a list that involves sorting my socks."

"Keep telling yourself that. You know you'll be sorry when I'm gone."

"Hey," I said. "Here's a thing. How about you tell me

what you're smoking so I can hop on the all-delusion-all-the-time thing you've got going there?"

He set his beer down. "Suddenly I've changed my mind." He pushed up out of the chair. "How does six hours of Hootie and the Blowfish sound?"

"Bite me."

"Now, now, Flynn. I thought you didn't want to play for the other team." He took a step, grinning.

And then the air behind him sizzled with a ribbon of vertical fire.

"Terric," I yelled.

I knew what that ribbon was. I'd seen it the last time Eli Collins had popped into my room and given me an ultimatum at gunpoint. It was a gate, it was tech and magic, and Eli was on the other side controlling it.

A hole in space yawned open.

Terric turned.

Eli Collins, the psychopath we'd been looking for, stepped through that hole.

Terric and I raised our hands, drew on magic.

Eli already had the gun aimed, bullets tearing through the air.

Magic is fast. Bullets are faster.

Terric took one in the chest. A second hit me in the throat.

Eli had a knife in his other hand. He slashed Terric's neck. Blood poured free as Terric fell to the floor, gasping.

Terric's pain and my pain hit me like a damn truck. I couldn't breathe. I fell to my knees.

And then Eli was standing over me, the gun trained on my head.

"Hello, Shame," he snarled. "I've been waiting a long, *long* time for this."

I pulled on Death magic.

He squeezed the trigger.

Magic is fast. Bullets are faster.

One shot in my head. Then heart, stomach, chest, lungs. One in each leg.

Everything was shock white, hot, burning. I couldn't think, couldn't reach the magic inside me.

I think I hit the floor. Watched with fading sight as Eli dragged Terric back through the hole in space. Maybe Terric was still alive. Maybe Terric was still breathing. I felt one more hot push of his agony.

And then I felt nothing. No heat, no pain. Because I wasn't breathing. I wasn't living.

Eleanor, next to me, screamed.

Eli Collins emptied the rest of the clip into my body.

I didn't feel a thing.

I heard Eleanor again, for a brief moment: *Shame! No! Don't go!*

I tried to answer but had no voice. The room filled with light. At the edge of that light I saw the tunnel, the road that led to death. The real, through-the-veil, no-coming-back death.

Like hell I was walking that road.

But my feet were not my own.

I got one last glimpse of my body, bloody and riddled with holes, staining the linoleum. Had one last thought that Terric would be pissed at the mess we'd made of the kitchen.

Eli yelled obscenities at my corpse from the other side of that hole. Then he closed the gate before I could even take a step.

And then I was dead.

Chapter 7

TERRIC

"Terric!"

The last thing Shame said—my name.

I spun as an explosion of pain tore through me.

Bullet. I staggered, but it wasn't a hand that caught me. It was a knife. I couldn't breathe, couldn't swallow around the pain.

Blood pumped from my throat, hot and slick, down my chest.

He'd slit my throat. Someone had slit my throat. The shock of that couldn't penetrate the horror I was already grappling with.

Shame was dying, right there on our kitchen floor.

For a slow, terrifying moment, I sifted the possibilities. Who could break into our home without us noticing? Who would know we would both be here together?

Then I heard his voice and knew who was behind me: Eli Collins.

We'd spent so much time looking for him, but he'd always known right where we would be. In Portland. Together. I don't know why he'd waited so long to attack. But Eli never did anything randomly.

I tried to raise my hands to push Eli away, to fight. Nothing about me was working. Blood loss, possibly poison, the bullet wound, and the pain of Shame dying. I felt cut in half from head to soul.

I was dying too.

Life magic caught fire inside me like lighter fluid under a match and devoured me whole.

God, not again. The healing Life magic forced me through was pure hell. It was always pure hell.

If I could breathe, I'd scream. If I could think, I'd turn Life magic on Eli to rip him apart. If I could move, I'd save Shame. But all I could do was endure.

Something deep and important inside me broke with a bone-shattering crack.

Please, no.

But I knew. Knew what that break had to be—my soul connection with Shame.

Shame was dead. Gone.

And my world went dark.

I woke with a soft grunt, lying on my back. Breathing. Hurting. Tied up.

My mouth tasted like piss and oil and blood—the remainder of whatever poison and magic Eli had put on the knife blade.

My chest felt like a block of ice were balanced on top of it: a cold I could not shake that held me pinned.

Shame was gone. . . . I pushed that thought away, buried it. I needed to remain calm. Needed to find a way out of this, whatever this was.

So I could kill Eli Collins.

I could not feel anyone near me, could not sense their beating hearts, their dying bodies.

I was alone.

"This is the first day, Terric Conley."

I jerked at the voice, a man's, cultured, but an American accent, echoing through the room. His words had the careful elocution of someone who had worked overseas for a decade or two.

I opened my eyes and saw nothing but blackness and blur. I wasn't blind or blindfolded.

"The first day will be the easiest," the voice said.

I blinked until my vision cleared. I was in a cage, thick bars reaching from floor to the darkness lost in the rafters. I was chained down to a cot by hands, ankles, waist. Shadows robbed the details, but I could make out an industrial fan high above me, and from somewhere over my left shoulder, a dim light shone. Shadows curved around pipes—old, rusting, and I thought I heard the steady drip of water leaking.

It smelled of dirt and coal and damp rust. A factory.

"The first day you will know what we want," the voice continued. The sound of footsteps echoed off the ceiling, the walls. It was a large room. Warehouse. The floor was concrete, uneven with the scratch of gravel and metal shavings.

Machine shop.

"The first day you can give us what we want without pain. Without cost." The man stopped just out of my line of vision.

I knew that voice. Where had I heard it before?

"The first day is free." He took two more steps, came into my line of sight.

Older man, gray hair brushed up away from his face, forehead creased from temple to temple, more lines winging out from around and below his heavy-lidded dark eyes. His nose was hooked and wide at the tip, his cheekbones hacked a shelf above sallow cheeks, and his lips were lost in a long jaw.

Krogher.

He was the man Eli said called the shots in the organization, the man who told Eli what to do. High-ranking government official of some kind who was far too interested in magic, Soul Complements, and the things he could do with both. Not CIA, not FBI, not several of the covert agencies we'd dug our way through while looking for Davy.

Powerful enough to hide from our very skilled investigation.

Krogher had been kidnapping people who had been poisoned by magic several years ago. He'd told Eli to carve spells into them. Spells that then made those people even stronger than Soul Complements. Spells that made those people walking, brainless bombs. Krogher had used them to try to kill Shame and me. It had almost worked.

We'd been looking for Krogher because we knew he had Davy. Sure, Eli was his dog, but Krogher was the one throwing the bones.

And now Krogher was right there on the other side of those bars.

"The first day, Terric Conley," he said. "Could be your last. If you cooperate with us."

I heard the scuff of shoes. There had to be at least two other people in the room. I should have felt their heartbeats, but there was nothing. I didn't even sense Krogher's pulse.

They'd found a way to block the heightened senses Life magic gave me.

Or they'd found a way to block magic from my reach.

"What do you want?" It came out harsh and dry, as if I'd been screaming for hours. I swallowed and wished I hadn't.

"You," Krogher said. "We want you, Mr. Conley. We want your cooperation."

"For what?"

"To unlock the mysteries of the universe. Well, the mysteries of magic. A mystery you carry in your blood and bones. Life."

I twisted my wrists and shifted my legs. It wasn't just metal and chain that had me tied down. There was magic worked into the metal and chain.

"Life magic isn't a thing," I said. "It is a way of casting magic. A discipline of using magic, of casting spells. That is all."

"Yes. We know that's all it *used* to be. But something happened to you over the years, over the battles you've survived. Life magic became something *in* you. Just as Death magic became something *in* Mr. Flynn."

"Where is he? Where is Shame?"

"You don't know?" He took a few steps closer to me, stopped just on the other side of the bars. "Strange. We thought you, of all people, would know exactly where he is."

He paused.

I pulled against the bindings, dragging myself up, but could only lift my shoulders a few inches off the cot.

"Where is he?" I yelled.

"We killed him," he said. "Eli Collins killed Mr. Flynn. He was too much of a risk. Too volatile for our needs."

Fury roared white hot over my body and raged in my head. Life magic flared, answering my anger, cold, deadly. It burned in me, coiled to strike.

But it could not strike. It was trapped in me, burning through me with no way out.

I couldn't cast a spell, couldn't make magic do my bidding. Couldn't kill Krogher.

"Bullets always trump magic, Mr. Conley," Krogher said. "How lucky we are that it is so. Mr. Flynn was a liability, a danger we could not control. You, however." He stopped close enough I could see the SIG Sauer in his hand. "You are the answer to our prayers. Although I would advise you to calm yourself. Too much Life magic will only . . . spoil our conversation."

I looked up into his eyes. Held that dark gaze. "I will kill you."

His expression didn't change. I'm sure he'd heard those words before. He was in a line of business that guaranteed threats. But this was the first time he'd heard them from the man who was going to follow through on that promise.

"So," he went on as if Life magic weren't cracking my bones. "As I was saying. This is the first day. And this is what we want: cooperation. From you. An all-access pass to the Life magic you carry."

"Why?"

"Now, now, Mr. Conley. We aren't here to answer *your* questions. We are here to get the job done."

"What job?"

"Let's just say we have investors who are very interested in magic. In how it has been used. In how it can be used in the future. We are interested in the secrets the Authority has been hiding for centuries. Especially secrets about how magic can break rules. Things like Soul Complements, for instance. Things like you, Mr. Conley. Things like Davy Silvers."

"Davy?" I said.

"Oh yes. We have him. And he is still alive. If you would like him to remain that way, you will cooperate."

"With what?"

"With me," a new voice said.

I turned my head. Out of the shadows walked Eli Collins.

"Hello, Terric," he said. "I hope you're enjoying your stay. We got you the best suite and the highest-quality, strongest-binding spells this side of purgatory. Nothing's too good for you, my friend."

Life magic flared again, but this time I repeated a mantra, tried to breathe slowly, tried to calm my mind. I was no stranger to the pain magic inflicted. I knew how to cope.

"See there?" Eli said. "I told you he'd fall in line. Because Terric always does the right thing. Don't you, Conley? You have such a hero complex."

"Did you kill him?" I asked.

"Who? Your little fuck-buddy Flynn?" He stepped up to the bars, a hypodermic needle in one hand and a black leather satchel with glyphs painted across it in the other. "Tell me you didn't feel the connection break. Tell me you can't feel, right now, a raw burning sickness chewing its way through your spine, screaming and puking in your brain. Tell me you didn't feel him die."

I was breathing hard, trying to keep Life magic from flaring and burning me up. "Did you kill him?" I asked again.

The door to the cage slid aside and he stepped into my prison.

He was close enough I could kill him with a thought.

Except the glyphs that bound me to the cot, the spells carved into the cell bars, the spells burned into the concrete floor, bound me too. I knew how to kill him, but Life magic refused to move, refused to take shape to my will.

He had done a very good job of locking magic up inside me.

Eli strolled over to the cot. Distantly, I heard the clack of Krogher's gun chambering a round. Heard that echoing throughout the warehouse, three, four, half a dozen other guns trained on me.

So there were at least six other people here. People I could not sense.

Magic is fast. Bullets are faster.

But I was two things: patient and vengeful.

Eli stopped next to my cot. Stared down at me through round gold-wire glasses. It had been some time since I'd seen him. Haggard, he hadn't shaved in probably a week, his hair was three missed appointments too long, and his clothes—a button-down white work shirt and gray gabardine trousers—were wrinkled and stained at the cuff.

Stained with blood.

"Did I kill Shame?" Eli bent at the waist, putting his mouth near my ear. "Yes. Just like he killed Brandy."

I jerked at that. "Your Soul Complement? She died of a heart attack."

Eli straightened, then placed the satchel next to him, his face immobile as his hands delicately manipulated the locks on it.

"She was under doctors' observation," I said. "Close observation. Shame didn't kill her. He couldn't have."

The locks gave with two soft *snicks*. I smelled sharp chemicals and hot plastic.

"Eli," I said, "there were cameras on her. Protection spells on her. She was under lock and key. We wanted to keep her *alive*. There was nothing in it for us if she died. Shame never touched her. He couldn't have touched her."

I knew I was reasoning with a madman, but getting through to Eli was the only card I had to play right now.

He didn't turn, didn't shift from the slow, measured motions of whatever he was unpacking onto the table or surface just beyond my view. Like a man caught in the trance of a dream he'd gone through too many times.

I looked the other way. Krogher was still there, the gun pointed at my head and his finger resting near the trigger. I knew there were other gunmen doing the same.

"He was there," Eli said so quietly my own breathing nearly drowned out the sound of his words. "He sat down beside Brandy. Covered her mouth so she couldn't scream. Stared in her eyes. Told her . . ."

He held up a knife, long and razor sharp, glyphs and spells cracking into shadows and sparks of light as he turned it. ". . . that he wanted to hurt her. For me. To make me feel pain. Her pain. To tell me . . ." He turned toward me the knife—a blood blade—in one hand. In the other hand was the hypodermic needle.

"To tell me that he was coming to kill me. For what I'd done to Victor. For what I'd done to Dessa. For what I'd done to you. What have I done to you, Terric? What have I ever done to you?"

"Shot me," I said with every ounce of calm I could call upon. "You nearly killed me, Eli. You wanted to kill me. You did kill Victor. And Dessa and Joshua. And many others."

My heart was pumping too hard, pain riding each beat. Shame never told me he killed Brandy. He'd acted just as surprised and angry as any of us that she had died before we could use her as a bargaining chip to negotiate Davy's release.

He'd lied to me.

Jesus, Shame. Why couldn't you trust me? Why couldn't you tell me?

"Only nearly?" Eli said, tipping his head so a bar of liquid light warped across his glasses, hiding his eyes behind the reflected fire of magic. "I *nearly* killed you. Well, I promise you I completely killed that filthy rat fucker, Shame."

"Mr. Collins," Krogher said. "We are on a schedule."

"Eli." I was breathing too hard. Trying to find the words of reason buried in my anger and hate. "I want you to listen to me very closely. Are you listening to me?"

"Mr. Collins," Krogher said again. "You have work to do. Get it done."

Eli paced over to me, stood there a moment, then bent, the needle aimed at my arm.

That was all I needed. He was finally close enough to hear me.

"Eli," I said. He shifted his gaze away from the needle hovering over my vein and met my gaze. "Listen very closely. I'm going to strip the oxygen from every molecule in your body. Do you understand me? When I get out of here—and trust me, I will—you will be more than dead. You will be erased from the earth."

He blinked several times. Then, "Without your Soul Complement, you are nothing, Terric. Less than nothing. Trust me," he said, shoving the needle in my vein and thumbing the plunger down. "I know."

The poison traveled faster than blood, pushed by the spells in the needle and the mix of magic and chemicals.

It burned hot, crackling like fire over my skin, then under my skin. It numbed me completely as it passed through me.

Eli turned away to his worktable again.

"Now," he said. "Let's get this show on the road." He was still holding the knife, but in his other hand was a glass bowl. "We'll need some blood for this spell. Sorry to say, this is going to hurt. A lot."

I braced for it. I centered my thoughts, stared him straight in the eye, accepted the pain that was coming, accepted that it would last for hours, days. Accepted that there would be an end to it.

"Better make it your best shot," I said. "Because when I get free, I'm going to tear you apart, put you back together, and tear you apart again until you beg me to kill you."

Eli's top lip lifted away from his teeth. Then he shoved the knife into my chest.

Chapter 8

SHAME

Okay. Let me just make this one thing clear: death was awesome.

To hear Allie speak of her one trip to death, it was a broken place that looked like a dark, twisted version of Portland. Zayvion, who had also spent some time caught on the other side, didn't remember much of it except light and pain.

They both got it wrong. I'd died, and now I was standing outside a bar. That made death officially awesome.

"Are you just going to stare at the door all day," Eleanor asked, "or are you going to buy me a drink?"

I turned. She leaned against the side of the building not too far from me. She was wearing the same thing she'd been in when I killed her—dark slacks and shirt—but instead of looking sort of see-through, she was solid, real, and grinning from ear to ear.

"El? What are you doing here?"

"You crossed over and I hitched a ride," she said. "Looks like that tie between us finally paid off. Also? You owe me a drink, Flynn. Hell, you owe me an entire liquor store." She pushed away from the building and took a couple of steps toward me. I could hear her bootheels on the concrete.

I grinned. "So we're both dead. That, my dear, is worth celebrating." I held my arm out for her. "Shall we see what's behind door number one?"

"Why not? This is your heaven."

"You taking bets we went up?"

"Trust me, Shame. If this was hell, we'd know by now."

She took my arm, and together, we walked through the door.

Death and a ghost walk into a bar in heaven . . .

Inside was all wood and brass, two walls of booze, and a shelf that ran round the top of the room, bottles shining like jewels caught in a halo up above our heads.

Heaven indeed.

A couple dozen tables filled the floor; a few candlelit corner booths rounded the edges of the place.

"My God," I breathed. Because the room wasn't empty. No, not at all. There were plenty of people here. People I'd known. People I'd loved. People I'd lost.

This wasn't heaven. I'd finally come home.

"Shame!" Chase called, waving me over to her table where she sat with Greyson.

"Go," Eleanor said. "But you aren't getting out of this place without buying me a drink, hotshot." She gave me a little shove, and I smiled again and headed over to Chase.

"So the rumors are true," Chase said. "They'll let anyone into this place."

Sight for sore heart, Chase was lovely. Hair pulled back in one long ponytail just the way she used to wear it when she, Zayvion, Terric, Greyson, and I were training in the Authority. Learning to use magic, learning to hunt the Hungers that used to cross through gates and give us hell.

We were brothers in arms. Maybe more than that. Chase had been all set up to exchange vows with Zay before her

Soul Complement, Greyson, rolled onto the scene. Their breakup had been hard on Zay. Then Greyson had been taken, experimented upon, and eventually he and Chase had been used and killed by a couple of crazy Soul Complements who wanted to destroy the world.

Proving once again that there was no happily ever after for Soul Complements.

Well, except maybe in death.

"Chase, darlin'," I said as I pulled up a chair and plunked down. "Aren't you looking fine?"

"For a dead chick, you mean?"

"Hey, now," Greyson, who was sitting next to her, said. "For any kind of chick." He looked like his original human self, brown hair, square face, football player good looks, and eyes that didn't reflect the hell he'd been through in life. He wrapped his arm across the back of her chair and gave me a warm smile. "Don't make moves on my girl, Shamus. I can still kick your ass."

"Still? Obviously death has addled your memory. You couldn't kick a baby duck's ass."

"Still ninety-nine percent bullshit and one percent pitiful, aren't you?" he said. "I didn't think we'd see you so soon. Did you drunk it down a flight of stairs or something?"

Images flashed across my vision, brighter, stronger than the bar, more real than the table, than my friends.

Bullets tearing holes through me. Terric falling . . . a knife.

I blinked, and they were gone.

"Shame?" Chase said. "Are you okay?"

"Fine," I said. It wasn't a lie. I felt good, better than I think I had in years. Not a single inch of my body hurt, and the grinding fear and hatred of the Death magic eating away inside me was gone. I felt free, light. And strangely, more alive than I ever had before.

"So, you two?" I asked. "I know things didn't go so well for you dirt-side. Despite your attitude," I said to Greyson, "it's good to see you both. Really good. I'm sorry we couldn't have done more to help you. That we didn't catch Leander before he . . ." I pulled my finger across my throat.

"Shame," Chase said, lifting her bottle of beer. "We're in heaven. There's nothing to apologize for. It's not your job to try to keep everyone safe. And besides. This? Not such a bad way to pass the time."

Greyson nodded. "Seconded. If you want to get technical, we have a lot to apologize for too."

"But the Soul Complement thing between you two?" I said. "That's good now, although I guess ultimately it's what got you killed."

"Well," Greyson said, "that is what got me possessed, turned into a half-beast killer, *then* killed."

"But now?" I asked. "Happy all around?"

"Happy all around," Chase said. "It wasn't being Soul Complements that got us killed. That just made us targets. Leander and Isabelle got us killed. Whack jobs."

"Note to the wise, Shamus. There is no crazier, wounded, desperate creature than a Broken Soul Complement," Greyson said.

Eli with a knife in one hand and gun in the other, hatred twisting his features as he fired again and again . . .

I pushed that image away. Didn't want to think about it. Didn't want that pain in my heaven.

"Isabelle and Leander aren't here, are they?" I asked.

Chase shrugged. "This is your heaven, Shame. Do you want them here?"

"Never."

She lifted her beer in a toast. "To your heaven. Go get yourself a beer. You know you want it."

I glanced at the bar, then back. "I'll just be a minute."

"Take your time," she said. "You might want to say hello to a few people." She pointed off to my right to a table where two men were sitting.

"Victor?" I said.

He saw me looking his way and held up his glass. And the man who sat across the table from him, with his back toward me, turned.

Dark hair, sharp features, dark eyes, and a wide smile—a smile I hadn't seen in over a decade.

"Dad?"

Chapter 9

TERRIC

Days, maybe weeks passed. I'd lost count of how long I'd been caged. There was no day or night, nothing to signal the passage of time except for pain. And the pain? Once it became constant, the hands of time were meaningless.

Eli was with me sometimes, just standing above me, silent, staring. Other times he was much more involved in my pain. Flaying skin from my bones, carving apart muscles, casting spells.

Hundreds of spells, hundreds of modifications to the magic I held inside me. Making it follow the routes he wanted it to follow. Making it into something it was not meant to be.

He'd done this to Davy all those years ago. Davy had never fully recovered, trapped between being a man and being whatever the magic that coursed through the spells set in his flesh by Collins the Cutter forced him to be.

I couldn't keep track of all the spells. I lost count of which he began, which he canceled, as often as I lost consciousness.

Eli held all the cards. He was slowly, surely digging into

the walls I held around the magic inside me. He was slowly breaking through the walls I held around the things that made me me. He was tunneling into my soul.

I'd killed people in my time. I'd Closed them—dug around in their heads and made them forget what they were, who they were. I was good at it—very good—and could surgically break anyone's ability to use magic.

But Eli Collins was waltzing the bloody ballroom around me. He was deeply, frighteningly good at tearing a mind, a body, and magic to shreds.

This was why Victor had wanted Eli Closed. Broken. Dead. This was why he'd made Shame promise to kill him.

And I knew it was why, no matter what we'd done to otherwise shut Eli down, he had found a way to glue himself back together.

Because he was a monster.

He killed Shame.

No, I couldn't think that now, couldn't deal with that. He was killing *me*. That was the only thing to focus on. That, and getting as much information as I could out of him about Krogher's plan.

"Terric," Eli said. "Are you awake?"

Showtime. I knew he saw my reaction to his voice, the change in my breathing. Since I was currently sitting on the floor with my wrists chained to the cell bars above me and I was blindfolded, I did what I could to manage myself. Stayed still, tried to keep my breathing soft, my mind calm.

I wanted to hear him coming. *Please, God, let me hear him coming this time.*

"Let's take that off, shall we?"

The rustle of fabric shifting against his skin as he bent toward me was loud as an ocean roar. He was just to my left. If I kicked, I'd hit him. And whatever weapon he had in his hand would be my reward.

I'd lost a pinkie knuckle last time I'd hit him.

Two for two?

I waited until I could feel the heat off his body, smell the sweat and vodka of his skin.

"We don't need this, do we, now?" he asked, his fingers fumbling at the blindfold over my eyes.

Low would be useless, ankles if I was lucky. I wanted meat. I wanted blood. Solar plexus, stomach, groin. A connection to any of those would make my day.

Fingers brushed over my eyes, every muscle in my body tensed for the blade, for the needle, for the pain.

Fingers stroked back along my temple. I felt his knuckles at the back of my neck.

My breathing was too hard. Too fast.

The blindfold fell away, revealing the needle that hovered in front of my eye.

He was extended, arm stretched away from his body. Unguarded. Vulnerable.

I kicked him as hard as I could.

Connected.

Turned my head just enough the needle plunged into my cheek.

Eli screamed, skittered away from me. And then there were hands—the others under Krogher's employ who saw to it I was bound, gagged, beaten. Then there were kicks, and a Taser just to round out the layers of pain.

Agony, for minutes, for hours. Worth it. Worth seeing the hate and the fear on Eli's face. Maybe I wasn't breaking as easily as all the others he'd carved up with spells. Maybe I was going to be his worst nightmare when all this was said and done.

It was a brutal hope. And one I held tightly to.

Another fist hit my face, took the lights out.

When I woke, I was strapped down. My left hand was stretched out, tied at the wrist, the elbow, the shoulder.

"That," Eli said, "was a very bad choice, Terric. I thought we talked about good choices. Choices you *should* make. But you're not going to listen to me, I see that now. So now we do this the hard way."

I took in the details I could while pulling mental walls around me, digging in, and holding against what I knew he was going to do to me. Again.

"Perhaps a pinkie wasn't enough punishment for your indiscretion. Perhaps we need to dig a little deeper."

The knife edge dragged down my neck, along the carotid artery. One slice and I'd bleed out in minutes, then down my armpit, axillary artery sliced, and I'd bleed out in minutes, and down and down, following the line of my veins all the way to my thumb.

"Let's have a little fun, shall we?" Eli said.

He leaned on the blade, pressing it just below my thumb knuckle, breaking the skin, deep enough I felt the familiar gush of blood and heard my own whimpering.

Left hand. It was only my left hand. I'd still have one thumb. I'd still have one hand. I repeated those words over and over again. Holding to them, using them as a shield against the strangling proof that Eli was fucking insane and by the end of this, I would be damaged beyond repair.

But not dead. As long as I breathed, I would have a chance to break free and kill him.

The knife released its bite. He hadn't chopped off my thumb. Hadn't gone through with the threat. But he could. Any second. Anytime he wanted. He had done worse.

"Do I have your attention, Terric?" He was still bent over me.

I looked up at him. "Why?" I rasped. "Are you lonely?"

He pounded a fist in my face. I spit blood. Eli wasn't shy about getting his hands dirty, or his fists bloody. He was also easy to rile up. It was good information to have, but I had no idea how to leverage it.

"What I am is generous," Eli said. "You are lucky to be breathing, Conley."

Lucky, my ass. He'd have killed me the second he stepped into my kitchen if he wanted me dead. And all the blood he'd drained, all the flesh he'd carved, all the spells he'd stitched into me weren't just for his amusement, weren't to kill me. He was aiming for an outcome.

I just didn't know what it was yet.

"But not as lucky as some," he said. He held the knife in front of my face, waiting for me to track it. I tried not to. Tried not to watch as the knife once again scraped cold against my cheek, pressed into the soft flesh under my jawbone, then throat.

I was breathing hard. Already running from the pain I couldn't escape.

Stay calm. Stay focused.

The knife moved away. And then the pain hit, a hard, fast slice across my pinkie. Second knuckle on what was left of that ruined digit.

I clamped my teeth together and yelled, pulling against the binding, pulling on Life magic.

Life magic that flared in me, filled me. Life magic that could not heal me, because Eli had taken care of that with the spells he'd carved into me.

"Good," he said. "Good."

This was what he wanted. I could hear it in his voice. He wanted Life magic. The Life magic in me. And it was right there for the taking.

Stay calm. Stay focused. Hold the walls.

Eli dragged something toward him with his free hand. Sounded like wires skittering across the floor. He attached them to the bindings at my wrists, then ankles.

"Are you ready, Mr. Collins?"

I jerked at Krogher's voice. Turned my head to see him, standing outside the bars of my cage, holding something that looked like one of the Beckstrom disks glued to a cell phone.

Behind him stood fifty people. Men, women, children. Blank-faced, unmoving.

"Just a moment, Mr. Krogher," Eli said.

He attached electrodes to plastic tabs pressed into my chest, five points set into the spells he had left there. If you drew a line between them, which Eli had done — in flesh and spell and whatever the hell he'd injected into me — it mapped a pentagram.

"Now," Eli said quietly, just to me. "I want you to know I'm not doing this for Krogher. I'm doing this for you. To make you pay for everything you've done to me, for the things Closers have done to me, for killing Brandy. Understand? See all those innocent people? Casualties of the war you lost three years ago when magic changed. Casualties you can't save. You know why? Because you are going to be the one who kills them. Oh, they won't take their last breath today, but this . . ." He dug his thumb into the ruins of my chest and I arched back in pain, screaming.

"This isn't just a pretty picture. This is a spell that will give us direct access to the magic you contain. I don't know how you hold magic in your body. Sure, those people out there can be vessels for magic because it nearly killed them . . . tainted magic. Maybe you almost died too, maybe when you and Shame were killing Jingo Jingo back in the day, it changed you, turned you into this hollow shell for Life magic. I would love to have studied you back then, but, well. All things come to those who wait. And today, I'm going to use the magic in you to charge the spells I've carved into those poor, brainless people out there. And when we use those spells, use those people, one shot and . . ."

He smiled. "Boom."

"Mr. Collins," Krogher said. "Move this along."

"If I were you," Eli said, near my ear, "I'd buckle up."

He straightened. Took three steps away from me. Checked on the wires, which I realized were clamped to the bars of the cage around me.

A cage that had Transfer spells carved into each bar.

Holy shit.

"No," I said. "Eli, no. You don't know this will work. You could kill these people."

"True," he said as Kroger pressed buttons on the device in his hand and each person stepped forward as if pulled by the same chain. "If they die, I'll just find some more. Hundreds of people were infected with tainted magic, scarred by magic. We have the records and can kidnap anyone we choose. We have reach, Terric. We have money, we have power. Now all we need is magic. So we have you."

The people surrounded the cage. I was sure they couldn't hear what he was saying, couldn't understand what was about to be done to them. Eli had carved enough spells into them; they no longer had free will. Each wrapped a hand around a bar.

"Don't," I said, scrambling for a way out of this, for a way to keep Life magic behind the crumbling wall I'd built in my mind.

"Too late." Eli flipped a switch.

Electricity hit like a hammer strike.

The cell bars flared with electricity and magic. A chemical stink burned my lungs as the spells Eli had been carving in my cage and the spells he'd been carving in me came alive, fueled by the Life magic I could not control.

Magic gushed out of me like blood from a severed vein and blasted into the people surrounding the cage. Each of them was carved with one spell. Each of them became a battery, a vessel for the magic to fuel that one spell. Walking bombs.

They screamed. But not all of them died. Death would be too easy, a kindness out of this hell.

I was Life magic, and life meant only one thing: suffering.

Chapter 10

SHAME

"Shamus," Dad said, "come on and sit down, son. We need to talk."

If he hadn't said anything I probably would have just stood there staring at him for days.

I cleared my throat. "Sure." I crossed over to him. "Well, it's . . . it's good to see you, Da."

I paused there next to his chair not knowing what to do next. We hadn't exactly left on speaking terms before he'd been killed. If he was as stubborn as I remember him being, he'd probably carried those grudges all the way up here to heaven and was ready to unpack them on me.

Dad pushed his chair away from the table and stood. He was younger than I remember him being, maybe in his late twenties, but he was still my dad. "Son."

And then he was hugging me, something I hadn't experienced since I was ten. I was surprised to realize I was about an inch taller than him, though he still had nearly twenty pounds of muscle on me.

"It is so good to see you, lad," he said as he gave my back a fond pat.

I swallowed, inhaled the scent of him, cigarettes and Old Spice. "You too, Da."

Then he pulled back, one hand on my shoulder while he gave me a long, long look.

Funny how even when you're dead you hope that your parents will be proud of what they see in you.

"You really gave them hell, didn't you, boy?"

"I got my hits in," I said.

He shook his head. "I knew you could handle it. Told your mother from the day you were born, you'd be the man who would stop Jingo Jingo. And the apocalypse too." He pointed at the empty chair between him and Victor and took his seat.

"Well, I had help," I started. But before I sat down, there was another father I had to say hello to.

I walked over to Victor. "I am so sorry. We tried. We couldn't get to you fast enough."

"When?"

"When you died. When Eli killed you."

"Ah yes." Victor gave me a look that was not unkind. His hair didn't have any gray in it now. I'd put him in his early forties. I guess those had been his glory years.

"I didn't expect you to save me, Shame. The struggle between Eli and me was a battle I chose. I knew what the outcome could be. I have no regrets."

He stood.

"But if we had been faster, just a little faster—"

"It is done," he said. "Let it be done. I am not unhappy with my life, nor with what I left behind. I'm not unhappy with *who* I've left behind: you, Terric, Zayvion. You're sons to me. In that, you've never failed me."

He rested his hand on my shoulder and then pulled me into a hug.

"We miss you," I said.

"Everything has an ending. It is the order in chaos."

Those were words I'd heard him say more times than I could count.

He released me with another pat and pointed at the chair for me to sit.

"We're both very happy to see you here, Shame," he said. "But we think you might have jumped the gun. There is so much more for you to do."

Bullets flying out of nowhere, tearing through me, searing hot. Eli must have started firing even before he opened that hole in space behind Terric. . . .

"That," Dad said, "is what we're talking about."

I blinked, and the memory went back to being a memory instead of a picture show.

"Don't follow you." I picked up the pint in front of me and took a long, hard pull. Good God. It was amazing.

"The Death magic that took housing in you, claiming you, is a very unusual thing," Da said. "In all of history, we don't think anyone has ever carried a piece of magic within them."

"It wasn't like I planned it," I said.

"*You* didn't plan it," Da said. "But you did stumble into the way it could be done. Soul Complements joining on the battlefield, using magic to die for each other, and to live for each other. When you screw with the rules of magic, it will screw you back. And what you and Terric did on the battlefield, that was a top-notch screwup."

"Yeah. Sure," I said. "We had a shot to kill Jingo Jingo and we took it, consequences be damned."

"And living with Death magic trying to eat you alive is the price to pay," he said.

"Was," I said. "It was the price to pay. Paid up. Everything has an end, right?" I lifted the beer. "Worth it."

Victor shifted in his chair and folded his fingers together while laying his hands on the table. I knew that glint in his eye. He was planning something.

"You know Terric is still alive down there," he said quietly.

Nice of him to sledgehammer my moment of happy.

"I . . . wondered. When I didn't see him here. . . ." I swigged beer, which, while delicious, wasn't really cutting it for me. I was in a whiskey mood.

As soon as that thought crossed my mind, the beer wasn't beer anymore. It was a glass of whiskey.

I took a sip. Correction, it was angel song in a tumbler, liquid heavenly voices raised in pure heat and pleasure.

I set the glass down, did a reality — well, a heaven — check. The bar was the same. The people there the same. Only my drink had changed.

Dad and Victor, however, were watching me as if they were working out exactly how to tackle a particularly difficult problem.

I leaned back. "So Terric's alive. That's a good thing, right?"

Victor raised an eyebrow, nodded. "It is. But it would be a better thing if you were alive with him."

"We're better apart," I said. "I *know* that. We've tried being together and . . ." I shook my head. "This is my heaven. I belong here."

"This is all of our heavens," Dad said. "Changing for each of us, as we meet, rejoin, or part. But you carry Death magic, Shamus, and there is no place death can't be."

"Which means?"

"We need you to go back," Victor said. "There are things you could accomplish, things you and Terric could accomplish that will make a difference for so many. Magic is on the brink of being used as a global weapon. So many will die. Too many. If we do nothing to stop it, the world will enter a war that will never end."

"Still can't let go of the old job, can you?"

"It's important, Shame. You left this fight far too early."

"I *died,* Old Man," I said. "Let's keep that clear. It's not like I strolled up here on a lark."

"That aside," Dad said, "Terric is still alive down there, half a soul without you, and soon to be only half-sane. You know how destructive Life magic can be. You know he was barely managing it when you were with him. And now, alone . . ."

"He's capable. He'll find a way to cope," I said.

That was a lie. The broken tie of our Soul Complement was a punched ticket to insanity. If he still had access to the Life magic inside him, he would be capable of doing terrible things. I didn't want to do that to anyone I cared for, to break him like that.

"So you want me to go down there and stop him? Kill him?"

"No," Victor said. "We want you to go back and save him, before Eli Collins kills him."

Just the thought of Eli killing Terric made me want to hit something.

"But if Terric dies, he comes here, doesn't he?" I asked. "I'm not going to lie to you. I feel good here. I feel right here. Better than I have for"—I lifted my hands, trying to find the words—"for as long as I can remember. I finally feel *good.* Maybe this is the best for us, for me, for Terric. Maybe death is as good as it gets for Soul Complements."

Victor finished his drink, then gave my dad a look. I suddenly remembered that these two had known each other back in the day when they were the young rebels raising hell in the Authority.

Shit.

"Here's the way of it, lad," Da said. "You and Terric have a chance to stop what Eli and the government behind him want him to do. Things are a little fuzzy from this height, but we are pretty sure if you don't, the world we knew, the one we all fought for, and died for, where magic isn't used as a weapon against humanity, will be gone, erased. All the people you care for, all the people *we* care for will suffer. You have a chance to change that. We think you should take that chance."

"How many apocalypses does a man need to stand in front of, Da?" I asked. "There must be someone else who can take this on. Someone living."

"No one else is the embodiment of magic, Shame," Victor said. "Not even Allie and Zayvion can do what you and Terric can do. Life. Death."

He was right.

"I don't even know that I can go back to living," I said. "And if it's a twelve-step program to zombiedom, I'm outs."

"We can help with that," Victor said. "Even if you're not tied to Terric, there is a draw, an affinity. As long as he is alive, you should be able to reach him."

"That's what started the last apocalypse, you know," I said. "Soul Complements slipping out of death to be together in the living world."

"Which we consider the precedent that proves our theory," Victor said.

"And you, son"—Dad pointed at me with his beer—"aren't returning to destroy the world. You're returning to save it."

"I suppose the two of you have worked out a way for me to do this?"

"We have ideas," Victor said.

"I knew you would," I said. "What's it going to take?"

Dad leaned forward. "Magic."

Chapter 11

TERRIC

There must have been a time when I was not in pain. Certainly I'd had a childhood. I'd been born, loved, cared for. I'd spent years running with Zayvion and Chase and Greyson. Those had been good years. Even with Shame.

And that's where my thoughts always stopped: Shame.

Surely there'd been some time in my life when I hadn't hurt since I met him. If life was pain—and it was—Shame had to be something else, right?

But all I could remember from my time with him was the pain.

He'd nearly killed me when we were twenty and the creature we had been hunting got past him and almost tore me apart. That had broken my ability to use certain magics: Faith magic, Blood magic. His mistake had changed me, changed my life. But it had been a mistake.

Yes, I'd forgiven. Because what he'd done to me had broken him more than me. He had never forgiven himself. He had spent years with the guilt, the regret. It was like watching a man slowly cut his way through his own throat. For years.

Years.

Shame's life had changed because of what he'd done to me. Shame had changed.

"Are you awake, Terric?" Eli asked.

I couldn't track time anymore, had given up trying.

Time was stretching out toward eternity. It had been days, weeks since Eli had tapped in to the magic I carried and used it to power up those people. Days of dead bodies scattered around my cage, eyes empty, staring at me, at their killer.

Faces I would see for the rest of my life, however long that was.

Then the dead were dragged away, blood and fluids mopped up by men with surgical masks who could not hear my screaming.

And always there was Eli, more torture, more pain.

And now there was now.

"I want you awake for this," Eli said.

I was strapped down again. Hadn't I just been standing?

Sitting now. A chair. Shackled by feet, arms, chest. The drugs they'd kept me pumped full of left the taste of burnt plastic and hot concrete in the back of my throat.

"You might be wondering what our endgame is." Eli sat in front of me now. There was a table between us. He took off his glasses and polished them with a yellow cloth that looked like a square of sunlight in shadows. Surrounded by gray and black as I was, it had been too long since I'd seen a color other than red.

"I'd want to know what this all adds up to if I were, well . . ." He pointed at me with his glasses. "If I were on the other side of the table."

I didn't say anything. Not because the back of my throat was numb. Because there was power in silence. Right now it was all the power I had.

Eli placed his glasses back on his face like a man who had been working too many hours. "Have you guessed? Do you know what this"—he gestured to the cage and warehouse around us—"is all about?"

I waited.

"You know this wasn't my idea, don't you?" he said. "I asked you and Shame to save me. To save her. I *begged*." His hand clenched into a fist and he was silent until his fist stopped shaking, until the color faded from his face, until the hatred in his eyes slipped back into madness.

His Soul Complement, Brandy, the other half of his soul, was dead. Yeah, well, so was mine. He and I had something in common. We each wanted to see the other person planted six feet under.

"If it were my idea," he went on, "I'd have left him alive, Shame. So he could feel what I've done to you. So he could suffer every. Last. Cut." He smiled. "It would have been . . . poetic."

My heart beat harder. Life magic flickered somewhere within me, responding to my need, but was so drained and far from my reach, I couldn't get at it. Yet.

Keep talking, Eli.

"But they . . ." He leaned back. "They wanted what you had. And they knew only I could get it for them. Life magic. I got to it, didn't I? I always deliver. I'm a genius, you know. And yet you aren't dead. That's impressive. Any other man . . ." His voice faded and he frowned. "Funny how it all works out. You and I, on the same side, serving the same cause. Maybe not willingly, but serving. Good little soldiers.

"It's the difficulties that make strong bonds, isn't it, Terric? And you and I, well, we've had our difficulties, haven't we? Now here we are. Each a half of nothing."

He stopped talking and just sat there, his eyes going distant, hollow. As if all the fire in him had been snuffed.

"It's not how I wanted things to go," he whispered. "At all. We really were on the same side once." He smiled, just slightly.

"Before . . . before the end of the world. But then all my memories came back. All those *years* taken away from me by Victor." He shook his head. "I enjoyed killing him. Wished I had more time to do it properly. But they always had the upper hand, these people." He gestured to the warehouse. "They had me, because they had her, Brandy. No matter what I did, no matter who I asked to help me, to save her, they've gotten what they wanted from me. And no matter what I've given them, she's still dead. . . ."

He closed his eyes for a moment. When he opened them, they were the eyes of a man broken. Defeated.

"Sometimes I think they wanted it. Wanted Shame to kill her. So I would stay with them, do what they asked. Revenge is a weakness of mine. Always has been. And while I dislike being predictable, being played . . ." He shrugged. "At least I'm the one who will see this to the end.

"Now, the endgame." He sat forward. Not close enough for me to touch him, but close enough the camera that was on the cage wouldn't see his face. I knew he did it on purpose. I just didn't know why.

"Pretty simple, really. The government wasn't happy to find out there were people who knew how to make magic strong again. People like you and me—Soul Complements. The only people in the world who can break the core of magic and unleash the power, the destruction. So yes, I threw my chits in with them. Made them an offer. Government assistance in getting my Soul Complement, Brandy, out of the loony bin. In exchange for a few tricks I'd learned. Tricks I played on Davy Silvers—carving spells into him, spells that changed him. You remember Davy, don't you? How you tried to save him and how you failed?"

My breathing picked up.

He waited. Waited me out. "Ask me," he whispered, a small smile on his face. "Ask me what I did to poor Davy."

I swallowed, the burn sliding farther down my throat. Felt like I hadn't had water in years. "Where is he?"

"Don't want to give me time to brag about my exploits?" he asked. "Fine. Since you didn't ask, I activated a few spells I carved into him all those years ago. And then I killed him."

I tipped my head back, my breathing ragged now.

Eli winked. His hand, which was in front of him and out of the camera's line of vision, lifted slightly and he crossed his fingers.

Lying? He was lying?

"I killed him because we got everything we needed to know from him. He was my blueprint, my plan for carving all those other people up with spells. Spells you've supercharged, thank you, Terric. Couldn't have done it without you.

"The program is going forward, thanks to your cooperation. It will be easy to find the Soul Complements in the world since there are so few and the Authority's records have long been accessed by the government. Then it will be even easier to take these magic-carved people, these drones, to each Soul Complement, trigger the magic they carry, and kill the Soul Complements. Of course it will also kill the drones, but magic has always come with a price, hasn't it?

"Once the Soul Complements are out of the way, no one will have massively destructive capabilities with magic. Well, except Krogher and his warehouse of walking bombs. I do believe that will make covert operations and worldwide negotiations quite a different game. Our government will be the only one in the world that has a stockpile of destructive magic. It is a limited resource, but hey, if you're the only kid with the toys everyone wants, the world is your sandbox."

No more winking, no crossed fingers. He wasn't lying about this.

"Why tell me?" I asked. "You know I'll stop you. I'll stop them."

"With what, Terric? Magic? You don't have that anymore. We drained you dry. To access magic again, to really access the power of it, you'd need someone who could use magic in perfect concert with you. What's that person called? Something . . . oh yes, a Soul Complement. No luck there. Shame is dead, dead, dead. He is dead, isn't he?"

I didn't know why he asked me that. He knew the answer.

"Just like Brandy, I suppose," he said. "Gone."

Eli might be right about Shame, but he was wrong about me. I wasn't empty. Magic still flickered in me. Close enough I could almost reach it. I just needed a little more time.

"They'll stop you," I said. "They'll break magic and stop you all."

"Who? The Soul Complements? I think you are grossly overestimating their abilities. After all, who is more dangerous than you and Shame? Who is more powerful than Life and Death? If we can kill him, if we can do all these *things* we have done to you, Terric, who do you think can stop us?"

I didn't say it. I didn't have to.

"Allie and Zayvion. That's who you're thinking of, isn't it?" His smile was a little less convincing. "Even they can't stop this machine. Krogher will take out the Soul Complements, and then he will have the world in the palm of his hand. I've seen the things that he wants magic to do. I've seen how he wants the world to end. . . ." He stared down at his feet. "It is not a pretty picture. For anyone."

"Now," he said, slapping both hands flat on the table. "Let's get on with this. Today, Terric, I'm going to take a burden off your mind. I'm going to Close you so you can't use magic anymore. No more responsibility, no more worrying if Life magic is doing harm to anyone. No more worrying about magic at all. You won't even remember it

existed, and if by some strange circumstance you do remember magic, you will have no idea how to use it."

Cold terror clenched my gut. If I couldn't use magic,
there was no chance I'd break out of this place. Without
magic, I had no cards to play. Without magic, I wouldn't be
worth keeping alive.

"Why don't you just kill me?"

"Kill you? No, not yet. I need you." He paused as if that
were an important admission on his part. Then, in a lighter
tone: "You are the liability insurance. Just in case we need
to load a few more spells, you'll be right here, easy for the
taking. Oh, we know you're drained of magic right now. But
you might surprise us. I always plan for surprises. Always.

"So, let's get on with this, shall we? It's been a while
since I've done anything old school, like Closing. I can only
assume I'll be a little rusty. We'll just muddle through together, won't we?"

He snapped his fingers.

I jerked.

Footsteps echoed in the warehouse, people walking this
way. Two guards led a boy and an older woman toward us,
both of them blank-eyed and filled with magic, one spell
carved into their flesh. They walked up to the cage and
wrapped their hands around the bars.

"There is a certain irony in your own magic being used
against you, to keep you from using magic, isn't there?" Eli
stood, walked to the corner of the room where a table was
spread with scalpels, hammers, wire, Void stones, mortar,
pestle, and more. Things he had used on me. Things he had
done to me.

He paused there, glanced over his shoulder to make sure
I was watching what he was doing. "This," he said, pulling
out a circle of metal with glyphs carved into it, "was the
beginning of the solution. The problem? If you can raise an
army of walking, mindless spell holders, how then do you

activate those spells? How then do you deactivate those spells? I began with this." He turned and held the disk in the fingers of his right hand.

"My first attempt was to use a Beckstrom disk. A very few still hold magic. Those that do are oddly well designed for activating magic, or for deactivating it. Think of it as a magnifying glass. Whatever spell you press into this metal, which is laced with the crystals of the well in St. Johns, will be strong enough to trigger a corresponding spell once.

"My theory was, if used correctly, it might even be possible for one disk to cancel every spell I've ever cast. Although the magic required for that is beyond you and me now."

He paused, and his eyebrows ticked just slightly upward, as if he were asking me if I understood what he was saying.

Why would he tell me how to cancel his spells?

"A failed experiment. The disks were a dead end." Again the look. Again the wink. "But then, one can't advance on success alone." He turned back to the table. "After a few adjustments, it was clear that control over the drones and spells would be achieved through technology rather than magic. So this . . ." He turned around again. This time he was holding one of the controllers I'd seen in Krogher's hands.

Hell.

"Wireless. Elegant. Useful." Eli took a step toward me with each word. "It controls every action of every spell-holding drone. Hold still, Terric. This is going to hurt quite a bit."

He pressed something on the plastic in his hand and I felt magic stir in the room. No, I felt the magic in the boy and in the woman open to his command as if he'd just unlocked windows in a storm.

Eli didn't even trace a spell in the air. He didn't have to. He triggered the spell the woman carried. It rushed out of her, straight from her hands into the bars of the cage, and followed the lines Eli had carved and cast in the floor. Magic hit my feet with the force and heat of lightning.

I grabbed for that magic, to turn it around, to stop it, to use it, to control it.

But the moment it touched me, the moment it ran the course of spells carved into my flesh, burned into my blood, I lost control of it, lost the ability to use it, couldn't even remember what it did or how it worked.

Closed. Magic was Closed from me.

And no matter how hard I tried to pull on it, to hold it, to use it, magic was locked away, walled away, removed from my reach.

Chapter 12

SHAME

Eleanor strolled over to our table. "What's going on here?"

"Eleanor?" Victor said. "It's so good to see you."

She smiled, surprised. "I still can't get used to people actually seeing me. Hi, Victor. How are you?"

"I'm wonderful, thank you. I'm so sorry for your death. You left the world far too young."

"No, don't worry about it," she said. "We'd gotten bad information, and were doing what we thought was right. But it was wrong."

Funny how hearing her say that unknotted something in my chest. I wouldn't have been fighting her, and consequently lost control of Death magic and killed her, if she hadn't been trying to kill me first.

I didn't blame her, though. It's hard to keep the communication lines clear in an apocalypse.

"And you must be some relation to Shame." She held out her hand for my dad.

He shook her hand. "Hugh Flynn. I'm his father. Pleased to meet you, Eleanor, is it?"

"Roth. Eleanor Roth. I work for the Authority in Seattle. Well, did."

"How'd you end up with this piece of work?" he asked, pointing at me.

"He chickened out at the last minute and didn't kill me enough," she said. "Then there was that binding thing. How *did* you do that, Shame?"

"It's a Death magic Bind." I looked away from her as I said it. "Souls are energy, life that can be stored and drained later. High-level, illegal, dark magic stuff."

"Which is why you owe me a drink," she said. "To celebrate my freedom from all those days tied to your angst."

"Please," I said. "I don't angst. I brood like a manly man."

Victor snorted and I threw him a grin.

"Celebrate," she said again. "Drink. You owe me one. Time to pay up."

She planted her hands on her hips, waiting.

"Well, gents," I said, "you heard the lady. Your nefarious plans will just have to wait."

I thought my dad might try to stop us, but he smiled. "Go on. If she's put up with you for this long, she's earned that drink."

Eleanor took the arm I offered her, and we walked toward the bar.

Behind me, I heard Dad and Victor start up a conversation about death and life and how to break the barriers between them.

"Why are you arguing with your father?" she asked. "This is supposed to be heaven, Shame. Weapons left at the door."

"A little tussle with the old man? Sounds like heaven to me."

She chuckled softly. Here, where she was real, and soft, and smelled like sweet cinnamon, I found myself liking that I could make her smile.

"How is this for you?" I asked. "You're untied from me, aren't you?"

"I think so. It doesn't feel the same." She took a stool and I sat next to her and flagged the bartender.

"Good," I said. "Good. Say, I wanted to ask. Did it hurt?"

"Dying?"

"No. Being tied to me."

"At first, yes. As time went on, it wasn't so bad. I just wish you wouldn't have spent every second of your life racing toward the grave."

The bartender came over, set two drinks in front of us. Mine: whiskey. Hers: chocolate martini.

"I never raced toward anything a day of my life."

"So I just imagined you wishing for death every waking moment, is that it?"

"Well, I might have been considering the grave. . . ."

"Please." She picked up her drink. "You couldn't get here fast enough." She lifted her glass. "Here's to the end. May it be just the beginning."

"Hear, hear!" I tapped my glass to hers and took a drink, watching her.

She pressed her lips against the glass, tipped it back, and closed her eyes as she held the drink in her mouth. She'd been not quite dead for years now. No eating, no drinking. This had to be the first thing she'd tasted in forever.

"Good?" I asked.

"Mmmmm." She opened her eyes. "Heaven."

"To heaven," I said.

"What about earth?"

"What about it?"

"I heard what your dad and Victor said."

"Look at you? Once a stalker, always a stalker."

She made a face at me. "So you're going to stop the end of the world?"

"That's the idea."

She leaned her elbow on the bar and twisted to face me. "I've been tied to you for what, over three years now?"

"Yes."

"And you couldn't hear what I said for almost the entire time, right?"

"Not since the first few months." I took another sip.

"Then listen to me now. You have a good heart."

"This old thing—"

She held up one finger. "It's still my turn. You have a good heart. I don't care what you show other people or what you want them to think you are. I lived with you."

At my look she rocked her head side to side. "Existed. Whatever. But I was there, Shame. Right next to you twenty-four-seven for almost four years. I've seen your bad days and your really bad days. But despite all the shit that's happened, you are a kind man. Sometimes I suspect you're even a hopeful man."

I blew air out between my lips.

She held up a warning finger again and I shut my mouth.

"But some of the things you've done, Shame. Some of your choices."

"Were awesome?" I prompted.

She rolled her eyes. "For a while there, I didn't think you'd ever pull your head out of your ass. If you'd used magic with Terric—don't give me that look—if you'd just relaxed about it and used magic together without being so damn determined that it would cause the world to explode, everything could have been so much better. You would have been better. He would have been—"

"—inhuman. Dead inside. All Life magic, no humanity, insane," I said.

"You don't know that," she said gently. "I watched you. I watched him with you. You made each other better, not worse. Just neither of you was willing to have a little faith that you were meant to use magic together. That maybe it would be the one good thing you had together that worked."

"Water under the bridge, darlin'."

She took another drink. "You too easily see the world as full of sorrow, and you too quickly assume that sorrow is all you deserve. Also, you are as stubborn as a mule in mud."

"Whoa. Someone can't hold her martini," I said.

"I think your dad and Victor are right."

"About what?"

"You don't belong here yet."

I swallowed the last of the whiskey. "I might not be staying long anyway. They think they can send me down to the green grasses."

"Even so, you *do* belong here." She reached over, pressed her fingers against mine.

I smiled. "You deserved so much better than what you got, love."

"Well, this isn't so bad." She patted my hand and finished off her drink.

"Sure, death is fine," I said. "But life is nothing but suffering."

"Not all of it," a voice said. A woman's voice.

I looked across the room. At my dad, who held open the door for a woman who had just walked into the bar. Dessa Leeds. The woman I'd loved.

I stood. Suddenly she was the only person I could see.

"Dessa?" I breathed.

She raised one eyebrow. "Hey there, charmer. Didn't think I'd see you so soon."

Beautiful in life, but here in death she was vibrant, more alive than ever. Red hair long and silk-soft around her shoulders, she was wearing a very simple pale green dress, short enough to show thigh, and sort of flowing as she walked toward me.

Her skin was moon-pale, her face a porcelain perfect heart, and those blue eyes....

I stopped breathing at the sight of her, and realized that yes, you not only breathed in heaven; your heart could pound so hard it was difficult to hear your own thoughts.

"Hey," I said. "You're here."

She lifted one hand and very gently drew her fingers down the side of my cheek. I closed my eyes at her touch, savoring that connection, wanting it to never end. Wanting her to never disappear.

"Shame," she said.

I opened my eyes.

"I'm so glad to see you before you leave."

I frowned. "Maybe ... maybe I can stay awhile."

"No," she said. "You have to go."

"Why?"

"Because only half of you is here." She placed her hand over my heart, and beneath the warmth of her palm was a cool hollowness, a blackness that only Terric could fill.

"Your father told me there's still work for you to do. Hero things."

"My father has a big mouth and overestimates my abilities."

She smiled. "There's someone counting on you back there."

"I know," I said. "Terric."

"Yes. But you made a promise to look after someone."

"Allie and Zay?"

"Their child, Shame. You promised to be there to look after her."

"Hold on," I said. "Her? They're having a girl? Zayvion's going to have a daughter? Lord, he'll go mental over that. How do you know all this? You weren't there when I promised to look after my goddaughter."

"Just call it a heaven thing. Okay," she said, "maybe I was

spying on you a little." She stepped closer to me. I could smell her perfume, feel the warmth of her body against mine. "Go be a hero, Shame."

She kissed me and it was heaven.

I lost myself to her. Lost myself and never wanted to find myself again.

She pulled back, finally, tipped her forehead against mine. "Don't hurry back. But don't be gone forever, okay?"

She looked up at me and I discovered that even in heaven, a heart can break.

"Dessa . . ."

Two hands landed on my shoulder. Firm. Familiar. "It's time, son," Dad said on one side of me.

Dessa stepped back. "See you, Shame. You know . . . that spying thing of mine . . ."

"Da," I said, glancing up over one shoulder, then the other. "Victor. Just a few minutes?" I might not be a love-'em-and-leave-'em guy anymore, but if the kiss had been that good, I had a list of other things I wanted to try out.

"Son," my dad said as he and Victor pushed me toward the window that now had a couple of spells painted on it. Transference and Crossing. Magic in heaven. Who would have guessed? "We might be too late as it is."

"Wait," Eleanor said. She ran toward me. "You're not going without me."

"No," I said. "Hell no. Stay. You've earned that."

"You're going. I'm going," she said. "Will this hurt?"

"Can't say this is going to feel good, exactly," Da said.

"Through the window?" I said, bracing for the impact and fall and impact.

"We'll give you everything we have, Shame," Victor said. "Godspeed to you, son."

Victor and Da jerked me off my feet at the same moment, and then they both said one word. A word that shattered all sound, shattered all light, shattered the heavens. Or at least my heaven.

Magic.

"Good-bye, Shamus," I heard Dad whisper. "Make me proud."

And then I was flying through the air, into the window.

I threw my hands out to try to protect my face. Glass exploded, sliced through me, shredded my clothes, my skin, my bone.

I yelled. And fell forever.

Chapter 13

TERRIC

Eli came by often to make sure I was drugged so heavily I couldn't feel the pain anymore. And even though that meant I couldn't think clearly, I was glad for it. Glad for the respite.

I didn't know why I was drugged. Without magic, shackled to this cage, I wasn't exactly the biggest threat on the planet.

A sound like a stone cracking steel rang out so loud I came awake gulping air.

"This," Krogher said, only inches away.

He'd never been this close to me. There had always been bars between us.

Eli stood by the small table, a Beckstrom disk in his hand, one of the ones he said didn't work, or sometimes worked as a magnifying glass, or something he'd said a long time ago. It had something to do with Davy and the drone and lies and control.

The disk was smoking, the metal a useless burnt lump.

Krogher was still talking. To me, I realized, much to my surprise. I stared at his lips, trying to focus on the words.

". . . final day for you, Mr. Conley," he said. "We want to thank you for your service to the United States government and its allies. I can assure you there will be a job waiting for you, a modest home, and a small amount in savings as a token of our appreciation."

I blinked hard. He was still there. So was Eli, standing to my side.

Not a hallucination, then.

". . . understand me?" Krogher asked. "I thought you said he'd be clear by now."

"He is," Eli said. "Just about now."

"This is your last day," Krogher said. "We'll be letting you go, Mr. Conley."

"Go?" I asked, my voice a shadow in the room. That didn't seem right. They were letting me go? I looked up at Eli. He raised his eyebrows. That didn't help me much.

"Where?"

"We are relocating you, Mr. Conley," Krogher said. "Of course."

Of course. Which meant not at all. I might be drugged out of my brain, but I wasn't stupid.

"But first, we must be certain that none of this will ever become a problem for us," Krogher said. "Mr. Collins, please proceed."

This was a problem. I knew what they were doing—making sure I never talked about any of this. If I were the one calling the shots, I'd know exactly how I'd achieve that goal.

"My pleasure," Eli said. Krogher walked out of the cage, his footsteps a fading echo across the walls and ceiling as he left.

"So," Eli said once he was sure Krogher was gone. "I am going to Close you, Terric. Wipe out all your memories. You know the most delightful thing about all this? It is up to me. It is in *my* hands to decide what you become. I can mold you. I can break you. Give you a good life, make every day a worthless, living hell. I am your god."

He smiled. "I have to say it is not a bad position to have landed in. But before I Close you, I want you clear and sober. I want you to really understand exactly what I'm doing to you. Would you like some coffee?"

He turned and I heard the rising treble of liquid filling a cup, smelled the rich, warm scent of coffee. My mouth watered. I couldn't remember the last time I'd eaten. Couldn't even remember water. Glanced at my arm. Cotton and tape there where an IV had been attached.

How long had I been here?

"What day is it?" I asked.

Eli strolled over and set the coffee down on a table next to the cot where I sat. He took the only chair in the cage, turned it to face the cot, and slurped the hot edge off his cup before sitting down.

"Wednesday."

"What month?"

"March." He watched me as he took another drink of coffee. Then, "Just one Wednesday since I pulled you out of your kitchen, as a matter of fact."

I was sitting, but my hands were no longer chained. I reached over, picked up the coffee, trying to keep it steady and not spill. My feet were free. I wore loose pants like something found in a prison or hospital, and a white T-shirt. I was barefoot and the floor was smooth, concrete, and cold.

One Wednesday. I tried to think through the implications of that.

Lifting the coffee was almost more than I could manage, but I didn't spill it as I drew it toward my mouth. I shouldn't be this strong. Not after what he'd done to me.

"It's been months," I said. I took a sip and held my breath against the pleasure and pain of it. I felt like I hadn't eaten in years. "At least that."

"Yes, at least that," he said, enjoying my confusion. "It seems like such a long time you and I have spent together. And yet . . . something tells you that's wrong. So. Do you have it? Do you understand it yet?"

The stone-on-steel sound that woke me. The burnt disk. I hadn't been sleeping. I'd been wrapped in magic.

Son of a bitch.

"Time," I said. "You cast Time."

"Head of the class. I guess I didn't scramble your brain as much as I thought I did. What has been months for you, six, if you'd like to know, has been only days. Six, as a matter of fact."

He'd cast Time and held the spell so we experienced a month a day. That was very precise work, something only a genius magic user would even try to attempt.

To break the spell and land us back in the correct flow of reality's time took a deft touch. And apparently blew the hell out of a Beckstrom disk.

No wonder Eli looked so tired. Holding that spell for nearly a week would exhaust anyone. I just hoped it had exhausted him enough to make him sloppy.

"And since I'm locking your life away in a box and melting down the key, I thought I'd tell you everything," he said. "Anything you want to know, I'll tell you. Think of it as my way of thanking you for not dying before I was done with you. Ask."

"How many people, spell holders are there?"

"Really, Terric? Business to the end? Save the world at all costs? I'd expected more from you."

"How many?"

"Drones? Just under a hundred. Each topped off with magic and showing no signs of decay."

"Who are they targeting first?"

"Soul Complements. Don't you remember me saying so? Maybe you were too . . ." He made the circle motion by his ear.

"When?"

"I believe I'll be briefed on that today. But if I had to guess?" He swallowed coffee. "Immediately. Krogher and his division don't like loose ends left behind. And they most certainly do not like people out in the world who can break magic and use it as a deadly weapon. Company motto: Sooner the enemy is dead, the better."

"Did you kill Davy?"

"No. I did much worse than that to him."

"What? What did you do to him?"

"I triggered spells carved into him so that he is no longer solid. No longer a real boy. He begged me. Begged me to let him go. So I did. Maybe not the way he wanted me to, but I think he got what he deserved. He is no longer bound to this world. Magic gave him a way out, as only magic can. If you know what I mean, Terric?"

He waited, studying my face. I had no idea what he meant. But then, madmen aren't easy conversationalists.

"Anything else?" He glanced at the watch on his wrist. "We are running a little behind schedule and I'd hate to keep the government waiting."

"Did you kill Shame?"

He paused, cup tipped halfway to his mouth.

"Oh yes. Very much so. I shot him. Over and over again. Until I saw him fall. Until I saw him take his last breath. You should know. You should have felt the snap of your soul from his, a bone break so deep the pain blinds. Did you feel that, Terric? Did you feel his soul and life severed from you?"

He had asked me that before. This time I answered.

"Yes," I whispered, the memory of that moment, of watching, feeling Shame die burning like acid across my mind. "I just wanted to hear it from your lips," I said. "Wanted to hear that you killed him. Because after this is done—these orders of yours—I'm going to find you, and

I'm going to kill you, Eli. It doesn't matter what you do to me. Doesn't matter if you Close my mind, take magic away, wipe my memories. I will find you. And then you'll be dead."

The corner of his mouth twitched upward. "Wouldn't that be something? I'd like you to try, Terric. Truly, I would. At least it would be something to look forward to." He took another drink of his coffee. "Now we really must get on with it. Let's have at it, shall we?"

"One last thing," I said. "There's no house and job at the end of this for me, is there?"

He shrugged. "You'll think there is." He tapped his temple. "That's all that matters, isn't it?"

I gripped my coffee cup tighter. He'd have to touch me to Close me. I'd have one chance at this. At knocking him out. At escape.

Eli stood.

Be tired, Eli. Be sloppy.

The shadows shifted outside the bars of my cage. A man stood just outside, shuffling forward as if sleepwalking. One of the drones. He held his hands palm out in front of him, thumb and forefinger touching.

I'd seen drones like him before. When Shame and I had tried to stop Eli from taking Davy. When Shame and I had tried to stop Krogher from killing Dessa. When Shame and I had failed.

The drone would be the power behind Eli's spell. But there would be no spell if Eli had a concussion. Hard to concentrate on spell casting when your brain was bleeding.

One more step.

Eli stopped, just outside my reach. Began drawing the spell.

My heart was pounding. I'd drawn that spell a hundred times before. I'd taken people's memories away; I'd taken away their ability to use magic. I knew what kind of concentration went into it.

Closing was not as easy as it looked. As a matter of fact, being a Closer was one of the hardest positions to hold in the Authority.

But I had no doubt that Eli could pull it off. In his right mind. Refreshed.

I gripped the cup, waited for that moment in the spell where he would have to draw the doorway, the opening between his mind and mine. It was a door that only the caster had the key to. I watched his movement so I would know his signature, know his exact lines and style of casting this spell.

So I would know the shape of the key that could set me free.

There. He set the lock, drew the key.

I surged to my feet. Swung with every ounce of strength I had.

Just as the spell triggered.

Just as magic broke free like water from a dam, blasting out from the drone outside the bars and into Eli's spell.

The mug slammed into Eli's head with a satisfying crack.

His spell opened its maw and swallowed my mind.

But not before I saw Eli fall, bloody. Unconscious.

And then I was nothing but what the magic wanted me to be.

I was no one.

Chapter 14

SHAME

The problem with falling is that there is always something to hit at the bottom.

I hit a fist.

Or rather, a fist hit me. Pounded my chest, broke a rib. Took another shot. Broke two.

Holy shit, that hurt.

Someone was yelling, cursing. Taking my name in vain. I didn't know who I'd pissed off, but there wasn't nobody having any fun here today.

"Fuck," I gasped, "you."

The beating paused. A woman's voice filtered through the hell in my head.

"Shame? Are you alive? You'd better stay with me, you son of a bitch, or I will carve you a new one."

Sunny. Sounded like Sunny. I wanted to open my eyes to find out, but it was everything—and trust me when I say everything—I had just to fill my lungs with enough air it could wheeze out of me.

Where the hell was I?

"Just keep breathing," she said as if that was an easy thing. "Dash! Get your ass in here. He's alive."

I thought she might be jumping the gun a bit on that one. I wasn't even remotely close to alive yet. Hell, the jury was still out on breathing.

"Jesus," Dash said. "Get this under his head. Here."

There was some movement around me, but I still couldn't see Jack, and couldn't feel squat.

"Hello?" yet another voice called out. Took me a second to place it. Finally got it. Cody Miller. The one guy I always got into the most trouble with back in the day. "You two find anything? What are you doing?"

"Calling nine-one-one," Davy said.

"Don't bother," Cody said. "They wouldn't know what to do for him."

"He's dying, Cody," Dash said.

"No," Cody said thoughtfully. "I think he's way past that."

"Can you help him?" Sunny asked. "Cody, do you know of some way to help him?" She sounded angry, but also a little worried. I might have thought it was sweet if I didn't also know she'd been the one slugging me repeatedly in the chest just a second ago.

Where the hell was I?

The lungs were working slightly better, though I couldn't get more than a mouthful of air down into either one of them. The rest of me either was numb or felt like crap.

Time to give the eyes a try again.

One, and a two . . .

Got it. Kind of. Was rewarded with blurry light. Then Dash's face, screwed up with concern, hovering over me. "I'm calling nine-one-one."

"Give him a minute," Cody said. "He's almost back."

"What the hell are you talking about?" Dash said.

"I am saying, he's almost got it," Cody said. "The hang of living. Well, when I say living . . ."

Shame? Eleanor floated over from across the room. *Remember why you're here. You have to live. You have to save the world, save Terric, save . . . everything. This is what you came back for. So live.*

There was something different about her, something I should remember. Oh, right. She was free. She was no longer tied to me.

That's right, she said. *I took the jump with you. But I'm here on my own terms now. You need to draw on life, on something, Shame, or you're corpsing out.*

"Go," I wheezed, trying to warn her, "away."

Dash backed up. So did Cody. But Eleanor didn't move away quick enough.

The hunger inside me was mindless, wild. Any life would do—it just had to be close to me.

No. Not Eleanor. Not again.

I fought for control, desperate not to hurt her.

She didn't have much life in her, but she was an energy. And she was in the hunger's reach.

No!

The magic in me, Death, was too strong. It snapped out, wrapped around her neck, pulled her down to me, and drank her up.

I heard her scream. Tried to let go of her, tried not to tie her soul to me.

And then I couldn't hear anything anymore because everything in me caught fire at the same time, all nerves firing, screaming. I'd be joining the chorus, only I didn't have air for it, and was pretty sure I was rattling around on the floor—kitchen floor—seizing like a mother.

Good times.

Something turned out the lights. Maybe just the overload of pain. Maybe Sunny punched my clock, bless her violent little heart.

I woke up in a bed—my bed. I was naked, clean sheets

around me, a pillow under my head. Didn't want to move and ruin the moment, but my face itched like a million ants were swarming over it.

I lifted my right hand to try to push some of the ants off the side of my face. My hand didn't make it that far.

"Hey, Shame," Cody said from somewhere to my right. "I thought you might be waking up soon. Welcome back."

I gave up on making my hand do what I wanted it to do. "I feel like shit."

"You should. You died." Cody was sitting in the chair, his feet on the wooden crate of ammo I used as a nightstand.

Right. I thought I'd heard something about that. Seemed to remember there being a bar or something. "Swell," I whispered. "How long?"

"As near as we can tell, you haven't been breathing for a week. The bullet holes look at least that old. Well, they *did*. Since you came to, you've healed. Well, you aren't bleeding and all the bullets were expelled, which isn't quite the same as healing, but it did seem to help you breathe better. You look like hell on a half shell, though."

I heard him, I really did. But my brain simply refused to process most of what he was saying.

I'd died. Why didn't I stay dead?

Eleanor floated up behind him. She was almost completely see-through. A black rope around her throat tied her to me.

No. I didn't mean to . . . not again.

"I'm sorry," I said. "God, I'm so sorry."

She flipped me off with both hands. Then she floated as far away from me as she could reach, arms crossed over her chest, turning her back toward me.

I'd seen her like that so many times over the years. She was angry. At me.

And she had every right to be. I hadn't meant to consume her again, to tie her soul to me. But I hadn't been strong enough to stop it from happening either.

"Shame?" Cody asked. "Are you okay? You're staring at me."

"I'm not okay."

"Can I—" he said.

"No. Nothing." I glanced at Eleanor one last time. Didn't know what I could do to fix what I'd done. Didn't want to talk to Cody about it. "I need to take a leak."

He pointed to the left. "Bathroom's that way."

"I know. This is my house, you idiot." I pushed at the sheet. It resisted my attempts to move it.

Jesus, I was tired.

"I heard talking," Dash said as he walked into the room. "Shame, why are you moving? You shouldn't be moving. Dr. Fischer is on the way. Where do you think you're going?"

"Bathroom," I said. I'd pushed the sheet down to my waist and was working on sliding a leg over to the edge of the bed.

"Here." Dash stepped to the side of the bed and half hauled, half supported me out of it. He didn't say anything about me being naked and dead, and I was too naked and dead to care.

Got me to the bathroom. I tackled the problem of the toilet by propping one elbow on the towel rack and trying not to pass out.

Having managed that, I decided to go for the gold.

Turned toward the shower. Who in their right mind built a shower three miles away from the toilet? Didn't care. I was going to wash this pain, blood, sweat, and hell off me, no matter how long it took for me to do it.

". . . got it," Dash said, suddenly appearing out of nowhere, his arm around my waist as he helped me toward the shower. "Almost there."

"Dash," I said as we crept ever closer and closer to the shower, which was already on and steaming up the room. Strange. No, Cody was over there, putting something in the shower. A plastic patio chair? What the hell?

". . . sit," Dash said, bending with me to fold me into the chair. ". . . dumb idea. If you die on us, Shame, I'm going to kick your ass, you understand?"

Whoa. Kind of harsh on a guy who'd just marched his naked ass halfway across the universe for a shower.

"Take it easy," Cody said to him. "Why don't you go make some coffee and check on Sunny? I'll stay here and make sure he doesn't drown."

Maybe Dash said something; maybe he and Cody got in a fistfight, danced the tango, or took up skeet shooting. Didn't care. There was water—warm, soft, life-filled water—pouring down over my body.

Eleanor hovered across the room, still as far from me as she could get. She refused to look at me.

"I'm . . . sorry," I said. "I couldn't stop it. I . . . El. I'll fix this. I promise."

She still wouldn't turn.

It would have to wait. She would have to wait. I was too damn tired to do anything but sit and breathe. Everything else, the whole damn living world, would have to wait until I had my feet under me.

Lost some time again. When I woke up, it was dark out. The lamp in the corner of the room glowed softly. I was back in my bed, propped up with pillows so I was not quite sitting. Had a pair of boxers on. I moved a little and bandages scraped against the sheets. Bandages on my arms, my legs, my chest.

I felt like a piñata, the day after the party.

"Are you awake, Shame?" Sunny asked. I heard her shift in the lounger chair set in the corner of the room.

I tried to get moisture in my mouth. "Who do I have to blow for a drink of water?" I rasped.

More rustling; then she sat on the bed next to me. "You don't have to blow," she said. "Just suck it, Flynn." She angled a straw into my mouth.

Funny. I sucked and the water hit my mouth with a shocking clean coolness full of flavor. Water had never tasted so good. I got a few mouthfuls of it down before Sunny took it away.

"You are a piece of work," she said quietly as if she didn't want to wake the other people in the house.

"What, this?" I said, trying a smile. God, that hurt. "It's nothing."

"Shame," she said, "you've been dead. For a week."

"Miss me?"

She didn't say anything for a second or two. Then, "We can't find Terric."

Gut punch.

"What? What does that mean?"

"He's not here in the house. He's not anywhere else either. A lot of old blood on your kitchen floor, and we're pretty sure not all of it is yours.

"I followed up on some leads on Davy. Think I have a pretty good idea where Davy's being held. Then I came back to get you. To make you come with me and kill the bastards who are holding him. Only no one had seen you. For days. And no one had seen Terric. So Dash, Cody, and I looked everywhere. We finally came here. Don't you ever lock your front door?"

"Why? What could go wrong?"

"Goddamn, Shame. This isn't funny. This isn't one of your play-it-loose-and-it-will-all-work-out schemes. People are dying here. Davy. Maybe Terric, if he's still alive. And you, you jackass. I need you to get your head in this. I need you to . . ." She waved her hand at me.

"Be a weapon so you can save Davy?" I asked.

She gave me a long look. One thing I had to give the

woman. She did not back down. Blood magic users. Tough as steel.

"Yes. I need you, and I need the Death magic you carry. You do still carry it, don't you?"

"I don't know."

"Can you? Know? I need you to know, Shame. Because if you don't have it, then I'm going to go after Davy without you. Tonight."

"Where?"

"There's a warehouse up in Washington. Outside Ephrata. I think he's there."

"You worked the Spokane lead?"

She nodded. "I think Eli's there too."

"Who else have you told?"

"Just a few Hounds. Well, and Dash and Cody."

"Who has Dash told?"

"No one," Dash said from the doorway. He looked a little rumpled in a T-shirt and jeans but had his boots on. He also had two mugs in his hand. I thought I smelled tea. "This is off the radar, Shame. We agreed we don't want to drag anyone else into it if we go get Davy."

"We?" I asked.

He walked in. "Sunny, Cody, and me. We didn't want anyone else in the Authority involved, which is why I haven't even told the boss man, Clyde. He'd just tell us not to do whatever it is we are going to do anyway. And we certainly didn't want to worry Zay and Allie."

Allie. The baby.

A memory scraped across all the raw and screaming in my head. Something about Allie. Something about her baby. "Is she? Did she have her daughter yet?"

Davy handed me one of the mugs. Half-full, black tea with honey and cream. I pulled it toward me and took a sip. Braced for the explosion of scent and flavor, lost myself to it for a minute or two.

This "living" was a heady thing.

"...girl?" Dash was saying. "Shame? Are you listening?"

"No. What'd I miss?"

"Did Allie tell you she was having a girl?"

I looked up at his cautious concern. Checked out Sunny, who was giving me the same look.

"No. Maybe. I don't know," I said, chasing memories. Someone had told me. Said she was having a girl. Told me more. That I had to save Terric, save the world. Kill Eli. Stop Krogher. No matter the cost.

"Has she had her? Or it? Has she had the baby?"

"Not yet," he said. "Any day, though. Why?"

I took another swallow of tea, filling my whole mouth with it, shuddering through the glorious riot of flavor. It burned all the way down. "We need to go now." I held the cup out for Davy, who took it. "Before the baby is born."

Then I pushed the blankets off.

"I don't think that's such a good idea," Dash said. "Dr. Fischer wanted you to rest. She said she'd be here in the morning to check on you."

"Which means she's writing a report for someone somewhere to read. Probably Clyde," I said. "We leave tonight."

"Shame," Dash said. "I think you need to get through a whole twenty-four hours of breathing before we drive your ass across two states."

"I can breathe in a car. You think Terric is there?" I got my feet over the edge. Held still to give my lungs a chance to catch up.

"We don't know where Terric is," Dash said. "We think Davy's there."

"Can't you tell?" Sunny asked. "I thought you could feel Terric. With that Soul thing you have?"

"No," I said. That was the truth, the hell I was not ready

to face. I couldn't feel Terric. At all. It might be because our connection had broken when I died. It might be because he was dead.

Or it might be because I'd died and come back not quite what I had been before. Something that didn't match to a soul anymore.

The hunger rolled in me and Eleanor arched back, pulling against the rope that tightened on her neck. I pushed at the magic, shoved Death away until it subsided.

Damn.

"So if you can't feel him . . . ," Dash was saying.

He knew the answer. Terric might be dead.

If he was, then I had myself some unlucky bastard to track down and obliterate.

"Do you remember what happened?" Dash asked. "Do you remember who shot you?"

"Eli." I pushed up onto my feet. The insides of me knotted up and lurched and threatened to become the outside of me.

". . . Shame," Dash said, in front of me with his hands on my shoulders. "Breathe!"

Right, as if it was that easy. Still, I gave the lungs a try, swallowed air. Enough to make the blackness filling the room step on back a bit. Note to the wise: Lungs plus bullets do not equal fun times.

"You can't do this. Not yet," Dash said.

"Dash," Sunny warned.

"You two might as well take the argument to the other room." I pushed Dash's hands off me, gently, because I didn't want to hurt him, and because really, that was all the strength I had in me. "I'm going to get some clothes on."

Sunny started toward the door. Dash, bless him, hesitated. "You dying—again—isn't going to help us find Davy. Or Terric. Or anything. Shame, you need to rest."

I gave him a small smile. He really was concerned about me, about Davy, about Terric.

"Well," I said as I shuffled over to my dresser. "As soon as we're sure I'm actually alive again—then we can worry about me dying again."

"Shame," he said softly. "This can wait. At least a day. Please."

I paused by the drawer, wondering if I had it in me to open the damn thing. "Eli shot me, and he took Terric. I think he took Terric. If Eli also has Davy, then that's where we're going. Where I'm going. Even if it's just to kill Eli and bury Terric's body."

Dash didn't say anything, so I did.

"I would kill for a cup of coffee, mate. That tea just isn't cutting it." Life would help too. Dash's life, Sunny's life. But I'd already done . . . something terrible to Eleanor. Trapping her, tying her down with that black rope of magic. I wasn't going to let that happen again. I didn't want to hurt anyone else.

"Jesus, Shame." Dash rubbed at his eyes. He looked tired. Of course, he'd spent a week looking for Terric and me, and when he'd found me I was dead. It hadn't been an easy go for him lately either.

"Coffee, Boy Wonder," I said. "And make it strong. We have a long road ahead of us."

Dash shook his head and walked out of the room. "Stupid, stupid idea."

I could hear Sunny telling Cody we were headed out.

All right, Shame. Time to really take stock.

I took a gander under the bandages. I'd apparently sprouted a collection of holes. One in each shoulder, deep enough I could stick my pinkie into it up to my middle knuckle—which, by the way, hurt like a bitch. They were bloody, but not bleeding, and were strangely cold. My body temperature was way below manufacturer's recommendations.

Five in my chest, two in my right leg, three in my left. Two in my right hip.

All of them deeper than I wanted to go digging around in, but the exit wounds were just as small as the entry wounds. Bullets didn't work like that. I should be fifty percent ground beef in the back with that many shots in me.

I guess that if one is already filled with Death magic, it might make dying a little more difficult.

I pulled on the dresser drawer, gulped air until I could see straight again, pulled out a T-shirt, and dragged the soft cotton over my aching skin.

Gun. I had been in the kitchen. Terric was with me. We were eating pizza. Doing our magic thing to that poor plant. And then . . .

. . . *blood. A knife cutting into his throat. Terric's eyes, as he fell* . . .

. . . *fell at Eli's feet.*

Son of a bitch.

My heart kicked against my ribs and I groaned, waiting for the pain to pass. Eli had gotten into the kitchen. Eli had shot the gun. Eli had killed me, something that did not sit well with me at all.

Eli had slit Terric's throat.

Everything inside me twisted again, agony I braced against and sweated my way through.

I glanced up at Eleanor, and this time she just stood there, blankly staring at me. She didn't appear to be in pain. But I could see the tears streaking her face.

I didn't know if it was withdrawals from death, or that I was allergic to life, but either way, something was irreparably wrong with me. With my body.

I needed life. Needing living. The Death in me was a bottomless hole, burning black in me. Hungry. And I was having a hell of a time fighting it.

In the end, I supposed it would win.

So I had some things to get done before I kicked off for good.

I had to find Davy for Sunny. Had to find Terric. Kill Eli. Kill Krogher, stop the drones. Save the world, no matter the cost. No matter what I gave up for it.

I was the last human on earth who should be given this responsibility. One look at Eleanor proved that. I'd shackled a woman who had jumped out of heaven for me.

What kind of monster was I?

I glanced up at the mirror, above the dresser.

The face of my nightmares looked back at me. I'd seen that look on the last Death magic user I'd killed. It was hunger and darkness and need. It was the thing that using Death magic was turning me into—a monster I could not sate or control.

Chapter 15

TERRIC

A hand tapped the side of my face. "Wake up, Terric. We need to go."

I wasn't sleeping. I was just sitting here, wherever here was. Prison. There were bars all around me, so it must be prison.

"Terric?"

The man in front of me was maybe in his twenties, blond hair. He was sweating and breathing as if he'd been running a marathon. His nose was bleeding.

I shook my head. Where was I? Why was I here?

"Let's go. Eli won't be out for long, and I can't hold this—"

The man flickered, disappeared.

Holy shit.

I scrambled up onto my feet. There was another man bleeding on the floor, a broken coffee cup shattered at my feet. I was in hospital clothes, and there was enough medical equipment in the room that it wasn't a big leap to think I was sick.

The bars didn't make any sense. What kind of hospital kept people behind bars?

Was I insane? That man who had just been here and disappeared could have been a hallucination.

Okay, so insane was looking like a probability. That would mean the man on the floor was a doctor or an orderly, and I was ...

... I had no idea what I was. I had no idea *who* I was.

That was terrifying.

Panic shot ice through my veins.

"Okay," I said, talking myself through this. "Okay. Names. Records. Something. Look for answers. There must be something here."

I knelt, gasped at the pain that squeezed my ribs. Broken ribs, judging from the bandages wrapped around my chest. And from the gauze packed around my left hand, I was pretty sure I was missing a pinkie.

Bars, bandages, missing digits. That painted a new picture. Not so much a medical facility as a place of interrogation. Torture?

A memory cracked open and spilled through my mind: knives in the hand of that man who was unconscious on the floor. Knives cutting into me.

Eli. His name was Eli, and he'd used more than knives to cause me pain.

He'd used magic.

Then the memory was gone and I grunted at the snarling headache that replaced it. I didn't even know who I was, couldn't remember why I was here, but I knew that I should not have been able to access that memory.

Maybe the hallucination had been right. I needed to get out of here before the man on the floor woke up.

I stepped over Eli.

Every motion hurt. Breathing hurt. It felt as if someone had taken a hammer to all the things inside me and left me shattered and bleeding.

Even so, I made it to the table covered with blades, saws, and other hardware.

If even half of those things were used on me, it was no wonder I was in pain.

No key for the door. I took one of the knives, walked to the bars, which were painted with designs or maybe a language. Nothing I could read. The lock was electronic.

"Terric." The hallucination man appeared on the other side of the bars. "You have to follow me. We need to get the hell out of here before they get the cameras back online. The blocking spell I cast won't last for long."

"Who are you? Where are we?"

"You've been Closed. Or at least partially Closed. He took away your memories. We're in a warehouse in Washington and we don't have much time before they find out I'm not dead, and you're not catatonic."

"Closed?" I managed.

"Magic." He searched my face for understanding, and found none. "Okay, fine. You want out of here, you'll just have to trust me on that. And if this knocks me out or . . . kills me, I want you to tell Sunny yes for me, okay?"

"Yes?"

"She asked me to marry her, then took off to Florida. Before I could call her, I got my ass handed to me by Eli and the rest of these fuckers. I never got a chance to give her my answer. It's yes. Now stand back."

He wrapped his hands on the bars and exhaled slowly. The symbols etched into the metal caught white fire, arcing from bar to bar to glow brighter, then run like hot oil down to the lock.

"Davy," a voice said behind me. "How nice of you to join us. I'd thought you were gone from the world for good."

I turned. Eli was no longer unconscious. He stood, his face covered in blood from that broken nose and sliced cheek.

He held a gun aimed at us.

"Shoot, you bastard," Davy said. "I'm coming for you next."

"You don't have the strength," Eli said. "And I should know." He shifted the gun just a fraction.

"I wondered if you would find that little loophole I couldn't plug," he said. "Some of those spells in your flesh just refuse to be canceled out, no matter what I try. But you must understand there are plans in place. *Plans*," he said to me as if I knew what he meant, "that would be the best for all of us to follow. While I would love to further my research on you, Davy, I will not let you get in the way of my plans."

Eli squeezed the trigger.

"No!" I threw myself in front of Davy.

Just as the bars around me went white-fire supernova from Davy's spell.

The first bullet burned through my chest, the second right behind it. I hit the bars behind me. Yelled as fire engulfed me. Tasted ash, oil, and blood.

I thought I heard Davy yell. And then everything went black.

Chapter 16

SHAME

By the time I'd pulled on a pair of jeans and laced up my boots, I was so tired, I wanted to weep. Nothing in me was working. My lungs stuck shut with every breath, my vision went black if I moved too fast, and my heart tripped like a three-legged bull in a china shop.

Eleanor refused to acknowledge me and made it a point to stay as far away as possible.

I eased down and sat at the foot of the bed. Didn't think I'd be getting up under my own power anytime soon. I'd never felt so broken. It wasn't just my body. It wasn't just magic. Deep down, in the core of me, where maybe my soul should be was a gaping wound. I was torn, empty, shattered.

Terric was gone.

Jesus. I didn't love living with him, but being without him was worse.

Dash stepped into the room with a cup of coffee. "You look worse," he noted as I accepted the cup he offered and took a small sip.

Coffee Mack-trucked my senses: hot, bitter, sweet, thick.

I held on as it took the corner down to my stomach, where it crashed in a burn that rolled out across my nerves.

C'mon, caffeine. Shamus needs to go out and play.

I looked up. Expected Dash to be saying something I wasn't listening to. But he was standing there, waiting. He'd brushed his hair back, found his glasses, shrugged on a gray jean jacket. It was startling how very alive, whole, and well he was.

Compared to the pale imitation of a human I'd seen staring back at me from the mirror, he was a beacon of life.

"Before we go," he said, "I need to know a couple of things. Can you tell if Terric is alive?"

"No. But . . ." I shook my head. "What we had, our connection. That's gone."

"Right," he said softly as he put two and two together and carried the conclusion. We were Soul Complements who had used magic together more than once. It meant we were tied. Soul to soul. If Terric were alive, I'd know it.

Wouldn't I?

Dash cleared his throat, but his voice shook just a little. "You think Eli took him?"

"Yes."

"Okay, can you access magic at all?"

Even the idea of it made me nauseated. And hungry. I licked my lips, tasting the old blood from cuts there. "I don't know."

"Let's find out."

"Really? Dash, I'm just . . . I think that's a bad idea."

"Before we get in the car. Before we go hunting Davy. Before we look for Terric, alive or dead. Before we run into Eli. I want to know, right now, what shape you're really in. I know this is hard—"

"Stow the sympathy," I said.

"Not sympathy, Shame. Let me lay this out for you. Sunny is too invested in finding Davy to think any of this through. Cody's in his own world, like he always is. I'm here to make sure you're going to make it through the night."

"Listen. It's sweet of you to worry," I said.

"No. It's practical. Sunny thinks you're the gun she can wave to get Davy back. But you're my friend, Shame. You died." He paused, letting that statement linger in the silence. Then, a little quieter, "I'm not going to let you walk into battle and die again. So prove to me you've got the legs to survive a rescue mission against the same people who kicked your ass to hell and back."

I glanced up at him. Saw maybe for the first time someone other than my ex-assistant and general nice guy. Sometime over the last three years, Dash had stepped into his own. He was keeping a clear head under ridiculous circumstances. Taking charge.

Man might make a fine head of the Authority one day.

Huh.

I hadn't known him when powerful magic was something anyone could use easily, although I'd read his record and known he had mostly stayed away from using magic, and instead dealt with the business sides of the Authority's needs.

But that man leaning against my bedroom wall had this possibly explosive magical situation under control and was determined to see it through.

Since the explosive situation in this case was me, and I was barely holding it together, I was impressed by his composure.

"What are we going to do, Dash?" I said. "Fight? Think you can take me?"

"Right now my grandmother could take you."

I smiled. "True." I swallowed another couple mouthfuls of coffee and left the cup on the edge of the bed. I pressed my hands into my thighs and pushed up.

"This is me. I am on my feet," I said. "Where's the battle, Chief?"

"Use magic," he ordered. "I don't care what spell. But you're going to show me what you got." He tipped his head down and made that hurry-up motion with his fingers.

I glanced over at Eleanor, who had her back turned to me, staring out my window. The black rope around her neck snaked toward me and latched in to my arm like a dark IV line.

"This is *such* a bad idea," I whispered.

"Why?"

"There's a good chance I'm going to hurt someone."

"Won't know until you do it."

I finally looked away from Eleanor. "You just won't let this go, will you, Spade? Why haven't you used this kind of determination to get Terric to date you?"

I was hoping bringing up his love life would make him pull back. Sore subjects usually do. But he didn't even flinch.

"Magic, Shame. Now would be good, but I can wait. Days, if that's what you need."

I glared at him. Would have continued the argument, but just standing there holding up my attitude was wearing me out. If I was going to cast magic, which apparently I was, then I'd better do it while I had the strength to control it. I didn't want to drink another person down.

I didn't want to hurt Eleanor.

Something easy, like Light, seemed a good bet, but what Davy really wanted to know, and what Sunny really wanted to know, was if I could handle Death magic.

In for a penny, in for a pound.

I took a breath, held it, then drew on the place inside me where Death magic sat.

It came to me, slowly, cold, and painful. Filled my bones with a weight that threatened to snap my bones.

Holy shit, it hurt.

But I stood, holding against the weight of it. I directed Death magic, sluggish, heavy, and raw, to Death something. But not a person. Or a ghost.

The dresser looked like a good enough target.

I turned toward it, held out my hand. Nothing. Magic was there, I could feel the lead weight of it in my chest, in my spine, filling my arm so that it was difficult to keep extended, but magic would not move through me.

Hell.

I trudged over to the dresser. Put both hands on it. Reached in for the magic again, dragging it forward.

Death, I thought. *Now.*

Magic responded by paralyzing me.

Shit.

Out of the corner of my eye, I saw Eleanor dim and flicker.

Magic oozed out of my bones, slithered through my veins, cold, toxic.

My hands cracked with black lines as Death magic carved new channels and paths in me. Paths that hadn't been open even before I'd died.

I couldn't breathe.

Well, that was inconvenient.

Magic poured out of my fingertips like oil and ink, puddling and spreading from under my palms, covering the dresser in the black and slime, dissolving wood and nails and brass, aging them all, decomposing, killing.

Death.

The dresser went ash gray and crumbled into a pile of dust.

I was still standing, mostly because I couldn't move. Just enough nerves were firing to let me know I was going to be hurting or unconscious—or both—when magic was done with me.

"Shame?" Dash said. "Shame?"

I tried to answer, to tell him not to touch me, for God's sake.

No go. Magic wasn't done with me yet. It crept out from

the ashen pile of rotted wood and across the floor to the outer wall, where it leaked beyond the bedroom to the plants that surrounded the house.

And killed them all in one quick strike.

An explosion of pleasure blew through me. I closed my eyes as the death of each plant rolled hot and sweet across my skin, my bones, my soul. It was sex; it was more than sex. It was death and life, wrapping around me in an embrace so sensual I lost all thought.

I wanted life. The life Death magic could give me.

Death magic drank down the easy, sweet life of plants, bushes, trees.

I wanted more. So much more. Cars rushed by on the road that wound above the house. Cars filled with sweet, blood-pumping life. That would be enough to fill me. To begin to fill this cold dark hole inside me. To ease my pain.

And then Eleanor was in front of me. She'd been crying, her eyes red-rimmed, her cheeks wet. She shook her head. *Stop, Shame. You don't want to kill innocent people. You don't want to lose your humanity to this darkness.*

She was right. I just couldn't move, couldn't get ahead of the magic that had swallowed me whole.

Eleanor must have seen something in my eyes. She smiled sadly, then reached out and pressed her hand over my heart.

For a moment, I felt her hand as if she were solid, real, alive. Or as if I were dead, ghostly like her.

Magic paused, eased its grip on me.

It wasn't much of a break, but I took full advantage of it.

Enough. I focused my will over it and drew the magic back to me, hauling on it, hand over hand, as if it were a rope, a chain that I could drag away from the living world and pack away inside me.

Magic snapped back with concussive force. I grunted from the pain but didn't let go of the magic. I forced it down, back into that hole in my brain, chaining it to me and drawing it in, tight, tighter.

"Shame." Dash was right in front of me now. I didn't know where Eleanor had gone. Dash looked angry. "Let go, Shame," he said. "Please, just let it go."

Nope, not angry, worried.

"So, that good enough for you?" I asked, though it came out a faint wheeze.

I felt like magic had just bad-touched me from the inside out. I was cold, sweaty, and I stank of it.

Dash didn't move. Didn't reach out to help me. After I got done breathing too hard, and my vision cleared, I realized why.

He wasn't worried or angry. He was afraid.

Join the damn club.

"That was delightful," I said. "Thanks."

"You think that's control?" he asked.

"Enough."

He clearly didn't believe me. That was okay, I didn't believe me either.

"You need a day to rest. Well, a year might be better, but at least a day, Shame. This can wait."

"No," I said. "It can't. We haven't had a lead on Davy and Eli for months. We do this now, while there's still a trail to follow." I gave the walking thing a try. After three wobbly steps, my legs and muscles got back on talking terms. As a matter of fact, I felt the best I had since rising from the dead. My lungs were on autopilot, and my heart pumped on its own, although very, very slowly, which was both odd and distracting.

The life from the plants had done some good.

"I'm fine," I said to Dash and his sideways looks.

"You look worse," Dash said.

"Ever thought about going into motivational speaking?" I asked. "Because you'd be amazing."

"Shut up, Shame."

That's my boy. I gave him a smile and walked out of the room, down the hall, and into the living room, where Sunny was pacing the perimeter.

"About damn time, Flynn." She slung a glare my way and then went ghost white. "What the hell happened to you?"

I paused, held out my hands to each side. "I got dressed. Like it?"

She looked over at Dash as though maybe he had something to say about my wardrobe.

"You'd better get used to it," he said to me. "Because you just disintegrated all the rest of your clothes."

The dresser. He was right.

Well, shit.

"How bad was it?" Cody asked, coming in from the kitchen with a plastic cup of pudding.

"What?"

"Death magic. You drained . . . something, drank some living thing down and it fueled you, right? But there must be a price."

At my look, he said, "I'm the guy who held all of magic until it healed, remember? You're an anomaly, Shame. I can see it in you. Before today, I wouldn't think someone could come back from the dead with that much Death magic gluing them together. What's it like?"

"Hungry," I said. "Cold. Painful."

He nodded and scooped pudding into his mouth. "And the price?"

"Having to answer dumb questions."

He ate another bite of pudding and waved the spoon at me. "By changing the subject?"

Sunny and Davy were silent, but I knew that was the question foremost on their minds too.

I didn't blame them. They were about to road-trip with Death, after all. You'd have to be an idiot not to want to know if I had magic under control.

"It's different," I said. "But I think I have a handle on it. And as long as I don't use it, I think I'll be okay. I think you'll all be okay. If that changes, I'll tell you."

I walked to the door and pulled my coat off the hook. "How about we get on with the rescuing of Davy and the saving of the world?"

"So you're good, Shame?" Sunny asked.

I just gave her a bored look. "I've never been good, babe."

She glanced at Dash again as if he were my keeper or something. "All right," she said, uncrossing her arms and picking up her duffel. "Let's go. And you can cut the 'babe' shit."

Dash strolled up to me. "So we're going to pretend you have control?"

"I'm going to pretend you didn't ask me that."

"And we're ignoring all that black blood that poured out of you, and gray light and magic that destroyed your dresser?"

"It wasn't blood," I said. "It was Death."

"So is that what we are paying attention to?"

"You're still standing. That's what we're going to pay attention to."

"My survival? Was that a problem?"

"No. Maybe. Hell, I don't know, Dash. Right now I have control over the magic inside me. I'll tell you if that changes. I don't want to hurt anyone."

"That's good to hear," he said. "So listen to me now. I don't want you hurt either. If you need help with that magic, if you need us to do something for you, or *to* you, tell us."

"Sure," I said. "I'll do that." Not that anyone could do anything. Still, he seemed comforted by my words.

His phone rang and I motioned for him to step through the door. I followed as he answered the call. Didn't bother to lock the door behind me.

"Dashiell Spade," he said.

Sunny and Cody stood by a black SUV that must be something Sunny rented. Sunny was glaring at me. Cody was finishing off his pudding and staring up at the trees that surrounded the driveway. I glanced up at the trees too.

Dead. Every one of them gray and white, needles rusted, leaves shriveled at the tips of branches. All the life sucked out of them. Not just the trees. All the plants, ferns, grasses, and brush were shriveled, brown, barren.

As if a month of winter had set down right here in my driveway and gone on a killing spree.

"Love what you've done with the landscape," Cody said. "You could open a business, you know."

"Who?" Dash said into the phone.

"The hell you talking about, Miller?" I asked Cody.

"Yard care. You're poison and weed whacker all in one. You can call it Death to All Shrubbery."

Okay, yes. Cody and I had run together a lot when we were younger. Before his mind had been broken, he and I use to swindle, gamble, and generally pal around. I liked him. But he was getting on my nerves.

I pointed at my chest. "Not in a joking mood, mate. Not even a little bit."

He ran the spoon across the bottom of the pudding cup, catching up the last dregs. "I think he's still alive, you know. Not that you asked me."

"What?" I asked.

"Terric." He looked up, those blue eyes of his giving me no clue how sane he was at the moment.

"How would you know?" I asked.

"Eleanor told me."

That stopped me cold. "You can see her? Hear her? Now?"

He frowned. "Not now, no."

"When?"

"She showed up in my bedroom telling me you were here and needed our help, which is when we knew something serious was wrong and came out to your place. I saw her when you woke up."

He'd seen what I did to her. That I'd used her to live, that I'd tied her to me.

"Cody, I didn't want to hurt her," I said.

"They're dead," Dash said, thumbing off his phone.

"What?" I asked.

"Simone Latchly and Brian Welling."

I knew those names. Soul Complements. They'd gone into hiding when we found out the government had suddenly gotten pissy about Soul Complements' ability to break magic.

"How?" Sunny asked.

Dash shook his head. "There was a bomb. They think there was a bomb. The villa they were staying in was demolished."

"Any other deaths?" Sunny asked.

"No. Just Simone and Brian. It was magic that hit them. An Impact spell was seared into the rubble."

We all stood there for a second. The only thing that could power a spell strong enough to take out two Soul Complements was another Soul Complement.

Or those spelled-up drones Eli and his boss, Krogher, had been making.

Son of a bitch.

This was it. This was the move we'd been waiting for them to make for months now.

And we weren't in any shape to shut them down.

"Let's go," I said. "If we find Davy, we find Eli. And before I make Eli eat his own beating heart, we make him tell us where the hell Krogher is, and where his drones are going to hit next."

Everyone was suddenly moving. I took the backseat because I knew I'd be useless as shotgun. Death twisted inside me, trying to get out, trying to slip my control, but I knuckled down on it.

If it slipped my control in a car full of my friends, I'd be well fed, and they'd be dead.

Sunny started the car.

Dash was next to me, already on his phone.

"We hit the warehouse first," Sunny said.

"Yes," I said. "Police, Hounds, and other officials will be crawling over the bomb scene, but I don't think Krogher or Davy or Eli is anywhere near it. The warehouse is the most solid lead we've had in months, right?"

"Yes," Sunny said.

"Good," I said. "Give me your phone, Miller."

Cody tossed it back to me. I thumbed through his contact list, finally found the number I wanted, dialed.

"Cody?" Zay answered.

"No, it's Shame," I said. "Things are about to get hot. You need to get Allie out of there. Somewhere safe. Somewhere off-grid where no one would expect you to be."

"Where the hell have you been, Shame? We haven't heard from you."

"I'll tell you later. You have to leave Portland. Go far away."

"We aren't going anywhere."

"Yes," I said, "you are. Krogher's got the bombs up and running. Two Soul Complements just bit it. You're on his list, and it's a damn short list."

"We *can't* go anywhere. Allie is in labor."

"What?"

"She's having the baby, Shame."

"No. That's a month away, isn't it?"

"It's right now. We were just headed to the hospital."

"You can't."

A hospital would be an easy target, an easy kill. It wouldn't take anything to get a person close enough to them to kill them. It wouldn't take anything to get a drone in to kill them.

There was a pause, then, "We'll call Dr. Fischer. We'll go somewhere safe. Where are you now?"

"I'm with Cody, Sunny, and Dash. We have a line on this—the warehouse—and are going to follow up. We'll be in touch. Just . . . look after her."

"Nothing's going to hurt Allie or the baby," Zay said in that soft voice that sort of made me want to take several steps backward.

"Good," I said. "We'll let you know if we have any info."

"Shame," he said. "Is Terric with you?"

My heart tripped, stopped beating for a beat or two.

"No," I said as evenly as I could. "He might be dead."

His silence said more than words.

"And you?" he asked.

"Holding it together. Mostly."

He knew it was a lie. He also knew I needed him to pretend it was the truth.

"Is there anything else I need to know?"

"Nothing important. We'll call. Just keep them safe, okay?"

"We're all going to be fine, Shame," he said. "You're going to do what you have to do, and then you are going to come back and hold my kid in your arms while I tell you you're doing it wrong. You are going to survive this. Do we have an understanding?"

"Sure," I said, "we have an understanding."

I hung up and glanced at the phone in my hand. The glass was cracked, the case broken into tiny brittle bits. Then even the light on the screen went out.

I'd killed it. In under a minute flat. The Death magic inside me had drained down the electricity. And I hadn't noticed Death slipping past me.

Not good.

"How far to the warehouse?" I asked.

"About five hours," Sunny said.

Great. Five hours of keeping the lid on Death. I closed my eyes, turned to the magic inside me, and concentrated on exactly two things: breathing and not giving Death magic an inch.

Chapter 17

SHAME

Sunny made the drive in three hours.

Dash stayed on the phone almost that entire time, checking in with Clyde and half a dozen other people along the way. Sunny placed a few calls too, to make sure the Hounds were there to watch over Zay and Allie.

I didn't bother to tell her that if Eli was involved in the drones killing Soul Complements, the Hounds would never see him coming.

He had that tech device that opened up holes in space he could walk through.

Just as he'd walked through one into my damn kitchen.

And killed Terric.

Death magic kicked at that memory and I pushed the outer world away again. Just me and Death in the dark of my mind, and I was the only one of us with the key to the door.

It wouldn't hurt for the Hounds to stay with Zay and Allie. After all, anyone with a gun pointed in the right direction can squeeze the trigger and take out any magic user, including Eli.

"...awake?" Dash said.

I opened my eyes.

Dash was leaning in the door of the car. He shifted back just a bit but didn't take a step away.

Apparently we weren't driving anymore.

"Are we there yet?" I asked.

He nodded. "Right over the hill."

I sat up, the upholstery beneath me crackling and crumbling to fall down around my feet. So much for Sunny's deposit on the car.

It was dusk now, the cloud cover already swallowing what little light remained of the day. We'd stopped on a gravel and dirt road that rambled off to the nowhere of fields and scrub brush horizons.

"Here." Dash handed me a protein bar and a bottle of water. "Sunny's scouting. She'll be back in about three minutes. Cody's taking a leak."

I took the bar, glanced at Eleanor, who was about six feet away from me, arms crossed over her chest.

"Eat," Dash said. "I'm getting tired of telling you how horrible you look."

I opened the bar, took a bite. "Tastes like crap."

"Peanut butter," he said. "It tastes like peanut butter."

"My point stands. You hear anything from anyone?" I broke the seal on the water, drank. It wasn't enough. None of it was enough to sate my hunger.

"Nothing useful. We've contacted all the Soul Complements. They know the danger and are as prepared as they can be."

"What about Allie?"

"Her contractions slowed. No baby yet."

"Is that normal?"

He gave me a small smile. "I was assured it's okay."

"Does that mean she won't have the baby for another few hours, or tomorrow, or what?"

"I don't know. This is life we're talking about. It's unpredictable. How are you holding up?"

"Swell, thanks."

"Shame."

I chewed on another hunk of crap, swallowed, and tossed the rest of the bar in the back of the car. I ducked up out of the door, stood by Davy, who leaned against the car and stared out across a field that ended at a hill and darkening sky. "I've got my thumb on Death's windpipe, but it isn't going to last forever. How long did you say Sunny would be gone?"

He glanced at his watch. "Should be back in a minute."

"And she went alone."

"She's the Hound, Shame."

"She's a Blood magic user out for revenge for her lover being captured and tortured," I said.

He nodded. "That too. Still a Hound."

"See, what you may not remember, Spade, is that Sunny got into the Hounding business fairly recently. Before that, she was all about blood, blades, and blowing things up."

"She won't go in there without us, Shame. Not without you."

"Really? Reckless is in her job description. We go after her. Now."

"We wait."

The ground beneath my feet cracked, new spring grass dead brown, crumbling and flicking away in the wind. Dash noticed, because Dash is not a stupid man. He moved away from the car, moved away from me, his hands out to the side as if ready to draw a weapon on me.

I didn't move, because I'm not a stupid man either. Dash is fast on the draw, and while I hadn't thought to look, he probably had a gun on him. Or two. Or twelve.

"What about that windpipe?" he asked. "Are you really going to push this right now, Flynn?"

"Of course," I said, wrestling to pull the Death magic back into my body and away from all the lovely living things. "Have I ever been the guy who followed orders?"

"You've always been dangerous," he said. "And my friend. But right now I think you're just dangerous."

"Then listen to the dangerous man," I said. "I'm going out there to get Sunny before she gets shot. Don't care if you follow, and kind of hope you won't."

"Shame, don't."

"Or you'll shoot me?" I spread my hands and gave him a smile. "Knock yourself out, mate. Bullets don't punch my ticket."

He took a breath, looked out over the hill, maybe hoping to see Sunny there. Nothing but empty sky.

I started walking. Got about thirty feet from the car.

"You walking out on me?" Sunny asked.

I turned. She was striding up the road toward me.

"Did you find Davy?" I asked.

She shook her head. "He has to be in there, though, Shame. It's heavily guarded and I can smell magic. I think they have an Illusion over it."

"The drones?" I said.

"I'm guessing. The access road half a mile back will get us in the back door."

I glanced at the SUV. Didn't think there was a single chance I could get in it again and keep Death magic from devouring my friends. "I'll meet you there," I said.

Sunny stormed up the dirt road and grabbed my shirt with both hands. "I don't care what your problem is. I don't care that you *died*, Flynn. You owe me a favor. This is that favor. So shut up, stow your shit, and help me get Davy out of that hole. My way. Do you understand me?"

"You are so missing the point here. Death?" I swallowed. "It's all I can do to keep it under control. Keep it away from hurting you."

She was so close, her heartbeat sent shivers of need across my skin. The exhalation of her breath against me made me dizzy with hunger. I wanted to drink her down, drink down her heat, her life. It was more than want. I needed it.

Thumb on the windpipe, Shame, thumb on the windpipe. It was not much of a calming mantra, but it was, apparently, mine.

Blinding-hot pain shot through my shoulder.

"What the shit!" I stumbled backward as Sunny pulled her knife out of my shoulder.

"Do I have your attention now?" she asked with a tip of her head. "Or do I have to use your blood in a spell to slap some sense into your thick head?"

Blood magic users. Crazy bitches with blades.

"Stabbing?" I panted, trying to swallow back the magic that wanted to kill her. "Did you want my help, or did you want to piss me off? 'Cause stabbing me is only going to get you one of those things."

"Shame . . . ," Cody said.

"Shut up, Cody." I put my palm over my shoulder to hold what remaining blood I had where it belonged. "You want me to be your weapon against Eli and everyone else who's hurt Davy, fine. But if you so much as scratch me again, Sunny, I will walk, and you will be lucky to still be alive."

"Shame . . . ," Cody said again.

"You don't get this, do you?" she said. "I *own* you, Flynn. For this, I own you. And I don't care what you say about the magic in you."

"I'm the only thing standing between you and an early grave," I said. "I'm on your side, you crazy fool."

"That's it," she warned.

"Hurry," Dash yelled, jogging our way. Where had he gone? "Cars are coming."

Cody sighed. "That's what I was trying to—"

"Get in," Dash said. "Now!"

Neither Sunny nor I moved. We were just stubborn that way.

And then Cody and Dash were there, shoving Sunny and me into the car, which meant we ended up in the backseat together while Cody took shotgun and Dash slid into the driver's seat and peeled out, taking the road at speed.

"Access road," Sunny said. "South."

"I heard you," Dash replied. "Cody, you know anything else we don't know?"

"I think Shame's losing control, and if we want him to be conscious and . . . well . . . human by the time we hit the warehouse, you'll want to drive faster."

"Hey," I said. "Give the stabbed guy some credit." But my heart was stuttering, no longer quite in working order, and my lungs had gone to hell. I needed to kill. Needed life. Needed to feed the death inside me before it killed me.

Or let it kill me and not have to pay back that favor I never should have promised Sunny.

The rope around Eleanor's throat had tightened and shortened. She was sitting so close to me we'd be touching if she wasn't pulling against the rope as hard as she could.

If we got too close, would I drain her the rest of the way down? Would I kill her? Again?

"Just get me to the warehouse," I said, or thought I said. From the speed of things whipping past the car to the conversation around me that sounded as if it were underwater, I was pretty sure I wasn't on reality's frequency.

Eleanor shoved her cold, cold hand into my head, right through skin, bone, and meat, and wiggled her fingers in my skull.

And for a second, all the world went silent.

There was no sound, no motion, no pain. No Death magic hunger. I drifted, just outside my body.

Took me a minute, but I finally realized Eleanor was talking to me. . . . *kill me, then you'd better make it worth it.*

Get a grip on the magic inside you. It's the only way you're going to save them all. Kill them all. Find him and use it with him.

"Him? Davy?" She was talking faster than I was thinking.

Terric. He's not—

"Shame!" A palm hit my face, hard.

Okay, so basically things were not going well in Shameland. I was being chewed out by a ghost I'd enslaved and slapped by . . . I opened my eyes . . . my gay ex-assistant, who, come to find out, had a decent right cross.

We must have stopped for a change of drivers.

"Dash," I wheezed. "You hit me again, I will drink you down to sixty-two."

He frowned. "What does that even mean? Keep breathing. We're about half an hour away."

How much time had I lost? "Warehouse?" I asked.

"Hospital. You're a mess."

Rolling me up to a hospital would be like sitting a starving man down to a smorgasbord.

"Stop the car," I said. "Stop it. Now."

Dash glanced up and I did a recalculation on the entire situation. Still nightish, still in the SUV. Sunny driving. Cody next to her. Dash risking his fool life to try to keep me alive.

"I'm better," I said. Whatever Eleanor had done to my head had at least restored my ability to lie. And to think. And to hold down Death magic. For now.

"I won't fight you," I said. "I don't need a hospital. They wouldn't know what to do with me anyway."

"That's true," Cody said. "They only treat the living. Dash, we're only about twenty minutes from the warehouse. We should take our shot while we can."

"Shame," Dash said. "We're not going in there unless we have proof Davy's there. Can you feel his life?"

It wasn't a bad idea to ask me that. I could tell how many

heartbeats were within a ten-mile radius, and Davy's heartbeat was one of the more unusual ones on the planet since Eli had carved him up with magic a few years ago.

Only problem was that I had crap for control. If I used it, if I tapped Death magic, it was pretty good odds I'd kill my friends and all the living souls within a mile.

"Get me close to the warehouse and I'll try," I said.

Sunny gunned the engine, and time slipped by, measured by my slow breaths and ragged heartbeats. Dash kept looking over at me with that face that said he was sure I'd be dead between one breath and the next.

I winked at him and he sighed. "This isn't the time to be flirting."

"I'm not," I said. I was going to tell him I knew that I was close to being dead or undead or whatever it was a Death magic user turned into when he lost control. "But you all will need to get clear of me real soon now."

Before I became a monster. Just like Jingo Jingo. A monster that sucked the lives out of people and chained up their souls for a bedtime snack.

Yeah. That.

Fifteen minutes crawled by. The car stopped and Sunny was out the door. Pretty sure I heard a shotgun rack a round. That'd be Sunny all right.

Cody turned in his seat. "Be careful how you look for him, Shame. Be careful what you see. You might not like what you find."

Well, that was unhelpful. I held my hand out for Dash. He helped me sit and left me there as he went around the car to open my door for me.

I thought I had my feet, but I didn't argue when his hand under my elbow steadied me as I stood.

The thing Eleanor had done helped, yes. But I was so far from steady, it was hilarious.

The clouds had given some ground, stars taking the stage

to shine up the place. I tipped my head up and wasted a precious second or two staring into the eternal nothingness.

I should have stayed dead. It would have been kinder to . . . well, everyone.

"Shame?" Dash asked.

"I got it." I leaned my hip against the car and closed my eyes. "Might want to step off a bit, though," I said to him. "You too, Cody. And Sunny. My control is crap." I waited until I heard footsteps in gravel moving away. Then I waited until their three heartbeats were at least twenty feet off. Not far enough—a mile wouldn't be enough for them to be out of my blast zone. But at least they weren't in arm's reach. I'd be able to look for Davy's heartbeat and pay no attention to theirs.

Who was I kidding?

The cold pressure of Eleanor's hand landed on my left wrist. She was there, standing beside me. Not that she could get away. Not that she could stop feeding me, and the hunger devouring me, or break the tie between us.

But she was there to do what she could to help.

I sort of loved her for that.

So here's how it went down. I took a couple of breaths that didn't ruin my lungs, cleared my mind, thought the happy, and hooked up just enough Death magic in my mental fingertips, thumb still pressing on the windpipe. I could send it out like a gentle breeze to tell me if any familiar heartbeat was tapping away in the space around me.

Easy. I'd done it a thousand times before. Did it without thinking most days. Had to push it away and ignore it so every damn heart wasn't thumping against my brain.

So of course I could do it now, right?

First, I felt my heart. Broken, cold, and wrong in just about every way. Ignore that. Move on, move out. Cody's heart, calm, steady. Stronger than almost anyone I'd ever met. Man had a solid grip on living after all those years of being mentally broken. He was a survivor.

Ignore him.

Next, Sunny. Blood pushing too fast, heartbeat too high. Worried about Davy, her heart racing with love and fear. She would be so easy to pluck. So ripe.

Ignore her.

Past her heart, I could feel the beat of Dash's life. A little elevated, but steady. A man who had dealt with all sorts of shit and just kept dealing. He knew what he was in for, maybe was the only one here willing to put me down if I went feral.

Yes, I knew that was an option, a rather high chance, actually. If it came to that, I figured Dash would pull the trigger. Over and over until I stopped moving.

He was a good man, but he worried too damn much.

Ignore him.

Push the magic past them. Fast, faster. Rabbits and birds and snakes and bugs. Kill them all. Crunch and crack and pop of life spilled over my tongue.

Now the warehouse. And in it, human hearts.

The warehouse thumped with the living. People working there, maybe three dozen, all in a ragged concert, pumping with life like good little governmental engines.

That would be enough. Or at least an appetizer for my needs.

No, I wasn't going to kill people unless I had to. I wasn't going to become the monster.

Focus, Flynn.

Guards around the place, at least another dozen. And inside the place. . . .

I could feel him: Davy. Not alive like anyone else in this world. Carved by magic, changed by magic. Not alive, but not rightly dead either. Davy. In a room on the ground floor.

Unconscious, I thought. But breathing. Carved up with spells. New spells squirming amid the old.

I nearly lost my concentration from the surprise of finding him. I didn't think it'd be that easy. Didn't think Sunny had really tracked him down.

But he was there.

And so was someone else.

Faint, faint heartbeat, too long between each pump, so close to death there wasn't enough life left in him to fill a thimble.

Terric. That was Terric's heart. I'd know it anywhere.

Terric was in there. Alive.

Concentration slipped, control shattered. Death wanted its due.

I gasped, frantically pulling Death back to me in fear it would touch Terric. Kill Terric. Terric, who was already almost dead.

Magic roared back into me so fast and hard I lost my knees and fell to the ground.

Hands helped me up. Dash's hands.

"Shame?"

"He's there," I said, pushing his hands away, pushing his help away, not trusting my control. "He's there."

"Davy?" Sunny asked. "Where?"

"Both," I said. "Both of them. Bottom floor. Main room." Dash let go, took all his heat and living and energy I refused to drain away from me.

Good. Smart.

"Guns. We need guns."

"We have them," Cody said, walking around to the back of the SUV.

"Are you sure?" Dash asked.

"He's there, Dash," I said. "Terric's there."

And I watched something change in him. Dash had thought Terric was dead from the moment he'd found me corpsed out in the kitchen. He hadn't expected us to find Terric. Not alive. Not after all this time.

"Alive," I added just to make sure he understood. Understood why we needed to be moving. Now. "Get moving, lover boy."

I didn't have a gun on me. Luckily, Sunny had thought of that. She pressed a Glock in my hand. Good God. Did a loaded weapon need a loaded weapon?

"Can you keep that pointed the right way?" she asked.

"You mean at Eli's head? I got that."

"Is he in there?" she asked, her heart kicking up a couple of notches. Oh, she wanted him dead.

Get in line, sister.

"I'm not sure," I lied. "Let's just assume he is."

"How many guards?" Dash asked.

"As soon as I'm close enough?" I said, striding down the road toward the compound. "None."

I chambered a round and tipped my head down. Sure, bullets are faster than magic. But Death never needs to reload.

Chapter 18

SHAME

No chain-link fence around the lot, just a vast spread of dirt and gravel set out between the low rise of hills.

The warehouse stood in the center of the gravel, a monstrous structure several stories high that might have once been part of a gravel pit operation. Metal on metal on concrete, it appeared mostly abandoned from the outside, but I knew differently. I could count how many lives were ticking down inside those walls.

Security? Yes. Six men spotted me, walking straight down the middle of the parking lot. I wasn't hiding; I wasn't hurrying. I was getting this job done.

Before they could squeeze triggers, I reached down into the center of the Death magic roiling in me and cut the chain.

Six hearts pumped out their last beats. Six lives filled me, fed me, fed the monster inside me. A monster that wanted more.

I knew where Dash and Sunny and Cody were—just behind me, guns drawn, taking care not to be seen. I didn't let the monster touch them, hurt them.

So far the deaths had been silent. So far there had been no need for guns.

That was about to change. I walked up to the front door—a thick slab of metal and warning signs. Pressed my palm there and let Death magic have at it. Rust ate away at the hinges until they crumbled. I pushed and the door fell inward, tripping the alarms.

An explosion of bullets from above hissed around us.

I did not care, did not pause, did not stop. Davy was in this building, and I was bringing him back for Sunny. Terric was in this building, and I was bringing him back for me.

No matter how many people I'd have to kill to make that happen.

The place was set up surprisingly like an actual warehouse. Crates of product stacked down long aisles, forklifts and dollies resting along walls. I didn't see any workers. Could be they didn't have a graveyard shift. Could be they'd seen us coming and run.

I turned left, strode down the aisle. Davy's heart was easy to track, easy to find. More gunshots cracked through the air around us. Didn't matter. The gunmen's hearts were easy to find. Hearts were easy to squeeze, to stop.

I flicked my wrist like throwing a knife. Death magic followed my will, and did what it was meant to do: kill.

Dash shouted behind me. Sunny yelled something back.

More hearts, beating faster, coming our way, stopped by bullets. That was fine with me. Easy to drink their lives, easy to drain them down.

Davy's heart pumped away, leading me on. Death magic stretched out in me, numbing and pushing aside my emotions, my worry, my control of my mind and body.

I pushed back, a part of my mind screaming, a part of my mind knowing I was losing ground to Death, losing control.

Death didn't listen. Death didn't care.

Another left, this time to a hallway that led to a metal door. Locked. I threw magic at it and it buckled, rusted, fell, sending up a cloud of dust.

Death was getting stronger. I was working hard just to stay conscious.

I pushed Death back, shoved the magic away, put it behind me just enough to see where we were.

A storeroom or workroom. Heavily soundproofed, wired up the yang. Magic glyphs painted on the walls up to the ceiling, and across the ceiling, glowing with faint blue light.

The walls were lined with bars. Cages. Jail cells. In each cell were people. The kidnapped, spell-carved people. Mindless as zombies.

In the center of the room stood a larger cage. Magic poured down the bars of the cage, too bright, and smelling of kerosene. I couldn't see what was in that cage, couldn't hear anything from it. If I were operating off my senses alone, I'd say there wasn't anything in there.

But my gut told me otherwise. Said it was an Illusion surrounding that cage. My soul told me who was trapped in there, dying in there.

"Terric?" I whispered, everything in my head going suddenly shock-blank.

"Shame!"

I turned. Dash ran my way. Behind him, Sunny supported a very bloody Cody in her arms.

"Dash! Two o'clock," Sunny yelled. She turned and half dragged Cody behind something that looked like a generator.

Bullets sprayed around us.

Jesus. Someone was shooting at us.

Dash tackled me. Yes, it hurt. I bitched him out about it as we crawled across stained concrete to a supply shelf.

He was bleeding. So was I. But bullets couldn't kill me. I was already dead.

"Fucking suicide," Dash yelled as he took aim across the warehouse to where the gunmen were gathered. "Walking right into the line of fire, in a warehouse full of guns. Fucking stupid fucking ass."

It was possible he was talking about me. Reality was knocking on my brain box and I was doing everything I could to open the door and let it in.

We were surrounded. Injured. Worse, the cage in the middle of the room had taken bullets too. If Terric was in there, if Davy was in there, they could have been hit.

No, they most certainly would have been hit.

Possibly dead. Probably dead.

"Can't just walk into a fucking gunfight in the middle of the enemy's fucking living room," Dash said.

I'd give him a hard time about his language going to crap when he was being shot at, but, well, we were being shot at.

"Stay here," I said.

"Fuck that. Where the fuck do you think you're going?" he said.

"To save them," I said. It was hard to talk, to make my thoughts fit inside words. Death snarled and howled and chuckled behind every pulse beat, behind every breath. It scratched claws against the core of me, against my mind, my sanity.

"Trust me," I think I said.

"Like hell. You're going to get yourself killed," Dash said. "They have guns."

"I'll take care of that. Stay back."

He reloaded, swearing the entire time, but didn't try to stop me. He put down some covering fire.

I strode out from behind the storage shelf. Death magic reached for hearts. Reached for pulse points. Greedy, hungry, it shut them down one by one, each life feeding the monster in me, making the monster stronger.

Almost stronger than me. Almost out of my control.

The magic-drenched cage was only a few yards away. I made for it as quickly as I could.

"You got this?" Sunny was suddenly at my side. What the hell was she doing here?

Death wanted that. Wanted her. Pulsing bright. Her life burning like a bonfire in the darkness.

No.

"Go back, Sunny," I said. "Get away from me. Now."

"Bite me," she said. "Where's Davy?"

"I'll get him. I'll bring him to you." *Alive,* I thought while Death magic churned and growled, hungry for killing. "Back off before I lose control."

"If you kill him, I will kill you, Flynn. Are you listening to me?" She grabbed my arm.

Death magic paused, a predator zeroing in on the scent of prey—on the scent of her.

No. I closed my eyes, jerked my arm away. Built walls in my mind as fast and hard and solid as I could. Walls I could trap the Death magic behind.

"Go!"

But it was too late. Death magic slipped my hold.

The pulse of Sunny filled me. I tried to pull back, couldn't. Tried to yell, but Death stole my breath.

Son of a bitch.

Death put my hand over hers, gazed in her eyes. At the worry there. The anger, the need.

I tugged and pulled, fought to move my hand away, move my body at all.

No!

And then Death drank her down.

Something inside me broke, shattered like brittle glass beneath a bootheel as I screamed and screamed and watched her die. I couldn't stop it. Couldn't save her.

Death magic did not care.

Sunny slumped to the warehouse floor, empty, dead.

Death used my mouth, my air, to laugh.

Fucking hell.

Death was drunk from the high of killing someone I cared for. My pain, fear, and anger had made her death all the sweeter.

If I had control of my body, I'd be puking.

Instead I focused my thoughts. Quiet, calm. Calm enough to recite a spell. Calm enough to draw the spell in my memory, deep within my mind.

Bind.

Death's heavy gaze turned inward. To me, my life, my soul, and the spell I was drawing.

I concentrated on the Bind spell, making it as whole and real as any other spell I'd ever carved. Then I pushed it outward from my center, to surround my body and the Death magic that held the wheel.

I had no idea if this would work. It probably shouldn't. But if Death was me, then I was it. The magic I called up from deep beneath the earth to fill a spell in me should answer me.

Maybe.

I mentally traced the last line in the Bind spell, angling it to catch up and bind the Death magic possessing me. I filled the spell with the magic that pooled deep in the earth beneath the warehouse.

A shotgun crack whipped through my brain. Pain flashed black, then hot white.

Then I was in control of my body again. Death magic squirmed and chewed at the Bind spell inside my head.

This was not good. Not good at all.

But better than a moment ago.

I wiped the blood off my face and took a second to get my bearings.

No more gunfire. But I could feel more hearts, more people coming, rushing this way. Maybe with bombs, maybe with magic.

They weren't here yet. And when they were, I'd kill them too.

I had to get the hell out of here.

"Shame!" Dash yelled.

I didn't look, didn't answer, too afraid I'd lose control and drink him down.

I jogged to the bars of the cage and wrapped my hands around them. They were filthy with magic, spells tied to spells that refreshed and renewed the current of magic that powered the spells carved into the bars.

It was horrifyingly beautiful. Genius. Someone knew his shit. Knew how to make magic bend to his will.

Eli Collins. He'd made this cage, set this magic. He'd been here.

I searched for his heart, didn't feel it. Not near.

I couldn't break magic and make it do what I wanted. Not without Terric using magic with me. Using the Death inside me was a very bad idea.

But there were other forces that could break a lock. Guns, for instance. I pulled the Glock Sunny had given me . . .

. . . *don't think about Sunny. Don't think about what Death did to her* . . .

. . . took aim at the lock, and fired.

Unloaded half the clip. Enough bullets, it broke metal and interrupted the stream of spells.

And then it was just a metal cage in the center of a warehouse.

With two men bleeding on the floor.

Davy Silvers.

Terric Conley.

Oh God. No. Terric.

The Bind spell in my head wavered as my concentration slipped.

One step at a time. Get them out of here before the Death magic in my head broke free, or the rush of people coming our way with guns showed up and killed us.

I couldn't carry them both out. Wasn't sure if I could even carry one out. Probably shouldn't touch them at all.

I should get Davy. I'd promised Sunny I would find him, bring him to her.

She was counting on me to come through for her.

... her eyes wide, as Death pressed my hand over her hand and she crumpled to the floor ...

I looked around for her.

"Sunny?"

She stood a short distance from me, next to Eleanor. who had gained some slack on her rope. Sunny seemed a little faded, a little see-through, just like Eleanor. Her eyes were wild, and a black rope around her neck tied her to my arm.

I'd caught up her soul just like Eleanor, which meant I'd used her, killed her, and stood aside while Death magic ate her alive.

Fuck. Me.

Eleanor floated over to me and pressed her fingers against my cheek. *Save them,* she said.

Right. Davy and Terric. My guilt, my horror would have to wait.

I walked over to Terric. He was curled on his side, bullet holes in his chest. The pool of blood beneath him was not new.

I knelt, the knees of my jeans soaking up blood, his blood. Turned him onto his back. His face was swollen, bruised. His shirt was bulky from bandages soaked in blood. His bare arms were burned, cut, and bloody.

Not just shot. Torn apart.

Tortured.

Fury caught fire in my chest and burned through me. Not a clean anger. This was a ragged, tearing rage. A rage that would break my hold on Death.

I pressed my hand against Terric's heart, felt the stagnant beat there.

He was alive.

Still alive.

Death magic wasn't going to make him better. Death magic was the worst thing to have around him right now.

I was the worst thing to have around him.

He was dying, even though he carried Life magic. He was in too much pain to heal himself.

I could take that on. Some of that pain. Give the Life magic inside him a chance to work.

I'd never done it before. Never heard of anyone taking on another's wounds like this. Back in the old days, we Proxied pain all the time.

But I was ... different now. A small part of my mind—probably that thing called "reason"— knew this was a bad idea. A very bad idea.

I didn't care.

I drew a Proxy spell in the air between us, tying it tight. His pain was my pain. Enough of it was mine that his heart could beat. Enough that he could breathe.

I relaxed my hold on Death magic, just enough it could feed the spell, then tightened my fist around that Bind spell again.

The glyph between Terric and me crackled with black lightning. His pain rushed into me.

Holy mother of God, that hurt.

But I'd just killed a few dozen people. Like it or not, I was filled with their lives. I was strong enough to endure his pain.

I pulled Terric's arm up over my shoulder, got him sitting.

Dash was yelling again. I still couldn't understand what he was saying. Caught a couple of words: *hurry*, and *out*, and *now*.

Someone ran up to me. It was Dash. That, finally, brought me out of the shock I'd been wading through.

Dash gathered up Davy, helping him to his feet. Davy was solid, though blue magic pulsed from his bare chest like broken neon. That was good, I guessed. It meant he was alive. But he wasn't conscious.

And then Cody limped over. Cody had blood running down his face, and one of his eyes was filled with it. He stopped next to Sunny, gave me an accusatory glare but didn't ask. Of course, he didn't have to.

I didn't want to answer anyway.

He picked up Sunny, her unbreathing body. Her empty shell. He stayed as far out of my reach as he could.

I got Terric standing and walked with him out of the cage. He was barely conscious. "Stay close," I said. Or I hoped I said. Because I was going to burn this place down to the ground, and I didn't want them in it when it went to ash and cinders.

They stayed close, Dash supporting Davy, Cody carrying Sunny.

It felt like it took a year to walk out of that hellhole. One foot in front of the other, dragging Terric at my side, enduring his pain, begging him to hold on until we got out, got away while I tried to hold Death down inside me.

"That is far enough," a voice rang out across the rafters. "Mr. Flynn. You will not take a single step more. Not with my property."

I knew that voice. It was Krogher. The man who had used Eli as his very own pet psychopath. The man who had been stockpiling drones, using people as walking bombs charged with magic.

The man who I assumed had killed two Soul Complements and hadn't even gotten to the meaty center of his plans.

I blinked. Focused on my surroundings. We were in the outer section of the warehouse, fully stocked shelves and crates around and behind us. Krogher was not there. I knew that bastard's heart too. He was off-site, not even close enough for me to get a hook on his pulse.

But this was his facility. He had cameras. He knew exactly what was going on.

And what was going on was this: There were half a dozen drones standing at the front of the warehouse blocking our only way out. Men, women, young and old, blank-eyed and silent.

Easy to kill. But I was tired of killing. Terrified to let loose Death's chain and not be able to pull it tight again. Killing was the fastest and easiest way out of this. The only way out of this.

Hell.

I sucked in a breath, loosened my grip. Death magic lashed out.

Nothing happened. It was like throwing a feather with all my strength. Lots of windup, zero results.

Eli must have done something with the spells he carved into those people to keep them safe from magical attack, to keep them safe from *me*.

Son of a bitch, that was smart.

As one, they raised their hands. As one, they released the magic stored in the spells carved into their flesh.

Holy shit.

Magic is fast. Bullets are faster. I raised the gun, aimed. Fired.

Two of the drones went down. Their magic released, rushing at us in spiraling red flames.

I couldn't pull up a Block spell fast enough. Didn't even have a split second to react.

Didn't have to.

Davy was somehow in front of me, in front of us all, faster than a living being could move. Those spells Eli had carved in him gave him abilities most people didn't have, one of which was not being solid when he didn't want to be. He appeared in front of us, and was a very solid and, in my opinion, highly suicidal being.

Sunny, who was nothing but a ghost, ran to him. She tried to pull him out of the line of fire. But even a ghost isn't faster than magic.

Davy spread his arms wide. Magic hit him like a wall of fire. Fast enough, hard enough, he should be on his heels. But instead he absorbed it, all those spells carved into him sucking it in. He lifted his hands and threw the magic back at them with a ragged yell.

Had I mentioned he was not quite a regular guy anymore?

The drones disappeared in the blast furnace of that magic. They fell. Not dead. Not yet.

But maybe now that they were all out of magic, I could put them out of that misery.

I released just the edge of Death magic again. Let it drink down their lives, all six of them.

It was like gulping acid. The changes Eli had made in them, twisting them from human into living bombs, made them toxic. Poison. There was nothing human left to them.

He'd carved out their souls and used that to fuel the magic in them.

Holy shit. I'd seen dark magic before. I'd used it. But I had no idea anyone could twist spells to do the horrors he'd done to these people.

My vision narrowed in, just a speck of light out there at the end of the tunnel ahead of me as I endured this new pain. Their ghosts clawed at me, fingers burning into my bones. They were mindless, screaming spirits, nothing like Eleanor or Sunny.

But finally they slowed, calmed. For half a second they looked human again.

And then they whisked away like smoke in a strong wind.

They were dead. Maybe at peace.

Now there was nothing but a pile of dead bodies between us and the only way out.

I heard the distant thump of helicopters. Krogher had the resources to bring in the national guard, the police force, and any other heavily armed reinforcements he wanted. Those helicopters were probably coming for us, bringing more men, more guns, more magic.

The grumble of truck engines approaching filled the air too. Filled with even more lives scrambling to take us out.

Delightful.

We were officially screwed.

Time to run.

So we ran. Davy was able to move under his own power now, and helped Cody with Sunny's dead body.

Sunny's spirit pulled against the rope around her neck. I knew she wanted back in her body.

I knew I should let her go. If I could figure out how to do that, maybe she'd live.

We reached the SUV and I leaned Terric into the backseat, sliding in beside him and breathing hard with his pain. Okay, his pain and my pain. Sucking down the lives and magic from those poisonous drones had been a very bad idea.

Terric was pale, bloody, and not breathing nearly enough.

"Go now, go now!" Cody said from somewhere near the front of the car.

The car lurched across the lot, speeding down the road.

Bullets cracked through the night air. I heard Dash tell Cody to call for help, heard Davy begging Sunny to live, heard Sunny's ghost yelling at me to fix her.

But something in me was terribly broken. If drinking Eleanor down had shattered the wall between me and the monster I feared, then killing Sunny had given that monster permission to use me as its little puppet man.

I didn't know how to break the tie between Sunny and me. I didn't know how long I could keep Death from killing again.

So I focused on Terric, on his pain. That pain was all that was holding us together. It was all that was keeping him alive.

And I needed him to be alive. I needed it more than breathing. But no matter how much of his pain I took, his life was slipping, thinning. His life was winding down, spooling out. He'd be dead soon too.

No.

"Pull over," I said.

Nothing. So I said it again, "Pull over. Now."

Shame, you bastard. Listen to me. Sunny punched me in the face.

The world rubber-band-snapped back down around me, sharp edges, sounds, motion.

Dash was driving, Cody in the front seat. He was on the phone. I had no idea who he was talking to.

Sunny's body was in the back of the car. Davy held her in his arms as he talked to her in a soothing, monotonous tone. Sunny's spirit was floating in front of my face.

Put me back, she demanded. *Cut this damn rope and put me back.*

"I . . . can't."

Then I'm going to cut it. She pulled a knife. Typical. Blood magic user dies and takes her knives with her. But it was just a ghost knife. She hacked at the tie between us, but it didn't change a thing.

She pulled her head back, glared at me. Had that stabbing look in her eyes.

"Sunny, don't—"

Too late. She buried the blade in my chest.

Yes, it hurt. But that blade was her energy, her anger, her pain. And therefore it was consumable. I absorbed the blade without even thinking about it. It faded. Was gone.

"Settle down," I whispered. "Just. Stop yelling. Let me think."

"Shame?" Dash asked, glancing at me in the rearview.

Terric moaned. I had my arms around him, his head resting on my shoulder.

No wonder he was dying. He was in my arms. I was killing him.

"No, no," I said. "It's going to be okay, Ter. Just hang in there. You're going to be okay. It's all going to be okay." I let go of him and propped his unconscious body against the door. I didn't know what else I could do for him. He needed a doctor. He needed an army of doctors. He needed magic. He needed life.

He didn't need me.

None of them did.

"Pull over," I said again. "Damn it, Dash, pull over."

"Cody, tell me you found us a safe hole," Dash said.

"There's a house just outside Umatilla," he said. "We can stop there."

"We got it, Shame," Dash said. "Just keep it together a little longer."

I crossed my arms and closed my eyes, turning my attention inward. I wrestled Death magic down, retraced the Bind spell.

But no matter how far I distanced my mind and magic from the real world, I could feel the heartbeat of every person in the car.

Worse, I could hear Sunny's ghost talking to Davy. Telling him she was sorry, and that she loved him. Telling him I'd killed her. And if it was the last thing she was going to do, she was going to kill me right back.

I kind of hoped she was going to follow through with that promise.

I measured the passage of time in the rise and fall of Terric's pain. Maybe it took an hour before we stopped. I didn't know. Didn't care. Cody and Dash handled the getaway.

"This is it," Dash was saying. "What do you need, Shame?"

I let the world return.

Dark, painful. Sunny and Eleanor hovering right in front of my eyes, one sorrow, the other pain.

Both my fault. Blood on my soul. If I still had one.

"Shame?" Dash tried again.

"Help me with him." I opened the door, got out of the car. My legs were heavy, numb in places and on fire in others. I was too hot, too cold, Terric's pain making me shake. I staggered away from the car and puked.

Serves you right, Sunny said. *Put me back. Put me back in my body, Shame, or I swear I will kill you.*

I wiped my mouth on the back of my hand. The oily film of Death magic smeared there along with blood. My blood.

"Better hurry up," I whispered, "or you might not get the chance."

I turned around, watched as Dash and Cody pulled Terric out of the car.

Davy was already walking to the house with Sunny in his arms.

Sunny shot me a dirty look. *Help him,* she said. *Please.*

I put my hand on the rope that tied her to me. Her eyes went wide with fear.

"I can't break this." I yanked on the rope and all it did was flex. "I've tried for years. I can't free you."

You freed me once, Eleanor said.

"Yeah, well, I did that by dying. So if you can kill me," I said to Sunny, "do it." I spread my arms wide.

She floated over to me. Stuck her hand in my chest, maybe looking for my heart.

Nothing. There was nothing there she could touch. And the longer her hand was in me, the more Death wanted to drink the rest of her down.

I licked my lips. "Hard to kill Death, love."

She jerked her hand away. *What* are *you?*

"Not to be fucked with. So please, for all of our sakes, don't. Just don't."

I turned and walked toward the house, ghosts on my heels.

Cody and Dash had managed to get Terric inside.

The house was nice enough—maybe someone's vacation home. Fully furnished, clean but smelled cool and stale from disuse.

Cody and Dash took Terric down a hall to a bedroom and laid him on top of the bed. Davy had already settled Sunny on the couch in the living room.

He sat on the floor beside the couch, one hand holding her hand, and looked over at me as I walked in.

"Good to see you, Shame." His voice was flat, his eyes yellowed and bloodshot. He looked like he'd just been scraped off the bottom of the devil's shit kickers.

"I'm glad you're alive, Davy," I said. "We tried to stop Eli, stop Krogher, when they first grabbed you."

"I was there. I remember." Steady stare. That man used to be my friend. Not anymore. Not after what they'd done to him.

And what I'd done to Sunny.

"You shouldn't have done it," he said.

"What? Try to save you?"

"Bring her here. With you."

"I don't know what you're talking about," I said.

Me, Sunny said. *He's talking about me.*

I waited to see if Davy had heard her. He didn't even blink, just gave me that dead man's stare.

"Sunny?" I asked. "You're right. I shouldn't have. But you know her. She wouldn't stay behind. She would have gone without me."

"Did you kill her?" he asked.

I didn't answer him. I couldn't. There were no words in me for what had happened, for how I'd lost control and she'd paid for it with her life.

But he knew. He must know. He closed his eyes and bowed his head over her hand.

"Davy, I—"

"Shame?" Dash walked into the room. "You should be in here."

I followed him down the hall to the bedroom. The door was open, but I didn't walk in. I didn't want to get too close to Terric. Didn't want to kill him. Didn't want to kill Dash or Cody or, hell, anyone else either.

"How's he doing?" I asked.

Cody shrugged. "I think you know. He's dying."

"We pulled over like you asked," Dash said. "We got him here. What's the plan?"

"This *is* the plan," I said. "I need to leave. As far as I can get from . . . all of you. I can't be near him. I can't be near any of you."

Dash closed the distance and grabbed my coat. He walked me backward until my back was pressed against the hallway wall.

"You are his Soul Complement," he said. "Leaving him is *always* the wrong choice. Using magic with him is *always* the right choice. Use magic and fix him."

The heat of anger, pain, and fear rolling off Dash made the Death magic in me kick. Here was another life, burning bright for the taking. And my Bind spell was failing.

Death lashed out, slipped my control.

Damn it.

Shame, no! Both Sunny and Eleanor stepped in front of me. Stepped between Dash and me.

I hauled back on the magic but was too slow.

Dash jerked away, his hands instinctively rising to protect his head from the attack.

It was just a taste, the lightest lick of his life. Any other man would have dropped to his knees, but Dash stumbled backward, his hand reaching for the gun at his side.

"I am doing everything I can," I said over the howl of magic raging in my mind. "But I am toxic. If I stay here I will kill Terric and all the rest of you with him. Don't you understand me? Don't you understand what I *am*? What I've always done to him? Death," I said in case he wasn't following. "Pain and death."

Dash wiped at his face with his arm, as if trying to scrub off blood. But when I took a life, when Death magic drained a life down, there were no marks left behind on the living.

He hadn't pulled the gun on me yet. Idiot. This was his chance, might be his only chance to put me down.

"If you walk out on him right now," Dash said, "I will spend my life making you pay for that choice. Every damn second."

I didn't know what it was. Maybe just the tone of his voice. The fear and frustration. He knew Terric was slipping away. He knew I was about to lose him. He knew he was about to lose him too.

Dash wasn't the kind of guy who harbored revenge fantasies. Just hearing that desperate promise—and there was no doubt in my mind he meant every word—brought everything into focus.

I got an upper hand on the magic in me—not just a Bind spell, I regained clarity—and shoved it down, down inside me, and threw the locks.

I broke out in a cold sweat. It was like coming up out of a swamp, sucking for air and sunlight. I was mostly just me again, no more puppet man, even though Death magic still twisted in my bones.

Shame? Eleanor said. *Is that you in there?*

"Yes," I said. "Mostly me."

Then while you are here, and sane, I want you to release us. Release Sunny and me. Now.

I glanced at Sunny, who had on her killing eyes.

If I released her soul to go back into that dead body, she'd be dead.

Everything suddenly looked clearer now that I had control over Death magic, so: win. But that didn't mean things looked good.

We were holed up in a house with one dying man, a dead woman, and a spelled-up man who was not quite real and maybe not sane. We'd broken into a government holding cell, taken Davy and Terric out of it. We had killed. I'd killed.

We'd taken down their spell-carved drones.

There was no way Krogher was going to let us go. Ever. As a matter of fact, the ease of us getting into and out of that warehouse made no sense. Even if they hadn't seen us coming, even with me walking around in my bubonic boots, we shouldn't have pulled that off that easily.

I didn't know why we weren't currently being shot at.

"You need to make my point a little sharper?" Dash asked.

Right, Dash. We'd been talking. Or arguing.

"No, I heard you," I said. "Right now, this minute, I'm listening. Tell me what we need to do."

He held one hand up, wiped his face again. "I don't know, Shame. We got away, but if Krogher is as powerful as you say he is and has Eli under his thumb with those gate devices, we could have an entire damn army up our ass any minute."

"Then why aren't we running?" I asked.

"*You* wanted us to stop."

"And you listened to me? I wasn't exactly thinking straight."

"What the hell, Flynn? Yes, of course I listened to you. Terric's dying."

"Okay, okay," I said. "Hold on. Can we call someone to heal him? A doctor. A doctor who can use spells?"

"He can't be healed," Cody said from where he was standing next to Terric's bed. I had forgotten he was in the room.

"We have to do something," Dash said. "Take him to a hospital so they can put him on life support, pain medications."

I was listening to Dash but watching Cody, who held my gaze.

Cody shook his head. "*You* can do something to help him, Shame," he said. "It won't be easy. You won't want to do it."

Cody always had an angle. He'd saved my ass plenty of times when we were running cons. He'd selflessly saved all our asses back when magic had almost ended our world and he'd stepped up to be the vessel in which dark and light magic could join and heal. I'd developed a pretty hefty trust in the kook.

"Will it save Terric?" I asked.

He inhaled and lifted his eyebrows. "I don't know. This trip took some unexpected turns. What you've done, how you've killed. Sunny."

So he knew about Sunny.

He knows you killed me, Sunny said. *He'll tell someone. And they'll put you down. You are on borrowed time.*

I'd been born on borrowed time, but I didn't tell her that. We needed solutions to our problems.

"Tell me what to do," I said to Cody. "Tell me what I can do to fix this. Fix Terric."

"You have to kill him."

Chapter 19

SHAME

"What the — ? No," Dash said. "Shame, don't listen to him."

"Killing Terric seems to be what we're trying to avoid here, Cody," I said quietly.

"You died," he said. "You came back."

"I have Death magic riding shotgun in my noggin."

"And Terric has Life magic," Cody said. "Dying shouldn't be more than a pause in living for him."

"No," Dash said again. "No one kills Terric. I can't even believe I have to say that. Listen, Shame, here's what we're going to do. You are going to cast Illusion on the house and car. We'll get a doctor out here. For Terric and Davy. Understand me? We'll get them stable. No more killing."

"Stable," I said, still looking at Cody. "Then what, Dash?"

"We'll build that bridge when we get to it. Can you access enough magic to cast Illusion?"

Cody clearly wasn't a fan of Dash's plan. But he shrugged, letting me make the decision.

What I decided was to placate Dash. A deathless plan sounded like a good, reasonable starting point.

"I can access the magic," I said.

Even though the Soul Complement bond between us didn't seem to be working, Terric wasn't dead yet. That meant I still had superior abilities with magic. But if he kicked off . . . well, when . . . I'd be of no use to anyone except as a killing thing.

I was pretty sure if Terric died, I'd go completely, gloriously insane.

So basically, they'd want to end me pretty quick.

"Good," Dash said, sounding a little more comfortable with the conversation now that it wasn't about dumping Terric in an early grave. "Cast it. I'm going out this door to talk to Davy. I will be right back in. And if you lay a hand on him, Shame . . ."

"You'll spend your life making me regret it, second by second." I gave him a small smile. "I heard you, mate. I'm still in here."

He glanced over at Cody, at Terric, then walked past me and down the hall.

"I'm not wrong," Cody said. "About Terric."

"About me turning him off and then on again?" I shook my head. "I don't think so, Cody. I can't bring him back, and I don't know that he'll want to leave death for me."

"You left it for him, didn't you?"

"Yes." And if I did kill him, and did it wrong, I most certainly didn't want the ghost of him tied to me. I wasn't dealing well with the two ghosts I was currently failing.

"Soul Complements," Cody said as if that explained everything. "If you kill him, he'll come back. *Should* come back."

"You don't know that. You can't guarantee that. You're guessing your way through this just like the rest of us."

"Sure, but it's a good guess. A strong bet." He took a few steps away from the bed and sat on the dresser. "I carried magic for a while, remember? I have a good feel for these things."

"Terric and me, the magic we carry, isn't a part of what you did with magic."

"Now, that's not true. Magic is magic is magic. But I understand why you're doing Dash's thing first. It's the safe move. You have never been much for the big gambles."

"Hello? Do you know me, mate?"

He held up one finger. "International art couriers."

"They wanted us to be drug mules."

Another finger. "Wilderness guides."

"Hit men for the mob."

"Investing in Apple."

I stopped pacing. "I don't remember that one."

He frowned, and then a smile crossed his face. "Huh. Must not have been you. Well, you really missed out on that one."

"Ass."

"So, are you going to get with the Illusioning or what?" he asked.

Eleanor and Sunny were in the room, close together and talking to each other with their backs turned to me. So apparently the dead girls were conspiring against me.

Great.

As for the state of Flynn, I was worried, exhausted. The adrenaline of fighting Death magic and the kick of energy I got from the lives I'd consumed were already wearing off. If I was going to access magic for a spell with any kind of control, it would need to happen now.

"Here?" I asked.

"Outside won't put any of us out of your reach, Shame," he said. "Not really."

"Still, you might not want to stick around for this."

"And miss the show?"

"They say *I* have a suicidal personality," I muttered. I closed my eyes and cleared my mind.

Not Death magic, not the magic I carried. I wanted the

magic that flowed beneath the earth, magic anyone could tap in to. Magic that in my hands would be powerful enough to make this house and about fifty feet around it disappear. Or at least fade into the surrounding flora.

It wasn't hard to tap in to the magic. Even here where it wasn't channeled and networked through man-made conduits and lines, even here where there was no well where it naturally pooled, I could feel it.

Easy to reach. Difficult to control.

To use magic, glyphs must be drawn. To draw a glyph correctly, you gotta be calm, centered, focused.

I was about as far away from any of those things as I'd ever been.

Terric was dying.

Everything inside me was dying with him.

I'd trapped Eleanor. I'd let Death magic kill Sunny with cold, brutal efficiency.

Krogher was on our tail, probably Eli too. Davy was grieving—rightfully so—and was screwed up in ways that made me think we might want to book him a rubber room.

Dash and Cody were hurt—those bullets hadn't all missed. Soul Complements out in the world were walking targets. It was only a matter of time before they'd be dead.

The world needed saving. Maybe, if we made it through the night, we could come up with an idea on how to do that.

But none of those thoughts churning through my head were going to help me cast magic.

So I pushed them away. Pushed everything away. I knew how to make the world go away. I knew how to be silent, detached, dead.

That's what I did.

And from the middle of that silence, I drew the glyph for Illusion. I wrapped it with Fade so the unavoidable flare of magic wouldn't be as strong or bright, and so I might have a chance of not giving us away while I was trying to hide us.

The spell rolled out from the center point of the glyph I sketched in the air in front of me. As quickly as it glowed yellow with magic, it faded out, a pale connection of threads that soaked into the floor and wafted out to cover the walls around us. It surrounded the house, the car, and made it look like there was nothing but landscape left behind.

Cody sighed. "I miss it," he said. "Have I told you that?" He was next to me now, holding a glass of water out for me. "Using magic. Making things happen. Changing the world with a flick of fingers and thought."

"You can't tap it at all?"

He shook his head. "I can fix it if it's broken, I think. The big break, light, dark. But otherwise, it's as insubstantial as air to me."

"That's what you get for saving the world, mate," I said. "A big fat nothing." I took the water. "How's Terric?"

"I think he has a few hours. At most. But I'm not a doctor."

I drank the water mechanically. It didn't do anything to ease my thirst. What I wanted, what the hollow emptiness inside me yearned for was right over there on that bed. Dying.

Don't do it, Shame, Eleanor warned.

No, Sunny interrupted. *Do. Kill your damn Soul Complement. I want to see your face when he breathes his last breath.*

That won't help anything, Eleanor said. *Shame, just be calm about this. Think it through. Make a good choice.*

"How many voices you got in that head of yours?" Cody asked.

"What?"

"I know what you did to Eleanor. I know what you did to Sunny. They're both still with you, aren't they?"

Tell him, Sunny said.

"No," I said.

"Really?" Cody said. "If I happened to have the goods to pull on a Sight spell, I wouldn't see two women chained to you?"

"Get the goods. Then you can tell me."

That's constructive, Shame, Sunny said.

"You know you can't lie to me," Cody said quietly. "I know your tells."

"Yeah, sure. I'm an open book." I took a few steps away from him, then a few back, trying not to pace toward Terric. "They're both still with me," I said quietly. "I don't know how to let them go. If I break the tie holding them to me, the magic, they'll be dead for good."

"So why break it?" he asked.

"Other than they both hate me for killing them? There's a natural order, isn't there?" I said. "Life. Death. A way to sort chaos. The way things should be?"

"I think," he said, "you, and maybe Terric, get to have some say over that. Life. Death. But the rest of us—including Eleanor and Sunny? If there was a way to break the rules of death, you'd know it."

Which brought me back to the thing I was trying not to think about.

"You think if I kill Terric, he'll . . . just come back to life somehow?"

"You and Terric . . . you aren't like most of us. Death in you, Life in him. Positive, negative. You push him far enough, that magic in him is going to push you right back. Life always finds a way to survive."

In theory.

"You don't know that, don't know this"—I pointed at my head—"won't kill him."

He shrugged. "I was the Focal—the vessel for dark and light magic joining, Shame. Held all the magic in the world together until it healed and became what it is now. And while I wouldn't say it was exactly a comfortable experience, it did leave me with a pretty good blueprint on how magic does and doesn't work. Or perhaps more correctly, how it can and can't work."

"Cut to the big reveal."

"Okay. Two choices. Wait for a doctor to come here and tell us all of Terric's organs are failing and it's time to say our good-byes, or step in and take that natural conclusion away from him."

"Natural conclusion?"

"Death. I mean death, Shame. How hard did you get hit back there?"

"I wasn't hit."

He paused and gave me that thousand-yard stare while looking straight at me. I set my shoulders so I didn't squirm under it. I hated his forever-judgment look.

"You were *shot*," he finally said. "Multiple times. Trained gunmen don't miss."

I looked down at my chest. He was right. There were holes in my shirt I hadn't started the morning with.

Jesus.

"I can't take death away from someone," I said.

"Why not? You're death, aren't you?"

He says you can undo this, Shame, Sunny said. *You can undo death.*

"I can't. I've tried."

Sunny threw her hands up in exasperation.

Cody didn't say anything. We'd gotten to the point in our relationship where we didn't have to use our words to tell the other person that we knew he was fooling himself.

"If you can kill people," Cody said, "it makes sense you can unkill them. You can remove the death that's devouring him. Draw it to you, tie it to you. Just like you took Terric's pain. Some of it anyway. Enough to give Life a foothold in him again. A chance to thrive."

"You saw that?"

"I see everything."

"If I touch him, his heart stops beating."

"It's not his heart you have to fix, Shame. It's his soul. Your soul and his, tied together, are stronger than either of you alone. That's the beauty of being a Soul Complement."

"Save it for the greeting card," I said.

"I'm telling you how I see it. You know I'm not wrong. You know you can't kill him. Even if you tried."

I wasn't specifically worried about *me* killing him. I could have the best intentions in the world. But if I lost an inch to Death magic, he'd be dead in a second. Death magic had been looking for the edge on killing him for the last three years.

Dash walked back into the room. Yes, he glanced at Terric first to see if he was still alive.

"Where's the trust, mate?" I asked.

He gave me a warning look. "Don't touch him. We have a doctor on the way."

I hooked my thumbs in my belt and leaned against the wall. "Don't think a doctor can do anything for him."

"He was shot, Shame. Doctors can do something for that. That's what doctors do."

He was right. He was making sense.

"How long?" I asked.

"Thirty minutes." He paced over to the bed, pulled a chair up next to it. "I don't care if you stay in the room, but I'm not going anywhere. You want Terric, you go through me."

Something dark inside me shivered with the idea of that.

You're sick, Sunny whispered.

I gave her half a nod.

Cody sucked air in through his teeth. "So we wait. Awesome. I'll go see if there's something to eat."

He walked out.

I pushed away from the wall, not knowing where to go, but not wanting to stay here either.

"Thirty minutes, Shame," Dash said. "Give me that. You owe him that. At least."

"I know, I know, Spade. Give it a rest," I said. I knew the debts between us. They were carved into my soul. "Have you heard from Zay and Allie?"

"I called. She's in labor again."

"Again? Does it usually go this way?"

"No."

Is the baby okay? Eleanor asked.

"Is the baby okay?" I repeated for her. She gave me a faint smile.

"Dr. Fischer is there."

That wasn't a yes.

"And the baby is . . . ?" I asked again.

Dash rubbed at his forehead and I finally noticed he was bleeding from a cut near his hairline. His hand was shaking pretty badly too. He'd been hit and probably hadn't done anything to take care of his wounds.

Since I was already pacing, I walked to the bathroom. Dug for bandages. I should have done this when we first arrived, but I hadn't been thinking. Still wasn't.

"The baby, Dash," I said again, since talking about other things helped me ignore the things I didn't want to talk about.

Found a bottle of rubbing alcohol and a clean towel. Took that back to the room and handed it to him. Didn't look at Terric. Didn't stand too close to the bed.

If I did, there wouldn't be anything or anyone who could pull me away from his side.

"They aren't sure." Dash tipped the alcohol onto the towel. "Zay sounded worried."

That wasn't good. I'd stood side by side at the end of the world with that man and he'd barely worked up a sense of concern.

"That's not all," Dash went on. "Clyde called. Anthony was just found dead."

"Son of a bitch," I whispered. Anthony was another Soul Complement. "How about Holly?" I asked.

"Can't find her. They are assuming the worst."

The worst being that she was dead too. Krogher wasn't wasting any time. That was the second Soul Complement pair in less than twenty-four hours.

How long before he had drones around Allie and Zay's place? How long before he wiped out the only people who could break magic and stop him and his magic army?

"We need a new plan," I said.

We had a plan? Sunny asked.

"You mean something other than walk straight in the front door, into live fire?" Dash asked.

"Worked for me," I said.

"No so much for Sunny," Dash said.

I pressed my palm over my eyes. "I know. If I could change that, I would."

Killing Krogher seemed like a good idea. It wasn't a smart idea. Probably wasn't the thing Terric or Allie or Zay or ... hell ... anyone would get on board with. But seeing the light snuff out of Krogher's eyes before any other Soul Complement died would do me worlds of good.

At least it would make Sunny's death worth something.

I couldn't think here so close to an almost-dead Terric. I needed air. I needed space.

"If you try to leave this house, I'll knock you out cold." Dash wasn't even looking at me. Couldn't have known I was walking out.

I glanced back at him. He pressed the towel against his temple, pulled it away, and stuck it over the blood on his thigh. His glasses hung loosely in his other hand. He hadn't looked away from Terric. "If you try to leave, I'll tell Davy to make sure you stay unconscious. I think he'd be on my side. He's pretty sure you got Sunny killed."

I peered down the hall to the living room where Davy sat

in the chair next to Sunny's dead body. He was staring at me. Angry. Unmoving. The neon magic that was dripping out of him like a torn artery leaking blood was just a smear of dull blue shining up the darkness of his T-shirt. Boy was a ticking time bomb.

I was his target.

"Do you think that?" I asked quietly.

"I think I'm not going to ask what happened back there yet. And I think you're staying here, with us, until I say you can leave."

"Who said I was going anywhere?"

Dash dug the towel into the hole in his jeans and sighed. "You're angry."

"So?"

"Have you looked in the mirror when you get angry?"

"No."

He pointed toward the bathroom with the bloody bit of the towel. Then folded it to press a clean patch against his thigh wound again.

I walked back into the bathroom.

Stopped dead when I caught sight of myself in the mirror above the sink.

Too thin, eyes too black, skin too pale with dried blood at the corner of my eye and down the side of my face and neck. That was your basic bar-brawl chic and could have been me any given Friday night.

But a dark light surrounded me, as if every edge had been carved out of thick ice with a hard brightness shining behind it. I barely looked human. I was stone cold.

Death.

It wasn't just inside me anymore. It was me. It made me. Every inch of me. From heel bone to brainpan.

So much for hiding the monster on the inside. The line between me and it had officially been destroyed. I wore it just as much as it wore me.

Looking in that mirror made a couple of things clear: The monster and I were not happy.

And the monster and I were not weak.

Good. We had work to do.

The doctor was a very nice, if extremely nervous woman with short, dark hair and thin-rimmed glasses. Dash promised she could be trusted with this sort of stuff.

Since this sort of stuff hadn't happened before, I had no idea what she'd put on her résumé to land the job.

Her name was Mina, and even though she seemed nervous at first, as soon as she got one look at all of us with our various injuries, she was all business. Quick. Efficient. Capable.

Ordered people around.

She took care of Terric first.

Dash stayed with him while I paced the hall, occasionally glancing in through the open door.

Coward, Sunny said. She picked at her nails with the knife she'd somehow gotten back. Not exactly comforting to discover she could remanifest a weapon. I foresaw a lot of stabbings in my future. *You aren't even standing by his side. Afraid to see him die, Shame?*

"Give it a rest. You're angry at me. I get it. I'm angry at me too."

I rounded the corner into the living room and almost ran into Davy, who was walking toward the hall. He tipped his head and looked past me. Right at Sunny.

Davy, she said. *Can you hear me? Honey, can you see me?*

He hesitated and I waited, wondering if I would have what it took to block whatever he might throw at me. Then his yellowed gaze ticked back to me.

"You should go," he said.

"Where?"

"Home. While you still can."

"And *that* didn't sound like a threat."

"Did you kill her?" he asked.

Might as well tell him, Sunny said.

No, Eleanor said. *Not yet.*

Why not? Sunny asked.

Do you really want Davy fighting Shame? Eleanor said. *Who do you think would win?*

Sunny narrowed her eyes, looked at me, looked at Davy.

It wouldn't be Davy, Eleanor said. *He'd kill him. And then you'd both be dead. Do you want that?*

Cody strolled out of the kitchen and took in the situation. Me, standing in the hall, Davy standing just inside the living room. Neither of us moving. Neither of us talking.

"Hello, boys," he said. "What did I miss?"

"Nothing," I said. "There's nothing here to see."

This house was suddenly crowded with too many heartbeats, too many people, too many ghosts. Death magic pounded at the lid I'd locked it under.

It wouldn't be long before it broke free.

Davy's only answer was to walk back to where Sunny's body lay, covered face to foot by a clean sheet.

Cody looked at me, back at Davy, then headed after Davy.

I didn't know if I should be happy or worried that he thought Davy was the bigger issue to be dealt with here.

But I knew it was just a matter of time before Davy and I had it out over Sunny's death. Only a matter of time before he tried to kill me.

Hell, maybe I'd let him. It wasn't as if I didn't deserve it.

I paced until I was back in the bedroom again, just inside the door. I leaned my shoulder against the edge and stared at Terric.

The doctor had removed the bullets and put Terric on an IV with pain meds and antibiotic. She hesitated over all the signs of torture he'd been through. Finally defaulted to a gel and clean bandages for the burns, brands, and cuts.

But the deeper wounds, the things they had done to his mind, his soul, and his magic, were beyond her care.

"How long has he been missing?" she asked.

"A week." Dash hadn't budged from his side. He stood there, steady on his feet, though he looked a couple heartbeats away from a drinking binge and self-administered unconsciousness.

"Was he wounded before that?" she asked.

Dash shook his head.

"The knife wound at his throat," I said quietly from the shadows of the doorway. "That was the first."

She startled and glanced over her shoulder at me. She must have forgotten I was lingering there, even though she'd made a point to nod at me when she first came into the room.

"All right," she said. "The neck wound is nearly healed. It looks to be much older than a week. From the bruising, bleeding, and swelling, I'd guess his internal injuries are more than a few days old also. Weeks at least. And the cuts, the removed finger?" She nodded. "Those were done weeks ago, not days ago."

"That can't be right," Dash said. "He was fine a week ago. He was with us, at Allie's party. Healthy."

"No physical wounds, anyway," I said.

"Did he suffer from some other kind of wound?" the doctor asked.

"Withdrawal," I said.

"Drugs? Alcohol?"

"Magic."

She paused in taping the IV to his arm and waited for me to deliver the punch line.

I gave her a steady stare.

"Okay," she said slowly. "Magic. Do you know what he was using? Which spells? Blood magic?"

"Life magic," I said. "It's complicated."

She took a moment to study Terric. "I'm not sure I understand the consequences of that addiction. Do you think it caused any of these injuries?"

"No," I said. "Those are from torture."

She placed his arm carefully back at his side and then pulled the blanket up to his waist. "Does he have family?" she asked.

"Yes," Dash said. "Brothers, sisters. His parents are still alive. He has a lot of family. Why?"

"We'll want to contact them. They should know."

Dash opened his mouth but closed it as soon as he put two and two together and realized what she was saying.

Terric's family should know that he was going to be dead soon.

Death magic thumped on the lid in my head. A fist. A heartbeat. A demand.

"How much longer does he have?" I asked.

Dash closed his eyes and turned his back on the bed.

"Not much, I think," she said. "Maybe a few hours."

"What about a hospital?" I asked calmly. "Better equipment? Would it buy us time? Would it buy him time?"

"Assuming he could survive the transport? His injuries are just too numerous. And many of them were inflicted with magic. There are spells *carved* into him. Spells I've never seen before. I've dealt with magical wounds for years now, but nothing like this. I'm sorry. I really am. Even if we take him to a hospital, we should still contact his next of kin."

Terric's next of kin. His family. Contact them and tell them he was dying.

I was having a hard time accepting those words.

Dash said something to her that I'm sure was appropriate and thoughtful. After a minute or two, he walked with her out of the room. There were other injuries, other people to take care of besides Terric.

The doctor could do some good for them.

But not Terric.

Spells carved into him. There was a reason she'd never seen those spells before. They weren't spells any sane person would think of combining and inflicting on a person. I only knew one magic user twisted enough to create this kind of magical torture—Eli Collins.

I walked over to the bed and stared down at Terric.

Death magic growing, pounding, raging. *Thump. Thump. Thump.*

"You are a pain in the ass, Terric Conley," I said quietly. "I've tried . . . tried to keep you out of the blast zone of my screwed-up life, but you just wouldn't walk away. Not even when . . . when I gave you my life on the battlefield there years ago. Idiot. Why didn't you just let me go then? None of this would have happened."

The link of pain between us was gone—wiped out by the meds pushing happy-feel-good through his veins. He wasn't hurting. He was resting peacefully.

This was the kind of exit everyone hoped for, right? Asleep. Quiet. Easy.

I pulled the chair up closer to his bed and sat. "If you had just let me die, I never would have done . . . the things Eli tortured you for. Killing Brandy. I really fucked that up, didn't I? But I guess you and I are good at fucking things up. Carrying Life and Death magic inside us, mate? Who does that? No one. Maybe we should have just taken our beating back on the field with Jingo Jingo. Let the bastard win. Lain down and died."

Terric didn't say anything. His breathing didn't change. I had no idea if he could even hear me. Probably not. His ghost wasn't here, so he wasn't dead. But he wasn't all that alive either.

People could linger for years like this . . . comas. Maybe that's what would happen to Terric. Maybe the life magic in him would do more than the doctor expected. Maybe it would hold him stable, and over time, he would heal.

Cody thought he'd heal a different way. By fighting against a quick, hard death.

A death I could give him. Darkness sparking light, magic snapping against magic, death closing the loop so life could begin again.

There was fire in that sort of thing. Maybe it was the fire Terric needed to survive.

Maybe it would kill him.

"Jesus, Ter," I whispered, leaning my face into my hands. "What the fuck am I supposed to do?"

He didn't answer. This one was all on me. This choice mine alone to make.

"This shouldn't be in my hands, this choice," I said, even though I knew he wasn't listening. "That's you. You've always been the reasonable one, the thoughtful man. You've always been right."

I wiped at my face and the wetness there. "The right thing would be for me to leave. Let you heal, hope you heal." I nodded, and blinked until my eyes cleared enough that I could see him.

"But I am a selfish bastard, mate. You know that. If there's a chance you can be here, with me to track Eli down and drag him to hell, I want you here, beside me. I . . . can't do this alone."

It was probably a mistake, this decision I was making. Everything else I'd done in my life had been a mistake, so why would this be any different?

I sat on the edge of the bed. Watched as my proximity made his chest stop moving, his lungs pause.

I placed my hand in the center of his chest.

"I'm sorry, Ter," I whispered. "But you were right. I can't live without you."

I didn't know how, exactly, to do this. Cody had said all I had to do was take his death upon myself just as I'd taken his pain upon myself. That would give life some room to thrive in him.

Don't leave me, Ter, I thought. *Not yet.*

I kicked free the lid on Death magic. It washed through me with its own pulse, humming in anticipation, feral.

If I did this wrong, Terric would die. Permanently.

Cold sweat drenched me. If I did this wrong, there would be no coming back. For either of us.

Careful, then.

I let Death magic pour out of my fingertips, cold and slow, sending it to cover his skin in that dark glass-edge light. Then I sent it deeper, into his body. Into his soul where Life magic flickered like a flame drowning in the wind.

He wasn't breathing. He still wasn't breathing.

Seconds ticked by, piling up into a minute. Two.

Undeath him, Cody had said. Take his death on as my burden.

Easy to say, but there was no spell for assuming someone else's final end. There was no operating manual for the Death magic I carried.

It was like aiming a flamethrower to light a candle—messy and destructive.

"C'mon, Ter," I said softly. "Let it go. Dying isn't your thing—it's mine. And I've got you now. You can just let go. And come back to me, mate. Please come back to me."

Terric exhaled, long and slow, as I gently killed him.

And then he didn't breathe again.

Chapter 20

SHAME

Minutes dragged by, measured by my own ragged breathing. But not Terric's. Terric wasn't breathing. The Life magic in him had been snuffed, smothered out by the touch of Death magic.

Come on, Terric, I begged. *Breathe.*

Cody had been wrong. Cody had been very wrong.

I'd killed him. My friend. My soul.

The rolling clack of a bullet chambering a round rang out in the silence.

"Shame," Dash said. "Back away from him now."

Terric's ghost wasn't pulling free of his body. He wasn't tied to me like Eleanor and Sunny. But he was not alive either.

"Last chance, Flynn," Dash warned. "Bullets might not kill you, but they will slow you down."

Terric wasn't breathing, still wasn't breathing.

Goddamn you, Cody. You said he'd live. Like me.

I pressed my palm over Terric's heart. "I'm sorry," I whispered. "I'm so sorry."

"Move," Dash said, "away."

I swallowed the tears, swallowed pain. Nodded. I'd done this, made this choice. The wrong choice.

He was gone. Gone. I'd killed him. Just like I always thought I would.

Death spread its arms and wrapped around me like a thick, soft blanket, and I let it. Let it feed on my shock and pain, leaving me dull, blank.

I moved away from Terric as Dash said, backing away from the bed.

I'd killed him.

Everything went silent under the weight of that reality. The world slid past me in slow motion.

Dash moved toward the bed, shifting his aim to keep the gun pointed at my head. He bent and pressed fingers against Terric's neck, feeling for a pulse.

I stared at Dash's gun. Wished it could kill me.

I wished I was the dead guy in that bed. Wished I'd never crawled out of heaven and off that damn kitchen floor. If I could give up something to change this, to change everything, I would.

But there was nothing I could do.

Yes, I'd find a way to die. Soon. Dash was right—bullets wouldn't do it. Something would, though. I was sure of that.

But before I found out how to take myself out of this world, I had someone to destroy.

Eli Collins.

Death magic closed around me tighter, a black wave that swallowed the last of me.

I did not fight it.

I started walking, clearheaded and calm. Revenge is a wonderful focusing tool, when applied correctly.

Through the house, out the door. Maybe Dash was calling my name. Maybe Sunny said something as I stormed through the living room. Maybe the doctor put down her cell phone and walked out the door behind me.

Maybe Death didn't give a damn.

Out to the front of the house, out to the dirt road that wound off the highway and back into these hills. Out past the Illusion spell I had cast to keep us safe.

Only I didn't want to be safe anymore.

Not one little bit.

Come at me, boys, I thought. *I'm not hiding anymore.*

I bent, unlaced my boots, pulled them off, and threw them into the ditch. Stocking feet pressed against the cold dirt. Dirt tied in to everything in this world. Dirt beneath my feet was dirt beneath Eli's feet.

And there was a world of magic flowing between us. Magic I was a part of. Magic I knew he was a part of.

"Mr. Flynn," the doctor said, her voice sounding miles away and small.

Eli was somewhere on this earth. I was going to find him, find his single, beating heart out of millions of beating hearts. Then I was going to tear him apart and drag him down to hell with me.

Death curled my hands into fists. I was angry, but anger was only the beginning.

Shame, Eleanor said. *Whatever you're thinking about doing, don't do it. Think about this. Think about what your actions will do.*

Death could drink down every life in a ten-mile radius. Every life in a hundred miles. But the only life I wanted ended was Eli's.

"Please, Mr. Flynn," the doctor said. "Let me see to your injuries." Her hand gently touched my shoulder.

Death turned to her, to the life pulse thrumming in her, and smiled, hungry.

No, I thought

No! Eleanor said.

The doctor smiled back. "Let's go inside."

Death was fast. My hand whipped out and cupped the back of her head. My other hand pressed against her heart.

It was enough to snap me out of the shock, to shake off some of the numb grief that held me down.

But Death had the edge on me. I fought for control of my own damn hands, my own damn body.

Too late.

Death magic wrapped her, skin to soul, smothered the life out of her, and sucked it into me. The flare of her surprise, followed by pain, fear, and then the gentle release of her consciousness was thick against my tongue, heavy in my belly.

God, what had I become?

Shame, Eleanor said. *Let go of her.*

I heard her, and had enough control that I lowered the doctor to the ground and stood back.

Her spirit stepped out of her body, ghostly and confused. There was a new rope attached to my arm, a rope that wrapped around her neck.

Death magic was sated for the moment. Not easy to shove away, but I leaned into it, pushed it down, held it back.

The doctor was crying. *Why?* she asked softly.

"I'm sorry," I said, the words numb against my lips.

You killed me with a single touch, she said. *That's not how we die. That's not how anyone dies.*

"I know," I said. I had no words for her. No words she'd want to hear.

Eleanor and Sunny took her away from me, as far as their chains would allow, turned their backs on me, and on her dead body, and whispered comforting things to her.

If you're going to do it, Sunny said. *Do it now.*

I must have been standing there for a while. Eleanor and the doctor—Mina—still had their backs to me, but Sunny was in front of me now.

"What?"

You killed Terric and he died. Then you killed Mina too, she said. *Which I'm guessing was because you lost control of the snake pit of magic writhing in you. I can only think of one reason why you didn't just force Dash to blow your brains out. You want revenge.*

"Eli," I said.

Good, she said. *I want him dead too. Kill the son of a bitch. Kill him for what he did to Terric. Kill him for what he did to Davy. And kill him for what he did to you, Shame. For turning you into this crap-fest of magic, and hatred, and pain. For making you kill the people you care about.*

"He didn't do that," I said. "That's on me. My choice. My weakness."

Some of it, yes, she said. *But you have to know this is what Eli wanted. What he counted on when he was torturing Davy, torturing Terric: to make you suffer. So make him suffer back.*

I shook my head. Blood magic users. Always looking for a way to turn pain to their advantage.

She was right, though. If there was a price to pay for all of these deaths, I wasn't the only one who owed dues. Eli had blood on his hands.

"Why are you on my side now?" I asked.

You're my only way out of this, if there is a way out. Also, fuck Eli.

Death magic curled inside me, tempting, seductive.

I nodded. Revenge made strange bedfellows, but killing Eli was something Sunny and I both wanted. I had my body again, control again. The magic inside me was a tool I could use.

I inhaled, drawing just the thinnest smoke of Death magic into my hands. It slipped through my veins, cold and invigorating and powerful. I spread my fingers wide, sent tendrils of Death out to search for Eli.

Thunder rolled against the predawn sky.

"Come on, you bastard," I whispered. "Let's hear your heartbeat."

Hundreds of heartbeats tapped against my ear, then thousands as Death magic reached out in an ever-growing circle, wider and wider, tens of miles, hundreds of miles. Millions of hearts pumping, living, thriving.

I only wanted one. I only needed one: Eli.

Every pulse of life in the world was different. Fast, slow, old, young, hot, cold. Like a million fragile liquid notes, streaming out, pulsing, tangling, joining, breaking to make one vast, beautiful, chaotic song.

One of those notes had to be Eli's. One single life.

I held my breath, sorting heartbeats, sorting lives, digging and sifting through the dirt of this world until only one heartbeat remained.

Eli's.

Got him. He wasn't far, less than a hundred miles north of here. Close enough I might be able to kill him from where I stood. If I could hold my concentration. If I could control the Death magic long enough to kill him.

Sure, I wanted to be there to see him take his last breath. But I had a clear shot. I intended to take it. "Burn in hell, you son of a bitch," I snarled.

I cleared my mind, set my feet to bear the weight of throwing magic that far—impossibly far—and aiming it that precisely. Rolled my shoulders, tipped my head down. One strike, clean. That's all I needed. It would do no good to take down a mile-wide swath of innocent people on accident if I lost hold of the magic. I aimed . . .

. . . and Eli's heartbeat disappeared.

"Son of a bitch," I yelled.

I scrambled to follow him, follow the sound of his life among the snarled sounds and beats of all those other lives. It would be easier to find a single grain of sand in a tsunami.

Too many currents washed over me, too many lives coming, going, living, dying, changing.

I lost him in all that living.

Goddamn it.

Ice raked down the side of my face. I opened my eyes, gasped in a breath, started coughing. When had I stopped breathing? When had I fallen flat on my back?

Eleanor knelt in front of me, her hand on my cheek. *You are insane, Shame,* she said not unkindly. *Trying to kill him from here. Not even you can do that.*

"We know that *now*," I said. "Are you okay?" Throwing that much magic could have hurt her, could have hurt Sunny and the doctor too.

Enough, she said. *But we need to deal with Mina, okay?*

"Mina?"

The doctor. We know how you can let go of her so she can live again.

"Who we? You and Sunny?"

Me. The doctor floated over to stand next to Eleanor.

I'd like to return to living, she said calmly. *It hasn't been too long for me to recover from this. I'd like you to let go of me, and I think I can help you with that.*

"You can't. No one can."

Not true. She crossed her arms over her chest. *I used to be a Death magic user, back before magic changed. I understand the way spells can be used for supporting life, for holding off death. Let me help you.*

This was a bad idea. Using the Death magic inside me seemed to be nothing but bad ideas.

Eleanor's hand slipped down to my heart. Not digging around in my chest looking for a way to kill me, just a cool, soft pressure there.

This is the right thing to do, she said. *You know it is.*

Her gaze searched my face. Not judging. Just waiting, patient. Something inside me that might have been my humanity kicked at the walls of grief and anger and darkness that surrounded me.

"All right," I said. "She goes back to living. How?"

Eleanor smiled. *There's my hero.* She moved away while I got myself back up on my feet.

Mina drifted closer to me.

Do you know the Resurrection spell? she asked. *It was being experimented with in hospitals several years ago.*

"Not a doctor," I said. "And I don't raise the dead."

That's okay. I know the spell. I can draw it, and then instead of filling it with magic, you can fill it with this — she touched the black rope between us — *and me* — she touched her chest.

Even the crazy parts of me thought that was crazy.

"What makes you think it will work?" I asked.

Strong theories. She gave me a smile. *If it doesn't work, what's the worst that can happen?*

I didn't have time to run through all the possible disasters, but the most likely was that she'd be dead and still tied to me just like now. It was, in theory, a low-risk proposition.

"I think this is a terrible idea," I said. "But if you want to try it, I'll do it. I owe you that. I owe you more."

Good, she said. *Good. Thank you. Where do you want me to draw the glyph?*

"Between us should be fine," I said.

Eleanor and Sunny moved off a bit to give us room. Mina stood in front of me and then drew the glyph for Resurrection.

She cast with an odd blend of styles: half how I would expect a Life magic user to cast spells, and half how I'd expect a Death magic user to cast. The glyph knotted and looped in such a way that I lost track of the lines between blinks. Mina drew it as if she'd practiced it a million times, confident, clean, smooth, without a pause.

It hovered there in the air between us, the lines of it fading in and out of my vision, as if she had scratched the color off the world to make room for the spell.

That's it, she said. *It's done.*

She took a step away from the glyph. I could see where magic would fit into it. More than that, now that the spell was completed, I could see where a soul fit into it.

A soul like Mina.

"Who the hell came up with this?" I asked. I'd lived in the know of the secret, dangerous magic all my life and I'd never seen a spell like this.

Please hurry, Mina said. *Before my concentration fails and the glyph breaks.*

"Has this ever worked?" I asked as I untangled the rope that tied Mina to me from the other ropes.

We've had good results in the operating room.

"But pulling someone back from death?" I guided her rope toward the spell. The spell tugged on the rope, on the ghost of her, like a magnet pulling to metal.

She didn't answer me. Maybe she couldn't hear me. The spell was drawing her in.

"Live," I said.

I released my hold on her, concentrated on sending her spirit into that floating glyph.

She poured into it with violet light, filled the spell, and triggered it.

Sunny and Eleanor drew closer to the spell, like moths drawn to a flame.

The spell arced through the air and hovered above Mina's body. It draped over her like lavender lace. The black rope between us dissolved.

Our tie was gone, broken. The spell really had carried her soul, her spirit. She should be firmly back inside her body now.

Good. This was good.

She'd been dead maybe a few minutes at most. All systems were go. Lots of people had been revived after a much longer death.

I took a few steps back so I wasn't deathing up the area around her. Gave her space to revive.

I waited.

She's not breathing, Sunny said.

Eleanor bent down next to her, touched her face. *Mina. Wake up, Mina.*

Shame, Sunny said. *Do something. Get someone.*

Someone could do CPR. Not me. With the Death pulsing through me, I'd either rekill or reghost her.

I jogged to the house. Maybe Dash could help. Or Cody.

"Help," I said as I stepped into the living room. "I need help out here."

Cody and Dash hurried into the room.

"Shame?" Dash said. "What?"

"The doctor. Mina. She needs help."

"What happened?" Dash asked as he stormed out the door. "What happened to her?"

I didn't turn. I didn't have to. I knew the exact moment he found her there, dead on the ground. I heard him call for Cody. I heard him tell him to call 911.

"Me," I whispered. "I happened to her."

Eleanor and Sunny were just outside the door, watching. We waited. A full minute. We waited two.

She's dead, Eleanor said. *Gone. Oh, Shame. She didn't make it.*

Sunny swore, and paced past me, her knife clenched tight in her hand as if it could protect her from me. Protect her from death.

"You killed her?" Davy asked.

I turned. I hadn't seen him in the room. Probably because he hadn't wanted me to.

He sat on the floor again, in front of Sunny's corpse. The

glow of blue magic leaked light through the bandages someone must have wrapped him in.

Mina. Bandages Mina must have wrapped him in.

His hair hadn't been cut in too long, and fell into his eyes. He didn't bother to brush it out of his way as he stared at me, waiting for my reply.

"Who?" I asked. Not that it would matter. The answer would be yes.

"Do you know what I'm going to do for you, Flynn? I'm going to give you a head start. If you're smart, you'll track down Eli Collins and kill him. Before I find you. And kill you for what you've done."

He hadn't moved an inch, but the rage in him was a palpable thing pushing out toward me.

"Well, then, mate," I said quietly. "Until we meet again."

I walked away. Away from the house, away from the dead bodies. I thought Davy might have the right of this situation.

My best use, hell, my only use right now, was Death. And Eli was the man we all wanted dead. After that . . . well, it would be interesting to find out if the spells Eli had carved into Davy, the things he had done to change Davy, would be enough to kill me.

Wind dragged cold across my sweat-covered skin, sticking my jacket to my back and sending a chill up my bare neck.

Dash yelled my name.

I ignored him and jogged to the SUV, got in, started the engine.

I might still be able to find Eli.

But I'd be damned if I was going to kill any more innocent people tonight.

Ever.

A gunshot ricocheted off the vehicle. I glance in my rearview mirror. Dash was there, took a second shot, for the tires, I thought.

Hit the car, missed tires.

Too bad, mate. But I had no time to stay and explain things. I had a killer to take down.

I pulled off to the side of the road about twenty minutes later.

I'd left my boots back in that ditch near the house. The gravel on the shoulder of the road was sharp and cold. That was fine with me. I just needed enough contact to the earth for Death magic to find Eli's heartbeat again.

Almost instantly, I caught a heartbeat that could be him about two hundred miles northwest of here.

Somewhere near Portland. But where, exactly?

Even with Death magic feeding on my anger and adrenaline, I was fatiguing, my legs shaking.

Careful, now, Flynn, I thought. *Don't blow this. Just focus on the area surrounding him.*

I concentrated on the Eli heartbeat, then pulled my perception carefully up away from the beat to his body surrounding that beat, to the room surrounding that body, then the building surrounding that room.

I knew that building. It was part of a shipping yard in St. Johns.

He was in Portland. Close to Allie and Zay.

And I could guess why.

Three Soul Complements died today, but Eli wasn't done doing Krogher's dirty work. Allie and Zay, my family, people I loved like siblings, were next on the list.

And I was so not in the mood to be fucked with.

I focused to take this shot—twice as far as the last time I'd tried to kill him. Magic flared, blurred; my concentration slipped. I couldn't keep that tight a focus from this distance. I was too damn tired.

I came back to my own body standing in the deserted road in the middle of nowhere.

Blood trickled from my nose, and I wiped it away absently. I had a headache that could swallow a city raging in my head, but I didn't care. I knew where that bastard was now.

I hauled my ass back into the SUV and checked to see if any cell phones had been left behind so I could warn Allie and Zay that Eli was about to come knocking.

Nothing.

Hell.

I revved the engine and tore off down the road to Portland.

Eleanor and Sunny had given up trying to talk to me. They sat in the backseat, probably planning my end.

A phone rang and I nearly hit my head on the ceiling.

"Jesus," I yelped.

It wasn't on me, not in the side pocket, not in the passenger's seat. I finally found it in the glove compartment. It wasn't my phone. Maybe Sunny's?

I glanced at the screen. Dash was calling.

I thumbed it on.

"What?" I said.

"Where are you?"

"Driving."

"Shame, listen to me." His voice was shaking. Yeah, well, he'd just watched me kill Terric. A good man. His friend. And there was the mess I'd made of Mina too. Plus, Sunny was still dead on the couch.

"Eli's in Portland," I said.

"What?"

"He's in Portland. Somewhere near St. Johns. I'm headed there."

"How do you know where Eli is?"

"I found his heartbeat."

Dash paused. "Did you call Zay?"

"No. You do that. Tell them he's nearby. Tell them he might have those drones with him. To kill them."

"Fuck. Okay. Shame, you need to listen to me. What you did to Terric—"

I chucked the phone at the door. It shattered and fell to the floor.

That might have been important, Sunny said.

"Shut up."

I was ragged-edge exhausted. The last hour of driving hadn't been exactly hands at ten and two, safety first. It was everything I could do to stay in the lane.

This had not been a good twenty-four hours, and before that I'd been dead.

I wasn't exactly at the top of my game.

So I was going to keep one thing ahead of me, one single thing I was going to get done: kill Eli. Nothing else would get in the way of that.

Shame? a voice whispered from behind me.

Not Sunny. Not Eleanor.

I glanced in the rearview mirror.

Terric sat in the backseat, no blood on his face, no pain in his eyes. He just looked annoyed.

Pretty much how I expected his ghost would look once it found me.

Eleanor and Sunny were ignoring him, staring out the window on either side. So either they couldn't see him, which was odd, or they didn't want to deal with him, which was more likely.

"Don't do this, Ter," I said, looking away from the anger that flickered across his face. "I didn't tie you to me. You can move on."

You idiot, he whispered.

I glanced in the mirror again. He was gone. Eleanor and Sunny hadn't even moved.

Okay. Apparently I was tired enough to be hallucinating.

My heart flopped painfully in my chest, slamming against bone. I swore my way through the agony. Heart attack?

Terric had died and decided to haunt me. Painfully.

Figured.

I blinked sweat out of my eyes and kept my foot on the gas. I was less than an hour away from Portland.

The highway took a bend, following the river. Dawn was wiping the stars out of the sky and leaving behind a swath of pale yellow and gray. Traffic, which had been sparse, thickened the closer I got to the city.

I didn't have time for a morning commute. I had a man to kill.

Traffic crawled down to a dead stop. The highway was blocked, a dozen black cars and a bulletproof box van parked across the road. Police walked between the cars, flashlights in hand, getting IDs. Looking for something. Maybe looking for me.

Krogher had connections. Police would be just the beginning of what he could throw at me.

The cops were headed to the truck in front of me. Which meant I'd be next.

Goddamn. If they thought they could stop me, they were wrong.

I took a breath, put the car in park, and got out.

Killing would be easy. But it would also be messy. I didn't have time for messy.

What are you doing? Sunny asked. *Shame, what are you doing?*

My stocking feet on the cold asphalt made no sound. In the pale light of morning, strangely unnecessary details stood out for me. The hole in my left sock heel, the smell of asphalt and tar, the I LIKE IT DIRTY written in the dust on the side of the truck.

And the Death magic that sat like a dangerous, but also nearly endless source, of magic in me.

I didn't have to be seen if I didn't want to be.

I didn't want to be.

I drew a quick Illusion, pulled on the magic within me, poured it into the spell. Asphalt cracked, growing things alongside the road turned brown, withered, died as Death drank them down.

And the Illusion caught silver fire, then fell around me like a spider-silk cloak.

No one saw me as I walked by. No one even looked my way.

I strode past the barricade of cars, past the armored van, to the last car on the other side of the roadblock.

The car was empty and convenient. I checked for keys. Got in, expanded the Illusion spell to cover the car—to make it look as if the car stayed behind.

The level of magic and skill it took to pull off a spell like that wasn't taught in kiddie school. It also wasn't easy.

Pain stabbed through my brain and I cussed and rubbed at my eyes until I could see some of the road ahead of me. It hurt like hell, but I didn't let go of the Illusion. Not yet. I turned the car toward Portland.

. . . you shouldn't be driving, Eleanor said. *If you pass out on the road, you'll kill yourself . . . probably.*

"Do you think I care?" I asked her. "Do you really think I give a damn about that anymore?"

How about car accidents? she said. *You could kill other people too. Innocent people. You can't tell me some part of you doesn't care about that.*

I looked over at her. "If I'd thought, for one second, that killing every man, woman, and child in a mile square, either side of that road, would have gotten me what I wanted, I would have drunk them down like cold water."

You don't mean that, she said. *You can't—*

"Shut up, El."

Just listen.

"Don't. Talk." I wiped the sweat off my face, swerved back in my lane, trying to hold that double Illusion spell just a little longer.

Shame! Eleanor screamed. *Look out!*

Terric stood in the middle of the highway. His ghost, anyway. He was not annoyed anymore. He was furious.

Turn back, he said, and I heard him even though I shouldn't at this distance, at this speed.

Hallucination?

I was going to hit him. Run him over unless I did something pretty quick to avoid it.

Would a ghost survive the impact of an automobile?

I lost the Illusion spell.

All I heard was Eleanor screaming.

And all I saw was Terric.

No time to avoid a collision. I drove right at him, braced for the hit. Ghosts don't offer a lot of physical resistance.

The car went right through him. More than that, he went right through me.

A stream of light and color and blinding pain flooded me, claimed me. Terric and I shared the same space for a split second, shared the same body.

I'd lived with a ghost for almost four years. Was living with two now, one of whom liked to punctuate her sentences with knives. I knew what it was like to be hit by a spirit, knew what it was like to be touched, knew what it was like to be stabbed.

This was nothing like that.

Everything that made Terric . . . well . . . Terric slammed into me. Memories, thoughts, fear, joy, hope, anger, a whirling cascade of faces, buildings, conversations, sensations of his life, the good, the very good, and the very, very bad.

Like taking down an entire bottle of whiskey in one shot.
He left me reeling.
Left me wanting. Wanting him.
Unfortunately I was still driving.
And then I blacked out.

Chapter 21

SHAME

I smelled bubble gum and cigarette smoke.

Opened my eyes. My lashes scraped across fabric. Blindfold. I tried moving my hands. Bound at the wrists with . . . I wiggled my hands . . . silk? Something that felt like a woman's scarf.

This wasn't right. I lifted my hands, ran into metal above me. Dragged my fingers across it, then out to one side, then the other. I was in a box. A metal box. Tied and blindfolded. The vibration of an engine transferred through the box along with the smoky bubble gum smell. Where the hell was I?

"Morning, sunshine," a woman's voice called out. "Are you awake?"

I knew that voice. Beatrice. One of Allie's, well, Sunny's Hounds. Which explained the bubble gum. And the smoke probably belonged to Jack, her partner.

I licked my lips. At least I wasn't gagged. I couldn't tell if Eleanor and Sunny were shoved in here with me. I couldn't feel them. Didn't hear them.

"Why am I in a box?"

There was some rustling around and then Bea's voice was just on the other side of the metal.

"We're taking you to St. Johns," she said, slowly and carefully as if I had a concussion.

"In a box?"

"Void stone box. You're pretty toxic right now, so we're taking precautions."

"Who are you working for, Bea?"

She laughed. "Come on, Shame. How long have you known me? Do you really think I'd take a job on the dark side?"

"If the money was right?"

"Okay, true. But there was no money. Dash called. Told us to track your ass down, hog-tie you, and lock you up. Also, to take you back to Portland. You've been a bad boy, Shamus. A lot of people aren't very happy with you."

"How did you find me?" I asked.

"Not hard to find an unmarked cop car driven off into the gully. Thanks for making it supereasy for us."

Hell. "Open the lid."

"Sorry. I can't. Just hold tight and think happy thoughts."

"Just because I'm locked up doesn't mean I don't have magic. You don't want to be in my way when I break out of this."

"Knock yourself out, babe," she said. "If you can break that box, I'll give you a standing ovation."

Death magic pooled in me, cold and sluggish as an icy stream. Bea wasn't kidding when she said the box was made of Void stones. I could reach the magic, could even bring it to the tips of my fingers. But it stopped there, like flame under water. Canceled, void.

I couldn't use magic to break out. I was tied up, bruised and banged up enough I couldn't tear my way out of the thing either.

"Eleanor?" I said quietly. "Sunny?"

No answer. I didn't know if that was good or bad.

So I closed my eyes and thought happy thoughts of Eli's head on a platter.

After maybe half an hour, the car stopped.

"Hold tight, sugar," Bea said. "We'll just be a minute." Doors opened, closed. I couldn't hear people moving or talking, but they weren't gone for long.

Another door opened. Sounded like a hatchback.

"Ready?" Jack said.

"You going to open this thing?" I asked.

The box slid, and I heard hands grabbing at the side of it, a couple of grunts as I was lifted, like a corpse in a coffin, out of the car, then carried.

"Really?" I yelled.

No answer.

I was pretty sure I was taken up some stairs, then maybe an elevator. When I finally came to rest, it sounded as though it was on something padded.

Footsteps backed away. Wooden floor. Silence. Another set of footsteps came near. Then a latch was popped on each side of the coffin and the lid was drawn away.

The rush of air told me two things: One, I was at the Den, the Hounds' headquarters in Portland. Two, I hadn't been sold out.

"Sorry for the ride," Cody said. "But you were down-hilling crazy, Shame."

"You think that was crazy? If you don't get this blindfold off me, I'll show you crazy."

He grabbed my arm, hauled back, and helped me sit, but he didn't help me out of the box yet.

He did, however, untie the blindfold.

I blinked, glad that they'd pulled the curtains on all the windows of the place. They'd done a little remodeling since the last time I had been here, put up some walls in the loft space to create a bedroom of sorts. A couple of bunk beds lined the walls, and a few cots scattered in the center. That's where they'd set the Void stone box—on top of a cot.

Only Cody was in the room with me. Well, Cody and Eleanor and Sunny, who stood on either side of the box. The black rope that tied me to the two ghosts remained intact.

Eleanor waved her fingers at me.

"What in the hell are you thinking?" I asked.

Cody drew out a knife and cut the scarf—it was pink and silk, probably Bea's—off my wrists.

"You were out of control. We needed your attention. Luckily, you drove off into a ditch and made it easy for us to find you and box you up."

"Where are Zay and Allie? Are they okay? Have you found Eli? Did he send the drones after them?"

Cody turned to one of the nightstands while I worked on removing myself from the box. I stood, and then thought better of it, took a step, and sat on a different cot.

He handed me a glass of water. "Drink."

I took it. Drained the glass. God, I was thirsty. And I hurt. Everywhere.

"I'm under strict orders to make you shower," he said. "I'll answer questions while you scrape some of the blood and grime off, okay?"

"Whose orders?"

"Dash's." He pointed to the door at the far end of the room. "Just shower, Flynn. You look like hell and smell worse."

"Allie and Zay?"

"Still having the baby. Still okay. Dash has people there. They know about Eli. Shower and we'll do another round of Q and A."

He pointed again.

I pushed off the cot and headed to the shower on sore feet and sore muscles. It even hurt to breathe in too deep.

I heard voices out in the main loft area, men and women,

but didn't bother trying to track them. Now that I was moving, I knew Cody was right. I was filthy, wounded, and exhausted. Fighting Death magic constantly, and letting it take over my body and do whatever it wanted with me did not appear to be a path toward health and happiness.

Who knew?

The bathroom was set up like a locker room, without the lockers. No-frills tile floor and walls, three shower stalls and changing areas to the left, bench down the middle, shelves for towels and supplies above mirrors, and sinks to the right, toilet stalls to the back.

I pushed my way into the first shower, tugged off my T-shirt, which hurt, then my jeans and socks.

Left it all on the floor in the corner, turned on the water, and got in.

Holy fuck, it hurt. Every nick, every cut, every bullet hole—and I had an impressive collection in various sizes— burned.

I braced my arm against the wall and let the water pour over me. When that pain became familiar, I looked around for soap, found a bottle that said BodyWash, and poured some of that fresh hell into my hands and over my skin.

"Son of a bitch." I clenched my teeth, scrubbed as hard as I could bear, digging fingers and soap into my wounds. "Goddamn."

"You okay in there?" Cody asked.

"I'm friggin' perfect, thanks."

I washed my hair, did one last sluice, then got out. I wiped my hair back and rubbed my face, then shook water off my hands. I'd forgotten a towel.

Opened the door. Cody was sitting on the bench. He looked up as I got out, his gaze taking in my wounds.

"Holy shit, Flynn. You need a doctor, you know."

"A towel," I said. "I need a towel."

He pointed to the shelf I was already walking toward.

They were perfectly nice towels. I'm sure they were relatively soft. But it felt as if I were sandpapering off a couple layers of skin along with water and blood.

"Where are we at on the clothing situation?" I asked.

He lifted a plastic bag out to me. "We asked one of the Hounds to stop by your place and bring you something. Of course, he found your dresser had been turned into a pile of ash, so he did a little thrift-shopping for you. You owe him twenty bucks."

I took the bag, opened it. Pulled out a yellow T-shirt with a picture on it. "A monkey in a space suit?"

Cody leaned my way to get a look at it. "Curious George. He's such a naughty monkey."

"Which Hound picked this up?"

"Sid. I can see why he got it for you. The resemblance is uncanny."

"Oh, for the love of—" I shrugged into the shirt, put on the boxers, which were thankfully new, not used, and then got into the faded, hole-riddled old blue jeans that were a lot softer than I'd expected.

"Do we have eyes on Eli?" I asked.

"Not yet. Hounds are looking, though."

"I can find him," I said as I walked out of the bathroom.

"There's something you need to know first. Before you do that. Before you do anything else, Shame."

"Before I put on these socks? Because my feet are killing me."

"Even before socks."

We were almost to the bunk room. "Do not make me play twenty questions with you, because I will use my fists. Out with it."

"It's just, well, right there in front of you."

I stepped into the bedroom area.

Right in front of me, about halfway across the room, stood a man. A little taller than me, good-looking with white hair pulled back in a band at the nape of his neck, he wore a plain white T-shirt, jeans and a smile.

"Terric?" I breathed.

He held his hands out to the side, and the corner of his mouth turned up in a smile.

For an aching moment, I wondered if I was seeing things. Seeing what I wanted, who I wanted. He could be a ghost—I certainly saw ghosts. He could be a hallucination—I certainly saw my share of those too.

But the way he held himself, his left shoulder hitched just a little higher than the right, his head tilted, was one hundred percent Terric.

One hundred percent real.

One hundred percent my brother, my Soul Complement standing there.

My heart kicked so hard I couldn't breathe fast enough to keep up with it. My vision went a little dark at the edges.

"Hey, Shame," he said, words I thought I'd never hear again, a voice I thought I'd never hear again. "Sorry for the box—"

He didn't get a chance to say anything more. I strode across the room, grabbed him by the T-shirt, and pulled him into a tight hug.

"Jesus, Ter. You were dead," I said, my arms locked around his shoulders, my heart thumping with a new kind of pain. I didn't want this to be a dream or hallucination. I wanted, with everything I had, for this to be real.

He returned the embrace, leaning into me a bit as if surprised but grateful for the contact.

"So I've been told," he said.

"I felt you die, Ter." He was solid, warm, and real in my arms. I could smell the soap and medicine that clung to his skin. "You're alive, right? Really alive?"

"I'm alive, Shame," he said. "Right here. Real."

"And you're okay?" I unlocked my arms, moved back,

the sleeve of his T-shirt still gripped in my fist. "Do you need a doctor? A hospital? Are you hungry?"

He knit his eyebrows, his glacier blue gaze searching my face. "I don't need a doctor. I'm feeling fine. Considering what I heard happened to me."

"You don't remember?" I couldn't let go of him. Not yet. I didn't want him to disappear. His hand was still resting on my shoulder too.

"I remember some of it," he said. "Of . . . us. Not the dying part."

"Good," I said. "Good. It's better you don't remember that. It was just blood and pain, you know, like you'd expect. Pain and dying. Bloody way to go. But boring."

"And now you're babbling," he said. "Are *you* okay?"

The knife sliced his throat. There was blood, his blood, everywhere as he fell to the floor, Eli above him . . .

I pushed that memory away. Terric was standing here, smiling, in front of me. I was going to hold on to that for all I was worth.

"Me? Yes. Of course. I'm good, mate. Good. What's the last thing you remember?"

"Dash." He glanced over at Cody as if checking to see if he'd gotten the name right for the man we'd worked with for years.

Cody nodded.

That was my first clue that everything was not okay with Terric.

"Dash told me I was taken and tortured."

This was Terric. Real, alive Terric. Felt like Terric. Sounded like him, smelled like him. I knew he was real.

But there was something about him, a sort of guarded pain he was carrying.

"You don't remember that. That's okay. What do you remember?"

"Not much," he said, finally letting go of my shoulder. "They think I was Closed."

Son of a bitch.

I glanced at Cody. "Think?"

"We haven't had a lot of time to deal with it yet," he said. "We thought it was important to get you two together as soon as possible. If he was Closed, it was a botched job."

"It's like Swiss cheese in here," Terric said, pointing at his head. "I do remember some things. My parents. You. Victor." He smiled. "I thought maybe we could talk to him about how I was Closed. He might have some idea how to deal with it."

He didn't even remember Victor was dead. That Eli had killed him. That we hadn't been able to save him before Eli tore him apart with his bare hands.

"I don't think," I said before the memory of Victor, and the still-fresh grief of losing him cut off my breath. "No," I finished. "I don't think we can talk to him about this. Are you . . ." I looked away to Cody again. ". . . is he all right?"

"He's standing right here," Terric said. He patted my shoulder just in case I hadn't heard him. "Do you want to sit down maybe?"

I realized I was still holding on to his shirt like a little kid who was afraid to get lost in a crowd. "Sorry," I said, unwadding my grip and letting my hand fall to my side.

"It's okay." He tipped his head down just a bit to catch my gaze. "It's nice to be missed."

Ah, Terric, I thought. *You don't know the half of it.*

"You were," I said. "Missed. Place went to hell without you."

"I can see that. You're wearing a monkey shirt. A very yellow monkey shirt."

"I'll be killing Sid for that later," I said.

"See," Cody said, "I told you it would work, Shame."

"What would work?" Terric asked.

I threw Cody a dirty look, but he hadn't been intimidated by me since . . . well, never.

"It's nothing," I said. "You know how Cody is."

"Shame killed you," Cody said.

I tipped my head back and closed my eyes, exhaled the flash of anger. "Goddamn it, Miller."

"Killed me," Terric said. "Shame?"

He thought it was a joke. Probably because Cody was the one who had said it and Cody hadn't always been the most reliable guy back in the day.

I lowered my gaze until I was looking Terric straight in the eye. "Cody's telling the truth. You were barely alive. He thought the Life magic in you wouldn't let you go, but wasn't strong enough to bring you back either. Maybe coma, maybe just years of dying, suffering . . ."

I cleared my throat. "So I did. I . . . killed you. I let Death take you down."

"You killed me," he said flatly.

"Yes."

"And that's what brought you back," Cody said. "Death triggered Life magic to put you back together, to raise you from the ashes. You crazy Soul Complement kids can break all the magic rules."

"All right," Terric said slowly. "Fine. I'm alive. But if you killed me, then you owe me. Big-time, Flynn."

"Anything," I said.

He took a couple of steps back and ran his hand over his hair, dislodging tendrils that fell over his eyes. "That"—he pointed at me—"officially freaks me out."

"What?" I said.

"Not that you look like a skeleton, have bruises and burns and cuts . . . everywhere and you don't seem to feel them. Not that I've never seen you look so burned out, raw, on the edge."

"Then what?" I asked again.

"How long have I been dead?"

"Not long."

"Really? You've never given in so quickly on anything, Shame. *Anything.* You always put up a fight over every last damn detail of every last damn thing. And . . . and now you instantly promise me anything I want to make up for something you did, no questions asked? How long have I been dead?"

"Too. Damn. Long," I whispered.

I didn't think I'd ever surprised him into silence before.

Maybe because I rarely told him the truth. Maybe because he could feel my pain.

"Okay," he finally said. "It's okay."

"So, are we good here?" Cody asked. "Because I am starving." He motioned for us to follow him out of the room.

"Why are we at the Den?" Terric asked.

"Well, there was a madman killing innocent people we needed to stop," Cody said.

I knew he wasn't talking about Eli; he was talking about me. I would have flipped him off, but he was right. I had been out of control, out of my mind.

But now that Terric was alive, the Death magic that twisted and turned inside me was easier to control.

"Madman," Terric said. "He means you, doesn't he?"

"Shut up," I said, then, "Yes."

"Who did you kill?" Terric asked.

"A lot of people," I said. "But that isn't what matters."

We left the bunk room and made our way out into the main area.

Dash leaned against the back of one of the couches, arms crossed over his chest, looking our way.

Jack and Bea were on the other side of the room, also on their feet, Jack's arm around Bea's shoulders.

"It matters," Dash said. "Tell us, Shame. If we're going to

deal with the fallout, we need to know where it's coming from."

"Food?" Cody said to Terric.

Terric looked at me, then at Cody and Dash. "I'm good." Then: "This won't be the first time I've heard Shame catch hell for some idiot thing he's done. Go ahead."

"Standing right here," I said.

"All right," Dash said. "Tell us."

All eyes on me. "I killed the people in the warehouse, gunmen," I said, "the six drones at the door." I took a breath, then, "I killed Mina and Sunny."

"Sunny?" Terric said. "Shit, Shame."

"Was it an accident?" Dash asked. He sounded hopeful.

"Not really. Death wanted them dead." I could tell them I'd tried to stop it, tried not to hurt them, but nothing I would say could excuse what I'd done.

"And where were you while Death was getting what it wanted?" Terric asked.

I looked over at him. Didn't know how to say I was there, but broken. Didn't know how to tell him that his death had been more than I could shoulder, and I had fucked everything up without him. Didn't know how to say coming back to life might have been the worst thing that had ever happened to me.

I didn't have to tell him any of that. Damaged memory or not, he knew me. Knew the guilt and other crap that crowded all my corners.

Jack, who lingered with Bea near the windows, whistled low. "Always knew you'd go Hannibal Lecter one of these days, Flynn. Sorry I'm here to see it."

"Then don't be here," I suggested.

He easily had a decade on me but was smoked down to a tough, leathery finish. Not the kind of man any sane person would pick a fight with. He gave me a steady look, sizing up a target he'd be shooting at soon.

Yeah, good luck with that.

"Is there anything else we need to know?" Terric asked.

"Eli's in town," I said. "Eli Collins. He wants us dead. Zay and Allie too."

"Zay and . . . who?" Terric said.

"Wow," Cody muttered. "You really did get your noggin scrambled."

"First," Dash said, "the current emergency. That's you, Shame. How out of control are you?"

"As compared to what?"

"Full-tilt serial killer."

"Pretty sure I can keep a lid on that."

"Pretty sure?" Jack said.

"I'm good right now. Better," I said. "It's all you're going to get from me, Dash. I'll do what I can."

"We can't just take your word for it," he said. "I'm sorry, but our friends died while you were doing what you could to stay in control."

"I'll watch him," a new voice said.

Davy Silvers paced into the room. He wore clean jeans and a T-shirt, his hair cut short and damp from a shower. The blue light that had been leaking out of him back at the house was gone. From how the T-shirt caught at his ribs and stomach, he was wrapped in a lot of cotton and gauze.

There used to be a time I'd describe him as a laid-back surfer dude. Not now. The words that better fit him were *simmering violence* and maybe *psychotic break*.

"I don't think that's a working solution," Dash said.

"I'll be working." Davy's gaze was locked on me even though he was talking to Dash. "Watching him. I'll stop him if he kills. Or anything."

"We're all on the same side here," Dash said in a calm tone.

"Right," Davy said. "Sunny's dead. How did that happen, Shame?"

"Davy," Dash said.

"It's okay," I said to Dash. "He's right. You watch me, Davy. You take your shot anytime you think you have it."

"Shame," Terric said. "This isn't how we handle this."

"There's a way we handle this?" I said. "We've never even dealt with this before. I'm walking death. You've been half Closed and killed. And Davy here, he's . . ."

"He's what?" Davy asked quietly.

"I don't know," I said honestly. "But you've been under Eli's knife, just like Terric. That worries me. What do you think he did to you for his gain? What loopholes do you think he carved into you? It should worry you."

"Yeah, that's right," Davy said. "I'm the problem here."

"No," I said.

"The problem," Cody interrupted, "is we're standing around talking when we should be getting lunch. Or breakfast."

"Our problems are Eli," I said, "and Krogher and his drones."

Davy swallowed hard, his hands curling up into fists. He gave me a very short nod.

Well, at least the guy who wanted to kill me agreed we both wanted to kill other people first.

I saw what Sunny saw in the guy.

Chapter 22

SHAME

Cody clapped his hands. "Now that that's *not* settled, let's eat. Bea, Jack, is there any food in this place?"

"Aw," Bea said, "just when things were getting interesting." She ducked out from under Jack's arm, then caught his hand and made him walk with her into the kitchen. "Don't you boys kill each other while we're gone, okay?"

Cody chuckled and followed them.

"So, why don't we deal with the real problem?" Terric said as he strolled over to a recliner near the window. He sat with the kind of ease of someone who had Life magic in his bones, and was therefore fully healed. "Eli and Krogher. What do we know?"

Born leader, that man.

I glanced at Dash, who had pulled off his glasses and was rubbing at the corners of his eyes. He was exhausted, pale from pain, and painkillers, and too damn much death and shooting and killing in the last twenty-four hours.

When he pushed away from the back of the couch, he limped, that thigh wound still giving him hell.

"What we know," he said as he sat on the couch, "is that Shame said Eli's heartbeat was in Portland. Near St. Johns."

"You can tell that?" Terric asked.

I nodded.

"We don't think Eli knows we're in town," Dash said. "But he knows where Allie and Zay live."

I paced over to a window to one side of Terric, pushed the blind aside with my finger. Morning now, all sunlight and happy skies.

"Every Hound in town has their ear to the ground," Dash said. "Jack and Bea were very careful to leave trails away from this place. If Eli is hunting for you, Shame—he's taking his time."

"Who says he's hunting for me? He's looking for Allie and Zay. To kill them."

"They haven't seen any sign of him."

"Has she had the baby yet?" I asked.

"Baby?" Terric asked. "Wait. Zayvion's having a baby? With . . . Who's Allie?"

I pressed the heel of my hand over the headache in my temple. Lord. This amnesia crap was only fun in the movies.

"She's his Soul Complement," Dash said. "I'll check in with them again." He pushed up onto his feet, exhaling on a soft groan, and pulled a phone from his pocket. Then he paced over to where Davy had stalked off to on the other side of room.

"So," Terric said to me, "Chase and Zay obviously didn't work out. Chase is . . . ?"

"She's dead," I said.

"Ah," Terric closed his eyes as if I'd just punched him in the chest.

Dash put his hand on Davy's shoulder and guided him to the collection of couches where he could sit and still keep me in his line of sight.

Sunny floated over to stand near Davy. She just looked sad.

"I'm sorry," I said to Terric. "It was a long time ago."

He pointed at his head. "Really sloppy work. Lots of holes."

"Do you have any idea who Closed you?" I asked.

He stared off in the distance for a minute. Processing Chase's death, maybe sorting through memories. He tipped his palms, then folded his fingers together loosely in his lap. "There's a lot of people who could have done it, right?"

"No," I said. "Not really. Magic's changed since the old days. It's not easy to power those kinds of big spells anymore. Soul Complements can do it—break magic into dark and light. So either Krogher has Soul Complements at his disposal, one of which also happens to be a Closer—"

"Faith magic," Terric added.

"Right, and uses Faith magic to Close, or he's using the drones for the power and he has a Closer on call. I just don't know who Krogher could hire to do it."

Anyone, Sunny said from near Davy. *Lot of ex-Closers in the world.*

Maybe. Not many I'd trust.

"You know how UnClosing works, right?" I said to Terric.

"Whoever cast the Close spell is the only one who can UnClose that person," Terric said.

Thus, our problem.

"Eli, maybe?" he said. "I don't know. I have bits, fragments. I don't know if they're memories. Is he a Closer?"

"No. He's an asshole."

"I'm getting that impression. Is it something Zayvion could handle? UnClosing me. Or someone else . . ."

Here's where he should say Victor, but he locked gazes with me. We might not be as connected as we were, but we'd known each other for a long time.

I looked away, unable to hold the thought of Victor's death between us.

"God," he breathed. "When? How?"

"A few months ago. Bloody. At Eli's hands."

"I don't even remember Eli being ... anything. Is that what started this? Victor's death?"

"No. We started this."

"How?"

"What do you remember about me? About us?" I asked.

"Well, you tried to kill me once and never forgave yourself."

"Yeah, sure. Which time?"

His eyebrows shot up. "Are you serious? How many times have you tried to kill me?"

"It's still in the low single digits." I gave him a smile.

He grinned. "So I see things are going well between us."

"Oh yeah. We're fantastic."

"Great." He watched me stare outside for a bit. "Dash gave me the quick rundown about ... well, I guess most of the changes with magic, and the drone people Eli made for Krogher."

"Is that all he told you about?"

"I know we're ... Soul Complements, or maybe something more. Life and Death? He was a little vague about the specifics."

I tried not to wince at the way he hedged around admitting we were Soul Complements. I'd never thought he'd had a problem with that idea. He had always been the one telling me to get over it and deal with the link we had with each other.

"We're Soul Complements," I said evenly. "We can use magic together better than most. And we can break it."

"All right," he said. "And you carrying Death magic and me carrying Life magic *in* our bodies. This is a thing?"

"No. It's just our thing."

"Why?"

"Because we absolutely suck at watching each other die

and have done ridiculous things, made sacrifices . . ." I shook my head. "We screwed up so many times with magic, I'm pretty sure this is our punishment."

"Being stuck with each other?" he said with a small smile.

"Terminally."

"I could think of worse," he said.

"Yeah, well, you also have amnesia, so you don't know how bad it is."

"I know you're still overly dramatic."

"Or I'm just right," I said.

"And you still have to get the last word."

"True."

"How about some sandwiches, boys?" Bea called out. She held a couple cups of coffee in each hand. Jack walked next to her with a platter of sandwiches.

Bea gave us the coffee, flashed her dimples, and carried the other two cups over to Davy and Dash. Dash thumbed off his phone.

Jack offered me the sandwich platter and a look that told me he'd prefer it if I were still tied up in the box.

"Thanks." I took a sandwich, as did Terric and Dash, who walked our way.

"Allie and Zay?" I asked around a mouthful. Ham, cheese, and tomato on rye. Not bad.

Dash took a drink of coffee, closed his eyes for a moment before tipping the cup away and easing down on the couch.

"No sign of Eli. No baby yet," he said.

Terric grunted. "Still can't believe he's going to be a father. Zayvion." He shook his head.

"Can you find Eli, Shame?" Dash asked. "His heartbeat?"

"I think so." Half my sandwich was gone and I'd barely tasted it. "You don't want to be near me when I do."

"If we're going to be the ones to take Eli down," Terric said, "to keep Zayvion and . . . Allie?"

I nodded.

"Allie safe," he continued, "I need my memories back so I can use magic. So that we can use magic."

"You don't remember how to use magic?"

"No. Whoever Closed me got that part right. I have memories of casting spells, I know there are glyphs involved, but using magic . . . I don't have it, Shame. And I can't begin to tell you how much I want that back."

The old fire flickered behind his eyes. Sure, he was broken. He'd paid prices that didn't just fade away with the wave of a magic healing eraser.

In some ways, not remembering what had happened in the last week, hell, in the last three years or more, was a kindness.

Right. As if kindness was ever in the cards.

"Can you access magic at all?" Dash asked. "The Life magic in you?"

Terric took another drink of coffee, then shook his head. "I don't even know what I'm trying to access. Giving it the name *Life magic* is just giving it a name like *purple giraffe*. I don't know how to get at it, don't know where to look for it, don't know how to manipulate it."

"We don't know who Closed you," Dash said.

"So we have Zay take care of it," Terric said. "UnClose me. Next to Victor, he's the best Closer I know."

"Still, he wasn't the one who Closed you. It won't work."

"If Zayvion is half as good as I remember," Terric said, "he'll make it work."

"He's in the middle of having a baby," I said. "And I don't think that's going as smoothly as they hoped. He's too preoccupied to be doing magical surgery on your brain. He'll fuck it up for good."

"Then you do it, Shame," Terric said. "You know me better than anyone, right?"

Could you? Eleanor asked.

All this talking to living people had made me forget that there were two ghosts standing in the room over by Davy.

"What?" I said to both Eleanor and Terric. "No. Absolutely not."

"You said we were tied," Terric said. "That we use magic together better than most. So use magic. On me. Open up my brain, Shame." He flashed me a smile. "Trust me, it's not an offer you're going to get more than once in a lifetime."

Yes, Eleanor said. *You should. You should do this, Shame.*

"No. Not having memories is bad," I said. "But having your mind broken because an untrained Death magic user—hello, me—tries to pop your lid is a one-way ticket to Lobotomyville, Terric."

"All right." He leaned back. Gave me that "how about we run this theory through its paces?" look. I hated that look. "Give me another option."

"We call a Closer from the old days," I said. "Someone who knows the drill."

"Okay, good. Now tell me how this Closer is going to access enough magic to break what's been done to me. You said only Soul Complements and Krogher's drones can tap in to that much magic."

I scowled at him. Hated when he made sense. Hated when he showed me how very wrong I was.

"You can access magic, Shame," he said evenly, as if carefully picking a lock and waiting to feel the tumblers give. "It's inside you. And you know how to use it. If Zay's not an option, then you're the only one who can get my memories back."

"Another Soul Complement could do it," I said. "Someone who was a Closer."

"Got one of those in your pocket?"

"No."

"So we go with my plan."

"What is the plan, exactly?" Dash asked.

"Crazy over there wants me to restore his memories," I said.

"I heard that part," Dash said. "You're not a Closer, Shame. If I remember correctly, you failed that part of the magic-user test."

I pointed to my chest. "Choir here, Bible boy."

"He has magic and ability to use it. He also has incentive to try to do it right," Terric said. "Good enough for me."

"Since when did you become the reckless one?" I asked.

Terric gave me a smile I hadn't seen in years. "Being tied to you? Please. I've always been the reckless one. Stop being such an old woman about this. No big risk, no blue ribbons."

Good Lord, he sounded like Cody.

"So what I'm hearing," Dash said, "is we have no plan."

This was a bad idea. A very bad idea. But I didn't have a better one.

Terric raised one eyebrow. Daring me.

There was a chance, a very small one, that this could work.

Plus, I could never turn down his dares.

"I'm not doing this on my own," I said. "Not without instructions and a Closer. Dash, call Hayden. Tell him we'll meet him out at Mum's inn."

Chapter 23

SHAME

"What happened to it?" Terric bent just a bit to see the inn out the car window.

The remodeling was in the "nuclear warhead came knocking" phase, about a quarter of the place demolished, a quarter of it propped up by wooden bracers and another quarter of it caged under scaffolding.

"Mum happened to it," I said. Then, at Terric's questioning look: "She's finally doing that remodeling she always wanted to have done."

I got out of the backseat—Dash had insisted on driving and Davy wouldn't stay at the Den no matter what we threatened him with—and paced away from the inn toward the river.

Before going in there, near Hayden—hell, near Dash and Davy—I needed some air. The food hadn't slaked my hunger, and the last life Death magic had sucked down—Mina—was gone.

Death wanted to be fed. It dragged against the inside of my skull, heavy, needful. Being around Terric helped. But I did not want to slip up now.

Sunny and Eleanor drifted alongside me. They hadn't said much since I'd been thrown in the box. Maybe being tied to me was draining them too. They seemed paler, thinner. Sunny caught me looking at her out of the corner of my eye and flipped me off.

Well, at least she wasn't any less angry at me. It was the little things that counted in a new relationship.

I opened the cage on Death magic, just enough to let it seep out from beneath my feet, seeking nourishment.

All those hearts beating hot behind me, easy to take.

Shame, Eleanor said.

But I wasn't reaching for the lives Death wanted. Wasn't reaching for what would sate it fully.

Trees, bushes, grass would have to do. I pushed Death that way, sent it toward the river, toward the tangle of green and brown and bloom, and drank its meager broth.

There was a never-ending hole inside me. All the plants in the world weren't enough to fill it. But it helped.

"Morning," Hayden said from the porch. "What's the emergency?"

"Hayden," Terric said. "It's good to see you. It's been a while."

Hayden frowned. "Saw you just over a week ago. You okay?"

"No," Dash said, "that's why we're here. We need your help."

Davy got out of the car and stood there a moment staring at me. I was half-turned toward the inn, so I saw Hayden take in the situation and lean back a bit on one leg.

"Shamus?" He somehow shoved an entire "what have you done now?" into the two syllables of my name.

I turned toward the house, elbowed Death magic back behind the walls in my head, and locked it down. I crunched my way across gravel.

"Nice to see you, Hayden," I said. "Love what you haven't done with the place."

"You boys in trouble?" he asked.

"Are trouble," I said.

Hayden grunted and stepped out of the way of the door. "Well, come on in. Let's hear what it is this time."

Terric and Davy and Dash all walked past him and through the door he held open with the stump of his arm. He'd lost a hand the last time we stopped an apocalypse. He hadn't let it slow him down much.

I was hoping he'd step into the inn before me so I could keep some distance between us, but he waited for me.

"Shame. You need a doctor, son?"

I shook my head. "Naw, I'm good."

You're a mess, Sunny said, floating into the room before me.

Hayden wasn't buying it either. "You're scratched up and bruised," he said. "You have that hungry look in your eyes, and you're wearing a monkey shirt. You're a mess."

"Yeah, well," I said.

"Killed anyone lately?" he asked.

"Define lately."

"Want to try that again?" he said.

"I'm upright," I said. "Let's call that proof that I am fine."

"There might still be clothes up in your room. Put on long sleeves before your mother sees those holes in you."

"She's here?" I stopped short, not wanting her to see me, not wanting to explain why and how I'd completely lost this fight with the monster within me.

I'd killed Mina. I'd killed Sunny. I couldn't tell my mother that.

"She's in the kitchen pulling together some food. If you're fast and quiet, you'll get past her."

I was neither of those things right now, so I just stepped into the inn, noisy and slow.

"Dear Lord." The interior was torn down to studs. Painting tarps covered the old marble floor. All the light fixtures were gone, leaving bare bulbs hanging from the ceiling. Sawhorses, a drawing table, and a pile of power tools cluttered up the place.

When Mum said she was taking it down to bare walls, she was not messing around.

At least this time the destruction was on purpose. We'd had to do a hasty rebuild a couple of years ago after that explosion we'd set off to try to kill Leander—a Soul Complement who'd gone to death, come back with a hankering for revenge, and tried to destroy the world.

Strange, how that story sounded familiar.

The clatter of dishes in the kitchen reminded me that I needed to get moving, and I did, even though it felt strange to leave Terric behind. I crossed the room, turned down the hall, and then up the stairs to my old room.

The door to every room was off its hinges, leaning against the wall opposite.

I strolled into my room. All my furniture was set to one side, boxes labeled and piled up neatly. A box marked CLOTHES was in the bedroom. I flicked open my pocketknife and slit the packing tape. Pulled out a monkeyless T-shirt, hoodie, underwear, jeans, and socks. Went into the bathroom, changed.

Sunny stood in the dry shower, her hands on her hips. *Gonna give me a show?*

"Don't care if you watch. You aren't the first ghost who's haunted me."

You haven't missed anything, Eleanor said.

I chuckled at that.

Tell Davy I'm here, Sunny said.

"I think he knows."

I don't care. I want you to tell him I'm still here.

"What would that get you, Sunny? He's already hurting over you being dead. Being undead? What do you think that's going to do to him?"

He needs to know, she said. *I need him to know.*

"Maybe we don't all get what we need," I said. "I didn't mean to kill you, Sunny, but that's on me. My fault. And if I can, I'll find a way for you to finish dying."

You're telling a ghost you want her more dead?

"Trust me," I said, looking straight into her faded eyes, "there're much better places to be than haunting my wreck of a life."

She didn't seem to know what to say to that, so I dressed, looked for shoes since mine were currently in a ditch somewhere between Umatilla and Irrigon.

Will you think about it? Sunny asked. *About telling Davy?*

Found a pair of sneakers, laced them up. "Yes," I said. "Just. Give me some time."

I ran my fingers through my hair again and headed downstairs. Hungry. I couldn't shake the hunger.

Everyone was gathered in the main dining area, sitting on sawhorses or leaning against the worktable or walls.

"Shamus?" Mum said as I walked in. Hayden had his arm around her. I figured he'd warned her about what I looked like, but maybe he hadn't warned her enough.

Her expression made me look away.

"You need a doctor," she said.

"I need food." I headed over to the tray of lemonade and finger food spread across a folding table and helped myself to a pile of food. I'd been careful to put on a hoodie to cover the bullet holes in my arms. All she could see were the cuts and bruises I sported on my hands and face. Well, that and the general deathness of me.

"I wasn't asking you, I was telling you," she said. "I'm going to call someone."

"Don't, please, Mum."

But she was already walking out of the room.

Fantastic.

"You know better than to argue with your mom," Hayden said.

"Pointless," I said around a mouthful of club sandwich that should taste like heaven but was plain as ash. Food wasn't what I was hungry for. I wanted life. I wanted death.

"I'm fine enough. Until we're done with this."

"With what?" Hayden asked.

Dash started in on the situation, telling Hayden we wanted him to guide me through the UnClosing I was going to throw at the walls in Terric's head. The big man wasn't having anything of it. I moved to the side of the room near the door and let Mr. Spade try to talk Hayden into our crazy scheme while I inhaled three sandwiches and a couple of tall glasses of ice-cold lemonade.

The food sat heavy in my gut but didn't feed my hunger. If anything, it only made me hungrier.

Great.

What did you expect? Sunny asked. *You know what that hunger wants. You know what that hunger is—death.*

"Shut up," I muttered. Maybe a little too loud.

Dash shut up and looked over at me.

Even though I wasn't talking to him, I went with it. "I'm doing it," I said.

"No, you aren't," Hayden said. "I've seen a lot of stupid in my years, but you've just Nobeled that prize, boy."

"We need Eli dead," I said. "For that, Terric and I need to be able to break magic. For us to do *that* with any kind of control, we have to unlock the walls in Terric's head. Whoever Closed him isn't going to just come on over here and do us a solid. Zay's out of the picture, Victor's dead—and so are half a dozen other Closers Eli made sure to off months ago. We don't have options. We just have you, Hayden."

"Don't think you do," he rumbled.

I glanced at Dash and Terric. Terric shook his head slightly. We'd known Hayden since we were young. Knew that when he dug in his heels, it would take a couple sticks of dynamite and a gallon of gasoline to budge him.

"Well, then I guess we just have me," I said. "I'd like to give you a say in this, Hayden, but you either step in to help or step out of the way."

"Is that how it is?" Hayden asked Terric. "Is that how you want it?"

"We were going to do it without you before Shame thought you might help," he said. "So, yes, I think that's how it is."

"No," Mum said, from where she stood in the shadows of the hall.

"Mum." I shook my head. "It's decided."

She walked the rest of the way into the room, closing the distance between us. Her heart was beating a little hard. Not fear of me—fear for me.

I kept my hands open, ready to block if she was throwing magic, or a knife. Growing up with a Blood magic user as a mother kept a troublemaker on his toes.

But when she was near enough, she just placed her hand over my heart. Her gentle touch stilled me more effectively than any blade.

She stood there, looking into my eyes.

My heart was beating at about half the rate of any living person, and I knew my body was cold to the touch, even after the hot shower, even through my layer of clothes. I'd died—the real no-breathing parade. And it was clear coming back to life had left me changed. Had left too much of me dead.

I waited.

"Do you hear yourself?" she asked quietly. "Do you understand that you can't undo the damage done to Terric because you aren't the one who damaged him?"

"I watched him die, in my kitchen, at the hands of a madman I couldn't stop," I said so quietly only she would hear me. "I am the one who damaged him."

"Terric's alive. You see that, don't you? Whatever happened to you—"

"I died too," I said. "Not figuratively. Eli *killed* me."

Ah, there was the shock, the sorrow. Her emotions ran blood deep, through the familial tie between us. I didn't want to say more, but I couldn't stop now. "Eli walked into my house and shot me full of bullets. Killed Terric too, sliced his neck, dragged him off to be tortured, and let someone Close him."

I could feel the edges of her sorrow, could almost taste it on my tongue.

The Death magic inside me yearned for that pain.

She must have seen that. Seen how her pain kicked up the hunger in me.

She stepped back. "I am against this, Shamus."

"I know," I said.

"I can't watch this," she said. "Won't."

"Then maybe you shouldn't be here, Mum."

She held my gaze a moment more, then turned her back on me and walked out.

I could count on one hand how many times she'd turned away from me. Each time she'd been right to do so. I had screwed up each of those times by not listening to her. Maybe I was screwing up now.

"You still think this is a good idea?" Hayden asked.

"I never said it was a good idea. But it needs to be done. Are you going to help or not?"

He looked off the way my mom had gone, then back at Terric. "I'm standing here, aren't I?"

Yes, that surprised me.

"Did Dash tell you what we need?" I asked.

"Other than matching straitjackets?" Hayden paced away

from the wall, pointed at Terric. "Cop a squat, Terric. This would hurt at the hands of an experienced Closer. An amateur like Shame isn't going to make this any kind of joyride."

"Amateur?" I complained.

Terric looked around, decided the floor would work and sat, leaning his back against the wall.

"You." Hayden pointed a finger my way. "Stand right here."

I stepped up next to him, expecting him to tell me how to draw an UnClose spell.

"If you ever treat your mother's heart like a toy you can tear apart," he said quietly to me, "if you ever look at her like a meal you can slice up and swallow like what I just saw—"

"I didn't—"

"—I will put you down," he said. "Do you understand me? Son?"

Death magic rolled over me at that threat, but I hauled back on it, locking it behind the thin barrier of my flesh and bones. "Yes, sir. I understand."

"Go apologize."

"That's a really bad idea," I said as Death magic kicked at me.

"You want my help, you go patch it up with your mom."

"She needs some time to cool down," I said. "So do I. Just. Just show me what I need to do with Terric. Then I'll talk to her. I promise."

I really needed him to listen to me. The hunger was gaining on me. If I were left alone, with my mom. . . . no. I wouldn't hurt her. I couldn't.

"Please, Kellerman. Just. Please."

"Fine," he said. "Against my better judgment. Faith magic spells used to Close a person aren't like casting Death magic. You must be mechanically precise. You must be controlled. You must be disciplined."

Great. I was pretty much none of those things.

"How *must* must I be?"

"Depends on how badly you want Terric's brains to remain unmangled. This is precision work, Shamus. You so much as deviate on any aspect of the spell, improvise or wing it, and he's losing memory, or brains, for life. Are you getting what I'm saying, or should I take you around the dance floor one more time?"

"I heard you. Precision. Discipline. My middle name. Then what?"

"You'll cast Close. Backward."

I glanced up at the big guy. "Is that all?"

"Not as easy as it sounds. You have to trace the original Closing spell from end to beginning. Hard enough if it was a spell originally cast in your signature. Damn impossible to trace someone else's handwriting backward. Blindfolded. With a handful of fire."

I knew how to fake another magic user's signature, but not good enough to fool anyone. Not exactly right. Only a few people in the world could pull off that kind of deception.

But I knew someone who could do it. An artist with magic. Good enough he'd run on the wrong side of the law for years taking forgery jobs.

"Son of a bitch," I said. "Dash, get Cody here. Now."

Cody showed up less than fifteen minutes later. Walked into the room, paused, then grinned. "We're UnClosing Terric, aren't we?"

"That's the idea," I said. "I need you to do it."

"Do what? I can't cast magic anymore, Shame. That's what I gave up for letting magic use me as a cocktail shaker, remember?" He walked over to the table, poured himself some lemonade.

Dashiell lifted a few fingers in greeting. Davy did the only thing Davy seemed to do lately—glare at me.

"Just because you can't use magic doesn't mean you can't draw a spell," I said. "Your hands aren't broke, Miller."

He held up his right hand and wriggled his fingers. "Hands, sure. But I'm not a Hand with magic. Not anymore."

"He's right, Shame," Dash said.

"I'll take care of magic part," I said. "You just draw."

"Just draw." He glanced at Hayden, who shook his head and shrugged.

"Putting aside for the moment that it's not going to work," Cody said, "why do you need Terric unClosed? Can't you still use magic, break magic, Shame?"

"Not reliably. Not with control. I need . . . I need Terric for that. It's going to take both of us to kill Eli. To stop Krogher. To do something about those drones."

To save the world before I destroy it.

With Allie and Zay down and every other Soul Complement in hiding, we were the only people left who could take them on. End them.

"All right," he said. "We UnClose Terric. Or try to. What's in it for me?"

"Saving the world isn't enough return on your investment?"

"I want something personal. From you."

"Like I don't break your nose?"

"Like you make me an unbreakable promise."

"Everything breaks," I said.

"Sealed with Blood magic. Terric's blood and your blood."

Terric spoke up from the floor. "Nope. I won't be a part of Shame's deals. Not after that poker game in Astoria," he said. "I'm Closed, not suicidal."

"Okay, your blood," Cody said to me. "You make me a Blood promise, that the two of you won't change how I mended magic. No matter what else you do together, you leave magic gentle like it is now, and I'll help you get his memories back."

I threw my hands up. "What the hell does you mending magic have to do with anything? We're not doing anything to *change* magic. We're trying to get Terric's brain back so we can *use* magic."

"Then it's an easy promise, isn't it?"

I'd heard those words out of Cody since we were teens. He usually said them right before I made a deal I ended up regretting.

"Don't care if it's easy," I said, drawing my pocketknife and slicing my left palm. "You got the promise. I won't screw with how you healed magic if you show me how to fix Terric." I held up my bloody palm, used the tip of the knife to draw a Binding spell between us. "Happy?"

He held his hand out for my knife. I gave it to him and he sliced his palm. "Good enough."

We shook, blood to blood, and I felt the binding of word and magic in the clasp of our hands.

"Good. Now . . ." Cody wiped his palm on his jeans. "Let's pry open his brain, shall we?" He strolled over to Terric and stared down at him. "Ready for this?"

"Should I do something? Bite down for pain?" Terric asked.

"No. You're fine," Cody said. "Shame, I need Sight."

"Not your magical slave, mate."

I stepped up to him and drew a clean Sight spell, then drew on the magic beneath the inn to fill it. The spell hissed to life, deep blue light carving three perfect concentric circles.

"Not too bad," Cody said.

"Considering it's perfect?" I asked.

Cody didn't answer, too busy looking into Terric through the Sight spell in ways I couldn't see. Well, I could see them, but I wouldn't be able to puzzle them out the way Cody did.

"I see the Close spell that was used on him," he finally said. "You might as well go do something. This will take me a minute to get a grip on it." He closed his eyes, his lips moving as if pulling words from a long-forgotten text.

Terric looked up at me. "Go. Apologize to your mom. You know she's worried."

Since my other option was to stand there while Davy and Hayden glared at me, I went. Took me a couple of minutes to find her. She wasn't down in the basement where the Blood magic well rested, hidden beneath the old marble. She wasn't in the kitchen, or outside, or in the main part of the inn. I finally found her at home — the second-story addition on the inn where we had lived when I was younger and where she and Hayden were staying now.

I didn't have to knock on the door. It was open.

"Mum?" I walked into the living room, across the honey brown wooden floors and throw rugs, into a space I knew as well as my childhood dreams. She was standing at the window, looking out, a locket in her hand.

I knew that locket, though I hadn't seen it for a long time. It held a photo of her and my da from their wedding day.

"Who sent you here?" she asked.

"Hayden," I said. "And Cody. And Terric. So: everyone."

"I don't want to hear the words they want you to say."

I paused. It would be easier to go back. To turn around. There were so many things broken inside me, so many holes Death had chewed through my humanity, I was flailing for solid ground. The last thing I needed was to fight with my mum, or worse, to hurt her.

"So this is me," I said. "And these are my words I want to say. I'm sorry for . . ."

What should I apologize for? Dying? Coming back to life? Being broken? Being willing to do anything to take Eli down, even if that put Terric at risk?

"Everything, I suppose," I said. "Dying, it . . . rattled me, and I wasn't all that steady to begin with. I know I'm alive-ish for a reason. Terric and I are the only ones who can take out the people who are trying to kill our friends. So I'm doing whatever it takes to see that it's done. Finishing this fight."

She didn't say anything. I waited there as long as I could. Death magic twisted in me, painful, hungry for the life in front of it. Her life.

"So, we'll be out of here soon. Love you, Mum." I turned to go.

"Shamus," she said, and I stopped in the doorway. She finally looked away from the window and turned toward me. "We aren't done talking about this, understand? When we've helped Terric, and when you've taken care of what-ever it is that is going on, you and I are going have a nice, long talk. For years."

I couldn't help smiling. "Sure, Mum."

She crossed the distance between us and gave me a hug.

I clenched my teeth and gently wrapped my arms around her while Death magic stabbed at my brain.

"Good," she said. "Now go finish this fight. We'll talk later."

"All right." Cody opened his eyes. "Terric, I think you'll want to be standing."

"Hayden told me to sit."

"That's because I thought you'd be on your ass when we got done with you," Hayden said. "But if Cody says stand, stand."

"I'll stand beside him." Dash walked across the room and stood next to Terric. "I won't get in the way unless you fall."

"You could get in the way, a little," Terric said.

Dash blinked back his surprise, glanced at me. I raised an eyebrow briefly. Yeah, that sounded like flirting to me too.

Maybe memory-less Terric had some advantages.

"Well, let's start with getting back your old memories before we make any new ones," Dash said.

"Fair enough," Terric said.

"Shame." Cody motioned me over. "Stand right here in front of Terric. I'll stay at your right, and, Hayden, you can be there on his left. I'll guide Shame's hand through the spell. I don't think a Closer cast the spell. Or if it was a Closer, he was sloppy. Too many inconsistencies. It's no wonder there are holes in your memories, Terric."

"Hurray?" Terric asked.

Cody nodded. "Not exactly cheer-worthy. Cleaner spells are easier to follow. This one's . . . rough. Hayden, let me know if you see anything I'm missing.

"Your job, Shame, is to concentrate on what you want the spell to do—UnClose him—as you and I draw it. When the glyph is done, you'll fill it with magic, his mind will unlock, and . . ." Cody snapped his fingers. "He'll get his memories back."

I glanced at Terric. "He might be oversimplifying things a bit."

"Not my first ride at the carnival, Flynn," he said. "Get cracking."

"Is there a way to erase the bossy parts of him?"

Cody snorted.

I shook my hands, cleared my mind. The thing none of us was really talking about was that my control of Death magic was in the gutter right now. If we got through this without me killing someone just to ease the pressure and feed my hunger, I'd consider it a raging success.

I held up my right hand, ring and pinkie finger tucked loosely against my thumb, index and middle finger pressed against each other and extended.

"Closing," Cody said, "is intention. It's about the spell and the function of magic, but it's also about the Closer's intention. Know who did the Closing and why, half your work is done."

"We don't know who did the Closing," I said.

Cody put his left hand on my shoulder, placed his fingertips on the back of my raised hand. "Sure we do," he said.

"Sure we do?"

"Who?" Dash asked.

"Eli Collins."

"Eli Collins ain't no Closer," Hayden said.

"I know," Cody said happily. Yes, happily. The jerk was enjoying this. "That's our break. That's what we're going to use to our advantage. Because I know his signature and could forge it blindfolded."

"This," Cody said, applying pressure on the back of my hand to raise my fingers level with Terric's forehead, "is our beginning. Let's take it to the end."

Chapter 24

SHAME

It took an hour, with Cody's fingers guiding mine, Hayden's occasional interruption to tell us to angle the glyph one way or another, and my keeping my mind as clear and clean and focused as I could manage.

Holding Death away from every beating heart in the room was exhausting.

I was breathing hard after the first fifteen minutes. By the hour mark, I was covered in sweat, shaking, and so hungry I'd pulled Eleanor and Sunny up on such a tight leash they were almost standing in the same space with me. Only Hayden's arm around my waist was keeping me on my feet.

Terric seemed to be doing pretty well so far. But then it wasn't the prep for this spell that was going to knock his teeth out. It was when I poured magic into it.

"Almost done," Cody said. "Just tie that line into the diagonal arc. Yes, that one." He paused. "Okay, Shame, I think you have it, his UnClosing. Hayden, do you see anything we missed?"

He took his time looking through the glyph I had carved,

a glyph that hovered in a milky white light in front of me like the flight paths of air traffic control over La Guardia.

"It's good," he said. "For what it is. Eli is no Closer. I wouldn't know how to make it better."

"So, cast?" I asked through my teeth. I was glad they were being extra careful, but I was counting down the seconds of consciousness here.

Terric was the one who answered. "Cast it, Shame."

I held his gaze with my own. Saw the trust implicit there and the feelings he had for me: friendship, caring, maybe hope. God, had we ever been that innocent?

"See you on the other side, mate," I whispered.

I drew on magic from beneath the inn, opened my hand wide, and let the magic fill the lines of the spell. It caught like a lit fuse, hot red liquid flowing through the glyph so quickly I barely had time to register that the spell was charged before it whipped out and wrapped Terric from head to boot.

He yelled, stiffened. Davy caught him as he fell, slowing his descent to the floor as he eased him down.

Terric was still yelling.

I had done it wrong. Cast wrong. Drawn it wrong. Somehow I'd connected the spell to me, as I had connected it to him.

I could feel his mind breaking open, dull teeth tearing at my body, my mind. I could see his memories. Not just the torture, not just the last few years, but all of his past. All of the things he'd been through with me, without me. All the things he'd endured because of me.

Jesus. How did anyone go on living after that?

"Shame?" Someone was shouting, their voice muffled and distant. "Shame!"

A hard slap, maybe two, landed across my face. Got my attention.

Hayden was looking down at me. Not worried. Angry. "Are you in there? Are you listening to me, Shamus?"

Eleanor was looking down at me too. That must have been the second slap.

"I'm here." My voice sounded so far away and strange, the very weirdness of it pulled me up to full awareness, sweating.

I was in the middle of Terric's head. Got the full double-vision thing of looking out of his eyes—he was currently staring at Dash, who looked worried for Terric—and out of mine, where Hayden still had on his ass-whupping glare.

Story of my life: Something goes down, everyone frets over Terric and blames me.

Terric laughed, and I could feel it, *feel* his laugh on my brain walls. "You think you're the one they blame?" he asked.

"Stop listening to me."

"Stop whining in my head."

"Your—?" I swore, then turned to look at him. He was sitting on the floor, Dash on one side, Cody on the other. Hayden was standing next to me, and Eleanor was at my left, kneeling beside me.

When I looked at Terric, I got that mirror-in-a-mirror sensation. I was looking at him while he was looking at me, while I was looking at me from him, looking at me from me.

"How the hell do Allie and Z do this shit?" I asked.

Terric bit his bottom lip, which I realized was bloody and swelling from all the screaming and whatnot that had just gone on.

"For one thing, they *want* to be connected this close," he said. "But for us . . ."

"This is a bad idea," I agreed. "I'll step back if you step back. And no nicking the valuables, on the way out, mate."

He smiled and I got a weird wash of him thinking I was adorable when I assed around and pretended not to be ter-rified.

Way too much information for me. I wasn't built to know

what a real human heart felt. Pretty sure if I ever had to deal with real emotion any real person should experience, I'd snap in half.

"Please," he said. "And I always thought I was the drama queen."

"Done being your brain buddy. Just shush up and step back."

No one else in the room seemed to have anything to add to the conversation.

I didn't know how much of what we were saying was going on in our minds, and how much was actually coming out as words.

I had cast magic, UnClosed Terric . . . I hoped . . . and we'd ended up sunk knee-deep in the mud of each other's minds.

"This might hurt," he said.

"I'd be surprised if it didn't."

There was a one-two-three countdown, a holding of breath and gritting of teeth, and then we both jumped back into our own thought space.

"Son of a bitch," I panted. Terric just groaned.

". . . coming, Shame," someone was saying. I blinked, looked around. Dash was hanging up his phone. "Here. We have to get moving."

"Where? Who? What?" I said. Hayden was already hauling me up to my feet. After a couple steps I finally got the hang of feet and legs and walking.

There were too many people in the room doing too many things: Hayden, Terric, Cody, Dash, Mum, Davy.

We were headed to the door.

The air sizzled and popped. I knew that sound—had last heard it in my kitchen before Eli had killed us.

"Gate," I yelled.

And then there was chaos.

Three men—drones—stepped out of nowhere, a flash of

light pouring through the room. They stood with their hands extended, fingers and thumbs together, focusing magic.

"Down! Down," I shouted.

Magic pounded through the air in a blast of heat. I lifted my hands in a Block spell, but I was too unfocused to cast, or even begin to pull a spell together.

Time stopped for a moment, my heart, all the people in the room, the magic, stopped.

I saw my mom falling, the spell the drones had cast—Impact—burning a fire through her. Hayden was midstep, trying to reach her, trying to block the magic with his own body.

Too late.

Terric was just closing off the line of a Cancel spell, impressive since he had to be at least as rattled as I was, and both Eleanor and Sunny were blank-eyed and frozen in place.

Davy was nowhere to be seen, maybe already out the front door.

Dash was halfway through firing his gun, not at the drones, but at the man I saw behind them, the man standing in the hole in space.

Eli. He waited for me to make eye contact. When I did, he nodded and held up something in his hand. A disk.

"Come and get me, dead man," he said. Behind him was a house. A manor. I knew that place.

He flipped the disk and caught it in his fist.

Hammer and steel cracked like a broken gong as he canceled the Time spell he had cast. Time cranked up again; the hole in space burned into itself, closing Eli away and leaving the drones behind.

Magic sizzled through the air toward Mum, completing the spell the drones had cast.

She fell.

Dash's bullets hit one drone in the chest, the next in the

neck. Terric's spell ignited and sucked down all the magic in the room.

I busted the chains on Death inside me and let it have its due.

Death drank down the lives of all three drones, who screamed, and fell, and died.

I turned. Mum was on the floor, Hayden calling her name. She wasn't breathing.

Cody ran to her and started CPR.

I stood there, numb, frozen. I watched her spirit, her soul, lift up out of her body. She looked around, confused.

"God, no." I couldn't lose her. She couldn't be dead, hit by a spell that wasn't meant for her. This wasn't how it ended for her. Not like this.

I took a step, held out my hand toward her. A smoky black rope shot out from my hand so fast I couldn't follow the path it took, couldn't lower my hand in time to redirect it.

Holy shit.

Eleanor screamed, *Shame, no!*

I jerked my hand away, trying to sever the stream of Death magic pouring out of me.

Too late.

The rope looped around my mom's throat and cinched in tight.

Her hands flew to her neck and she pulled against the tie between us.

Death magic had taken her, claimed her spirit. I could already feel the heat of her energy feeding into the vein in my arm.

"Oh God," I breathed, not wanting to believe what I was seeing. Not wanting to face the horror of having just tied my mother's ghost to me.

Mum stopped struggling and seemed to see me—really see me. *Shamus?*

She looked down at her body, where Hayden had gathered her in his arms, where Cody was slowly standing back up, the CPR having done no good.

Ah, son, she said, her ghostly eyes closed. *No.*

"I didn't mean, I didn't want . . ." I put my hand over my face and wished the world would go away. Wished I could be gone, dead. Wished I hadn't done this to her, killed her. Worse: tied her to the monster inside me.

Terric walked up from behind me, then stopped next to me, his hand gripping my upper arm.

The contact was a shock of electricity. But instead of blowing me off my feet, it grounded me, cleared my head, steadied me.

"I got you," he said. There was Life magic in his touch and kindness in his tone. "Do you have your mother's spirit?" he asked. "Did you tie her to you?"

I nodded.

"You did *what*?" Hayden bellowed.

"How about the others?" Terric asked. "The drones? Do you have them?"

"No," I said. There was nothing inside them for me to take."

Hayden gently lowered Mom back to the floor, then stood.

Man clocked in over six four and was half again as wide. "Did you kill your mother, Shame?"

"I—"

"He saved her." Terric moved to stand between me and Hayden. Terric was a little taller than me but was still dwarfed by the size and muscle of the older man. If this came down to a physical fight, I had no doubt Hayden would mop the floor with both Terric and me.

"What do you mean?" Dash asked. He still had the gun in his hand, probably to put me down if needed. Smart.

"She's tied to him, which means she isn't dead," Terric said. "He has her spirit. We have her. And we'll find a way to heal her."

"Then find a way *now*," Hayden yelled.

A phone rang. It sounded like it was coming from Dash's pocket. He finally set the safety and answered the phone.

"I said now," Hayden said again. "Or so help me, you two, I will make you wish you'd died with her."

"We didn't kill her," Terric said. "That Impact the drones threw killed her. Understand me, Hayden. Shame caught her when she fell. He may have saved her."

Hayden uncurled one massive fist and pointed at Mum. "Do something for her."

"All right." Terric gave me a hesitant smile. "It's going to be all right, Shame. Relax."

He so didn't know that. "Don't tell me what to do."

Mum, who still stood near her body, cleared her throat. *Listen to him, son. This is all ... all going to be fine.*

"No," I said, the rise of tears choking back my voice. "I don't think it's going to be fine. You're dead!"

Terric pressed his palm on my shoulder. "Just trust me for once."

He walked over to Mum's body and knelt. He breathed deeply and cleared his mind. Faith magic user. Terric had been one of the best many years ago. When he wanted to access his inner calm, it came snapping. With just a couple of breaths, he drew tranquility around him.

It was a technique Victor taught all his students—this Zen state of mind. One I'd never really gotten the hang of.

Terric stretched his hand out toward me and not knowing exactly what he wanted, I stepped over and clasped it.

Then he closed his eyes and prayed.

Great.

Terric had a thing about praying when he cast magic. It wasn't required, and the prayers he spoke were derived from very old texts. But in each syllable, between each word, he hung his faith, his belief and trust that the good in this world, and the worlds beyond our reach, would be there to support his actions, to guide his choices.

That was another part of Faith magic I'd never gotten the hang of—the faith part.

Early on in my training, Victor had declared that if I couldn't even manage patience, peace, and trust, I'd have zero chance surrendering myself to faith.

He hadn't been wrong.

Terric kept praying, the same few verses over and over again in a voice just above a whisper.

Mum moved to stand a little closer to Hayden and put her hand on his, not that he noticed. *Oh,* she said. *I see. I see what he's doing.*

I'm glad she could see something, because all I saw was her unbreathing body.

Terric opened his eyes, the last word tumbling from his lips, a gentle light pouring from his hand into Mum's body. The soft yellow glow of healing, of Life magic doing what Life magic does best—thriving—filled her.

Mum glowed for a moment. Then the glow was gone.

"Did you?" I asked. "Is she all right?"

Hayden was on his way to her again, knelt on the opposite side of where Terric still knelt, Mum between them.

"She's breathing," Hayden said. "By God, she's breathing. Call an ambulance."

I think Cody or Dash called 911.

Davy showed up with a blanket to cover her.

I didn't know what good an ambulance would do. Mum might be breathing, but she was still tied to me, her spirit, her soul, caught by the Death magic in me.

Shamus, she said, *can you break this tie between us and let me back into my body?*

The last time I'd tried that—with Mina—she had died.

I just shook my head, not willing to risk that with my mom. "I can't—"

Maybe this time it will work, Eleanor said.

"No." The last time it hadn't worked. The doctor's spirit had stepped back into her body and died.

I didn't know how long I stood there. Long enough for Hayden to get Mum bundled in the blanket. Long enough for Terric to be standing next to me again. Long enough the ambulance pulled up to the place.

What a mess they'd find. Three dead bodies, a burned room, and a woman in a coma.

". . . need to go now," Dash was saying from somewhere ahead of me.

Terric pulled on my arm, Cody pushed at my shoulder. We were moving, running.

"Go, go," Cody urged. Out the back hallway. Out the back door into the shaded afternoon light beneath the trees behind the inn.

"Where are we going?" I asked. "Why are we leaving?"

Sunny and Mum and Eleanor floated there next to me, looking just as confused as I felt.

"Did you see where the drones came from?" Dash asked. "When the gate opened. Shame, did you see where they came from?"

"Yes. Kevin Cooper's manor. His house—the one out in the West Hills. I'm sure that's where Eli was standing."

"Kevin Cooper?" Dash asked. "What does he have to do with the drones?"

"Not him," I said, "Eli. Eli was there. Right outside Kevin's house. He told me to come and get him."

"Wait," Terric said. "You saw Eli? In a flash of an instant, you knew where he was?"

"It wasn't like that," I said. "Time stopped. You didn't feel that? Hear that?"

He shook his head but had gone very pale.

"Eli stopped time. Long enough for me to notice him. Long enough for him to show me that he was holding a disk."

"Why?" Dash asked. "Why would he want you to see him? You want him dead."

"That's why," I said. "This confrontation. Our confrontation, he and I. Without Krogher in the middle of it pulling his strings. He wants us to come to him, me to come to him. And finish this fight."

"I hate to say it again, but *why*?" Dash asked. "He has the gates, he has fucking disks, apparently. He has the drop on us."

Terric shook his head. "Not now. Not if Shame and I use magic together. Break it. Break the core of it into dark and light so we can change the world if we so choose." He was silent a moment, then, "Eli's Soul Complement is dead. We have the upper hand now. He's choosing the ground upon which we kill him."

"Kevin's house," Cody mused. "Dash, where are Allie and Zay holed up?"

Dash shook his head. "They haven't told me. Just said they'd be safe and that Dr. Fischer was with them."

Cody turned and looked at me. "Shamus. How much money would you bet that Allie and Zayvion are hiding at Kevin's house?"

"Damn it. Call them," I said. "Dash, call Zay or Dr. Fischer and find out where they are. Now."

Dash pulled out his phone, dialed.

But driving wouldn't get us there fast enough. We might already be too late to stop Eli's attack.

"Can you open a Gate?" I asked Terric.

You would have thought I'd asked him to fly to the moon and back.

"No," he said. "Shame, I haven't been a Faith magic user for years. You broke that in me, remember? Closings, opening gates . . . that's all Faith magic."

"All right. Fine," I said. "Can *we* open a Gate? Together. If we break magic?"

He shrugged one shoulder. "I don't know. Maybe. Do you want to test our control over magic by tearing a hole through the fabric of reality?"

"I vote no," Cody said.

"Why not?" I asked.

"Because I don't want to be at ground zero of a nuclear explosion," he said. "But hey, I like being alive."

Dash hung up. "You were right," he said. "They're at Kevin's. But they haven't seen any sign of Eli or the drones."

"He was at Kevin's house," I said. "I'm sure of it. With that gate thing of his, Allie and Zay won't know they're surrounded by drones until they are right up their asses."

"I sent Stone to keep an eye on Allie," Cody said. "For a magical gargoyle made of rock, he's . . . sensitive to such things, fluctuations in magic. He'll warn them."

Not fast enough. Not good enough. Not enough for them to kill Eli.

I was already striding out to the parking lot. "Warning isn't the same as stopping," I said. "Or killing."

"I can do it," a low voice said. I glanced over at the cover of trees.

"Davy?" Sunny said.

"Davy?" I echoed. "What are you doing out here?"

"Watching you."

"Easy," Dash said. "Just take it easy, Davy." His tone made me do a double check for guns in Davy's hands.

No guns, but from the look in his eyes, I was pretty sure ol' Davy Silvers would rather kill me with his bare hands.

Looked like Cody should be worried about two nuclear reactors in the area.

What's wrong with Davy? Mum asked me.

He's angry about Shame killing me, Sunny said.

Oh, Shamus, Mum said.

"I didn't mean to," I said.

He's going to kill you, Sunny said. *And I'm going to enjoy every minute of it.*

Sunny! Mum used her teacher voice, and Sunny shut up. *I understand you're angry he killed you. Fine. He killed me too.*

"God," I groaned. Just what I needed. Arguing ghosts.

But, she continued, *we are not in hell yet. And as long as we are on this earth, alive or in spirit, we do our job. Take care of magic, keep it out of the hands of people who would use it to harm others, and save the innocent.*

Your own son is one of the people who harmed others with magic, Sunny said. *He killed Eleanor too.*

It's more complicated than that, Eleanor said.

We should be keeping magic out of his hands, Sunny said. *We should be stopping him.*

Death magic demands many sacrifices, Mum said. *It's what you do with those sacrifices that makes them worthy of the price. I trust you, Shamus.*

Dash was still talking too, but I had sort of lost that side of the conversation. The ghosts were arguing pretty loudly for beings that had no lungs.

"Shame?" Terric's hand on my shoulder shot an electric pulse through me again, and once again I felt grounded, connected. Life magic flared and died in his eyes, and he knew the cool darkness of Death magic rolled through me.

Like lightning and thunder, we were a storm rising.

The clash of our magics wasn't unpleasant. It wasn't even that uncomfortable resistance of one magic tearing against the other. Something had changed between us again. Life magic set me straight and clear, and Death magic, apparently, returned the favor for him.

Soul Complements. Maybe we didn't have to be living in each other's heads like Allie and Zay. Maybe we didn't have to go insane. Dying had brought us closer to each other. I was having a hard time finding something wrong with that.

Being drawn closer together wasn't exactly how we wanted things to go, but right this minute, it wasn't so bad.

"So you killed Sunny?" Terric asked quietly.

I couldn't lie to him. He'd know if I did. "Yes."

"Is she tied to you?" Terric asked.

"What?"

"Sunny. Do you have her soul?"

"Yes."

"Okay." He turned and once again stood between me and the man who wanted to see my guts on the floor. "We'll find a way to make this right, Davy. But right now Allie and Zay are in danger. We stop Eli; we kill him, kill Krogher, stop the drones. Once that's done, we'll make amends. Even if what you want is our deaths."

"Whoa, wait," I said. "*Our* deaths? You didn't have anything to do with me killing anyone, Terric. This is on me. I clean up my own messes. Do you understand me, Davy? This is on me."

He nodded but was looking at Terric, not me. "I understand you. If you want Eli, I can get you there."

"How?" Dash asked.

Davy unbuttoned his shirt, revealing the spells carved into his skin.

Oh, mercy, no, my mum whispered. *The poor thing.*

There were so many spells carved into the meat of him that I couldn't even see his skin. His entire chest was just a crossing and recrossing of black lines that pulsed with that strange blue neon.

"He left me his calling card," Davy said calmly. "And a few other things."

"Other things?" Terric asked.

"Ah, crap," Cody said. "I think this is going to hurt."

And then Davy pressed his palms together, blue magic surging up the lines of his arms to the tips of his fingers, completing an overarcing spell carved through him. When he pulled his hands apart, the air around us sizzled and burned.

No, not just the air. Magic. Davy had opened a Gate.

Then he said one word, and we all fell through.

Chapter 25

SHAME

I hated gates. Zay and other people who could open the damn things seemed to love jumping through them. But whenever I stumbled through one, it felt as if someone inserted hot peppers up my nose, into every other orifice, and kicked me off a cliff into the salty deep.

Unpleasant, and I almost always ended up puking.

The magic Davy shouldn't have been able to access landed us in the driveway in front of Kevin's house.

Every inch of me burned, but at least I wasn't going to lose my lunch. I had no time for it.

Eli was walking up the front steps. Eli was almost at the door. Eli was almost close enough to hurt two of the people left in this world whom I most wanted to be safe.

"Hey!" I yelled.

He looked surprised as hell that we were right behind him. I thought for just the barest second that he glanced at Davy and gave him a nod. What? Were they in this together? But then I didn't have any time to pick out the subtleties of what the fuck was going on.

Half a ton of rock tumbled out of the sky, all wings, claws, and fangs.

Stone the gargoyle.

He had probably been roof-side and noticed both Eli and our arrival at the same moment. He tore down out of the sky aiming straight at Eli.

Good boy, Stoney.

Two things happened at once: I unleashed Death magic. Terric reached out with Life magic.

Okay, three things happened.

Eli opened a gate in the ground behind him and stepped back into it just as Stone lunged for his throat. He and Stone fell through it and were gone.

"Son of a bitch." I was running to where Eli and Stone had just been on the porch. I was also yarding back on Death magic so it wouldn't consume everything living in its path. Terric, I assumed was doing the same with Life magic.

Dash and Cody were a couple steps ahead of us, but they pulled up short when the door opened.

"Stop right there." Kevin stood just inside the expansive entryway, a semiautomatic rifle in his hands. Correction, a semiautomatic rifle in his hands pointed at us. "What the hell are all of you doing here?"

Kevin was the kind of guy you might miss in a crowd— thinning hairline, sad eyes, and average in most every other way. But when he was holding a gun, he was riveting.

"Eli was outside," Terric said. "Stone tackled him. They gated out. Could be gating back at any minute. Are Allie and Zayvion all right?"

"No one comes into the house," Kevin said. "Not even you."

"Kevin," Dash said, "it's all right. We're here to help."

"How'd you get here?"

"Davy opened a Gate," I said.

Kevin turned his gun on Davy.

What we had here was a powder keg and a book of lit matches. Nothing but boom ahead.

"We came to stop Eli," I said. "We can leave. Terric and I can leave."

"It's not Terric and you that I'm worried about," Kevin said. "Step back, Davy. Way back. Now."

"Davy? Davy's not the problem," I said. Kevin wasn't making any damn sense. "He brought us here to hunt for Eli. If Eli isn't here, we're gone."

"Sure he brought you here," Kevin said. "Because he's under Eli's orders to do so."

"What?" I said.

Bullshit, Sunny said. *Davy's not working for Eli. He was tortured by him. Held captive by him.*

"You sure about that?" Dash, who couldn't hear Sunny, asked Kevin.

"One hundred percent," Kevin said. "Back off the property, Davy Silvers, or I will drop you where you stand."

Davy held up his hands. "Kevin. You're wrong. I would never take orders from Eli."

He sounded like Davy. Looked like him—well, like a version of him who had recently been hammered through hell. The Davy I knew would rather slit his own throat than work for the man who had turned him into a monster.

"Back up," Kevin repeated.

No, Sunny said. *Shame. Don't let him kill him. Don't let him shoot.*

"Davy," I said, "you'd better listen to him, mate. Just step outside and we'll get this all sorted."

Davy didn't move, didn't say anything.

"Davy?"

That wasn't Davy behind those dead eyes. Maybe hadn't been Davy for a long time.

Shit.

Magic can do wonderful things. Back in the day it healed the sick, fed the poor, made the world an easier place to live in. Of course magic back then always came with a price: You used it, and it used you.

The price for using magic was pain.

Then Cody healed magic, turned it into its new extra-gentle form and made it so using magic didn't cost much because it didn't do much.

Those spells carved into Davy were dark magic. Eli had carved spells from a time when magic was broken, raw, and extremely deadly.

Spells that would kill a man. Spells that would change a man. Spells that destroyed anything they touched.

And in those black hashed and looped designs were a few more spells. Things that would take care of Eli's enemies. Things that would take care of Krogher's problems.

Davy wasn't just a blueprint that Eli had used to carve the drones into bombs; Davy was his master weapon.

His very first, very best, flesh-covered bomb.

Right here, at Kevin's house, where Allie and Zayvion and Terric and I had gathered. Two sets of powerful Soul Complements. Maybe even the most powerful Soul Complements. Maybe the only Soul Complements left in the world. The only people who could stop Krogher and his drones.

And we'd brought Davy here—Eli's walking weapon. We'd let *him* bring us here. All together now, cozy and easy to kill.

Fuck. Me.

I triggered Death magic, sent it straight for him, at the exact moment Davy threw his hands down and out to the side. He arched back, his entire body consumed by the blue flame of those spells.

Magic called up from the wells beneath the city, magic called down out of the cloudless sky, a firestorm of hell.

Magic Davy should not be able to access, if he were just human. Magic that was damn near impossible to pull on anymore.

An ungodly immense amount of raw magic.

There was no way I could block it.

And then the world exploded.

Chapter 26

SHAME

There is maybe one thing good about carrying Death: You can't die. There are, however, a lot of bad things about carrying Death. Example? Sometimes dying is a kindness.

In the middle of that explosion, as magic ripped through the walls of the house, as magic was set to do one thing—kill all the people in that house, especially the Soul Complements and their unborn baby—I decided there was one more thing Death magic was good for: absorbing energy.

Even magic.

I threw Death at Davy's magic like a heavy blanket, swallowing down the force of it, devouring the heat of it, taking on the explosion as an energy I could drain and diffuse. Did it too.

The blast rerouted to the middle of my head.

Pain.

Heat.

A riot of magic—the magic Davy had tapped—pulverized through my mind and body.

Eli had done more than carve spells into him. He'd filled him with tainted magic. Just like the magic that filled the drones. Back in the warehouse when I'd drunk down the magic in the drones, it had made me sick.

This? This might be my ticket out of here.

I screamed and burned and bled and broke, tainted magic pouring over me, pumping through me. I didn't know how Davy had held this so long, didn't know how he was still alive.

And then, in an instant, there was silence.

That was just a different kind of pain.

A hand lay cool against the back of my neck. He walked me into the house, took me to a bed, made me sit. The magic was gone. So was the porch, melted to slag and ash.

Hell.

The ringing in my ears was so loud, I couldn't hear my own thoughts.

Shuttering darkness and blasts of light still rolled through my brain, across my eyes, but I was pretty sure that was Terric at my side, Terric who had brought me here.

"Rest," he said maybe from somewhere in my head, his hands still on me, words carrying a soft yellow light. Life magic. Healing.

The next time I woke up, I didn't know where I was. This was not my bed, not my bedroom. I was alone. Well, just me and the ghosts of three women. I was on top of the covers, a light blanket over my torso.

Go slowly, Mum said from where she sat on the bed next to me. *That was a lot of magic to consume.*

Consume? I wondered if I said that out loud. From the look on Mum's face, I hadn't.

I pulled my hands up to my sides, bent elbows, and pushed up to sitting.

Bloody hell, that hurt.

Sunny sat cross-legged on top of the dresser, her head resting against the mirror behind her. *I didn't know,* she said.

"Know?" Excellent. That was actual audible speech. My bell had been rung pretty damn hard, though. It had taken a lot to get that word out.

The details of exactly what had happened were on the other side of the blast zone in my brain.

About Davy, Sunny said. *I didn't know that he was carved up and triggered to kill you. Well, you and Allie and Zayvion and Terric.*

Ah, the details were coming back to me. "Did he? Kill?"

I looked around the room expecting to see everyone I cared about dead and tied to me. But the only ghosts in the room were Mum, Sunny, and Eleanor, who shook her head.

No one died, Eleanor said. *But your mom's right. That was a lot of magic to absorb. You're kind of smoldering with death and darkness.*

"Yeah?" I asked. "Is it sexy?"

She grinned. *Oh yeah. Real sexy.* That was the first time I'd seen her smile, really smile since I had bought her a drink in heaven.

Hold on. Heaven? Images and memories flashed and burned through my mind. All that magic I'd absorbed must have rattled a few things loose.

I'd died, gone to a bar in heaven. I'd seen Eleanor there, and Chase and Greyson, and Dessa. Dad and Victor too.

Shamus? Mum said.

"Hold on. Having a Dorothy moment."

Dad and Victor had thrown me out of heaven and cast me down here.

They'd told me I didn't have much time. That if I didn't stop Krogher and Eli and the drones, the world would end. I searched those memories for exactly how the end might come, but came up empty.

Undoubtedly it was something involving magic.

"How long have I been here?" I asked. "How long since Davy bombed out on us?"

It hasn't been longer than an hour or two, Mum said.

Felt like years.

I got out of the bed, keeping one hand on the wall just in case walking was going to be an issue. Nope. I felt pretty good for a guy who'd just taken a nuclear blast to Oz and back. "Where's Terric?" I asked. "Where's Dash and Cody? I have to go. We have to go find Eli."

I was fully clothed, still had my shoes on.

Like we'd know? Sunny said. *We can't get that far away from you.*

"Then let's get moving." I opened the door onto a nicely decorated hallway. Figured out where I was.

I'd been to Kevin's house a couple of times and recalled needing a map to navigate the place. It had been in his family for generations, a family of some wealth who liked living on the grand side of the scale.

I was on the lower floor, in one of the bedrooms that was probably a servant's quarters back in the day.

The hall led to a sitting room and a few other rooms that I guessed were libraries or something, and finally I was in one of the main living areas, which was roughly the size of a small ballroom.

There was no one in the ballroom, but I heard voices from farther down the hall.

Great. More walking.

The voices were in a meeting room that was done up in wood and leather and fine artwork.

Terric, Dash, and Cody sat at the table on one side of the room with Kevin, who had a shotgun propped next to his knee.

"Started the party without me?" I asked.

They all looked my way.

Terric stood, walked over to me. "I didn't think you'd be up. Not so soon." But in his eyes was *not at all*.

"I'd hate to miss out on the plans for kicking Eli's ass," I said. "We are kicking Eli's ass, aren't we?"

"Yes," Terric said, placing his hand on my shoulder and guiding me over to a chair. "But there's something else we have to deal with first."

"Tell me it involves ordering pizza."

"No," he said. "You want a drink?"

"Is it that bad?"

"Yes."

"Then make it a double."

He walked over to the small refrigerator recessed into the wall and pulled out a beer, brought it back to me.

I opened it, took a drink and then one more. How long had it been since I had a beer?

"Okay," I said. "Tell me."

Terric looked over at Cody and the rest of the people at the table.

"It's kind of complicated," Cody said. "But we think Davy booby-trapped the house."

"Think? That's a yes/no sort of situation, isn't it?"

"Sure, if we could get a straight look at it," Kevin said. "But that spell, whatever the hell that was he hit the place with, left something behind."

"Okay." I held up a finger, then finished the beer. Because, priorities. "I just got cracked in the head with exploding tainted magic he carried. I'm guessing Eli sewed a Beckstrom disk into that poor guy's chest, so explain everything to me straight and clear. Use small words."

"Davy's spell created another spell," Terric said. "We think it's a trap."

"Spells can do that? Never mind. A trap for what?" I asked. "Keeping us in, or keeping us out?"

"Both," Cody said. "Maybe. Or maybe it's something more."

"Like?"

"The possibilities are pretty damn endless," Dash said, finally joining the conversation. "We can't figure it out."

"Still missing the details." I glanced at each of them. "I said small words, not no words."

Terric stood and walked toward the door. "It would be easier to show you."

I heaved up out of the chair and followed him. The others stayed behind.

"How are you doing?" he asked, keeping his pace slow enough that I didn't have to strain to keep up.

"Just spiffy."

He glanced over at me. "With less bullshit," he said. "How are you doing?"

"I killed my mother, Terric. How do you think I'm doing?"

You didn't kill me, Mum said.

He didn't say anything for a bit. Then, "You didn't kill her. And I think you're doing better than I expected, considering what you're dealing with."

"Yeah, well, maybe you don't know what I'm dealing with." The people I'd killed. Losing ground to Death magic. Hell, the only thing I had to look forward to was penance via silver bullet through the head once we took care of Eli and Krogher.

Terric made a little hmm sound, then said, "Death, trip to heaven, dire warnings from your dad, killing Sunny, Mina, your mom—"

He didn't kill me, she said again.

"—killing me, taking the brunt of an explosion meant to kill half a dozen people even though you knew that tainted magic is probably the only thing that will end you. Kind of hoping you'll bite it after you take Eli and Krogher out? Silver-bullet penance." He looked over at me again. "How am I doing?"

"The hell, mate?"

"I heard your thoughts, Shame. When you UnClosed me, you were an open book. There isn't anything in you I didn't see."

"And that's not creepy how?"

"You saw the same in me, I'm sure."

"No," I said. "I didn't. All I saw was the spell we were trying to trace to UnClose you."

"Really? I told you. You never pay attention."

"Sure," I said, "next time you get a hatchet job on your brain that I have to unhatchet, I'll try to take the time to appreciate the scenery."

We stepped into the actual ballroom of the house. Yes, the house had a ballroom.

"You know we still have a chance at this, right?" he asked.

"At what?"

"Life. Maybe a decent one at that. You and me." At my look, he added, "Not you *and* me like that. But both of us. Alive. No silver bullets necessary."

I stopped.

He stopped too. "What?"

"You really think that somehow, if we survive taking out Eli and Krogher and those walking drone bombs, you and I are going to just go along like nothing happened? Live our lives the way we were before we both died?"

"Live our lives however we want to," he said. "Why not?"

"Oh, I dunno, mate. Maybe because we *died*? I don't know about you, but I am not the same since the revolving grave door. Not at all. Something in me is broken. I am pretty sure I'm not a thing that should be allowed to live."

Shame, Mum said gently.

"That's the truth," I said. "That's how I'm doing. So if you want to believe that there's some kind of happiness ahead of you, good on ya. But it won't include me. The only thing ahead of me is a grave."

He looked over my shoulder, maybe bored. Maybe angry. "Are you done?" he asked.

I shrugged.

"I know what you are, you idiot," he said. "I'm your other *half.* If I say we live we live."

"And if I say we die?"

"Well, then you and I will just have to see who wants it more." He gave me a hard smile and I couldn't help smiling back.

"Yeah," I said, "I suppose we will. But money's on black here. Death ends us all."

"Keep telling yourself that," he said. "Every time you've died, you've come back. So far, Life trumps. My money's on red."

"You're delusional."

"Not even a little."

"So, where's this problem spell Davy cast?"

"You can't see it?"

I looked away from him and at the room. It was a big space. Stage at one end that could seat an orchestra, staircases from above spiraling down to the center, lots of marble with plenty of room to waltz.

The room was humming with blue magic—Davy's spell. The lines of the spell webbed from wall to wall to ceiling to floor, but each line was so thin and glass blue, I couldn't see all of it at once.

"What the hell is that?" I asked.

Terric had his hands in the front pockets of his jeans. He shrugged. "Like Dash said, we're not quite sure yet."

I craned my neck to look at the ceiling. "Does it go through?"

"Yes. Up about thirty feet from the roof, and out thirty

feet on each side of the house. It's like we're wrapped in a ball of twine. Magic twine."

"So, where's Davy?"

Terric pointed to the center of the room and the center of the spell. I don't know how I'd missed him. Well, since he was completely covered in the glasslike magic, he just looked like a man-sized knot in the center of the thing.

Davy? Sunny said. *Should I . . . Shame, should I touch him?*

She was asking me? "Have you tried to reach him?" I asked Terric.

"Yes. When any of us touch the magic, the whole thing heats up."

"Hot?"

"Energized. Powered. Cody thinks this is the trap Eli wanted to lay for all of us. And if we touch it to try to defuse the bomb, cut the wrong wire, it's going to go off."

"Go off and do what?"

He gave me the shrug again. "Blow us all up? Break magic? Infect us all with tainted magic? Wipe Portland off the map? Lots of theories, little data."

"Did you eat a bowl of Valium this morning, Conley? You are way too relaxed about all this."

"I've recently been reminded to enjoy the little things."

I gave him a quick smile. "Go ahead, Sunny," I said, "see if you can reach him."

Terric looked around, didn't see her, but nodded. "Can she talk to you?"

"Yes."

"I bet that's been interesting."

"You don't know the half of it."

"Let me know if she says anything, okay?"

"I'll give you the CliffsNotes."

Sunny walked through the web of magic. Her passing

didn't disturb the spell at all, didn't even make one single thread waver, flare, or move. As soon as she realized she didn't have to worry about the spell kicking to life if she touched it, she walked the straightest line to Davy.

The rope between her and me stretched out with her, but it was a big room. There was only so far she would be able to go before she reached the end of her rope. Literally.

I walked up as close to the spell as I could, stepping over and ducking the thin blue lines.

Davy? She stopped next to where he knelt, close enough she could touch him.

"She's there," I told Terric. "Next to him."

She reached out and gently touched the tangle of blue that cocooned him.

The entire spell pulsed, one flood of blue that lit every line simultaneously, then faded away.

But for that moment, I saw the spell. Saw all of it at once. Saw what it must be.

"I'll be damned," I said. "It's a Gate."

"The entire thing?"

"Yes, didn't you see it light up when Sunny touched it?"

"No. That's all you."

I guess I had seen it change because of my connection with Sunny. "Who casts a Gate spell this big? And where the hell does it open to?"

"I don't care," a new voice said behind us.

I turned.

Zayvion Jones was walking into the room. Had on boots, jeans, and a sweatshirt, only it looked as if he'd been sleeping in them for a couple of days. Plus, he needed a shave. "Shame, Terric."

I'd seen that man face down the magical apocalypse at the end of the world. He hadn't looked half as tired as he did now.

"You look like hell, mate," I said.

He paused, then took a full breath. "Don't touch the Gate, don't go through the Gate, don't do anything with this thing. We're going to the hospital. Now."

"The baby?" I asked.

"C-section. The sooner we get there, the higher the chance the baby survives."

He said it calmly, but I could see how those words hurt him. No wonder he looked like crap. Forget about magic and Gates and bombs. He was up to his neck in his own personal hell.

"And," he said, his voice wavering. He cleared his throat. "The sooner we get to the hospital, the higher the chance Allie will survive."

Every word came out flat, but oddly weighted by pain. And I knew why. He was not only dealing with Allie dying; he was connected to her. He was dying with her.

"Son of a bitch," I said. "I'm sorry, Zay. Go. We got this."

"No. I don't want you to have this. We don't know what it is and I am not going to take the risk of the two of you fucking around with it. I'll handle it."

"No," I said. "That's a bad idea."

He wasn't listening. "You're not going to touch it or trigger it. Do you get me, Shamus?"

"Sure," I said. "I hear you. I'm not going to do anything to fuck this up, Zay. Go. Take care of Al and give us five minutes to see if we can find a way to get you and her out of here."

His gaze weighed me, then turned to Terric. "What the hell happened to you two?"

"Just a death thing," I said. "It's all good."

He ignored me. "Terric?"

"Eli's a vindictive bastard," Terric said. "We're handling him."

Zay looked back at me, one more time at Terric, then nodded. "Five minutes, and then I'm leaving no matter what this thing is set to do. He turned and started out of the room. "It's not a Gate spell."

"You can see it?" I asked.

"It looks like the glyphs on the Beckstrom disks."

"Huh," I said to Terric. "Maybe he's right."

"I am," Zayvion said, even though he was already in the hall.

Terric pulled a disk out of his pocket.

"Where the hell did you get that?" I asked.

"Eli dropped it when Stone tackled him and fell through that hole in space Eli opened up."

"Filled with tainted magic?"

"Nope. Feels pure. I'm guessing it's a relic from the old days. Charged back when magic was strong. Clean."

"It's charged?"

"Yes. And changed. He carved a spell over the original spell."

"Gimme."

He hesitated.

"Other half of you, remember, mate? Trusty-trusty."

He dropped it in my hand. I tipped it, light and shadow tunneling through the carvings.

"Not Gate," I said.

"No, it's something he told me would cancel the magic in the drones."

"Wait a minute," I said. "Eli *talked* to you?"

"Funny how chatty he is when he's torturing a man." Terric said it calmly, but I knew him. Hell, I was connected to him. I could feel the wave of heat, anger, and shame that rose in him at the memories of what Eli had done to him.

As I said. Not having his memories would have been a kindness.

"This disk cancels the magic in the drones?" I asked. "All of the drones?"

"I don't know. He said we could use it to cancel the spells he cast. I think. He wasn't being very clear about it."

I handed him the disk. "Well, I am all for crazy plans built on dubious hunches. Let's do this."

"Do what? Shame? What?"

"Trigger the spell."

"You told Zay we wouldn't do that."

"I lied. I do that. We'll cast Block when we trigger it. Should keep Zay and Allie out of the blast zone."

"We don't know what the blast zone is."

"We'll take an educated guess."

"And we're not going to tell anyone that we're doing this, why?" he asked, putting the disk back in his pocket.

"Too many people get involved and we'd have to make a new plan."

"What plan?" Dash asked. He, Cody, and Kevin were all walking into the room.

"The plan of Zay and Allie getting to the hospital as soon as possible," I said.

"No." Dash shook his head. "I'm pretty sure I already heard that plan from Zayvion. You two have something else cooking."

"We think Davy's spell is part of how we can stop the drones," Terric said.

"Why?" Dash asked. "I don't remember Eli being on our side."

"Eli's on Eli's side," Terric said.

"What does that mean?" Kevin asked.

"He's more than happy," Terric said, "to use friends, enemies, and anyone and anything else to get what he wants."

"Okay," Cody said. "Do you know what Eli wants, Terric?"

"Destruction," he said. "Krogher's destruction for using him as a weapon and a tool. Shame and my destruction for killing Brandy. In that order."

"Aw, we're number two on the list?" I said. "Disappointed."

"How does this"—Dash pointed at the spell that spun out around Davy—"stop the drones?"

"Might be a Gate," Terric said.

"Who says?" Kevin asked.

I held up my finger. "It looks like a Gate to me. Zay doesn't agree."

"So we're going to trigger it and find out," Terric finished.

"That's a terrible plan," Dash said. "Eli carved this into Davy and then he led Davy and us here to set it off. You said it yourself, he wants you two destroyed. This isn't a Gate—it's a damn trap."

"Probably," I said. "And we're going to set it off. We will also cast Block, to keep the explosion to a minimum. Kevin, I'd like you to stay with Zayvion and Allie. Just because we're following Eli's bread crumbs doesn't mean he isn't planning to kill them while we're in the woods."

"I'd like to go on record as being against this idea," Kevin said gruffly.

"We'll be sure to have our secretary put that in the notes," I said. "Go. Keep them safe for me, okay?"

"I will," he said. "And you two had better stay a step ahead of the grave. I do not want Zayvion on my ass for letting you go get killed in a permanent sort of way."

"We have a few aces up our sleeve," Terric said.

Kevin gave us both one last look. "This isn't good-bye, boys." He turned and waved his hand above his shoulder as he walked out of the room.

I hoped he was right.

"Now." I clapped my hands and rubbed them together. "Let's do this."

"I'm coming with you," Dash said.

"Bad idea," Cody and I said at the same time. "Jinx, mate," I said. "You owe me a beer."

"It's all a bad idea," Dash said.

"I'm with Shame and Cody on this, Dash," Terric said. "You should stay here."

"Yeah, well, I'm not going to listen to you either, Terric. So let's get this done." He pulled a gun out of his pocket and chambered a round.

I couldn't help appreciating his attitude. Somewhere along the line he had picked up the habit of being armed at all times. I liked it.

If this spell was a Gate, that meant it would swing both ways. It was just as likely to let something through to us as to let us through to something.

And if something was coming through the Gate . . . well, magic is fast. Bullets: faster.

"I don't suppose you'd keep Dash here for us, would you?" I asked Cody.

"You want me to argue with the gunman?"

"Great," I said. "Then this is a plan. Fantastic. Sunny," I said, "I need you to touch Davy again. When I say three, okay?"

"Sunny?" Dash said. "She's here? She's dead."

"Shame tied her soul to him when he killed her," Cody offered up helpfully.

"Jesus, Shame," Dash said. "That's worse."

Yeah, well, we could discuss my screwups later.

"Did you hear me, Sunny?"

I heard. I'll touch him. She'd been involved in magic for years. She knew the only way to get Davy out of this mess was to set the spell free to release him.

And we were about to find out if setting the spell free would release him alive or dead.

But promise me that you'll catch him if he dies, she said.

I nodded. It meant I'd have both of them haunting me for the rest of my life. But I owed her . . . well, at least a chance to be with him again.

"If Davy lives," I said to Cody, "he'll need help."

"Already have nine-one-one coming this way," he said. "I'll make sure he's taken care of."

"Ready, then." I glanced at Terric. "Block?"

"Got it," he said, finishing the last lines of the spell. We'd have to fill it with magic at the same time we were triggering Eli's spell. A tricky bit of work.

This really was a bad plan.

"One, two, three." I put my hand on Terric's right wrist just as Sunny reached into the tangle of blue around Davy and kept her hand there. The entire spell lit up again.

Terric and I drew magic up from the ground beneath us in perfect sync. I am not ashamed to say I moaned a little from the pleasure of it. We set the Block spell thrumming with magic while we focused on Eli's spell.

It was so easy to draw on magic with him, so easy to set it spinning down the threads of the spell, to guide it to the core of the spell, to twist it just a bit so that as the spell activated and Davy was cut free.

Davy yelled and toppled from his knees to the floor.

"Holy shit," Cody said. "He's alive, Shame. Tell Sunny he's alive."

I'd be happy to pass along that news, but the spell spun where Davy had knelt, burning with blue fire that caught red. Thunder fired somewhere above us, and the air sizzled.

In the center of the room was a hole. Not just a hole in space, but a break in reality, a tear in magic. Zayvion had been wrong. It was a Gate.

Go, Mum was yelling. *Now, Shamus, now!*

I ran for it, Terric right beside me. Dash was on our heels. We tucked our heads and jumped.

Chapter 27

SHAME

Hit solid ground on the other side.

Concrete floor.

The Gate slammed shut. Thunder so loud I covered my ears, palms sticky with blood.

A hand grabbed at my shoulder, dragged me up by my hoodie.

I reached out, got ahold of a shirt. Terric. Blinked until the burning in my eyes, ears, and mouth backed off a bit.

We were in a room that might have been an art gallery. Beige walls carved out alcoves of more beige walls, track lights running across a white ceiling with the glyph for Lock painted across it in black. The torn-up strip-wood floor looked like it was made of old pallets and was painted, carved, and burned with dozens of glyphs: spells for containing, draining, binding.

Terric panted beside me, hand on my shoulder, mine on his. Dash was gone. He hadn't made it through the Gate.

Magic users only? Or maybe it was a door made just for Terric and me.

There, right in front of us, was Stone the gargoyle. He

was on all fours, wings extended, head down, and lips pulled back from his teeth. But he was not moving.

He looked like a statue. As if someone had found his "off" button.

Ah, Stoney, no.

"Here they are," a voice behind us said. "The Soul Complements."

We pivoted.

Eli Collins stood about forty feet away from us, wearing the white shirt, suit/vest combination I usually saw him in, his sleeves rolled up, wire-rim glasses hiding his eyes.

But nothing hid the automatic rifle in his hand.

Behind him was an alcove as wide as the room, filled ceiling to floor with what looked like security camera monitors.

"Good to see you again, Shame, Terric," Eli said. "I'm glad you finally accepted my invitation. Although it did take you long enough."

"And you're not shooting us, why?" I asked.

"You don't die easily. Either of you. Good news for me." He licked his lips, smiled. "Well, killing you would have been nice too, but there is so much more I want now that you've proved you can keep on ticking. Death. Life." He waved the gun between us. "Revolving door for the two of you."

I could kill him from here. One quick strike with Death magic. Totally worth a few bullets. I reached for the Death magic inside me.

And got nothing.

"*There* it is," Eli said. "You're getting it now. No magic, unless I say you can use magic, Shame. And no leaving this room unless I say you can leave." He pointed to the glyphs on the floor. "You are locked down. Just like Stone."

"Bullshit," I said.

"Just ask Terric," Eli said. "Terric, tell the poor boy how

good I am at keeping a person exactly where I want him to be."

"What do you want, Eli?" Terric asked.

"I want my Soul Complement back. I want Brandy. Alive. And I want you two to make that happen."

"The hell," I said. "Brandy's been dead and buried for months."

"She has not been buried. She was never buried." He tipped his chin toward the alcove to his left. Not an alcove, a room with a door open just enough I could see the foot of a cot.

"She is waiting for the man who *killed* her to bring her back to life."

Eli stared straight at me, that gun pointed at me.

"I can't bring her back," I said evenly. "My return from death was a fluke, a onetime shot, Eli. I can't bring people back to life. I don't have that power."

He lifted the gun, aiming at Terric. "You will make sure she lives," he said to him. "You"—he pointed the gun back at me—"will fetch her soul for me."

"Not going to happen," I said.

"That's unfortunate." Eli took two steps to the side so we could see the monitors behind him. "Every spell-filled drone under Krogher's control is there on the screens."

A dozen screens. On one of them: Zayvion and Allie, on the way to the operating room. Good. They'd gotten out of the house. Another: my mum in ICU, Hayden beside her. The Den. The Inn. Two other remaining Soul Complements eating somewhere in Rome. Cody. Kevin and Violet and their kid, Daniel. The police department. Every hospital in the city.

All being stalked by a walking bomb.

Son of a bitch.

"What are you doing, Eli?" I asked.

"Krogher isn't the only one who has control of these

weapons," he said. "I worked a loophole into each of those spells I carved into them. I've found it prudent to have a back door, seeing how consistently I have been betrayed.

"With one word, I can trigger every spell simultaneously. And then . . . well. You lose. Everything."

"I can't bring her back," I said.

"Oh? Then maybe I should show you just exactly how I can trigger a bomb." He took several steps over to the monitors.

"He'll do it," Terric said. "He'll bring Brandy back."

I looked over at him. Terric knew I could not do that. I didn't have a road to heaven or hell or anywhere a soul might be and had never put a soul back in a body successfully.

"You'll have to let me heal her first," Terric went on, like a teacher who was reciting a lecture on a subject he'd been over a hundred times before. "And then Shame can get her soul."

Calm words, yes. But Terric's heart was racing. And no wonder. He had just offered his torturer a little private time with him in the back room.

"Fuck. Fine," I said, going with whatever plan Terric had. "If you want this to work, I need to see what Terric does. So where he goes, I go."

Eli tipped his head, the light sliding down the lenses to pool shadows under his eyes and in the hollows of his cheeks.

We were promising a madman things we could not deliver—that was going to end well.

"Jesus, Eli," I said. "You and I want mutual destruction. But I don't want all those people dead because you're being a dick. You keep your finger off the big shiny red button of doom, and I play by your rules."

He nodded. "I can do worse than kill you," he said quietly. "You understand that, don't you, Shamus?"

"Sure."

He strolled closer to us, to where we were held imprisoned, trapped by magic. "Keep that in mind. While you go retrieve her soul." He fired six or eight bullets into my heart.

Bastard.

I went down. Terric's hand on my shoulder, but no magic in his touch. He couldn't use magic here, locked in these damn spells, just as I couldn't use magic here locked in these damn spells.

It was, in a sick and twisted way, kind of funny. Eli was betting everything on killing me to go find Brandy's soul, expecting, of course, that the Death magic in me would bring me back . . . even though he had blocked me from using Death magic.

Not like him to be so stupid.

I was so going to kill the fucker.

"Those are Void stone bullets," he said. "To keep your options limited, Shame. Now, Terric, drag him outside the circle."

I didn't know what Eli did to cancel the Binding spells that had held us in place, but I was dragged ten feet or so.

Magic hit me like a falling anvil. I cussed and moaned.

Outside the circle sucked more than inside the circle.

Life magic flared in Terric's hands, poured over my wounds, both burning and numbing as it washed through me. Pain backed off a bit, so that was good.

"It's going to be okay," Terric said. "It's going to be fine."

I was pretty sure it wasn't going to be either of those things, but you know, nice of him to say so.

"Step away from him," Eli demanded, "or the next bullets are in your head."

Terric placed his hand on my shoulder, squeezed. He had that killing fire in his eyes. He stood. "Let me see Brandy," he said.

Now would be a good time to ambush Eli, if I could move. I tried moving.

Nope.

They walked to the cot in the other room, Eli behind Terric, the gun at his back.

I was a mess. Death magic tried to fill all the cracks and corners of me while the Void stones held it, and all other magic, at a distance. I reached for Death magic, but it hovered just beyond my reach, a heavy, caustic power snarling to be used.

Bloody. Hell.

Maybe a master Death magic user couldn't die, but that didn't mean he couldn't suffer.

Shamus, Mum said. *Son, can you hear me?*

I could; it was just difficult to talk. And breathe. "Yes."

"He's going to kill you and then have Terric revive you. Do you understand that?"

"Yes."

"We have a better idea."

"All ears."

Eleanor bent so her eyes were even to where I sat in a sort of useless pile.

She was beautiful. That might be a strange thing to be thinking when I was apparently dying, but not for the first time I wished I'd known her when she was alive. Maybe said yes to that date she'd asked me out on all those years ago.

Now listen carefully, she said. *Eli has some spells on Brandy's body that should help a soul reenter her. It's like the spell Mina cast except much more advanced. He's obviously had some time to work out the kinks.*

He's coming back, Sunny said. *Eleanor, they're coming back. Hurry.*

I think I can step into her body, Eleanor said. *It will buy you and Terric some time. Probably not a lot, but maybe enough for you to kill him.*

They're back, Sunny said. *Shame, they'll hear you if you talk.*

So be ready for that, okay? Eleanor finished.

I'd seen what happened to Mina. Reentering her own body had killed her.

There was absolutely no way I was going to put Eleanor through that. She might think Eli had the spell worked out, and yes, he was a genius, but he was also stark raving batshit insane.

"No," I said.

My turn to call the shots, she said. *Plus, I wasn't really asking your permission. Just letting you know what I'm going to do.*

Terric knelt beside me again. He placed his hand on my chest and the warmth of Life magic washed over me like soothing water, taking the pain down a notch again.

"Brandy's body is alive," he said quietly. "Eli wants me to drain your life. Just enough that you cross over to death. Coma."

The look in his eyes told me he wasn't going to do that.

Tell him, Eleanor said.

If Eli has a word to trigger the spells carved into those people, Mum said from where she was standing just behind Terric, *he has a word for canceling them. He always has a back door. Make him give you that word in exchange for Brandy's soul.*

Crap. That was not a bad idea. We'd been trying to unweapon Eli and Krogher, and all these people they'd taken and spelled up for months now.

And this was our chance. It wasn't a very good chance, but then, it was the only shot we had.

"Help me stand," I said to Terric.

He shifted so he could pull me up by the arm and shoulder, putting his face near mine.

Eli was at a distance, blocking Brandy's room, the gun still in his hand.

"I want a guarantee," I said. It came out a little soft, so I put more air behind it. God, that hurt.

"If I bring her soul back, you tell us how to cancel the magic in all those drones." That came out stronger.

Eli smiled. "And why would I do that?"

"It's sad how you think you're negotiating with a man who cares if he lives. I die, maybe I take Terric with me this time. Maybe I don't come back. That makes you shit out of luck, mate. No me, no soul."

"I'll kill your friends."

"Death doesn't scare me, Eli. Not even their deaths. I know what's on the other side. Been there. Drank the beer."

He hesitated. He had the gun, sure. But his plan revolved around us staying alive. Mostly.

"You told me the disks could stop them," Terric said.

Eli nodded slowly. "So you do have all your memories back. I'm impressed. I saw you—through Davy—as you cast that bastardized UnClosing spell. I hadn't expected it to be successful."

"The drones," I said. "The spell. The deal."

Eli made his decision. Had probably made his decision before we'd walked through that Gate spell.

"Bring me her soul, and I'll tell you how to disarm them," he said. "But I promise you, a single word will set them off. And then we'll see just how comfortable you really are with your friends' deaths, Shame."

"Just take me to her," I said.

Terric walked with me across the room, which hurt like every level of hell. I would use the pain to feed the hole of Death magic in me if I didn't have half a pound of Void stones stuck in my chest keeping me from using Death magic.

Eli backed into Brandy's room, and Terric crossed in front of me so he could walk on my other side.

"What are you doing?" he whispered.

"Eleanor will try to possess her."

"If she can't?"

"I'll buy you a beer in heaven."

The room was larger than I'd expected. Walls and wooden floor covered in an overlapping tangle of spells, an empty cot by the wall, and in the center of the room, a cot where Brandy slept, covered in spells and tubes, surrounded by medical equipment.

Eleanor drifted over and stared down at her for a long moment. Eli, or someone, had cut Brandy's dark hair even shorter to keep it out of the way of the tubes that ran into her nose and down her throat. She was that corpse-y shade of gray, her cheeks and eyes scooped out by shadow, no color in her lips at all.

The labored hiss and clack of the machine that kept her breathing seemed too loud in the quiet of the room, in the utter stillness of her.

"Now, Terric," Eli said. "Send Shame to fetch her soul."

Terric tightened his grip around my ribs. Instead of draining the life out of me, he just poured a little more into me, easing my pain a bit.

I slumped against him and sent that Life magic to connect to Eleanor and the resurrection spells on Brandy.

Okay, Eleanor said. *I think I see how to do this.* I felt the rope between us stretch, tugging at my arm.

And then it snapped.

I gritted my teeth, but a groan still escaped me. That disconnection hurt above all the other pain.

"Shame?" Terric said.

I opened my eyes and stood on my own two boots. Terric kept his arm across my back so I didn't lose the steady bleed of Life magic he was feeding me.

"It's done," I said. "She's in there."

"So quickly?" Eli asked. "Proof, Shame."

"Fuck you. See for yourself."

He waved us back with the gun, and we took a couple of steps away from the cot.

"Give us the spell, Eli," Terric said. "Tell us how to disarm the drones."

The machines around the cot were beeping and flashing. Eleanor was in that body, struggling to live.

I just hoped she wasn't in pain.

"Brandy?" Eli said. "Wake, my love." He briefly drew his finger away from the trigger and pressed one of the buttons on the machine just above her right shoulder.

Magic flowed. That was pure magic, untainted magic, unhealed magic, light magic. The only way to access pure light magic now that it had been all muddled up with dark magic was by having a Beckstrom disk from the old days.

So that's how he'd powered all these spells. Jesus, he must have found a vault of them.

I was going to have to have words with Allie's stepmom, Violet, and tell her the security on her labs was crap.

That is, if I survived.

The spells across Brandy's throat flared a soft green.

Her eyes flew open, rolled back in her head, then focused on the ceiling. She arced back, arms pressing against the mattress, legs stiff, as the machines beeped even louder.

Eli was sweating and breathing hard. He hadn't thought it would work either.

"Back out of the room. Now."

"Tell us the deactivation spell," Terric said.

"You need a Beckstrom disk." He moved between machines, flipping switches. No gun on us, hardly paying attention to us. I couldn't kill him with Death magic with the Void stones rattling around in my chest.

I glanced at Terric.

"And?" Terric said.

Eli turned toward us again, gun in his hand. "Get the hell out of the room."

We backed toward the door. Stepped over the threshold.

"It's Sleep," Eli said.

"That's the spell?" Terric said. "Just sleep?"

"Use the magic in the disk. Cast Sleep. It will drop them cold."

"Will it kill them?"

"Oh, Terric. What I did to them? They are already dead."

He could be lying. We'd find out pretty quick, hopefully before I bled unconscious. All we had to do was cast Sleep and send that spell precisely out to hit each of the drones on those monitors. Drones that were scattered across the world.

It was going to take a hell of a lot of concentration on our part to send a spell by remote sight. But hey, Soul Complements, rule breakers, blah, blah.

"Can you feel her?" Terric asked as we slogged across the floor to the monitors. "Are you still connected to Eleanor?"

"No. Why?"

"That means the spell worked," he said. "That's how we get your mom and maybe Sunny back into their bodies again."

"Swell. Let's deal with one disaster at a time," I panted.

He dug the disk out of his pocket and held it in the palm of his hand, the watery blue light from the monitors catching against the glyphs carved into it.

"Sleep," he said.

"I heard him. You'd better cast it, mate. I'm wrecked." I walked over to the wall and pressed my back against it, locking my knees. From here I could see into Brandy's room. The monitors were to my left.

Good God, I wished I had a smoke. Or painkillers. Or a drink. Or a working gargoyle. Or no bullets in my heart.

Terric stood at an angle to me so he could see the monitors and, from the corner of his eyes, Brandy's room.

Any minute now, Eli was going to figure out that wasn't Brandy in that body. A soul knew a soul. And Soul Complements, even the crazy ones, couldn't be fooled for long.

"Hurry," I said.

The Zen thing Victor had taught all his students came in damn handy. With a single breath, Terric cleared his mind. Another breath, and he was focused on the spell, drawing it in the space between us.

He didn't need to pull magic out of the networks to fill the spell, didn't need to pour Life magic from his body into it either.

All he had to do was tap the magic in the Beckstrom disk, and stay focused on the spell reaching out to each of the people he saw on the monitors.

Terric finished the spell, glanced at me.

I gave him a nod and he triggered the disk.

Magic flared through that spell and burned the room into a supernova. Spell after spell on the walls, the ceiling, the floor, triggered and filled with magic, burned to life, blew.

Son of a bitch. Those spells weren't just set to keep Terric and me where Eli wanted us. They were a bomb ready to go off.

And that damn Sleep spell had been the trigger.

The room filled with spells: Impact, End, Pain. More. Spells I didn't even know the names for. All of them aimed at killing Terric and me, at tearing us apart into so many pieces we'd never glue back together again.

We had one second, maybe not even that, before the spells all hit. Time to make a choice. Who would win?

Death?

Life?

Eli?

Then magic blew us to bits.

Chapter 28

SHAME

In that explosion of power, we made our choice.

Without a word, without so much as a nod, Terric and I reached into the spells as they exploded. We grabbed them with our hands and dragged that raw fire and pain toward us, into our bodies, into our souls.

All magic in the world is joined. Like thousands of rivers, lakes, pools, it is connected by rocks, soil, air, and those who use it.

It is us.

It connected Terric and me, tied us by the soul, made us whole.

Soul Complements.

We could break magic, deep at its core. We could rewrite its rules. If ever there was a time to go all in—to break magic and make it do anything we wanted it to do, this was it.

We broke magic, splitting it like a melon beneath the machete of our will.

It was no longer just Life and Death that filled us. It was no longer the soft, nearly useless force that filled the world.

It was darkness and light, pure, deadly, and intoxicatingly strong.

Magic that anyone could use for a price — pain.

Just like the good ol' days.

All the magic in the world paused, waiting for our hands to guide it. To use it, to make it into whatever we wanted it to be.

The room was silent.

First we kill Eli, I thought, knowing Terric would hear me.

First we stop the drones, Terric thought. *Then we take care of Eli.*

I was still full of Void stone bullets, and yes, they still hurt like hell. But light and dark magic pulsed through me, through Terric, and back to me, in a constant loop, one part adrenaline, the other part morphine. I felt no pain.

We didn't have to talk it out, didn't have to decide who was doing what. We were in perfect sync now, not a horrifying nonperson as I'd feared, but two people perfectly locked together in ways I'd never imagined possible.

Soul Complements. It was strong. Powerful.

Terric and I weren't lost in each other's minds; we were found.

Oh, we could get into so much trouble, I chuckled.

Focus, Flynn, he said.

We focused. It was easy to throw magic, dark and light across any distance. Easy to break the spells carved into the drones. And so we did.

One by one, the drones fell, empty of magic, powerless. All of Eli's work undone, all of Krogher's plans ended. The monitors went blank as the spells that connected the drones to Eli's network and control were broken.

And since we could take the shot, we threw magic at Krogher too. Found where he was hiding in this world, stopped his heart, ended his life with a single thought. It was a much more merciful death than he deserved.

But with Krogher dead, my mum in ICU was safe. Allie, Zay, Cody, Davy, the hospitals, the police department, the remaining Soul Complements, and every other target in Krogher's crosshairs was safe.

But we were not done using magic yet. Were not done with this great power at our disposal. Eli wasn't dead yet.

We strode to Brandy's room, shoulder to shoulder, step in step.

Eli backed away from her cot, gun aimed at her still form. He must have seen us coming, must have known what we had done. He pulled the trigger. The rattle of gunfire filled the air as bullets tore through her body.

"Eleanor!" I said.

Eli swung the barrel our way. "If I can't have *her*," he yelled, "then I'll be damned if you can have *him*." He aimed at Terric.

"No!" I yelled.

We were already throwing magic. To stop him. To end him.

Magic is fast.

Bullets are faster.

A dozen bullets hit Terric. Bullets I couldn't stop.

"You son of a bitch," I growled.

Terric stumbled backward, fell to his knees just as our magic, all magic, pounded into Eli.

I dropped to the floor next to Terric, catching him before he hit the ground.

"Terric?"

"Don't let him live, Shame," he gasped.

I glanced over at Eli. Magic enveloped him, burning Eli alive, searing red and black as it devoured him, his flesh, his bones, until only his ghost remained, standing above a pile of ash at his feet.

"This, I said, to the dead man, "is done between us, Eli Collins. This"—I pointed to the world around me—"is mine.

I rule here. Death rules. I will know if you return. And if you do, I will kill you and burn even your soul to dust. Do you understand me?"

Eli screamed, hatred twisting his face into inhuman rage. He ran at us, but before he could take more than two steps, he faded and was gone.

It was not a cruel enough death for that sick bastard. It was not nearly enough suffering to make him pay for all he had done to hurt the people I loved.

But by God, it felt good to snuff out his flame.

"You're going to be okay," I said to Terric, easing him the rest of the way to the floor.

His pressed hands over his gut, but too much blood covered the floor around him already. Too much of his blood covered me.

"I should have bet on black," he whispered.

"No," I said. "No. You are not going to die. We got this."

"Don't . . ." He inhaled but couldn't seem to get much air in him. ". . . tell me what to do." He tried to smile, but I knew how much pain he was in. I could feel the slow, slow beat of his heart as if it were my own, the numbing shock that was drinking him down, taking his thoughts away, making this world fuzzy and distant, taking him away from me.

He was dying.

Just because we had all the magic at our fingertips didn't mean I could heal him. There weren't spells that could heal instantly. The only healing—real healing—I'd seen magic accomplish was when Life magic filled Terric. But now that we had broken magic, all it was good for was destruction.

I had all the magic in the world in my hands and I still couldn't save the one man who I would give up my life for.

I wasn't ready to let go of him. Not now. Not ever.

Shame? Mum said. *You have to let him go, son. Don't trap his soul. Don't chain him to you.*

She was right. I shouldn't trap him. I should let him go.

The only problem? I never was very good at doing the right thing.

There was a slim chance I could save him. Not by tying his ghostly soul to me. That wasn't saving; that was enslaving.

Life magic could save him. I just needed to unbreak magic, join dark and light together the way Cody had joined it together—by holding it in my body long enough for light and dark magic to blend and heal. And then Terric would be filled with Life magic again, right?

It would heal him. It wouldn't let him die no matter how many bullets were in him.

Joining magic, all magic in the world, wasn't an easy thing. Cody alone had been strong enough to endure that particular hell. Lots of people had tried to join light and dark magic in the past. Lots of people had died. Breaking it wasn't easy, but it wasn't deadly.

It was the joining of magic that would probably kill me. Still, it was worth it.

Time to put all my money on red.

"We had a good run, mate," I said to him, even though he was beyond hearing me now, barely breathing. "Come on up and have a beer someday."

I stood, strode into the other room.

Shame? Mum said again. *What are you doing?*

What I was doing was installing a nuclear reactor into my body. A little distance between me and the guy I was trying to save seemed prudent.

"Love you, Mum," I said. "And, Sunny? I'm sorry for . . . hell. Everything."

She just nodded.

I glanced over at Stone. He wasn't moving, poor little gargoyle. Well, hopefully this would fix that too.

I drew magic to me, dark magic, light magic, all the magic in the world. I opened myself to it, surrendering to it, giving in, giving up. Without hatred, without fear, without anger. Just peace and calm. Very Zen.

I thought Victor might be a little proud of me for that.

Then I commanded it to join together again, to heal and mend using my body as the focal point and as the vessel to do so.

I knew I'd pay a price for this. More than pain. I would pay with my life. But Terric would live.

Worth it.

There was a moment of intense pleasure as magic filled me up and took over every part of me that made me me. And then as I tried to make dark and light join once again, magic tried to unmake me.

Chapter 29

SHAME

"Wish I'd brought my camera." Terric sat next to me, his jeans rolled up, bare feet over the edge of the concrete bricks, a river flowing by below his feet.

My feet too. I was sitting next to him. We were in a city. European, I thought.

"Paris," he said. "You really should travel more, Shame."

"So . . . is this your dream?" I asked. "Or . . . oh Lord. Is it your heaven?"

"No, it's Paris. Really. These aren't our bodies, but . . . you know." He gave me a crooked smile. "Soul Complements break magic, break rules. I thought you and I needed a second or two to talk. And it's been a while since I've been here."

"Talk about what? Wasn't I in the middle of fixing magic? Joining it again?"

"That. You can't heal magic, Shame. Only Cody can."

"You know this because?"

"Those records I've been looking into? They talked a lot about Soul Complements, and a little about the rare—very rare—children of Soul Complements. Cody's mother and father . . ."

"Mikhale and Sedra," I said.

"Soul Complements. And only the children of Soul Complements can actually heal magic, though Allie's dad did some crazy experiments trying to prove that wrong."

"Well, *there's* information that would have been nice to know before I made myself magic's chew toy. Thanks, Ter."

The breeze picked up. Chilly with the first drops of rain.

"There's a way out of this. I think," he said.

"Paris?"

"You dying, idiot."

"Go on."

"I can heal you. You managed to hold magic long enough for me to get Life magic back, mostly, so thanks for that. I should be able to heal you enough for you to give the magic over to Cody to fix. Permanently."

"That will work?"

"Sixty-forty."

"And magic?"

"I'm guessing Cody will make it what it was before: gentle, blended. Except for when Soul Complements break it."

"Great," I said. "There's just going to be someone else, another Eli, another Krogher, who will find a way to tap magic, to make it into a weapon again. To hurt people with it. Kind of tired of putting out the world's fires, mate."

"Right," he said, "I've been thinking about that too. What if no one can use magic, *no one*? Then we won't have anything to worry about. Magic will still be there, flowing like water beneath the earth, and maybe someone will find a way to tap in to it, on occasion, on accident, but otherwise . . ." He shrugged.

"So, what? We make it so spells don't work?" I asked. "We make it so that even if you draw a perfect glyph, magic won't come to your calling?"

"That's the idea, yes."

"And when you say no one can use it, you mean there are no exceptions? Not even for you and me?"

He looked away, at the bridge and city downriver. When those blue eyes turned back to me, there was more than a bit of a gleam in them. "Well . . . maybe we could make a small exception."

"And now I like this idea."

He grinned. "Good." It was raining harder now, most of it falling right through us. He stood up and held his hand down for me. "Then don't die."

I took his hand.

It was cool, warm.

Filled with magic.

Life magic.

I opened my eyes and inhaled just enough to know that I shouldn't go overboard on that breathing thing yet. A lot of magic burned and snapped inside me. Well, all magic, really. I still carried it all, despite Terric's little let's-ghost-off-to-Paris trick.

He knelt above me. His mouth was moving, so I assumed he was talking, but I wasn't getting any of it.

He pressed his hand against my chest and one hard strike of magic rocked me.

And blew all the air out of me.

I inhaled again—it still hurt—but this time he had my full attention.

"The hell," I wheezed.

"You don't get to die, remember?"

"Don't tell me what to do."

That got a smile out of him.

"We need to get out of here," he said. "You need a hospital. And Cody."

"Me?" I was going to scoff, but the room spun, and then I was on my feet, Terric holding my arm over his shoulder.

"...healed," he was saying. "Life magic hit me like a damn avalanche, and I'm fine. You, on the other hand, look like pounded hell. You have to let go of all that magic before it burns you up."

"Wait," I said. We were still in the room Eli had brought us to, which was burned and slashed from the explosion of magic we'd harnessed. Stone growled next to my leg. I looked down at him and he tipped his big face up at me.

"Stoney! Good to see you, buddy."

Mum's and Sunny's ghosts were still with me, but I was missing someone.

"Eleanor," I said, finally remembering.

Terric paused. "I think she's dead, Shame."

"I have to know. I need to."

So we limped into the room where Eli had kept Brandy's body.

No signs of fire and magic here. Just blood. Blood covered the floor, blood soaked the white blanket and sheet covering her, blood sprayed the wall.

All the machines were silent. Unplugged.

"Closer," I told Terric. He helped me walk the distance.

Her eyes were open. A single tear ran down her cheek.

"She's alive," I said, hope leaping into a sort of panic. "Heal her, Ter. You can heal her."

"Shame," he said quietly. "There wasn't much I could do for her body before. And now ... with that many bullets and her barely being alive for months? Eleanor would be trapped, Shame. A vegetable at best."

"*God*," Sunny said. "*Shame, don't do that to her. Better death.*"

I pulled away from Terric, kept my feet, which I think surprised both of us. I eased down and sat on the edge of the cot where Eleanor could see me. Where I could see her, there behind Brandy's eyes.

"Hey, El. You are amazing," I said. "We saved them all.

Allie, Zay, Cody. And we think we can save Mum and Sunny too. Because of you. What you did in here? How brave you were? I'll never forget that. I hope you'll save a drink in heaven for me, love."

I put my hand on her chest, or what was left of it. Eli had reduced her to a gory mess.

I still had Death magic somewhere in the tangle of magic in me. If I pulled the right thread, I could ease her pain. Ease her passing. I owed her that. I owed her more.

I wasn't expecting this to be simple. But I wasn't going to leave her here to suffer. I called Death magic to me.

What did you know? It was simple. Death magic slipped over my hand like a velvet glove, dark and soft and blessedly painless. I wrapped her in it as gently as I could and let it drain her life away.

Eleanor closed her eyes, tears caught in her eyelashes, and then exhaled her last breath.

Her ghost stood beside me and smiled. *This,* she said, *was a very good choice, Shame.*

She gently cupped the side of my face and kissed my lips, cool and sweet as rain. *You two look good together,* she whispered. *Using magic. Soul Complements. Keep it that way.*

I reached for her, to tell her thank you, to tell her I was sorry, but she faded away and was gone from this world. Gone from me for good this time. I knew I should be happy she was finally free, but I was going to miss her dearly.

". . . chance for your mom and Sunny. Now, Shame," Terric was saying.

Magic rolled in me, cutting and chewing on all my tender places.

I got myself on my feet again, started toward the door. "We fix Mum first, okay?"

Terric walked on one side; Stone padded ahead of us. "Just keep breathing," he said. "And we'll get to your mom and Sunny."

He tested the door to see if it was locked. It wasn't. That's how certain Eli was that we wouldn't be walking out of this place. Asshole.

My one and only goal was reaching the outside door to the sidewalk beyond. And when I achieved that, my one and only goal was not passing out while Terric asked someone walking by if he could borrow their phone.

Someone finally said yes.

He called for Dash, not surprisingly. Dash made it to where we were in record time.

He double-parked and got out of the car.

"My God, Terric. Shame," he said as he jogged over. "I didn't think I'd see you two alive."

"We need to get him to the hospital, where Maeve is," Terric said.

"Sure, yes," Dash said. "Can he walk?"

I pushed away from the wall, Stone's head under my hand. He walked with me toward Dash's car.

"Holy shit," Dash breathed. "What happened to him?" Then he was opening the door and Terric was helping me into the car.

Stone jumped in and settled on the seat next to me. I slouched down, one arm over Stone's shoulders. He burbled and locked warm, smooth marble wings around me, holding me secure as Dash raced to the hospital.

If Terric responded, I was long past hearing him.

Chapter 30

SHAME

It took me three tries to convince the gargoyle I needed to get out of the car without him attached to me. He made disapproving grumbles but finally unlocked his wings.

Dash was waiting with a wheelchair, which I thought was completely unnecessary, until I tried to drag my ass out of the car.

Stiff, swollen, and aching from feet to teeth, I felt like someone had fed me through the meat grinder. Twice. And set me on fire just for good measure.

So I got in the chair and let him push me. Stone, finally, caught the hint that gargoyles should not be seen or heard and took off into the shadows.

"Mum's right?"

Terric looked down at me. "Have you heard anything we've said?"

"No."

"We're almost there."

I looked around for her ghost. Mum and Sunny were still tied to me, drifting along in front of Dash.

"This is it," Dash said.

Terric opened the door and Dash pushed me into the room.

Hayden sat at Mum's side, holding her hand. If the machines that had been in Brandy's room were overly loud, these were very quiet, almost hushed about the readings they were taking from her.

Hayden glanced up, smiled when he saw Terric. "Good to see you," he said. Then his gaze drifted to me. "Good God, boy. What did you do?"

"Found a way to save Mum," I said. "A spell."

"Did you?" Hayden looked from me to Terric. "Did he?"

"We," Terric said. "It's a refined Resurrection spell. We think it will allow her to reenter her body and stay there."

"And?" he asked.

"We've only tested it once," Terric said.

"You aren't going to test it on her," Hayden said. "I won't risk her life on a maybe."

Mum crossed her arms over her chest. *Tell him I want you to do it.*

"He won't listen to me," I said.

Tell him I love him but he is being a bloody idiot.

"Uh, Mum says she loves you but you're being a bloody idiot," I said.

He looked a little startled at that. "She wants you to do this?"

Yes, she said.

"Yes," I said.

Hayden rubbed his hand over his beard, then took her hand again. "All right."

"Do you want me to cast?" Terric asked.

I groaned my way out of the chair and caught a glimpse of myself in the mirror in the bathroom to my left.

No wonder everyone was looking at me as if I were a monster. My skin was burned, blistered in patches, and peeling in others. That feeling of being stiff and swollen I hadn't been able to shake since Terric re-Lifed me was not just a feeling. I looked like I was having the worst allergic reaction ever.

And I was. Magic wasn't sitting well with me at all.

But it was my eyes that really did the freaky. Magic pooled there, shifting like aurora borealis fire across the iris and whites of my eyes.

My body was burning up, burning out. I didn't know how much longer it would be before my flesh and blood were gone.

Wiped out by magic.

The faster we got Mum and Sunny back to their bodies, the better. Otherwise, they would be riding the friendly skies heavenward with me.

"Yes," I said to Terric, "cast."

He closed his eyes, then cast the spell, brilliantly, beautifully, perfectly. The glyph hovered in the air, then gently drifted down to spread across her torso.

"Shame?" Terric asked.

"Go on now, Mum," I said to her ghost. "Terric's going to pour Life magic into the spell. You'll feel the pull, and then you'll be free."

"Almost," Terric said. "I'm going to pour Life magic in you, Shame, and you're going to send that magic into the spell. It's how we did it before."

"I didn't have all this magic in me before," I said.

"You had Death magic. You still have Death magic."

"You boys do know what you're doing, right?" Hayden asked.

Hell, I hoped so. I put my hand on Terric's shoulder, Terric pushed Life magic through me, and I channeled it into the glyph.

This time my eyes were open, so I saw Mum pause, then slip down into her body, like a feather caught in a draft.

The tie between us broke, and sure, it hurt, but it was worth it.

She opened her eyes, saw Hayden, smiled.

It worked. Oh thank God, it worked.

And then the machines were making noises, and Hayden was on his feet, and the nursing staff was rushing into the room, and somehow Terric and I were out of the room, out in the hall, even Dash left behind, caught up in the chaos of Mum's return to life.

"Sunny," I said.

You won't make it, Sunny said.

"You won't make it," Terric said. "We'll take care of her after we take care of you."

"That's not how it's happening, mate," I said. "If it is the last fucking thing I do, I'm going to fix what I can. I broke Sunny—"

More like killed, she said.

"—and I'm going to fix that. Where is she?"

"Dash said they put her up at Kevin's place."

I concentrated on Kevin's house, imagined his overly large living room, held it clear and focused in my mind. Then I drew the glyph for gate and poured some of the too much magic in me into it.

Got it right enough on the first go. That was Kevin's place on the other side of that hole I'd sizzled into space. I grabbed Terric's sleeve and pulled him with me through the spell before my concentration slipped.

Stumbled to one knee but made it.

"Where?" I asked again, although breathing was getting to be a real problem.

My body was not built to carry all magic. Not like Cody, who had acted as the Focal the last time two Soul Complements—Allie and Zay—had tried to fix magic.

Unlike Cody, this was eating me alive. Ending me.

This way, Sunny said, running for the hall.

I followed her, my feet growing heavier with each step. I pressed my shoulder against the wall to steady myself. Terric slipped his arm around me and together we walked down to the room Sunny's ghost had disappeared into.

Terric was talking again, and I wasn't listening again. Something about Cody and magic and blah, blah, blah.

Sunny lay on the bed, still as death, though they'd hooked her up to machines too. Davy was on top of the covers next to her, on his side, his arm across her waist, his head tucked against her shoulder.

"Davy," Terric said. "Move back. We know how to get Sunny back in her body. We have a spell for it."

Davy drew his head away from her and shifted on the bed.

"What happened to you, Shame?" he asked, his voice raw as if he'd spent a year yelling, or sobbing. "Eli?"

"Self-inflicted wounds, mate," I said. And, "He's dead. Now move over so I can give you your girl back."

Davy moved. Terric drew the spell again, just as perfect, just as precise. Sunny's ghost stood by the bed, biting at her thumbnail.

I know I won't be in perfect shape, she said. *I mean, I was dead for over a day. There's going to be complications. But do you think I'll be a vegetable, Shame?*

"No," I said. "There's still life that wants to thrive inside you. It won't be easy, but you'll land on your feet."

Shame, she said. *I want you to know I appreciate you doing this.*

"My fault to begin with," I said, or tried to. The room was sliding down a long, long tunnel in front of me. "Wish I could do more."

And then Terric sent Life magic through me. Even though I was drowning in magic, I guided it, willed it to reach into Sunny and help her live, live, live.

C'mon, Red. We're betting it all on you.

The tie between us snapped, a hard *ping* of pain that rolled through me. And like the camel's back, I broke.

*　　*　　*

"Here," Cody said. "Just lay him down." Cody was leaning over me, his face close enough to mine I couldn't help hearing every word he said.

"Give it up, Shame. You can't hold that magic. I can. Let go and let me have it."

"Take," I said through swollen lips, "it."

Terric's hand was in mine, a fact I noticed as soon as he raised it into my line of sight.

Cody leaned back just far enough that Terric could trace a Transference spell in front of him.

I did my best to concentrate on those lines he drew with our clasped hands.

And as we used magic together, we were once again close enough to hear each other's thoughts.

Wow, Terric was terrified I was going to die.

Like that'd be a new thing.

Don't go delirious on me, Flynn, he thought.

Not delirious, I thought. *World would be better without magic.*

The world will be better, magic will be better, as soon as Cody heals it. Let go of it, Shame. You've done all you can. It's over. Let it be over.

Maybe for the first time in a long time, I didn't even argue with him.

Magic followed the spell Terric had traced. We cut into the magic inside me, light and dark, and let it pour out into the spell that strobed black and white between us. Then we sent that spell into Cody's chest.

Streams of aurora borealis flame twisted and poured around us.

Cody closed his eyes and let the magic fill him, his hands moving through complex spells. He tied and blended and wove darkness and light together with the instinct and soul of an artist, making magic into an amazing tapestry.

He healed magic, made it whole, and at the same time made it into a radiant expression of what magic could be: hope, peace, love, miracles. Things I certainly couldn't see in it. Things it would never be in my hands. Things I was glad he could make it be.

It was better this way. Magic was better when it was gentled, healed by Cody.

But for this to work, we had to hit him with everything, give him all the magic to mend and weave back together.

Okay, all the magic except the Death magic I kept cupped in my palm.

All the magic except the Life magic Terric held behind his back.

You do know we're cheating, I thought to Terric.

Terric's smile flashed through my mind, and left behind the taste of cloves. *This isn't cheating. It's keeping our possibilities open.*

Then all the magic, well, *almost all* the magic in the world, was in Cody's brilliant hands, body, and brain.

I was just me again, tired, empty, raw, Terric a steady warmth beside me and in my mind.

Cody inhaled, exhaled, and sent magic back out into the world, healed and whole.

And our new world began.

Chapter 31

SHAME

"...are you listening to me?" Allie said. She snapped her fingers twice. "Hello? Planet Earth to Shamus Flynn."

"Coming in loud and clear, m'dear." I was currently lounging on their couch, a half-drunk beer on the table next to me, my feet propped up on Stone's back. He was snoring softly, a stuffed puppy in his hand. Kind of adorable.

Zayvion was off getting Allie some iced tea from the kitchen. Probably just an excuse for him and Terric to talk about how magic had gone quiet and invisible since Terric and I gave it back to Cody and Cody gave it back to the world.

Which left me in the living room with Allie, who looked pretty damn good for a woman who'd just had a baby a week ago, my mum, who was on the couch with a thick wool blanket and Hayden's arm wrapped around her, even though it was plenty warm enough in the room, and Davy, who sat on the floor in front of Sunny's wheelchair.

Mum was moving pretty slowly, and resting a lot. Even with Hayden doting on her hand and foot, I knew what I'd done to her had left permanent damage. She'd aged in the short week since she'd returned to her body, her hair now a cascade of pure silver.

Sunny had recovered too, although she wasn't up to walking yet. The doctors had told her she probably never would. She had told them to shove it. She planned to be walking down the aisle with Davy in a year.

Davy was healthy enough to take care of Sunny, and had already said his apologies for being used against us. Unnecessary apologies. We'd let him down far more than he'd let us down. All the spells Eli had carved into him were dead now, leaving behind a wicked sort of full-body tattoo. Very tribal. I was sure it was going to look boss with the wedding ring he'd soon be wearing.

Terric had gotten out of the mess with a missing pinkie finger, and I'd somehow kept the aurora borealis glow in my eyes. It was still freaky. Sunglasses were now a permanent wardrobe item.

"So," Allie said, "you heard me warning you that I am going to make you hold your goddaughter, right?"

"Uh, right. Sometime, sure."

Allie fixed me with a look and eased up out of the rocking chair with the baby in her arms.

". . . in the future . . ."

She raised one eyebrow and nudged my legs with her foot. I drew my boots off the gargoyle and sat up straighter.

". . . when she is much less fragile . . ."

Allie plopped the tiny pink-wrapped bundle of baby Beckstrom-Jones into my arms.

". . . holy crap."

Sunny and Mum laughed.

"Language," Allie said.

This was the first time in my life I'd held a baby. Suddenly I was all thumbs and elbows, and every joint went stiff as I held perfectly still.

"Well, this was great," I said. "A miracle of life. Glad to be a part of it. You can take her back now."

"Oh, I don't think so." Allie walked over to the chair and sat down, smug as a cat.

"Please?"

"Nope."

"You're doing fine, son," Mum said from over her cup of tea.

The baby squished up her face and opened her mouth.

"What's she doing?" I asked, alarmed.

"Her name is Ramona Jozette, and she is yawning," Allie said.

"You can handle a little baby yawn, can't you?" Sunny asked.

"No," I said. "I most definitely cannot. Take her back before I break something." I sort of lifted my arms awkwardly, trying to hold her out for Allie to retrieve.

"Suck it up, Shame," Allie said. "You are officially in training. I expect full babysitting days out of you in the future."

"You should know better than to leave her with a guy like me, Beckstrom."

"What? A Death magic user who might at any moment drain the life out of her?" She gave me an innocent look. "Oh no. That's right. You can't do that anymore. *Nobody* can use magic anymore. Because you broke it."

I grinned. "You say that like it's a bad thing."

"What's a bad thing?" Zayvion strolled into the room, Terric a step behind him. "Hold on. Is that my daughter in your arms, Shame?"

"Yes," I said. "Thought she and I could have a little talk. Somebody's got to tell her all her daddy's dirty secrets."

Zay gave me a smile and his brown eyes were just brown. No more gold for him, no more magic for the man who had stood at the front lines on this city's battlefields for years, protecting it from the people who were trying to destroy it.

No more worrying about protecting his daughter from the things people with magic might do to her—a Soul Complement's child.

It had turned out to be, I decided, one of my favorite side effects of me trying to swallow magic whole, and it trying to tear me apart. Maybe his kid would have a chance to grow up in a place that wasn't so full of fear and pain.

"Tell her anything you want," Zay said, handing the iced tea to Allie. "I've got nothing to hide. She knows I love her."

"Is that right, Rami Jo?" I asked the baby, who had her daddy's thick black hair and her mommy's nose. "Did you also know that your old man was a very bad man back in his day before he grew up and turned soft and fatherly?"

"Unlike her uncle Shame," Terric said, "who is still a bad man and never grew up."

"Or your uncle Terric, who is a terrible liar, and owes me for saving his life. Again."

Terric settled onto the couch, took a swallow of his tea, and grinned. "Asshole."

"Language," Allie said.

Mum laughed again. "I don't think she understands it yet, sweetheart."

"It's the principle," Allie said.

I carefully shifted the baby so I could hold her in one hand. Her little body lay down on my arm but didn't even reach the crook of my elbow.

"Hey, look at that," I said. "I think I'm starting to get the hang of this. She's like a little football, isn't she?"

Zay crossed the space between us in three strides and plucked her out of my hands. "You know what? You are doing that wrong."

There it was. Promise complete. I held his daughter and

he told me I was doing it wrong. I grinned, leaned back. "What? I wasn't going to punt her."

"I know," he said, but his body language had gone daddy lion protective. Oh, her future dates were in for a world of hurt.

I looked over at Terric, who threw me a small smile. We were going to have a hell of a lot of fun teasing him for the next couple of decades.

Ah, who was I kidding? Fatherhood looked good on him.

"So, magic," Allie said, swinging back on the subject. "Now that we're all up and about, tell us exactly what you two did. I tried talking to Cody, but he was elbow deep in figuring out why Stone was still working after what you did."

Stone's ears pricked up at the sound of his name and he trotted over to sit on the floor between Allie's and Zay's chairs.

"We broke it," Terric said. "Killed the drones who were too far gone to be saved. Killed Eli and Krogher. Then Shame tried to put dark and light magic back together. Idiot."

"Well, if you'd managed to take a couple bullets like a man and not go whining to heaven about it, I wouldn't have had to mend magic."

"His attempt," Terric went on, "gave Life magic a hold in me. It healed me, then pulled him back from the brink of death. Which reminds me, I did the math. I've saved your life more than you've saved mine."

"Bullshit."

"Holy hells, Shame," Allie said. "Language."

"When we finally worked the fucking Transference spell," I said.

Allie threw her hands in the air and rolled her eyes.

"Shame," Mum warned, but she was trying not to smile.

"All the damn magic flooded into Cody, and he shitting fixed it. So you can blame that son of a bitch, not us."

"Okay," Zay said. "Allie and I used Cody to mend magic too, three years ago. Magic still worked afterward."

"Yes, but it was softer and gentler." I shrugged.

"Maybe it gets weaker each time it's broken and healed?" Davy suggested.

"Could be," Sunny said.

I took a drink of my beer and Terric glanced at me over his glass of tea, one eyebrow twitching upward. The thing we hadn't told them was we each could still use magic. He could use Life magic and I could use Death.

Magic wasn't gone from the world, far from it. We'd just made sure it was just a lot harder to get to now. Nigh impossible to reach. Well, except for us.

"Just because glyphs, spells, and blood can't hold magic," Hayden said, "doesn't mean people won't try other things."

"Sure," Terric said. "If magic can be accessed, humankind will find a way to do so."

"Are there any back doors into magic that you two know about?" Zay asked. "Any loopholes?"

"Nope," I lied.

"Terric," Mum asked. "Is that true?"

I made an offended sound. "Right here."

Terric just gave me a told-you-so look. "You have my word on it," he said. "No back doors."

Okay, seriously. Terric was turning into a first-class liar. Warmed my little black heart.

Zay just made a *hmm* sound.

He and Zay had the kind of friendship that didn't allow for a lot of lies. For all that we had grown up shoulder to shoulder, he and Zay had been up for the same position in the Authority. They had trained together, worked together, and had both been Victor's star pupils. They knew each other better than brothers.

Of course Zay and I knew each other better than brothers too. Which is why he was right to be suspicious of my answer, at least.

"If that answer ever changes," Zay said, "you'll come to

me, right? Both of you will." It wasn't so much a question as a command. As if he could call the shots.

Well, I guess old habits die hard.

"Of course we will, Daddy Jones," I said. "The day that the *truth* we are telling you suddenly turns into a lie, we'll be sure to give you a call."

"Good," he said. "Don't forget it."

Rami Jo made a cute little cooing sound and Allie and Zay exchanged a look that was more than love. Stone's wings shivered in delight and he hummed softly back to her. I had a feeling baby Rami Jo was going to be Stone's favorite little buddy ever.

"We're glad you're both okay," Mum said. "You are okay, aren't you?"

"Breathing all day every day," I said.

"And the Soul Complement stuff," Hayden asked, "is that finally good between you two boys?"

"Oh yeah," Terric said. "All good." He made a kissy face at me, so I flipped him off.

Like he said: all good.

Chapter 32

SHAME

The door of the diner behind Terric opened, letting in the warm June wind, a little sunlight, and a man I'd invited to lunch.

The man was Dashiell Spade. He caught sight of us and headed our way.

"What?" Terric asked me from over the slice of pie he was eating.

I tugged down my sunglasses just enough to gaze over the top of them. "I thought a movie might be fun tonight. You like movies, right, Terric?"

"Some movies. Sure."

"Good. I got tickets." I slid them across the table to him, pushed my sunglasses back into place.

"You and me?" He didn't touch the tickets but took another bite of pie and gave me a wary look. "What do you want, Shame? And don't make me come in there"—he waved his fork toward my head—"to find out."

It had been a couple of months since we'd broken magic and changed the world.

We'd figured out a few tricks of being Soul Complements, the first of which was how to block what we were thinking from each other. Some other tricks too, like how to use Life magic and Death magic so no one noticed we were doing so.

Worked best if we did it together, but wasn't so bad if we did it alone.

Life and Death didn't eat away at us like before. Terric had found a very old joining spell. It looked a lot like an infinity sign. We'd both had it tattooed, his on his left arm, mine on my right. Whenever we were around each other, magic sort of . . . balanced between us.

Eleanor had been right all along. Using magic together did make it better for both of us.

And we'd gotten good enough at blocking our thoughts that we didn't even have to concentrate on it much anymore.

Which meant I could plan something, like a movie, and he wouldn't know.

"Hey," Dash said, stopping by the table. "How's it going?"

"Dash," Terric said, throwing a look my way. "Nice to see you."

I took a bite of my pie and ignored Terric. "Pull up a seat," I said. "Terric was just telling me there's a movie he's excited to see. He has two tickets, but I have to bail on him. You two should go."

"Uh, okay." Dash snagged a chair from the other table to set next to us. "If you want me to?"

"Of course he does," I said. "Go on, Ter. You deserve a little downtime. I know how much you've been looking forward to this."

Just let go, mate, I thought. *And maybe let a good thing happen for once. The man likes you. It wouldn't kill you to let him know you like him back.*

Terric leaned back and studied me as if he were seeing new words in a book he'd been reading all his life.

Because suddenly you've decided I should date him?

Because you want to, I thought. *If I'm wrong, I'm wrong. No worries. I just . . . I want you to be happy.*

I am happy.

And behind those words was so much more. He was happy to be alive, happy I was alive, happy we weren't being hunted, hurt, killed. Happy we had finally accepted that, like it or not, we would always be together. Soul Complements, brothers, friends. Not such a bad thing.

"Terric? Everything okay?" Dash asked.

"Yes, yes. Sorry. Yes. If you're game, I have two tickets," Terric said. He picked up the tickets, read them. "And it looks like it starts in half an hour. How convenient." He tapped the table with a fingertip. "Let me settle our bill. I'll be right back."

He got up and walked over to the register. I ate pie.

"You put him up to this, didn't you?" Dash asked.

"Naw, not really. He's wanted to do this for years."

"But the movie and the second ticket for me was your idea."

I put my fork down and picked up my coffee. "Maybe."

"Shame," he started.

"Okay, yes. Hey. I have good ideas. This was one of them. Live life to the fullest, I always say."

"You never say that."

"Are you deaf? I just said it."

"You've made a lot of enemies, you know," he said. "People will find out it was you and Terric that broke magic and put it back together. They'll think you somehow made it so none of the spells work anymore. They'll think you two are what's standing in the way of them getting magic back."

"Nobody's getting magic back, and the world's a better place because of it," I said.

"They won't believe you. You'll have a target on your head."

"Aren't you gloom and doom today? Also, like I care?" I took a drink of coffee.

"You should," he said, holding my gaze. "For your friends, your mother, hell, for me, if no one else. I already saw you and Terric bloody and dead once. I don't ever want to see that again."

"Everyone dies, Dash," I said. "Can't promise that when we die, we'll go gentle."

"Just promise it won't be anytime soon."

"Cross my heart," I said.

Terric strolled over to the table. "Ready?"

Dash stood, smiled. "Looking forward to it."

Terric pointed a finger at me. "Your mom wants you over for dinner tonight."

"I'll be there."

"And Sunny said she and Davy are up for poker night at our house, six o'clock on Thursday."

"I'll be there too."

"Don't forget to pick up groceries today. We're out of coffee."

I shook my head. This was what my life had become. I was roommates with a walking to-do list.

"Go away, Terric. Dash, make him go away."

"Actually, I'm in no hurry," Dash said. "We could catch a later show. How's the laundry situation, Terric?"

"Now that you mention it, those socks aren't sorting themselves."

I picked up my fork and gripped it like a dagger. "Just because I like you doesn't mean I won't stab you both in the neck. Go."

"Groceries," Terric said again.

I made a shooing motion with my free hand.

"Bye, Shame," Dash said. "See you tonight."

"Well," Terric said, "see you sometime."

Dash raised his eyebrows and Terric smiled.

They headed toward the door.

I took a deep breath, glad for the peace and quiet in the diner.

No more ghosts, no more magic. Just a collection of worn-out people sitting at worn-out tables talking over worn-out problems. I picked up my coffee, drank the last cold dregs of it, then got up and walked out into the June sunlight.

Got about three strides down the block before a bullet cracked into the brick of the building right over my shoulder, and a second buried itself into my arm.

"Son of a bitch." That hurt. But it wouldn't kill me.

Spotted the gunman taking off down the alley toward his car there. I'd seen him before. He looked like the killer I'd been after a few weeks ago, Stuart. One of the killers from Victor's hit list.

Well, well. Things really were looking up. I grinned and strode down the street toward him, drawing Death magic into my hand. Magic, my magic, and yes, Terric's magic, was invisible now. It was also much more of a laying-on-of-hands type of thing.

I caught up to the guy and shoved him against the brick wall with a single touch of Freeze.

"Mr. Stuart?" I said, leaning my weight into my hand on his shoulder and magic holding him. "I think you and I need to have a little talk."

I lifted my other hand filled with Death magic and patted his chest. "Your killing days are over, mate. Time's up."

Death magic hit. I stepped back, took my hands off him. He crumpled to the ground, his heart beating too hard, then not at all.

The coroner would say heart attack. Not uncommon for someone his age with such poor eating and exercise habits.

Right. I pulled a handkerchief out of my pocket and pressed it against the bullet wound in my shoulder. I'd ask Terric to heal it later.

I stepped over the body and started off to my car.

Okay, so maybe I hadn't found peace, exactly. And yes, I still had Death riding my bones, and Terric still had Life to grapple with. We were okay with that. For the first time in our lives, we were even pretty okay with each other.

Maybe that was as good as it was going to get for me, for us.

As far as I was concerned? It was plenty good enough.

I got in my car and pulled Victor's hit list of killers out of the glove compartment. Crossed poor heart attack Mr. Stuart off the list and glanced at the next name.

Last-known address: Tacoma.

I tucked the list back in the glove box and dug a cigarette out of my pocket. Lit up, rolled down the window, and exhaled smoke into the sunny day.

Tacoma was just a few hours north of here. Sorry, Terric. Groceries would have to wait. I started the engine and grinned. I had plenty of daylight, a full tank of gas, and a man to kill.

Life just didn't get any better than that.

Read on for an excerpt from
Devon Monk's thrilling new novel,

HOUSE IMMORTAL

Coming in September 2014 from Roc!

*They named the comet Mercury Star. Not for how brightly
it burned, but for the star-shaped hole it punched into the
land and the rich, strange mix of minerals it left behind.*

— L.U.C.

The way I saw it, a girl only needed three things to start a
day right: a hot cup of tea, a sturdy pair of boots, and for the
feral beast to die the first time she stabbed it in the brain.

"You missed, Matilda," Neds called out from where he
was leaning in the cover of trees several yards off.

"No," I said, "I didn't. This one doesn't have a brain to
hit. Kind of like a certain farmhand I know." I pulled the
knife out of the crocboar's skull and sank it into the thrash-
ing creature's eye.

It lunged at me, its three-foot tusks and long snout lined
with crocodile teeth slashing a little too close for comfort.
Crocboars weren't smart, but they had the teeth, claws, and
tough skin to make up for it.

"Now you made it mad," Neds said.

"Not helpful." I jumped out of the way and pulled out
my other knife.

"I've got the tranq gun right here," he said. "And a clear
shot."

"No. Wait. I want the meat clean."

Keeping property out here in the scrub meant occasionally trapping and taking down feral beasts before they dam-

aged crops or the domesticated animals. Crocboar weren't good eating, since they were too filled up with the nano that laced the soil of this land. But they made terrific dragon chow.

The beast thrashed some more, ran out of steam, folded down on its knees, and fell over dead.

Just like that.

"Can't get over how quick these things fall," Right Ned said.

"Who are you calling brainless, by the way?" Left Ned said.

I shook the slime off my gloves—crocboars excreted oil—and glanced at Neds.

Most people stared, eyes wide and mouths open, when they first met Neds. There was good reason for it. Neds had two heads but only the one body, which was never the most normal sort of thing.

Both of him had sandy blond hair cut short and soft blue eyes that gave him an innocent shine, when most times he was anything but. He was clean-cut good-looking, a few inches taller than me, tanned and hard-muscled from farm-work—something you could tell even though he wore a dark green T-shirt and baggy denim overalls.

He'd left the touring circus and was looking for a job, when he saw the ad I'd taken out at the local feed store. I wanted a farmhand to help with the land and the stitched beasts my father, Dr. Case, had left in my keeping. Especially since my brother, Quinten, hadn't been home in over three years, something that worried me terribly.

Most people had been scared off by one thing or another in that ad: the hard work, the beasts, or me—a single women holding down her own chunk of land far enough from a city that I was barely covered by House Green and wasn't even on the power grid. Neds never complained about any of that. He'd been a fixture on the farm for two years.

"Bring the net over," I said. "We have some dragging to do."

It didn't take us long to throw the net over the beast and tug it tight so the rough hide caught in the rope fiber.

I took one last look around at the trees and the dry summer underbrush. Nothing else moved; nothing reared for an attack. So that was good.

"Who gets this one?" Right Ned asked, tossing me a rope. "Pony or the leaper?"

"Lizard. I think it's about ready to molt. It should be nice and hungry."

"Just tell me we don't have to boil down scales today, and I'm happy," Right Ned said.

I took a rope and slung it over my shoulder, and Neds did the same.

"No boiling," I said as we dragged the half ton of dead and stink behind us. "But we could have a little fun and see if we can scrape a few scales free while it's eating."

"Never have seen the fun in that," Left Ned said. "But if it pays extra . . ."

"Same pay as every day: food, roof, honest work, and the pleasure of my conversational company."

"About that raise?" Left Ned said.

"When we clear a profit, you'll get your share," I said.

Right Ned slid me a smile, and I grinned back. We'd had that conversation since the day they'd wandered up the lane.

Lizard wasn't hard to spot since it was approximately the size of a barn and was napping behind the electric fence. It was harmless as long as you didn't move fast around it, didn't look it straight in the eye, and didn't poke it.

"Never have asked," Right Ned said. "Where'd you get the lizard? Did your Dad make it too?"

"Yep. Stitched it up piece by piece." We stopped dragging, and Neds and I bent to the task of pulling the net free of the beast.

"What's it all made of?" Right Ned asked.

"Iguana, if you'd believe it," I said. "Of course bits of other things too—crocodile, kimono. No boars."

"And how do you explain the wings?"

"No idea. Mom always said Dad had a whimsical side to his stitchery. Said if he was going to make living creatures, he may as well make them beautiful."

I threw the last of the net off of the crocboar and straightened.

The lizard stirred at the commotion and shifted its big shovel-shaped head in our direction.

"You stand on back with the tranquilizer," I said. "I'll heave this into the corral. Plug it twice if it gets twitchy. Takes a lot to put it down. Are we gold?"

"We're gold," Right Ned said. He stepped back to give me room and pulled out the tranq gun.

"You know, no one says that anymore," Left Ned said. "Gold isn't what it used to be."

"Gold is just the same as ever," I said. "People aren't what they used to be."

I hefted the front half of the dragon kibble up off the ground, dragged it a little closer to the fence. It was heavy, but I was an uncommonly strong girl. My dad had made sure of that.

"Did you ever ask your father why he stitched a dragon?" Right Ned asked.

"Lizard."

"Four legs, four wings, reptile the size of a house." He raised the tranq gun at the beast, which had opened its slitted yellow eyes and then raised its head, lifting up onto its feet. "Dragon."

"All right, 'dragon.' Who knows? Mom said it was during his scatty years, shaking off his time after he left House White. Maybe just to see if it could be done."

"So your dad gets a pink slip and stitches together a

dragon." Right Ned shook his head, and I was pretty sure there was admiration in that smile. "Wish I'd met him. He aimed high."

"I wish he'd aimed smaller." I heaved the first half of the crocboar over the metal wires. "Then maybe Lizard would go catatonic like most stitched creatures of a certain size."

I heaved the other half of the lizard's breakfast over the fence. It landed with a squishy *thump*.

"And maybe it wouldn't be such a big, smart pain in the hole to deal with." I backed away from the fence but did not turn my back on the lizard. That thing was cobra-fast when it caught sight of something it wanted to eat.

"Do you think it could survive on its own if it were set free?" Right Ned asked, his voice muffled just a bit from holding the gun ready to fire if our fences failed.

"I suppose. Well, maybe not in the city. It's never been on dead soil. Large things unstitch there, don't they?"

Left Ned answered, "Can't keep a stitch that big alive in the city. Hard even to keep the smaller bits alive unless they are very, very expensive and very, very well made. It's not because of the soil, though."

"Sure it is," I said. "It's all about the soil. Out here in the scratch, we still have devilry in our dirt. Makes stitched things stay stitched."

"Never thought you were the sort of girl who believed in magic, Tilly," Right Ned said in the tone of a man who clearly did not believe in the stuff but had spent years taking money from people who did.

"Stardust, nanowitchery. Whatever you want to call it, Lizard there is breathing because of it."

Lizard finally got a solid whiff of the dead thing and smacked at the air, sticking out its ropelike tongue to clean first one eye, then the other. It started our way, with that half-snake, half-bowlegged-cow waddle that made a person want to point and laugh, except by the time you got around to doing either of those things, lizard would be on top of you, and you'd be bitten in half.

It opened its big maw, scooped off a third of the beast—quick as a hot spoon through ice cream—lifted its head up, and swallowed, the lump of meat stuck in its gizzard.

"All right, gold." I said as the lizard made contented *click-huff* sounds. "Looks like it's not going to attack the fence. Or us." I pulled my gloves off and smacked them across my thigh to knock off the rest of the dirt. "So, are you hungry? 'Cause I could eat."

Neds shifted his finger off the trigger, set the safety, and leaned the barrel across his shoulder. "I wouldn't mind a hot breakfast."

"Good," I said as I headed up the dirt lane toward the old farmhouse. "It's your turn to cook."

Left Ned complained his whole way through it, but he and Right Ned put up a decent egg-and-potato scramble.

I made sure Grandma had her share of the meal, ate more than my share, then did the dishes, as was only fair. Just as I was drying the last plate, there was a knock on the door.

Neds stopped sharpening the machete they called a pocketknife. He glanced at the door, then at me. We didn't get visitors. Ever.

Grandma, in the corner, just went right on knitting the twisted wool spooling up off the three pocket-sized sheep that were puttering around at her feet. The sheep were another of my dad's stitched critters, built so they grew self-spinning wool. I'd tried to breed them, thinking I could sell them and make a little money for the repairs on the place, but like most stitched things, they were infertile.

I wiped my hands on a kitchen towel and opened the door.

"Are you Matilda Case?" the stranger asked in a voice

too calm and nice for someone who was holding his guts in place with one hand.

"I am," I said, even though the Neds always told me I shouldn't go around giving people my name without having theirs first. "You're a long way from the cities. Do you need a ride to a hospital?"

The stranger was a couple inches shy of seven feet tall, had a broad sort of face with an arrangement of features that fell well into the rustic-and-handsome category—five-o'clock shadow included. His mop of brown hair was shaved close by his ears and finger-combed back off his forehead so that it stuck up with a bit of natural wave, which had passed for fashion maybe a hundred years ago.

His shirt, under the brown coat he wore, was high-collared and buttoned and might have once been white. That, along with his dark breeches and military boots laced and buckled up to his knees, gave him a distinctly historical sort of look. Brown clothes meant he was non-House: not owned by or affiliated with any of the eleven Houses that ruled the modern world's resources, from technology and agriculture, straight on up through defense, fuel, and the gods we worshipped.

I had changed out of my filthy hunting clothes into a pair of faded blue overalls and a checkered shirt. It wasn't at all House compliant, but then I'd been off-grid and below radar all my life. Just the way my brother wanted me to be.

"Unless you're here to sell me something," I said as I leaned the door shut a bit. "In which case, I'll just save you what air you've got left and say, no, there's no Matilda Case living here."

He didn't smile, but his eyes pulled up a bit at the bottom and something that looked like humor caught fire in them. That's when I noticed the color of his eyes: cinnamon red, like mine when I was injured.

I took a step back, startled, and he took a step forward.

Neds racked a round into the shotgun he'd had propped by his knee, and then all of us in the kitchen held perfectly still.

Well, except for Grandma. She just kept on singing her knitting song about sunshine through lace and liberty's death, her fingers slipping yarn into knots, smooth and liquid for a woman of her years.

"Not a single step closer," Left Ned said, his voice always a little colder and meaner than Right Ned's. "You have not been invited into this home."

The stranger looked away from me, and I thought maybe for the first time he noticed that there was a house, a room, and people around us. A whole farm, really: a hundred fifty acres tucked back far enough in the rolling hills of Pennsylvania that the nearest fill-up station was thirty miles away.

He certainly noticed Neds—both heads of him. And the gun.

Since Left Ned was talking, I knew he was willing to bloody the stranger up a little more if that's what it took to keep him out of the house.

"I'm looking for a doctor," the stranger said. "Dr. Renault Case."

"He doesn't live here anymore," Right Ned said calmly, everything about his voice the opposite of Left Ned's. "If you need someone to take you to a town doctor, I'd be willing. But there's no medical man here to help you."

The stranger frowned, sending just a hint of lines across his forehead and at the corners of his eyes. "You think I came here for help?"

I nodded toward his gut. "You are bleeding rather strongly."

He looked down. An expression of surprise crossed his face, and he shifted his wide fingers, letting a little more blood ooze out, as if just noticing how badly he was injured. If he was in pain—and he should have been—he did not show it.

Shock, maybe. Or expensive drugs.

"I didn't come here looking for help from Dr. Case," he said, his cinnamon gaze on me, just on me, and the sound of his blood falling with a soft *tip tip tip* on my wooden floor. "I came here to warn him."

"About what?" I asked.

He hesitated.

Left Ned spoke up. "Say it or get walking."

"His enemies are looking for him. For him and his works. I came to offer him protection."

It was a dramatic sort of thing to say, and he had a nice, deep, dramatic sort of voice for it. Chills did that rolling thing over my arms.

But there was only one problem.

"He's dead," I said.

"What?"

"My father, Dr. Case, has been dead for years."

That, more than anything, seemed to take the starch out of him. He exhaled, and it was a wet sound as he tried to get air back into his lungs. I almost reached over to prop him up, afraid he might just pass out and further mess up the clean of my kitchen floor.

He was a big man, but like I said, I'm strong.

"Are you certain?" he asked.

I was twelve years old when the men in black and white came to the farm. I'd hidden, like my father had taught me, up in the rafters of the barn. I'd watched those men kill him. Kill my mother too. I'd watched them search our house and carry out boxes. I'd watched them pick up my parent's bodies, put them in a black van, and then use our garden hose to clean up the drive so not even a drop of their blood was left for me to cry over.

"Very," I whispered.

"I . . ." He swallowed hard, shook his head. Didn't look like that helped much. His words came out in a slur. "I thought . . . I should have known. Sooner. We thought . . . all our information. That he lived."

"Neds," I called.

The stranger's eyes rolled up into his head, and he folded like someone had punched him in the ribs. I instinctively put my hands out to catch him, got hold of his jacket shoulders, and pivoted on my heels, throwing my weight to guide him down to the floor without knocking his head too badly.

I crouched down next to him.

Neds strolled over. "What are you going to do with him, Tilly?" Right Ned asked.

"I don't know. Check his pockets, will you? See if he has a name." I was already pushing his hand to one side so I could get to his wound. It was deep and bad. Might have been from a crocboar. Might have been from any number of beasts out on the edges of the property.

I could mend this, mend him enough to get him to a hospital hours away, in my old truck, on these old roads. If he hadn't lost too much blood, he might survive.

I stood. "I need the sewing kit. The medicines."

"Tilly," Right Ned said, "I don't think that will work."

I was already halfway across the kitchen, heading toward the bathroom, where I kept all the supplies for taking care of Ned and Grandma.

"Tilly," Left Ned snapped, "stop. Listen."

I did not like being bossed around by that man. Either of them. I turned.

Neds hunkered next to the stranger, his shotgun within easy reach on the floor beside him, his shoulders angled so the shirt stretched at the seams. He'd pushed the man's jacket sleeve back to reveal his arm up to his elbow.

Stitches. The man had a thick line of gray stitches ringing his entire forearm. Not medical stitches, not medical thread. Life stitches like mine.

I instinctively held my own hands out, turning them so they caught the light. Thin silver stitches crossed my palms and circled my thumbs. Just as those same silver stitches made paths across my arms, my legs, curved up my stomach, beneath my breasts, and around one shoulder. Just as those stitches traced my left ear to the curve of my jaw and ran a line across the back of my neck. I kept my hair free to cover them up. If I wore gloves and long-sleeved shirts and pants, no one knew I was made like this.

Made of bits.

Not quite human.

I'd never once in my life seen or heard of anyone — of any person — stitched like me.

Until this man. This stranger bleeding on my floor.

ALSO AVAILABLE

FROM

Devon Monk

IN THE NATIONAL BESTSELLING ALLIE BECKSTROM SERIES

Magic to the Bone
Magic in the Blood
Magic in the Shadows
Magic on the Storm
Magic at the Gate
Magic on the Hunt
Magic on the Line
Magic without Mercy
Magic for a Price

"Fiendishly original and a stay-up-all-night read."
—#1 *New York Times* bestselling author
Patricia Briggs

Available wherever books are sold or at
penguin.com

facebook.com/acerocbooks

R0129